Social Transformations in Hardy's Tragic Novels

Megamachines and Phantasms

David Musselwhite
Senior Lecturer in Literature
University of Essex

First published 2003 by
PALGRAVE MACMILLAN
Houndmills, Basingstoke, Hampshire RG21 6XS and
175 Fifth Avenue, New York, N.Y. 10010
Companies and representatives throughout the world

PALGRAVE MACMILLAN is the global academic imprint of the Palgrave Macmillan division of St. Martin's Press, LLC and of Palgrave Macmillan Ltd. Macmillan® is a registered trademark in the United States, United Kingdom and other countries. Palgrave is a registered trademark in the European Union and other countries.

ISBN 1–4039–1662–4

This book is printed on paper suitable for recycling and made from fully managed and sustained forest sources.

A catalogue record for this book is available from the British Library.

Library of Congress Cataloging-in-Publication Data

Musselwhite, David E., 1940-
   Social transformation in Hardy's tragic novels : megamachines and phantasms / David Musselwhite.
      p. cm.
   Includes bibliographical references and index.
   Contents: Introduction – The interrupted return – The exploding body of The mayor of Casterbridge – Tess of the d'Urbervilles : "a becoming woman" – Tess : the phantasmatic capture – Retranslating Jude the obscure I – Traversing The well-beloved – Retranslating Jude the obscure II.
      ISBN 1-4039-1662-4
      1. Hardy, Thomas, 1840-1928–Fictional works. 2. Hardy, Thomas, 1840-1928–Political and social views. 3. Literature and society–England–History–19th century. 4. Social change in literature. 5. Tragic, The, in literature. I. Title.

PR4757.F5M87 2003
823'.8–dc21

2003051790

10 9 8 7 6 5 4 3 2 1
12 11 10 09 08 07 06 05 04 03

Printed and bound in Great Britain by
Antony Rowe Ltd, Chippenham and Eastbourne

In loving memory of my father

**Rev. E. C. Musselwhite
(1915–1996)**

Contents

Preface and Acknowledgements   viii

1 Introduction   1

   A: Megamachines   1
   B: Phantasms   13
   C: Phantasmatical megamachines and mega-phantasms   19

2 The Interrupted Return   23

3 The Exploding Body of *The Mayor of Casterbridge*   50

4 *Tess of the d'Urbervilles*: 'a becoming woman'   89

5 *Tess*: the Phantasmatic Capture   108

6 Retranslating *Jude the Obscure* I   145

7 Traversing *The Well-Beloved*   155

8 Retranslating *Jude the Obscure* II   170

Notes   191

Bibliography   216

Index   222

Preface and Acknowledgements

The essays that follow are offered primarily as a study of Hardy's four major tragic novels – *The Return of the Native, The Mayor of Casterbridge, Tess of the d'Urbervilles* and *Jude the Obscure.* As such it is to be hoped that they will appeal to lovers of Hardy as well as to students and academics.

However, the two, perhaps rather unfamiliar, words that figure in my title – 'megamachines' and 'phantasms' – are there to indicate also a commitment to two major bodies of literary theory: the first to the work of Gilles Deleuze and Felix Guattari, particularly to their two major texts, the *Anti-Oedipus* and *A Thousand Plateaux*, and the second to the rather less well known work of the psychoanalytical theorist Jean Laplanche whose principal theoretical concept, the *fantasme*, was first elaborated in an article with J.-B. Pontalis in 1964. I offer introductions to both these bodies of theory in my 'Introduction.'

Nevertheless, it has been put to me that my work is 'highly recondite and opaque' and that I am likely to alienate my reader, particularly with my 'Introduction' with its battery of unfamiliar notions and concepts – 'territorialization', 'deterritorialization', 'reterritorialization', 'body-without-organs', '*corps morcelé*' and the rest – that stand like a dragon at the gate. All I can say is that I have tried to be as clear as possible and, indeed, if my book has a secondary purpose, it is the attempt to use the readings of Hardy to make the work of Deleuze and Guattari and Laplanche and Pontalis as accessible as possible to those who frequently find much literary theory jargonistic and rebarbative. Here I can only ask for patience on the part of the reader and suggest that before throwing the book to one side he or she at least attempt a reading of the chapters dedicated to the respective novels before returning once again to the theoretical apparatus: I think the most rewarding reading will probably be one that is prepared to jump backwards and forwards between the theoretical introduction and the actual studies of the novels. To suggest such a strategy is in part a tribute to Hardy to the extent that it indicates the measure in which the complexity and sophistication of his work can be used not only to *illustrate* (a truly reprobate proposition) the theoretical models deployed but in fact can be seen frequently to *anticipate* them in their intricacy and acumen. Not least of my concerns has been to lay to rest all that patronizing indulgence towards Hardy's 'regionalism' and 'provincialism' implicit in James' 'poor little Thomas Hardy.'

Having said all that, it would be disingenuous of me to pretend that in addition to hoping to appeal to a 'general' or, more likely, a 'student' audience, I haven't at times had fellow academics and critics, and 'Deleuze-and-Guattarians' and 'Laplanche-and-Pontalisians', in mind and that occasionally my address is to them, sometimes by way of questioning their interpretations of complex notions, at others by way of inviting corroboration or, again, questioning of what I have put forward here. This must account for the one or two – o.k., three or four, I hope not many – occasions when I have perhaps pursued a theoretical point to what might appear abstruseness. What I have in mind, for example, are my attempts to explain the notion of the 'body without organs' in my 'Introduction'; or my examining the relationship Deleuze and Guattari postulate between 'writing' and 'incest' in the chapter on *The Mayor of Casterbridge*; or my very compressed summary of Deleuze's study of Masochism in the first chapter on *Tess*; or my venturing into some conjectures on the 'Death Instinct' in the second chapter on *Tess*; or the discussion of the notion of '*Autrui*' in the second chapter on *Jude*; or, finally, my determination at many points in the text to establish the affinity of two notions – the '*body without organs*' and the '*phantasm*' – which Deleuze and Guattari have sought to keep quite separate from each other: indeed, they suggest rather that the two are inimical to one another.

Again, all I can say is that I have tried to be as clear as possible in examining and accounting for a number of critical terms and notions in Deleuze and Guattari's work that seem to me to have either been ignored by most commentators on their work or simply misunderstood by them. In fact, with very few notable exceptions, most accounts of the work of Deleuze and Guattari that I have read have seemed to me far more complex and bewildering than the original material – truly intimidating and all too often appealing only to a coterie of fellow initiates. It is my hope that in the readings of Hardy that follow I have managed to deploy many of Deleuze and Guattari's major concepts – by no means all of them – in such a way that even those most hostile to theoretical pretensions might find themselves understanding and at ease with what I am saying. Happily the work of Laplanche and Pontalis, largely because it is less well known, has not suffered from the baroque accretions that have gathered about the Deleuze and Guattarian *œuvre* but, again, I hope my extended account of the notion of the *phantasm* both in my 'Introduction' and the second chapter on *Tess* will make what I consider to be one of the most powerful and most important theoretical models that I have ever encountered accessible to a new and wider audience.

I began this work more years ago than I care to remember and early drafts of various chapters were offered as seminar papers at a number of universities – Southampton, Oporto, Cardiff, Hull and Warwick among others – to audiences that were variously sceptical and disbelieving, on the one hand, and supportive and enthusiastic, on the other. I benefited greatly from these encounters and there can be no question but that the final product is both more sharply defined and more focused as a result. As the work became more consolidated and nearer to completion my greatest encouragement has come from a number of close and valued colleagues here at Essex who have read and commented on more drafts than I had any right to expect anyone to read. Elaine Jordan has throughout been a wonderful close counsellor and mentor whose critical expertise has again and again ensured that I did not embarrass myself by some egregious *faux pas*. Her impatience that I get this thing finished was sufficiently sharp to keep me to my task at those moments when my own spirits flagged. Another colleague, Val Morgan, read the final chapters and her detailed comments on them – together with always striking suggestions for improvements of detail – helped greatly as I brought the project to a close. Another close colleague and friend, Leon Burnett, whose critical approach to literature is almost at the antipodes to mine, has also, over many years, encouraged and supported me and he knows how grateful I am for his unobtrusive but effective cajoling. Outside of Essex I am grateful for the totally unexpected and flatteringly supportive interest in my work from Keith Ansell-Pearson at Warwick: as one of the principal Deleuze and Guattarian scholars in the country his enthusiastic response to my work came at a time when such support was most needed. Perhaps my greatest, debt, however, is to Tracy Ryan with whom over the past three or four years I have enjoyed one of those too easily derided 'virtual companionships' via email, during which many of the ideas that emerge in the final text have been tried and tested for the first time. She has also offered me the luxury of an 'ideal reader' – the informed, independently minded, passionate lover of literature – for which I am particularly grateful.

On the practical side I want to acknowledge here a particular debt of thanks to Judith Stinton and Lilian Swindal of the Hardy Archive in the Dorset County Museum and to Nick Lawrence at the Dorset County Library in Dorchester. It is thanks to them that I was able to gather what evidence I could surrounding the truly appalling death of Mary Channing in 1705. Finally, last and most recently, I must thank Erna von der Walde for her careful proof reading of a number of the chapters and her many careful adjustments to the final text.

1
Introduction

A: Megamachines

> Strange Anglo-American literature: from Thomas Hardy, from
> D. H. Lawrence to Malcolm Lowry, from Henry Miller to Allen
> Ginsberg and Jack Kerouac, men who know how to leave, to
> scramble codes, to cause flows to circulate, to traverse the desert
> of the body without organs.[1]
>
> The exemplary case of Thomas Hardy: his characters are not
> characters or subjects: they are collections of intensive sensa-
> tions, each one is such a collection, a package, a bloc of varying
> sensations.... A subjectless individuation. And these packages
> of vital sensations, these collections or combinations, trace
> their paths of fortune or misfortune, there where-ever their
> encounters take them, or where-ever their unhappy encounters
> take them, sometimes as far as death, as far as murder.... These
> clusters of sensations, these individuals, file across the land-
> scape as though tracing a line of flight, or a line of deterritor-
> ialization of the earth itself.[2]

It had always been a source of some amazement to me, given the
fulsomeness of Deleuze's frequently expressed admiration for the work
of Thomas Hardy, that even recent studies[3] of the latter's novels rarely
attempted to draw on the theoretical potential of the two major texts,
Anti-Oedipus and *A Thousand Plateaux*, that he had composed with Felix
Guattari.[4] I found this all the more strange when, in an almost casual
moment, I first set Hardy's four major tragic novels – *The Return of the
Native, The Mayor of Casterbridge, Tess of the d'Urbervilles* and *Jude the
Obscure* – alongside the typology of social formations – 'territorial',

'despotic' and 'capitalist' – offered by *Anti-Oedipus*[5] and found that a good many parallels could be drawn between the work of the English regionalist novelist and that of the Parisian theorists. The latter speak, for example, of the requirement that all social formations – which they describe at times as the *socius* or, in the term derived from Louis Mumford, *'megamachine'*[6] – *code* or *inscribe* the flows or forces of desire that invest or run through them. In the course of their analysis they concentrate on three social regimes in particular: the *territorial* formation which *codes* the flows of production and desire directly on the body of the earth; the *despotic* formation which irrupts into and takes over the *territorial* formation and *overcodes* the flows and potentials of the earlier formation and reinvests them in the body of the despot and the accompanying apparatus of the state; the *capitalist* formation which, far from *coding* or *overcoding*, indulges in a vast operation of *decoding* and *deterritorialization*, scrambling and setting free all the codes – of money, labour, desire – in a frenzy of deregulation and speculation that threatens to blow the *socius* apart. That this does not happen is primarily due to capitalism's propensity to institute ever more artificial, archaic and residual *neo-codings* and *neo-territorializations* – institutions and axiomatics, rules and protocols – which are nothing more than elaborate *simulacra* or *simulations* of the real.[7]

On turning to Hardy, it seemed to me that *The Return of the Native*, with the massive brooding presence of Egdon Heath, could clearly be read as a drama steeped in a *territorial* formation, with its fetishes and its cultic residues, that was threatened by those forces that either disturbed its cohesion – Clym and Wildeve – or disavowed its magnetic allure – the tragedy of Eustacia Vye. If *The Mayor of Casterbridge* is about anything it is about the fateful consequences that must ensue when the passionate avatar of an erstwhile *territorial* formation, with his 'rule of thumb' approximations and *viva voce* contracts – the hay-trusser Henchard – is challenged and overcome by the dispassionate representative of a new 'despotic' order, with his scales and steelyards and legalistic niceties – the fair-haired intruder Farfrae. Finally, if *The Return* can be regarded as tracing the *codings* of a 'territorial' formation – the markings and engraftings upon the body of the earth – while *The Mayor* recounts what happens when those *codings* are over-taken and subsumed by the more severe *overcodings* of a despotic regime, then *Jude the Obscure* can be seen as offering us the bleak prospect of a world that has lost all its codings, lost all its mappings, grammars, bearings, and where existence is a sad migration that culminates only in a blank wall of exclusion or a black hole of perverse capitulation – the post-mortuarial world of capitalism.[8] *Tess of the d'Urbervilles* is both anomalous and exemplary with regard to these patterns of *territorial coding*, *despotic-over-coding* and *capitalist decoding* to the extent that it does not confine itself to an account of either just *one* (as in *The Return* or *Jude*) or even of *two* (as in *The Mayor*) distinct regimes but traverses, in effect, *all* of them from the *territorial* backwater of Marlott, through the benign but nevertheless structurally *despotic* regime of Talbothays[9] and the harsh, featureless desert of Flintcomb-Ash to the *artificial, reterritorialized* exotic seaside resort of Sandbourne.

To understand Deleuze and Guattari's typology of social formations it is necessary, first, to have some idea of their account of the evolution of consciousness. This is because in their broader scheme the evolution of consciousness provides, as it were, an analogue, or model, of the stages of human history, and the evolution of social formations.

At the basis of Deleuze and Guattari's work is a theory of 'flows', memorably described in the opening pages of their *Anti-Oedipus*:

> *They*[10] are at work everywhere, functioning smoothly at times, at other times in fits and starts. *They* breathe, heat, eat. *They* piss and screw. What a mistake ever to have said *the* id. Everywhere there are machines, not at all simply metaphorically: machines driving other machines, machines being driven by other machines, their couplings and connexions. An organ machine is plugged into a source-machine: the one emits a flow which the other one cuts. The breast is a machine that produces milk, and the mouth a machine coupled with it. The mouth of the anorexic wavers between several functions – whether it is an eating machine, an anal machine, a speaking machine, or a breathing machine (asthma attacks). Thus we are all handymen, each with his little machines. An organ machine for every energy machine, always flows and interruptions. ... Amniotic fluid spilling out of the sack and kidney stones; flowing hair, a flow of spittle, a flow of sperm, shit, or urine that are produced by partial objects and constantly cut across by other partial objects which in turn produce other flows, interrupted by other partial objects.[11]

Everywhere there are machinic flows and desiring machines: flows of milk and of urine, flows of blood and of semen, flows of hair and of faeces – but also flows of sunshine and flows of rain, of minerals and sap, of grass and of goods. The larval unconscious is constituted by such pre-singular and pre-individual flows, molecular and partial, cutting across each other, interrupting each other, appropriating from each other.

This molecular unconscious is deliriously productive, pre-personal and impersonal – even inhuman – and knows nothing of persons – 'The unconscious is totally unaware of persons as such';[12] or of lack – 'Desire does not lack anything...';[13] or of meaning – 'The question posed by desire is not "What does it mean?" but rather "How does it work?"'.[14] The unconscious works and does not represent; it is a machine rather than a set of beliefs. It is only with Freudian psychoanalysis and the development of the Oedipus complex that 'The productive unconscious makes way for an unconscious that knows only how to express itself – express itself in myth, in tragedy, in dream'[15] or that 'The unconscious ceases to be what it is – a factory, a workshop – to become a theatre, a scene and its staging.'[16]

There is no more critical distinction in Deleuze and Guattari's work than that between, on the one hand, the molecular, larval, productive unconscious and its partial objects and, on the other, what they term 'molar' constructs such as persons, wholes and totalities.

> The real difference is therefore between on the one hand the molar machines – whether social, technical or organic – and on the other the desiring machines, which are of a molecular order.[17]

It is 'molar' wholes or totalities that deprive desire of its very being, which inscribe lack in desire:

> Anthropomorphic molar representation culminates in the very thing that founds it, the ideology of lack. The molecular unconscious, on the contrary, knows nothing of castration, because partial objects lack nothing and form free multiplicities as such.[18]
> Desire does not lack anything; it does not lack its object. It is rather the subject that is missing in desire, or desire that lacks a fixed subject.... Desire does not express a molar lack within the subject; rather the molar organization deprives desire of its objective being.[19]

– by, for example, bi-univocalising or polarizing the heterogeneous and volatile partialities of desire about the crass axis of a gender identity assigned by the arbitrary erection of a sovereign/despotic phallus. In other words a detachable partial object (the penis) is arbitrarily elevated to the status of a detached complete object (the phallus) in relation to which one is designated masculine or feminine, either way defined by acknowledgement of lack – castration or absence:[20]

the libido as energy of selection and detachment [of partial objects] is converted into the phallus as detached object, the latter existing only in the transcendent form of stock and lack (something common and absent that is just as lacking in men as in women).[21]

That is, the postulation of a whole/ideal of which one must inevitably fall short introjects into the unconscious a sense of lack and impotence that must deny and disavow the molecular energies of desire.

For the phallus has never been either the cause or the object of desire, but is itself the castrating apparatus, the machine for putting lack into desire, for drying up all the flows . . . [22]

Nevertheless, for this larval unconscious to evolve beyond a state of capricious productiveness and haphazard connections and permutations it is essential that it find for itself or is afforded a surface of inscription, somewhere, some body, on which it might be coded, organized, subjected to discriminations and discrete articulations. The generic name for this surface of inscription is what Deleuze and Guattari describe as the *body without organs*.

There can be no doubt but that Deleuze and Guattari's notion of the *body without organs* and its accompanying and complementary notion of the *corps morcelé* – the *body in pieces* (that is the motley assemblage of flow-producing organs) – have proved to be amongst their most bewildering and intractable.[23] It is possible to trace the genealogy of the notion of the *body without organs* to four major sources. The first of these is to Artaud's radio broadcast of 1949, *To Be Done With the Judgment of God*, where the phrase itself occurs towards the very end when Artaud calls for the 'emasculation' of man and his reduction to a 'body without organs':

When you have given him [man] a body without organs, then you will have delivered him from all his automatisms and restored to him his true liberty.[24]

The second source, which has many parallels with Artaud, is the *programme*, which is to be clearly distinguished from a mere *fantasy*, of the masochist who demands that his limbs and organs be tied and stuffed and gagged and sewn up in order that the intensity of his desire be not blemished or compromised by climax or discharge.[25] It is by such means, thirdly, that a *plateau* of intensity or *plane of consistency* is attained which Deleuze and Guattari compare with the *plateaux* of aggressive and affective intensities that Gregory Bateson found in Balinese culture and which were carefully constructed in order to preempt and ward off climactic and violent resolution.[26] Finally, and this is the fourth source, this *body without organs* or *plateau of intensity* or *plane of consistency* is compared to the affective, immanent, body of Spinoza's *Ethics*:

> How does Spinoza define a body? A body, of whatever kind, is defined by Spinoza in two simultaneous ways. In the first place, a body, however small it may be, is composed of an infinite number of particles; it is the relations of motion and rest, of speeds and slownesses between particles, that define a body, the individuality of a body. Secondly, a body affects other bodies, or is affected by other bodies; it is this capacity for affecting and being affected that also defines a body in its individuality.[27]

In other words, the *body without organs* is something like the construction of an *erotic* or *affective field* or *surface of inscription* displaced and differentiated from the organic body and its physiological *needs* and as such a *field* or *surface* it becomes the arena of all kinds of flows of intensities which might gust across it from one horizon to another. Despite the complexity and even the mystification and sometimes, quite frankly, the sheer *bluster* the notion attracts in Deleuze and Guattari's work, I think it is fairly easy to come to terms with the notion of the *body without organs* by simply considering the status and function of a *field* in any human activity ranging from the erotic to the commercial, from sport to intellectual endeavour: any such *field* is a *virtual* rather than a *real* (i.e. *organic*) field and becomes the arena of all sorts of capricious and arbitrary affective intensities and events. A *body without organs* is anywhere where we live out and register and inscribe our desires whether it be a Ferrari or a Barbie Doll, a much-loved landscape or a glove – or, indeed, a *taste* or a *moment*: recall Proust's *madeleine* or Lorca's *five in the afternoon*. As far as 'making' or 'becoming' a *body without organs* is concerned – apart from the more obvious instances of the erotic allure of all *uniforms* – consider what happens whenever one girds oneself for a sport: what does the scuba-diver, or the baseball player, or the Tour de France cyclist, or the skate-boarder gain from his gear? It's not just functionality – whatever they may plead: it's to enjoy the affects and intensities of a *body without organs* differentiated from, and displaced and indifferent in relation to, its *organic* support.

This might be all very well for the adult or adolescent, it might be thought, but in what way can the child be said to 'construct' his or her *body without organs?* That is, an *affective* or *virtual surface of inscription*, or *plane of consistency* differentiated off from its merely organic body. The suggestion that Deleuze and Guattari make in the *Anti-Oedipus* is that the nursling discovers this *virtual*, separate *surface* or *plane* in the exceedingly modest encounter with its first *burp!*[28] but perhaps a more radical and even more primordial source is to be found in the affective recall of the lost *placenta*.[29]

The *placenta* – literally 'a little plate' or *plateau* – becomes the first *ideal* or *lost object* or *virtual surface* where the child might experience and inscribe, negotiate and marshall, the flows of desire that assail it. It might even be that this insulatory function of the lost *placenta* – functioning here as a second, virtual, skin – that accounts for the magical properties – protection against drowning, for example – attributed to the amniotic sac or *caul*. One can only conjecture that an unhappy or botched after-birth might have severe consequences at a later date for what is jeopardized thereby is the very constitution of the first affective surface.[30] It is this that endows the *body without organs* with its fragility and instability for while, on the one hand, it is turned towards the domain of organic and physiological *need*, on the other, it is turned towards the world of human *meaning* and *abstraction*; on the one hand towards the *molecular* flows, on the other towards *molar* identities.[31]

What it is important to understand at this stage is that between the *flows of desire* and the *body without organs* – between the *corps morcelé*, (the body in pieces, the scattered organs and their associated flows) and the ungendered *surface of inscription* (the *body without organs*) – a number of relationships are possible.

The first of these can be described as aggressive-paranoid where the *body without organs* fears the *corps morcelé*, which it regards as dangerous and threatening, ready to gouge and annihilate, to devour and eviscerate:

> An apparent conflict arises between desiring machines and the *body without organs....* Beneath its organs it [the *body without organs*] senses there are larvae and loathsome worms.... This is the real meaning of the paranoiac machine: the desiring machines [the *corps morcelé*] attempt to break into the *body without organs*, and the *body without organs* repels them, since it experiences them as an over all persecution apparatus.[32]

It is the fear of the body of its own desires: what it represses from within returns from without. The illustration I often appeal to here is that of Robinson Crusoe, so dressed in skins as to become virtually a drum, a kind of Humpty Dumpty (another classic example of a *body without organs*), and his dread of the cannibals who represent the *corps morcelé*, the dismembered body in pieces of his own desires. But here we might briefly cite the case of Henchard who, in his fetishistic oath, forswears and disavows his own passionate self. Henchard's self-constitution of himself as a molar identity, a 'character', that is, deprives his desires of their objective being. Or, again, Eustacia Vye who, by postulating for herself an ideal love, by failing to acknowledge the molecular, germinal allure of the heath and by hypostatizing it as some kind of molar, personal, enemy, finds herself filled with a cosmic sense of lack which nothing can assuage, while she herself is gouged, burned, scored, pierced, entwined and, finally, engulfed by the very forces she has disavowed.

The second relationship between the *corps morcelé* or the flows of desire and the *body without organs* is, in some ways, the reversal of the first. Now the *body without organs*, far from shunning the flows of desire as a potential threat, instead deliriously embraces them and clutches them to it in a gesture of euphoric defiance and triumph. This switch is described by Deleuze and Guattari as a 'miraculation' of desire: 'now I feel all powerful, I can conquer the world, I can change the weather...'

> An attraction-machine now takes the place, or may take the place, of a repulsion-machine: a miraculating-machine succeeding the para-noiac machine.[33]

This, in a sense, is the condition of Henchard in his heyday as mayor: all powerful, dominating the market, impatient of any check, and attempting to control the elements. It is, of course, central to Henchard's plight that he oscillates so violently between the paranoid/aggressive and the manic/miraculating phases.

The third relationship between the flows of desire and the *body without organs* is what Deleuze and Guattari term the 'celibate' phase:

> Let us borrow the name 'celibate machine' to designate this machine that succeeds the paranoiac machine and the miraculating machine, forming a new alliance between the desiring-machines and the body without organs so as to give birth to a new humanity or a glorious organism.[34]

It is, perhaps, the most difficult to describe for here we are in the domain of the saint and the mystic. Rather than being embroiled either in the paranoid or the manic phases here the subject finds itself blissfully aloof from the intensities that might swamp it and free to scan and peregrinate dispassionately but ecstatically all the moments of the earlier phases.

> The subject itself is no longer at the centre, which is occupied by the machine, but on the periphery, with no fixed identity, forever decentred, defined by the states through which it passes. . . . The subject spreads itself out along the entire circumference of the circle, the centre of which has been abandoned by the ego.[35]

It is the immaculate transcendence of the visionary, transpersonal and transhuman. In the past I have invoked this notion of the celibate moment to account for the great mystical poems of Emily Brontë/Ellis Bell,[36] but here what comes to mind is the provocative sub-title of *Tess of the d'Urbervilles* – 'A Pure Woman': for what Tess does, it seems to me, is to peregrinate through a whole travail of serial intensities remaining for ever untouched by them. The debate as to whether she is passive or active is, in this context, singularly inept: active/passive might be invoked at the manic/depressive levels but here the very dichotomy itself becomes meaningless – the 'passivity' of the contemplative might be his or her most active engagement.

The fourth relationship between the flows of desire and the *body without organs* is one of breakdown. The system overloads, the intensities become too much, the pain and even the pleasure intolerable and the *body without organs* and its desires spring apart; the body sheds its desires and retreats into catatonic withdrawal, refusing to feel, to eat, to breath, to live. The world becomes a madhouse of hectic and disassociated intensities peopled by the living dead. Following upon the manic-depressive world of Henchard and the celibate world of Tess, comes the profoundly schizoid world of Jude and Sue, a world of fragmentation and a loss of mapping, a scrambled, cipher-less world of disembodied voices and graveyard inscriptions.

Let us turn now to a consideration of the evolution of the various models of the social regime that in so many ways can be seen to be analogous to the evolution of the stages of consciousness we have just described.

At the level of social formations the first great surface of inscription – or *body without organs* – is the body of the earth itself.

The territorial machine is therefore the first form of *socius*, the machine of primitive inscription, the 'megamachine' that covers the social field.[37]

The founding task for the constitution of the *socius* (the social formation) is the coding of all the intense germinal flows on the body of the earth. Prior to this moment one might imagine a great unformed primaeval chaos of promiscuous generation, an undifferentiated delirium. Here and there, perhaps, isolated nomadic hunters might follow the flows of the seasons or of the great herds – ('The great nomad hunter follows the flows, exhausts them in place, and moves on with them to another place'[38]) – but always already there are sketches of arrest and territorialization in the nomad's camps and temporary dwelling places – ('But a pure nomad does not exist; there is always and already an encampment...'[39]). What constitutes the *socius* is the seizing upon the undifferentiated flows and the stapling of them into the body of the earth.

A kind of collective searing takes place as the intensive germinal flows are brazed or cauterized into grids of alliance coextensive with the surface of the earth. In the territorial formation so created men and women become, so to speak, the adjuncts and the organs of the earth itself, parasites swarming on its body like fleas in the mane of a lion. The flows of milk and blood and hair and semen – as well as of sweat and tears – commingle with the seeds and roots and strata of the earth itself – as well as with the wind and the sunshine, the rain and the heat. This intimate embrace of men and the earth is marked not just by the scars of toil but by initiatory cruelties, festive tattooings, painful libations:

> The primitive territorial regime codes flows, invests organs, and marks bodies.... The essence of the recording, inscribing *socius*...resides in these operations: tattooing, excising, incising, carving, scarifying, mutilating, encircling, and initiating.... It makes men or their organs into parts and wheels of the social machine.[40]

In the territorial formation there are no individuals, only collective assemblages of organs – hands, mouths, tools – or of organs belonging to the collectivity – a collective anus, a collective vagina or a collective phallus.

The method of the primitive territorial machine is in this sense the collective investment of the organs; for flows are coded only to the

extent that the organs capable respectively of producing and breaking them are themselves encircled, instituted as partial objects, dis-
tributed on the *socius* and attached to it.... It is the collective
investment of the organs that plugs desire into the *socius* and assem-
bles social production and desiring production into a whole on the
earth.[41]

Differentiated from yet close to the germinal flows, what the territorial
formation fears is anything that might threaten its intensities or disin-
vest its collective and molecular codings. It works to exorcise, then, to
conjure, to keep at a distance those practices that would convert its
qualitative intensities into quantitative abstractions – the offices of the
smith and the merchant, for example:

> The primitive machine is not ignorant of exchange, commerce, and
> industry; it exorcises them, localizes them, cordons them off,
> encastes them, and maintains the merchant and the blacksmith in
> a subordinate position, so that the flows of exchange and the flows of
> production do not manage to break the codes in favour of their
> abstract or fictional qualities.[42]

– or the advent of any regime that would subject its collective energies to
private appropriation.[43]

It is just such a catastrophe that occurs with the advent of the Despot.
With the arrival of the Despot all the complex and multivalent codings
of the territorial regime are subjected to severe over-coding. The practices and institutions of the territorial formation are not destroyed but
re-deployed and re-articulated about the figure of the Despot himself:

> The full body as *socius* has ceased to be the earth, it has become the
> body of the despot, the despot himself or his god.... In place of
> mobile detachments from the signifying chain, a detached object
> has jumped outside the chain;* in place of flow selections, all the
> flows converge into a great river that constitutes the despot's con-
> sumption.... It is the social machine that has profoundly changed:
> in place of the territorial machine, there is the 'megamachine' of the
> State.[44]

(*i.e. the 'despotic' moment is like the emergence of the 'phallic'
moment in the evolution of consciousness: in a sense the awe and
privilege accorded the phallus and its 'despotic' status is a derivative
of the 'despotic' moment at the historical/social formations level.)

The intense qualitative flows of the territorial regime are subjected to measure, strict calculation and quantification. Bargaining and evaluation give way to exact exchange, gift and spectacular festival to equivalence and mean propriety. The marking of the earth and the marking of the body give way to an imperial ledger and an implacable accounting. Cultic divination gives way to the imperial decree; the dance upon the earth is superceded by the letter of the law. The world becomes at one and the same time more ordered and more joyless. Instead of the generous exuberance of cruelty there prevails, instead, the infinite dread of a nameless terror. The pertinence of this model of the over-coding of a territorial regime by a despotic regime to an understanding and reading of *The Mayor of Casterbridge* hardly requires demonstration – indeed the basic 'application' is almost banal. That having been said, however, what a more sustained comparison of the model and the novel reveals, as will be shown below, is a complexity of compatibility and reciprocal illumination that is truly astounding.

While territorial societies work by means of codings and despotic societies by means of over-codings, the capitalist formation works by the scrambling of all codings. Capitalism is, therefore, that which haunts all social formations – the fear of their loss of codings, of falling back into undifferentiated chaos and unbridled anarchy:

> In a sense, capitalism has haunted all forms of society, but it haunts them as its terrifying nightmare, it is the dread they feel of a flow that would elude their codes.[45]

Requiring as it does the unfettered free-play of labour and of money, capitalism (to use Edmund Burke's great term) *volatilizes* previous formations. It constitutes a massive process of deterritorialization. (Here one thinks of the bleak featureless wastes of Flintcomb-Ash in *Tess* and the processes of rural depopulation registered at the end of the novel. But it is also the world of Jude, a world of lost mappings and unavailable lodgings, of ciphered texts and railway timetables). Capital, self-generating, self-producing, migrates about the globe like a locust swarm, its massive unfettered energies dedicated to waste: the more it wastes the more it grows and the more it grows the more it needs to lay waste. Genocide, famine, ecological disaster, market collapse, unemployment, food mountains, wine lakes: these are not the aberrations of capitalism but its conditions of existence. It works by obsolescence and waste. What prevents capitalism blowing itself apart, what prevents it from consuming itself, is, on the one hand, the elaboration of ever more complex axiomatizations of its own practices, ever new formulae and formulations – the New Deal, monetarism, tariff reforms, statistical manipulations, a 'Third Way' dare one add? – and, on the other, the resort to archaic, anachronistic and ever more artificial reterritorializations:

> Civilized modern societies are defined by processes of decoding and deterritorialization. But what they deterritorialize with one hand, they reterritorialize with the other. These neoterritorialities are often artificial, residual, archaic; but they are archaisms having a perfectly current function, or modern way of 'imbricating', of sectioning off, or reintroducing code fragments, resuscitating old codes, inventing pseudo codes or jargons. Neoarchaisms, as Edgar Morin puts it. These modern archaisms are extremely complex and varied. Some are mainly folkloric, but they neverthless represent social and potentially political forces (from domino players to home brewers via the Veterans of Foreign Wars).[46]

In this sense the capitalist world is a kind of gigantic Disneyland or Theme Park or, indeed, a sea-side resort (think here of the always slightly dubious role sea-side resorts such as Sandbourne and Budmouth play in Hardy's novels) – a world of images and simulacra, of second and third order simulations of simulations, where war appears to be no more than an arcade game and endemic unemployment an economic boom. The sheer schizophrenic delirium of such a world has its subjects perpetually in search of a *line of flight* – either in the hope of some sort of transcendence or escape or in a forlorn resort to palliates and analgesics – a *line of flight* towards oblivion and death.

B: Phantasms

> Phantasms are produced by an unconscious combination of things experienced (*choses vécues*) and things heard (*choses entendues*).[47]
> If we ask ourselves what these phantasms of origins mean to us . . . [w]e see then how it can be said of them that not only are they part of the symbolic order, but that they *translate* via the mediation of an imaginary scenario that seeks to effect a purchase on it, the inscription of the most radically institutive symbolic order on the real of the body. What does the primal scene mean for us? The link between the biological fact of

conception (and of birth) and the symbolic fact of filiation, between the naked act of coitus and the existence of the triad of mother–infant–father. In the phantasms of castration the real–symbolic link is even more obvious. Let us add, as far as the phantasm of seduction is concerned, that it is not only, as we have already shown, because he had found a number of real acts of seduction that Freud was able to make of the phantasm a scientific theory, so discovering via this detour the function itself of the phantasm; it is also because he wanted to account for, in terms of an origin, the advent of sexuality to the human being.[48]

The history and the genealogy of the phantasm as a theoretical concept have always been and, indeed, remain troubled. Here, for example, it will be noted that I have chosen to translate the French *fantasme* by the English *phantasm* rather than by the *fantasy* used in the available translation. The problem is that in the original German, and in the French translation of the German, there is only one word (*Phantasie*, *fantasme* respectively) whereas there are available in English two words (*phantasm/fantasy*) or, at least, two spellings (*phantasy/fantasy*). Now, one of the primary concerns of Laplanche and Pontalis' paper is to establish the *fantasme* as something quite other than what we would normally characterize as a 'fantasy' or 'daydream' or, even, mere 'wish-fulfilment'. The *fantasme* they seek to establish as a major psychoanalytical object – indeed what they term several times as the 'psychoanalytical object *par excellence*' – is rather like the kind of 'scene' or 'scenario' in which we find ourselves when in a kind of hypnagogic trance or second state – as in a dream or reverie – we as subjects don't just simply produce the scene but are in fact a part of it. Putting it another way: whereas we as subjects tend to invent and elaborate *fantasies*, the *phantasmatic event* is something that occurs or happens to us, or *possesses* us, quite independently of any design on our part, in moments of shock or crisis, or of reverie or distraction. They are liminal or inaugural occurrences. For Laplanche and Pontalis, it is this second, encompassing, inaugural or 'institutive' *fantasme* that may be said, in fact, to be responsible for *producing* us as human subjects in the first place – hence its crucial place in psychoanalytical theory. The phantasm/*fantasme* is located at the very interface – it *is* the interface – between need and desire, between the merely organic body and the socially determined human being.[49]

It seems to me that this more radical, genetic, *fantasme* is better translated by my *phantasm* than by the normal *fantasy* with its connotations of escapism and irresponsibility and which, I think, detracts something from the *gravitas* of the original concept. It should be said, however, that Laplanche and Pontalis are at pains to stress, that the *fantasme* as *phantasm* – in my sense of the 'deeper', 'genetic', scenario – and the *fantasme* as *fantasy* – my lighter, irresponsible wish-fulfilment – frequently reveal so many similar elements or characteristics (what might be a simple day-dream at one moment might be revealed to be a genetic and formative event at another) that one runs the risk of ignoring this affinity between the two by using different terms to describe them. Nevertheless, it seems to me that an important distinction has to be always kept in mind between the *fantasme* as *phantasm* and the *fantasme* as *fantasy* and this distinction is usefully flagged by the use of the two distinct terms and this I shall proceed to do in what follows. I think it is important, for example, to be able to distinguish, while reading *Tess of the d'Urbervilles*, between Angel's *fantasy* of Tess as a pure unblemished daughter of nature, and the place of Tess in the *phantasmatic* (in fact, *masochistic*[50]) scenario which constitutes his subjectivity; or to distinguish between the Tess who is frequently the object of voyeuristic *fantasy* and the Tess who is *phantasmatically* constructed by the narrative – a *phantasmatic* construction of which the voyeuristic *fantasy* is but one component.

In the chapter on 'Tess and the Phantasm' below I attempt to give a summary of Laplanche and Pontalis's 1964 paper and of Deleuze's development of the notion of the phantasm in his early work. In the chapters on *The Well-Beloved* and *Jude*, particularly the latter, I go on to examine Laplanche's development of the theory of the phantasm in his more recent work[51] particularly with regard to his account of the role that *translation* plays in relation to *repression* and the part played in analysis of processes of *de-translation* and *re-translation*. I also address to some extent the link that Laplanche establishes between *untranslated*, that is *repressed, enigmatic signifiers* and the *categorical imperative*. Finally, in both the *Tess* and the *Jude* chapters I venture to make some suggestions as to the link between the phantasm and the death instinct and what might be entailed in what Lacan, characteristically, elliptically refers to as the *traversal of the phantasm*.[52]

I do not want either to repeat or anticipate that work here but nevertheless some account of the phantasm might be useful.

Lately I have grown into the habit of thinking of the phantasm, with what degree of seriousness I am not sure, as *the most powerful device known to man!* I make this claim largely because, on the one hand, the phantasm is the very mechanism (Laplanche and Pontalis's word for this is an *agencement* – so difficult to translate) by means of which the biological creature that is the newly-born child becomes a human being, while on the other, it is the phantasm again that can be seen to offer the human being the best hope of something like the transcendence and ecstasy associated with the notion of the Nietzschean *eternal return*.

The first and most distinctive feature of the phantasm is that it constitutes the interface between the merely animal entity that is the infant (*infans*, we recall, meaning 'unable to speak') child and the emergence of the human being. It marks, that is, the boundary between animal need and human desire, between the *res extensa* and the *res cogitans*,[53] between the *lived* and the *heard*. At its most elementary the phantasm can be seen quite simply as the moment in which the mere adding of a word to a material circumstance constitutes or, in effect, *declares* it as a meaningful event: what are a *walk*, a *drink*, or a *party* but tiny phantasmatical events? – just as being *declared* man and wife, or a fête being *declared* open. In the literature of psychoanalysis the prototypical phantasm is possibly that sudden emergence into the child's inconsequential sighings, reported by Freud, of the phonemic clusters of 'fort!' and 'da!'[54] that articulate for the first time the penumbra of comings and goings around it and make them part of a human experience. The phantasm, then, – and this is perhaps its most critical function – articulates the biological on the social and the cultural, the purely physiological on the human. The 'Oedipus complex', for example, is the 'nuclear' phantasm as far as human sexuality is concerned for what that complex/phantasm *translates* is the naked act of biological reproduction into the social relation that is the family. It is this which leads Laplanche and Pontalis to speak of phantasms as *'originary phantasms'* for in a phantasm such as the Oedipal phantasm what we find accounted for and, indeed, constituted for the first time, is the question of the *origins* of gender; just as in the phantasm of the primal scene we have broached the *origins* of human life and in the phantasm of seduction the *origins* of human sexuality.

Life as a whole, to the extent that we properly experience it and so *grow* (rather than simply become older) can be regarded as being made up of a whole series of liminal events and phantasmic thresholds. Any major event will shape and determine and articulate and frame our affectivities and predilections, our sexual proclivities and our erotic choices. Indeed it might be argued that it is the phantasm that determines our sense of political and cultural identity and that the nation itself is no more, nor less, than a phantasmatic production. The phantasm, that is, in the last resort, constitutes our ideological armature.

Phantasms, moreover, while in many cases 'typical' – that is, we have all experienced phantasms of the primal scene, seduction, castration – are not in any sense standard or universal in their content or form but are derived from the contingent events that surround us and the collective wisdom – the *dit* or *rumeur* – of our community. What frequently happens in the phantasmatic event is the *unconscious* implanting of the *unconscious* phantasms of those most intimately concerned with our care and well-being – our parents and teachers. These *phantasms* or *scenarios* can remain encysted and unmetabolized for years in our unconscious, frequently in a scrambled or ungrammatical form, determining our whole existence. It is these *latent* and *untranslated* residues that Laplanche describes as *enigmatic signifiers* and compares in peremptory power to the *categorical imperative*. This situation prevails until some fortuitous later event or impasse prompts the endeavour to reach down to these buried memories and seek to *translate* them and bring them into consciousness in the form of a coherent, and now conscious, narrative. In an important sense no phantasmatic registration is instantaneous: always there is at least a minimal delay between the occurrence of the event and its registration – even the *Fort! Da!* requires at least a double take, at least an initial repetition. But the delay involved with the major phantasms associated with sexuality – because the *first*, infantile, event occurs *too early* when we are not prepared for it while the *second* event occurs only after puberty, when it is *too late* to prevent it happening – is what most strikingly marks the characteristic temporality of the phantasm – *that its effect is always an after-effect* – what Freud terms *Nachträglichkeit*. This term appears in recent translations of Laplanche's work as *'afterwardsness.'*[55] It is this delay or hiatus peculiar to the phantasm that has encouraged me to speak of Tess's 'phantasmatic capture', the hiatus between the death of Prince and the murder of Alex, in the chapter below.

The strange temporality – the delay, the 'afterwardsness', *Nachträglichkeit* – of the phantasm has another important effect: it means that when one attempts to come to terms with the phantasm – when one attempts to *traverse* it – one finds oneself immediately caught up in a *resonance* between at least *two times*: the *earlier* and the *later* events. Moreover, as both Laplanche and Deleuze have shown, no phantasmatic experience is ever a discrete event, a phantasm sufficient unto itself, but it always echoes and recalls and repeats other phantasms and events[56] so that once the pendular motion of resonance is set in train it can accumulate momentum to the point where each and every phantasm or event echoes and repeats every other phantasm or event so that all seem to proclaim the 'same' thing in a transport of univocity (that is, literally, *all saying the same thing*, like a great 'Hallelujah!' chorus) – it is this that links the notion of the phantasm to the Nietzschean *eternal return* such as it is described by Pierre Klossowski:

> I deactualize my present self in order to will myself in *all the other selves whose entire series must be passed through*... At the moment the Eternal Return is revealed to me, I cease to be myself *hic et nunc* and am susceptible to becoming innumerable others.[57]

There remains one more feature central to the phantasm and the eternal return, already evident in these quotations from Klossowski: they are centred on loss and absence. One of the primary characteristics of the *phantasm* that distinguishes it from *fantasy* and wish-fulfillment is that it emerges not as a compensation for something that has been lost but as the very mechanism (*agencement*) that *institutes* loss in the first place: that institutes, that is, that differentiation of roles and positions which brings into existence the play of human desire:

> The 'origin' of auto-eroticism [that is the moment of the phantas-matic intervention] would then be the moment when sexuality dis-engages itself from any natural object and finds itself handed over to the phantasm and so creates itself as sexuality.... But one could just as well say that, on the contrary, it is the intervention of the phan-tasm that provokes the disjunction of sexuality and need.[58]

What is engineered by the phantasm is the preemptive loss of a *virtual* object more precious than any *real* object, more precious than the self itself – whether it be the lost breast, the lost phallus, or the lost child – all those many avatars of the '*petit a*' of Lacanian psychoanalysis. It is this ineffable loss that accounts in great part for the hold and the ineluct-ability of the phantasm. The lost (virtual) object – child, phallus, breast, a hanged woman, even, perhaps – becomes the will o' the wisp *quasi-cause* of all our elective affinities. In the traversal of the phantasm that constitutes the eternal return what is lost and dissolved is the self itself, what Deleuze describes as the *moi dissous*, in a radiancy of transcend-ence. This dissolution of the self in the repetitions of the eternal return gives Deleuze a Death Drive at the opposite remove from the regressive material and mechanical repetitions of the Freudian Death Instinct.[59]

'A hanged woman': Hardy's fascination with the figure of the hanged woman, Elizabeth Martha Brown, executed in 1856, and its having in part inspired the denouement of *Tess of the d'Urbervilles* is well established.[60] Nevertheless I was not prepared for the overwhelming role that this particular phantasmatic event plays in both *The Well-Beloved* and *Jude the Obscure* – even though in both these late novels, written more or less in harness with each other, what we find is more a studied *process of dephantasmatization* than one of simple and unconscious submission to the phantasm that has held him: it is as if the phantasm so clearly brought into the light of day at the conclusion of *Tess* had so starkly confronted Hardy with an insight into the appalling heart of his imaginative universe that it could no longer simply be acquiesced in and indulged but must be confronted and exorcised. Once I had become alerted to the role of the phantasm in the fashioning of Hardy's novels it was not difficult for me to find myself reading *Tess of the d'Urbervilles* as little less than a brilliant exploration, from beginning to end, of the phantasmatic constitution of a subjectivity. *Tess* is unquestionably Hardy's masterpiece and whatever reservations one might have about the morbid obsession that informs the whole one cannot but marvel at the intricacy and precision of his psychological acumen. It was at this point that my readings of the later novels – *Tess, The Well-Beloved* and *Jude* – led me to formulate an *a priori* hypothesis with regard to *The Mayor of Casterbridge*. I had already completed what I had thought was a fairly satisfactory chapter on *The Mayor* when I decided that if my understanding of Hardy's *modus operandi* in the other novels was correct then this novel, too, must have its origins in an originary phantasm. That this proved to be yet another tragic and appalling execution of a woman, while it satisfied my theoretical blood-lust, shocked me not just by its inherent horror but by the almost deliberate way I sensed that earlier studies had avoided mentioning it. Finally I, too, returned to *The Return of the Native* but in this instance it was far easier to establish the phantasmal – indeed *Oedipal* – background to the later chapters of this novel for much of the work had already been done by both Hardy's biographers, Gittings, Millgate and Seymour-Smith, and by John Paterson in his excellent *The Making of 'The Return of the Native'*.[61]

C: Phantasmatical megamachines and mega-phantasms

Enough has been said to explain why Hardy's work lends itself so readily to a phantasmatic analysis but this still doesn't get round a problem of theoretical consistency: how can you start off with a study of Hardy based primarily on *Anti-Oedipus*, that notoriously anti-psychoanalytical text, and end up with a series of readings obsessed with the *phantasm*, the psychoanalytical object *par excellence*? Given the fact that Deleuze himself has so anathematized the notion of the phantasm[62] isn't it just obtuse or simply shameless eclecticism to juxtapose the work of Deleuze and Guattari with that of Laplanche and Pontalis?

Well, no. After reading Deleuze's execration of the notion of the phantasm in 1977 it is interesting to go back to Foucault's celebrated essay on Deleuze of 1970, 'Theatrum Philosophicum'.[63] This is the essay, it will be recalled, in which Foucault makes the staggering announcement that 'perhaps one day, this century will be known as Deleuzian.'[64] What is remarkable throughout that essay, which is an admiring account of Deleuze's two most personal, and most brilliant, books, *Différence et Répétition* and *Logique du sens*, is the close association that Foucault establishes between the work of Deleuze and the theoretical concept of the *phantasm*, so much so that he can climax his discussion with the rhetorical question:

> After all, what most urgently needs thought in this century, if not the event and the phantasm[?][65]

Others have complained of Deleuze's tendency to change direction in his work without offering any explanation and, really, nothing is quite so astonishing as Deleuze's disavowal of the notion of the phantasm which plays such a major part in both *Différence et Répétition* and *Logique du sens* – indeed it is the central concept of this second text. And this is the point: the very strength of Deleuze's disavowal of the notion of the phantasm is perhaps the clearest evidence possible that the *phantasm that haunts the later work of Deleuze and Guattari* – Anti-Oedipus *and* A Thousand Plateaux – *is nothing less than the originary phantasm itself.* Thus, while this is not the place to pursue the matter at length, I believe it can be shown that many of the most distinctive concepts of the later work – the *body without organs, agencement, Autrui, strata, the refrain, planes of consistency, lines of flight* – can be traced back to the phantasm. This means that any study employing the theoretical framework of *Anti-Oedipus* and *A Thousand Plateaux* is, sooner or later, bound to come up against the encysted and disavowed material of the phantasm – in many ways the *categorical imperative* that drives the later work. In other words the modulation that my study of Hardy undergoes from the theoretical framework of *Anti-Oedipus* and *A Thousand Plateaux* to that set out initially in the essay on the *'fantasme originaire'* is not the evidence of an opportunistic eclecticism but an inevitable consequence of the phantasmatic latencies in the Deleuze and Guattarian text. The *body without organs,* for example, about which I have already had something to say, far from being a notion threatened by the phantasm –

> The BwO is what remains when you take everything away. What you take away is precisely the phantasy [*fantasme* in the original], and signifiances and subjectifications as a whole.[66]

– is the very site, the double screen, oriented on the one hand towards the world of molecular biological flows and on the other towards the constitution of discrete, molar, identities, where the *phantasmatic interface* between the *lived* and the *heard* takes place. Foucault grasps the affinity of the two notions perfectly:

> Phantasms do not extend organisms into an imaginary domain; they topologise the materiality of the body...phantasms form the impenetrable and incorporeal surface of bodies...[67]

And when Deleuze asks 'What is an *agencement?*'[68] he comes up with an answer which is little more than a paraphrase of the Laplanche and Pontalis descriptions of the *phantasm* – which, it will be recalled, they, too, described as an *agencement*:[69]

> First of all in an *agencement*, there is as it were two faces or two heads at least. There are the *states of things*, states of the body (bodies interpenetrate, mix themselves with one another, affect each other); but also there are the *statements (énoncés)*, regimes of statements: the signs reorganise themselves in a new fashion, new formulations appear, a new style for new gestures (*gestes* – here it could be new adventures as in *chansons de gestes*) (the emblems that confer a knighthood, the forms of oaths, systems of 'declaration', of love, for example ...)[70]

As far as the notions of *strata* and *Autrui* are concerned I draw some attention in the chapters on *Tess* and *Jude* below[71] to their debt to the phantasm and I am confident that further links can be made to establish a similar genealogy for the other major concepts – the *refrain, lines of flight, planes of organization* versus *planes of consistency* – and so on and so forth.

And when all is said and done it should not come as a great surprise that a series of models of the social formation – the territorial, despotic and capitalist regimes – derived, in the first place as we have seen, from a series of models of the unconscious – schizo-paranoid, manic-depressive and Oedipal[72] – should find themselves compatible with another series of models closely concerned with the same theoretical terrain. I have also already intimated the extent to which we might consider the phantasm as constituting our political and cultural identities, or our 'ideological armature', or even the sense of the 'nation' itself.[73] It seems to me to be but a short step from this to considering the social formations described in *Anti-Oedipus* as little more than 'mega-phantasms' or, perhaps, 'phantasmatic megamachines' – indeed I have already alluded, in the essay on *Jude*, to something I have called 'the collapse of the feudal phantasm', by which I mean the feudal world order, in Shakespeare's *Troilus and Cressida*.[74] Having said all that and made one last claim for the power of the phantasm it is ironic that my last chapter here should be concerned with a world bereft of its phantasms. Yet when we recall the characteristic and distinctive temporality of the phantasm – its *afterwardsness, Nachträglichkeit* – then the phantasms that determine *us* have probably yet to be traversed.

2
The Interrupted Return

The Return of the Native offers us a powerful account of what constitutes a primitive territorial formation and the threats that assail it. The massive brooding Heath, as has been so frequently remarked, dominates the story and there is something awesome, magical, inhuman in its Titanic presence.

A Saturday afternoon in November was approaching the time of twilight, and the vast tract of unenclosed wild known as Egdon Heath embrowned itself moment by moment. Overhead the hollow stretch of whitish cloud shutting out the sky was as a tent which had the whole heath for its floor.

The heaven being spread with this pallid screen and the earth with the darkest vegetation, their meeting-line at the horizon was clearly marked. In such contrast the heath wore the appearance of an instalment of night which had taken up its place before its astronomical hour was come: darkness had to a great extent arrived hereon, while day stood distinct in the sky. Looking upwards, a furze-cutter would have been inclined to continue work; looking down, he would have decided to finish his faggot and go home. The distant rims of the world and of the firmament seemed to be a division in time no less than a division in matter. The face of the heath by its mere complexion added half an hour to evening; it could in like manner retard the dawn, sadden noon, anticipate the frowning of storms scarcely generated, and intensify the opacity of a moonless midnight to a cause of shaking and dread.

In fact, precisely at this transitional point of its nightly roll into darkness the great and particular glory of the Egdon waste began, and nobody could be said to understand the heath who had not been there at such a time. It could best be felt when it could not clearly be seen, its complete effect and explanation lying in this and the succeeding hours before the next dawn: then, and only then, did it tell its true tale. The spot was, indeed, a near relation of night, and when night showed itself an apparent tendency to gravitate together could be perceived in its shades and the scene. The sombre stretch of rounds and hollows seemed to rise and meet the evening gloom in pure sympathy, the heath exhaling darkness as rapidly as the heavens precipitated it. And so the obscurity in the air and the obscurity in the land closed together in a black fraternization towards which each advanced half-way.

The place became full of a watchful intentness now; for when other things sank brooding to sleep the heath appeared slowly to awake and listen. Every night its Titanic form seemed to await something; but it had waited thus, unmoved, during so many centuries, through the crises of so many things, that it could only be imagined to await one last crisis – the final overthrow.[1]

The moment is massively critical and inaugural, recalling, as it does, the opening chapters of Genesis and the division of the waters from the land and of the day from the night. One is reminded, at times, of that other great doom-laden, brooding, glooming, opening scene, when the flood has made and is about to turn, of Conrad's *Heart of Darkness*. Here the massive brooding power of the Heath – its imperiousness, arbitrariness, indifference – recalls nothing so much as the *natura naturans* of Spinoza's *Deus sive Natura* (God or Nature)[2] while the 'black fraternization' of the heath and the sky seems to look forward to Heidegger's celebration of the embrace of the *earth* and the *world* in his account of the origins of the work of art.[3] This opening of *The Return of the Native* is, indeed, an *originating origin*. For here, with its characteristic mark of a signal attentiveness, the *être aux écoutes*,[4] a 'watchful intentness,' what we have is nothing less than the *originary phantasm*[5] of a kind of cosmic primal scene with all its passion and violence:

The sombre stretch of rounds and hollows seemed to rise and meet the evening gloom in pure sympathy, the heath exhaling darkness as rapidly as the heavens precipitated it.... Intensity was more often arrived at during winter darkness, tempests, and mists. Then Egdon was aroused to reciprocity; for the storm was its lover, and wind its friend. Then it became the home of strange phantoms; at it was found to be the original of those wild regions of obscurity which are vaguely felt to be compassing us about in midnight dreams of flight and disaster, and are never thought of after the dream until revived by scenes like this.

(pp. 54–5)

It was an awareness of the seismic genetic power of this proto-human, pre-Olympian even, Titanic act of fecundation that prompted Lawrence's celebrated account of the novel:

What is the real stuff of tragedy in the book? It is the Heath. It is the primitive, primal earth, where the instinctive life heaves up. There, in the deep, rude stirring of the instincts, there was the reality that worked the tragedy. Close to the body of things, there can be heard the stir that makes us and destroys us. The [earth] heaved with raw instinct, Egdon whose dark soil was strong and crude and organic as the body of a beast. Out of the body of this crude earth are born Eustacia, Wildeve, Mistress Yeobright, Clym, and all the others.... The Heath persists. Its body is strong and fecund, it will bear many more crops beside this. Here is the sombre, latent power that will go on producing, no matter what happen to the product. Here is the deep, black source from whence all these little contents of lives are drawn. And the contents of the small lives are spilled and wasted. There is savage satisfaction in it: for so much more remains to come, such a black, powerful fecundity is working there that what does it matter![6]

The Heath is not merely one other, albeit superhuman, protagonist of the plot, nor is it simply an inert, picturesque and evocative background – but it is the very plane of consistency, the matrix, the affective field, within the boundaries of which the drama must be framed and then take its place. What the Heath represents, in conjunction with the flows of production, distribution and consumption that are registered upon it as their surface of inscription, is the great primitive *body without organs* of the earth – the *territorial megamachine*:

The earth is the primitive, savage unity of desire and production. For the earth is not merely the multiple and divided object of labour, it is also the unique, indivisible entity, the full body that falls back on the forces of production and appropriates them for its own as the natural or divine precondition.... The *territorial machine* is therefore the first form of the *socius*, the machine of primitive inscription, the 'megamachine' that covers a social field.... The social machine has men for its parts. . . . Flows of women and children, flows of herds and of seed, sperm flows, flows of shit, menstrual flows: nothing must escape coding. The primitive territorial machine, with its immobile motor, the earth, is already a social machine, a megamachine, that codes the flows of production, the flows of means of production, of producers and consumers: the full body of the goddess Earth gathers to itself the cultivable species, the agricultural implements, and the human organs.[7]

Resistant to cultivation and considering 'civilization' to be its enemy, 'the untameable, Ismaelitish' (p. 56) Heath is the primal, primitive ground – germinal, intense – of the territorial *socius*. It is on Egdon and in relation to Egdon that the drama and the conduct of the characters are to be determined, played out, and evaluated.

Massive and molar to the unintimate eye the Heath is essentially, as Hardy tells us in the Preface, a conglomerate – 'a bringing together of scattered characteristics.' To the attentive ear and the attentive eye – to, perhaps it should be noted, the childlike eye for much of the narrative stance is almost as if taken from the eye of someone like Johnny Nunsuch who plays such an important part in the plot – what the Heath presents is not an undifferentiated totality but a teeming, molecular multiplicity. Take, for example, the voice of the Heath:

> It was the united products of infinitesimal vegetable causes, and these were neither stems, leaves, fruit, blades, prickles, lichen, nor moss.
>
> They were the mummied heath-bells of the past summer, originally tender and purple, now washed colourless by Michaelmas rains, and dried to dead skins by October suns. So low was an individual sound from these that a combination of hundreds only just emerged from silence, and the myriads of the whole declivity reached the woman's ear but as a shrivelled and intermittent recitative. Yet scarcely a single accent among the many afloat tonight could have such power to impress a listener with thoughts of its origin. One inwardly saw the infinity of those combined multitudes; and perceived that each of the tiny trumpets was seized on, entered, scoured and emerged from by the wind as thoroughly as if it were as vast as a crater.
>
> (pp. 105–6)

Or the pool outside Eustacia's dwelling:

> The month of March arrived, and the heath showed its first faint signs of awakening from winter trance. The awakening was almost feline in

its stealthiness. The pool outside the bank by Eustacia's dwelling, which seemed as dead and desolate as ever to an observer who moved and made noises in his observation, would gradually disclose a state of great animation when silently watched awhile. A timid animal world had come to life for the season. Little tadpoles and efts began to bubble up through the water, and to race along beneath it; toads made noises like very young ducks, and advanced to the margin in twos and threes; overhead, bumble-bees flew hither and thither in the thickening light, their drone coming and going like the sound of a gong.

(p. 249)

And finally the 'nest' in which Clym meets Eustacia:

He was in a nest of vivid green. The ferny vegetation around him, though so abundant, was quite uniform: it was a grove of machine-made foliage, a world of green triangles with saw-edges, and not a single flower. The air was warm with a vaporous warmth, and the stillness was unbroken. Lizards, grass-hoppers, and ants were the only living things to be beheld. The scene seemed to belong to the ancient world of the carboniferous period, when the forms of plants were few, and of the fern kind; when there was neither bud nor blossom, nothing but a monotonous extent of leafage, amid which no bird sang.

(p. 264)

These are not simple descriptions but strange anatomizing x-rays where beneath organic forms mineral skeletons are to be perceived, where flora and fauna suffer subtle deformations into machined and fossilized shapes, where the geological ages of deep strata are briefly glimpsed on the surface. In the descriptions animal, vegetable, mineral, machinic flows commingle with each other in rich and undifferentiated profusion.[8] The 'acoustic pictures' that come to Eustacia and Wildeve in the darkness conjure up images of many of the locales that figure in the course of the story:

they could hear where tracts of heather began and ended; where the furze was growing stalky and tall; where it had been recently cut; in what direction the fir-clump lay, and how near was the pit in which the hollies grew...

(p. 139)

As many – including Hardy himself[9] – who have attempted it would testify the geography of the Heath is notoriously difficult to pin down for in many ways the spots labelled Blooms-End, The Quiet Woman, Mistover Knap are – like the idiosyncratic times they enjoy –

> 'Twenty minutes after eight by the Quiet Woman, and Charlie not come.'
> 'Ten minutes past by Blooms-End.'
> 'It wants ten minutes past by the captain's watch.'
> 'And 'tis five minutes past by the captain's clock.'
> On Egdon there was no absolute hour of the day.
>
> (p. 186)

– autonomous affective fields not totally subsumed into a coherent whole. Throughout the text we are made aware of the discrete affective intensities of many of the sites of the action – the Reddleman's 'brambled nook' (pp. 141, 205–6), the 'hollow' of the dicing scene (p. 293), the 'lawnlike oasis' of the dance at East Egdon (p. 319), 'Shadwater weir' (p. 436). These affectivities seem to swarm across the Heath like the spectral heath-croppers who witness Wildeve and the Reddleman's dicing (p. 293) or the migrant birds that converge upon the Reddleman – among them the wild mallard which alone brings with it gusts of 'Northern knowledge. Glacial catastrophes, snowstorm episodes, glittering auroral effects...' (p. 141) In fact much of the drama of the narrative can best be understood in terms of a life and death struggle between the molecular flows and intensities of the Heath and those molar forces that would disavow or appropriate them. It is this that makes the Heath such a classic instance of the Deleuze and Guattarian *body without organs*: one face turned always towards the molecular flows while the other is turned towards molar composites.[10]

Closest to these molecular intensities, most intimate with, almost symbiotically at one with them in this almost pre-social world of untrammelled flows, is the Reddleman, the last of the great migratory nomads.[11] We are told (pp. 131–2) of his seasonal migrations in search of reddle, his long peregrinations, his aloofness, isolation and 'Mephistophelian' mysteriousness. The Reddleman moves with the flocks and the seasons and the flows of the earth – sometimes, indeed, he seems closer to the animal (even subterranean) world than to the human, as when, for example, we behold him spying upon Eustacia and Wildeve:

> Near him, as in divers places about the heath, were areas strewn with large turves, which lay edgeways and upside-down awaiting removal by Timothy Fairway, previous to the winter weather. He took two of

these as he lay, and dragged them over him till one covered his hair and shoulders, the other the back and legs. The reddleman would now have been quite invisible, even by daylight; the turves, standing upon him with the heather upwards, looked precisely as if they were growing. He crept along again, and the turves on his back crept with him. Had he approached without any covering the chances are that he would not have been perceived in the dusk; approaching thus, it was as though he burrowed underground.

(pp. 135–6)

After the Reddleman, those closest to the flows are, of course, the heath-dwellers. This collective group at times barely exists as individuals but more as an assemblage of random organs and features scattered about and stapled upon the *body without organs* of the Heath:

The brilliant lights and sooty shades which struggled upon the skin and clothes of the persons standing round caused their lineaments and general contours to be drawn with Düreresque vigour and dash. Yet the permanent moral expression of each face it was impossible to discover, for as the nimble flames towered, nodded, and swooped through the surrounding air, the blots of shade and flakes of light upon the countenances of the group changed shape and position endlessly. All was unstable: quivering as leaves, evanescent as lightning. Shadowy eye-sockets, deep as those of a death's head, suddenly turned into pits of lustre: a lantern-jaw cavernous, then it was shining; wrinkles were emphasized to ravines, or obliterated entirely by a changed ray. Nostrils were dark wells; sinews in old necks were gilt mouldings; things with no particular polish on them were glazed; bright objects, such as the tip of a furze-hook one of the men carried, were as glass; eyeballs glowed like little lanterns. Those whom Nature had depicted as merely quaint became grotesque, the grotesque became preternatural; for all was in extremity.

(pp. 67–8)

Significantly we first meet them when they are tending the fires on the Heath, a collective ministration, where each individual operates less as an individual than as an integral appendage or organ of the Heath itself – 'like a bush on legs' (p. 65).

Furze-cutting itself, their principal occupation, reduces the cutters themselves to something like the status of parasites as illustrated in the description of Clym at work:

The silent being who thus occupied himself seemed to be of no more account in life than an insect. He appeared as a mere parasite of the heath, fretting its surface in his daily labour as a moth frets a garment, entirely engrossed with its products, having no knowledge of anything in the world but fern, furze, heath, lichens, and moss.

(p. 339)

Perhaps nowhere is the proximity of the heath-dwellers to, and affinity with, the flows of the heath more clearly indicated than in the account of the ritual Sunday haircuttings – a kind of comic festival of cruelty, where the body is marked, tribal tales recounted, flows of hair and blood offered to the four corners of the heavens, and manhood reaffirmed:

These Sunday-morning hair-cuttings were performed by Fairway; the victim sitting on a chopping-block in front of the house, without a coat, and the neighbours gossiping around, idly observing the locks of hair as they rose upon the wind after the snip, and flew out of sight to the four corners of the heavens. Summer and winter the scene was the same, unless the wind were more than usually blusterous, when the stool was shifted a few feet round the corner. To complain of cold in sitting out of doors, hatless and coatless, while Fairway told true stories between the cuts of the scissors, would have been to pronounce yourself no man at once. To flinch, exclaim, or move a muscle of the face at the small stabs under the ear received from those instruments, or at scarifications of the neck by the comb, would have been thought a gross breach of good manners, considering that Fairway did it all for nothing. A bleeding about the poll on Sunday afternoons was amply accounted for by the explanation, 'I have had my hair cut you know.'

(pp. 227–8)

Finally, there is a further comical illustration of this continuity of flows shared by the collective and the object of its labour in the mattress-making (the mattress itself a kind of 'mini-heath' or *body without organs*) scene at the end of the book:

They sat down to lunch in the midst of their work, feathers around, above, and below them; the original owners of which occasionally came to the open door and cackled begrudgingly at sight of such a quantity of their old clothes.

'Upon my soul I shall be chokt,' said Fairway when, having ex-
tracted a feather from his mouth, he found several others floating on
the mug as it was handed round.

'I've swallered several; and one had a tolerable quill,' said Sam
placidly from the corner.

(p. 468)

The collective is not just imbricated in production, however, for it
takes upon itself also, albeit in an *ad hoc* and seemingly casual way, the
establishment of alliances and marriages. That is, it is the collective that
cuts into the intense endogamous filiations of descent closest to the
flows of the earth and establishes, instead, sets of lateral, exogamous
alliances and distributions. In fact a good deal of the heath-dwellers'
conversation turns upon issues of kinship, courtship, genealogy, and
eligibility. Almost the first real topic of conversation concerns the marriage of Thomasin and Wildeve (p. 69) while it could be argued that the
major tragedy of the book is set in play by Eustacia over-hearing the idle
chatter of Sam and Humphrey:

'I say, Sam,' observed Humphrey... 'she [Eustacia] and Clym Yeobright would make a very pretty pigeon-pair – hey? If they wouldn't I'll
be dazed.'

(p. 163)

A remark that Eustacia takes very much to heart:

.... the heathmen had instinctively coupled her and this man together in their minds as a pair born for each other.

(p. 164)

It is this collective interference which preempts any possibility of the
relationship between Clym and his cousin Thomasin (that is, a dangerously close *endogamous* filiation), that at one point we sense lies very
much upon the cards.

At all levels, then – at the level of production (furze-cutting,
tick-waxing), at the level of consumption (bon-fire nights, parties,
dances – ''Tis well to call the neighbours together and to hae a good
racket once now and then...' p. 72); at the level of the formation of
alliances – the heath-dwellers enjoy that collective investment of the
earth which is characteristic of territorial formations. It is typical of such
a collective formation that it should resent and disapprove of that which

betrays its very essence. Hence their incomprehension at Eustacia's private fire:

> To have a little fire inside your own bank and ditch, that nobody else may enjoy it or come anigh it!
>
> (p. 79)

At practically every point in the book we find this basic rift returned to – between the molecular intensities of the Heath and the abstraction of private appropriation. Take, for example, the following bizarre scene – perhaps the most climactic of the novel for it so emphatically lays bare the extremities at play:

> The incongruity between the men's deeds and their environment was great. Amid the soft juicy vegetation of the hollow in which they sat, the motionless and the uninhabited solitude, intruded the clink of guineas, the rattle of dice, the exclamations of the reckless players.
>
> (p. 293)

On the one hand the 'soft juicy vegetation', the dark germinal intensities of the earth; on the other, the 'clink of guineas, the rattle of dice', quantified, abstract flows subject to all the vicissitudes of chance, the extreme limit of decoded, deterritorialized, flows.

Perhaps nowhere are the vicissitudes that threaten the institutions of the territorial formation more clearly indicated than in the various appropriations to which the Mummers Plays are subjected in the course of the narrative. That these plays themselves are already an appropriation of earlier festivals is not beside the point:

> The plays traditionally enacted in western England by village mummers (meaning literally 'wearers of masks') were the descendants of earlier plays originally performed at pagan festivals to celebrate the equinoctial conflict between summer and winter. Later, Christian champions and their opponents of the crusading period took the place of the pagan deities representing natural forces, Summer becoming St. George, Winter becoming Saladin or even, in versions played elsewhere at the same time as the Egdon Heath performances, the great folk demon Napoleon.[12]

The great fertility cycle of the territorial formation has been appropriated and overcoded by the champions first, of a feudal, courtly order

(St. George and Saladin), and then by a latter day despot, Napoleon. Vestigial traces of both appropriations are echoed in the text in the figures of *Christian* Cantle (who is presented as a totally inadequate specimen of manhood – a 'maphrotight [for *hermaphrodite*] fool', 'No moon, no man' (p. 76) – compared with the robustness of the turf-cutters) and of *Grandfer* Cantle obsessed with his youthful exploits in the 'Bang-up Locals' formed to repel Napoleon (p. 73). In the course of the narrative the Mummers' Play – already, as we have seen, despotically overcoded by St.George – is further compromised, and its rituals sub-verted, this time for *private* ends, by Eustacia Vye. That this *private* and *individualistic* appropriation must lead to a total *scrambling of codings* is evident by the account of what happens to the distinguishability of the protagonists when the embellishment of their costumes is the occasion of personal rivalry:

> The result was that in the end the Valiant Soldier, of the Christian army, was distinguished by no peculiarity of accoutrement from the Turkish Knight; and what was worse, on a casual view Saint George himself might be mistaken for his deadly enemy, the Saracen.
>
> (p. 179)

It is significant, then, that the two men who come to grief on Egdon Heath should represent those very offices or institutions which the territorial formation must at all costs keep at a distance for fear that its codes become 'abstracted' and 'fictionalised' – the merchant and the technician/smith.[13] On the one hand Clym is a diamond merchant or dealer from Paris; while Wildeve is a trained engineer. Both threaten the intensive germinal flows and codes of the heath with quantification and abstraction – indeed, Clym's philosophical idealism – his positivism – is little more than a cerebral form of the same threat. It is hardly surprising that when he announces his educational plans to the hair-cutting group – which so quintessentially embodies the unconscious economy of the territorial regime – he is met with scant enthusiasm:

> ''Tis good hearted of the young man,' said another. 'But, I think he had better mind his business.'
>
> (p. 229)

This is Clym's initial dilemma – torn between the germinal flows of the Heath –

Clym had been so inwoven with the heath in his boyhood that hardly anyone could look upon it without thinking of him...If anyone knew the heath well it was Clym. He was permeated with its scenes, with its substance, and with its colours. He might be said to be its product. His eyes had first opened thereon; with its appearance all the first images of his memory were mingled; his estimate of life had been coloured by it; his toys had been the flint knives and arrow-heads which he found there, wondering why stones should 'grow' to such odd shapes; his flowers, the purple bells and the yellow furze; his animal kingdom, the snakes and croppers; his society, its human haunters.

(pp. 226 & 231)

– and an abstract humanitarian ambition based upon an embryonic and, Hardy intimates, half-baked socialism –

A man should be only partially before his time...To argue upon the possibility of culture before luxury to the bucolic world may be to argue truly, but it is an attempt to disturb a sequence to which humanity has been long accustomed.

(pp. 230–1)

– Clym is already deeply divided even before his problems are compounded by his fascination with Eustacia and his break with his mother.

Eustacia Vye is, by far, the most complex character in the book but this complexity derives less from an inner problematic than from an external dislocation. For Eustacia's initial plight derives from the fact that she is not torn between just two regimes – say, as in the case of Clym, the territorial regime of the Heath and the abstract, quantitative regime of a capitalist, commercial world – but from the fact that she finds herself adrift across all *three* regimes – territorial, despotic, and capitalist – as well as the artificial, *reaxiomatized* and *neo*-territorialities with which the capitalist regime makes up for its devastations.[14] She was born, we are told, in that classic example of the *neo-territoriality*, the sea-side resort:

Budmouth was her native place, a fashionable seaside resort at that date. She was the daughter of the bandmaster of a regiment that had been quartered there – a Corfiote by birth, and a fine musician – who met his future wife during her trip thither with her father the captain, a man of good family.

(p. 120)

As a result of her parents' deaths she comes to live on the heath with her grandfather but 'She hated the change; she felt like one banished; but there she was forced to abide.' (p. 120).

> Thus it happened that in Eustacia's brain were juxtaposed the strangest assortment of ideas, from old time and from new. There was no middle distance in her perspective: romantic recollections of sunny afternoons on an esplanande, with military bands, officers, and gallants, stood like gilded letters upon the dark tablet of surrounding Egdon. Every bizarre effect that could result from the random weaving of watering-place glitter with the grand solemnity of a heath, was to be found in her.
>
> (pp. 120)

Thus Eustacia is already torn between the 'grand solemnity of the heath' and 'watering place glitter', between the germinal intensities of the earth and the artificial glitter of a seaside resort.[15] And as if this initial division were not enough, Eustacia is obsessed, too, by a line of imperial despots:

> Her high gods were William the Conqueror, Strafford, and Napoleon Buonaparte.... At school she had used to side with the Philistines in several battles, and had wondered if Pontius Pilate were as handsome as he was frank and fair.
>
> (p. 122)

To a very large extent it is this infatuation with the courtly, romantic, despotic ideal, in the form of the longed for 'great lover', that constitutes Eustacia's principal tragic flaw, for this fascination with the 'molar', complete, person or hero disguises from herself the manifest allure held for her by partial objects and local intensities. For what else can be betokened by her almost fetishistic delight in her telescope and hour-glass? (To interpret these simply as 'symbols' is surely no less than to vulgarize Hardy's intelligence.) And how else can we explain the evident thrill Eustacia derives from her sensuous contacts with the vegetation of the heath?:

> A bramble caught hold of her skirt, and checked her progress. Instead of putting it off and hastening along, she yielded herself up to the pull, and stood passively still. When she began to extricate herself it was by turning round and round, and so unwinding the prickly switch. She was in a desponding reverie.
>
> (p. 108)

> When her hair was brushed she would instantly sink into stillness and look like the Sphynx. If, in passing under one of the Egdon banks, any of its thick skeins were caught, as they sometimes were, by a prickly tuft of the large Ulex Europaeus – which will act as a sort of hairbrush – she would go back a few paces, and pass against it a second time.
>
> (p. 118)

Eustacia's mistake is to disavow her own intense affinity with the heath by hypostatizing the latter as a global enemy – "'Tis my cross, my shame, and will be my death.' (p. 139). It is this disavowal that puts her at risk for whereas the scarred and mutilated bodies of the heath-dwellers attest their belonging to the heath and afford them a certain immunity, Eustacia's haughty disdain leaves her particularly thin-skinned. As a result the heath consistently succeeds in getting through to her – she is pricked, scored and consumed by the heath and its ministers. Her relationship with the heath becomes a kind of reciprocal 'cannibalism'. On the one hand her acceptance of the burial urns from the barrow is attributed to 'a cannibal taste' for such things (p. 249) while, on her last walk across the heath, it is she herself who seems to be engulfed in the entrails of some 'colossal animal':

> Skirting the pool she followed the path towards Rainbarrow, occa-sionally stumbling over twisted furze-roots, tufts of rushes, or oozing lumps of fleshy fungi, which at this season lay scattered about the heath like the rotten liver and lungs of some colossal animal.
>
> (p. 420)

Absorbed by the gigantic body of the heath Eustacia's fall into Shad-water Weir resembles nothing so much as being flushed away by some vast urinary duct.

It is notable that this propensity to self-division and instability, amounting almost to schizophrenia, is not just confined to Clym and Eustacia but afflicts other characters too, even one such as Mrs. Yeob-right who seems at first to have such a strong sense of her self and her own identity:

> The air with which she looked at the heathmen betokened a certain unconcern at their presence, or at what might be their opinions of her for walking in that lonely spot at such an hour, this indirectly implying that in some respect or other they were not up to her level.

The explanation lay in the fact that though her husband had been a small farmer she herself was a curate's daughter, who had once dreamt of doing better things.

(p. 83)

It is characteristic of her that she tends to regard the world in totalizing, aloof and 'molar' terms:

What was the great world to Mrs. Yeobright? A multitude whose tendencies could be perceived, though not its essences. Communities were seen by her as from a distance; she saw them as we see the throngs which cover the canvasses of Salaert, Van Asloot, and others of that school – vast masses of beings, jostling, zig-zagging, and processioning in definite directions, but whose features are indistinguishable by the very comprehensiveness of the view.

(p. 248)

At almost the moment of her death we have her vision of the ants:

In front of her a colony of ants had established a thoroughfare across the way, where they toiled, a never-ending and heavy-laden throng. To look down upon them was like observing a city street from the top of a tower.

(p. 351)

And yet even she is attracted by the 'molecular', 'infinitesimal' appeal of the Heath:

Occasionally she came to a spot where independent worlds of ephemerons were passing their time in mad carousal, some in the air, some on the hot ground and vegetation, and some in the tepid and stringy water of a nearly fried pool... she sometimes sat down under her umbrella to rest and watch their happiness, for a certain hopefulness as to the result of her visit gave ease to her mind, and between important thoughts left it free to dwell on any infinitesimal matter which caught her eyes.

(p. 339)

At the very end it is probably fitting that the character that has done most to disavow and break free of the allure of the Heath – with regard to what constitutes a desirable alliance (that of Clym and Eustacia) she represents a principle of moral authority quite at odds with the wishes of the collective – is herself brought low by that most earthbound of creatures, the adder, and the two regard each other at the end in a spirit of inveterate malice:

> Mrs Yeobright saw the creature, and the creature saw her: she quivered throughout, and averted her eyes.
>
> (pp. 358–9)

Finally, there is Diggory Venn, whose bewildering switching of roles between that of prosperous dairy farmer and itinerant Reddleman with moments, too, of Mephistophelean spookiness, threatens at times the very coherence of the text – Hardy's own rather testy account of the reasons for his final transformation into Thomasin's eligible lover some evidence of the stress.[16]

To a considerable extent we can account for these instabilities in terms of the instability of their encompassing milieu, the gigantic *body without organs* of the Heath itself which we have recognized as the precarious threshold or interface between molecular flows and molar identities, between, on the one hand, the subhuman world of purely biological and cosmic drives and pre-personal singularities and, on the other, the human world of discrete sexual and social identities.[17] The frantic patterns of flight and return, the conflicting appeal of the intensities of the Heath and the securities of a professional identity, the pull of Dionysian abandonment set against recognition of the importance of strict marital fidelity, are all part and parcel of the contradictory swirls of affect that traverse the primary plane of consistency.

It is at this point that we can turn to an alternative account of, and explanation for, the instabilities of text and characterization to which we have drawn attention. Nevertheless, what is remarkable about what is, in effect, a complete change of critical perspective is that once the empirical evidence has been marshalled it is again the theoretical model offered primarily by *Anti-Oedipus* that provides the most satisfactory diagnostic tool.

John Paterson's account of the genesis of *The Return of the Native*[18] provides us with an indispensable archeology of the novel. What Paterson's study reveals is the different strata that constitute the novel in the course of its evolution from what Paterson terms an 'Ur-novel' begun in 1877, through the serial publication of January 1878 and the first book edition of November 1878, to the establishment of the Uniform Edition

of 1895 and the Wessex Edition of 1912.[19] It is Paterson's thesis that
what began as a primarily pastoral novel was centred upon the tribula-
tions of a rustic innocent, Thomasin, who, thanks to a faulty marriage
certificate, finds herself unwittingly living in sin with a rather feckless
and seedy *roué*, Wildeve, while, at the same time, she is also the victim of
the cruel attentions of a local witch, the dark and promiscuous Avice
Vye, a former lover of Wildeve. The atmosphere of this Ur-work was
predominantly bucolic and magical – very like the world of *The Romantic
Adventures of a Milk-Maid*. The manuscript evidence suggests that some
sixteen chapters of this Ur-novel were written before Hardy sent it to
Leslie Stephen, the editor of the *Cornhill Magazine* where he had hoped
to have it published. Stephen was nervous about the proposed story:

> 'he feared that the relations between Eustacia [i.e. Avice], Wildeve,
> and Thomasin might develop into something "dangerous" for a
> family magazine.'[20]

Hardy took the hint and withdrew it from the *Cornhill* and subjected the
story to a massive process of what Paterson terms 'bowdlerization' – that
is the wholesale toning down of the whole set of rather *risqué* relations
existing between the three protagonists: Thomasin was no longer to live
with Wildeve in illegal conjugality, Wildeve was made less of a *roué* and
the nature of his past relations with Eustacia were left rather vague while
Eustacia herself (the name changed from Avice) was no longer a witch
except perhaps metaphorically or as a term of abuse. 'Hardy's reappraisal
of the Ur-version,' however,

> went far beyond the narrow requirements of bowdlerization.... Of
> this fact the almost total transfiguration of Eustacia Vye offers the
> most dramatic proof.[21]

From a figure primarily steeped in folk-lore Eustacia is transformed into
the romantic heroine of the final version:

> in the course of revising the Ur-chapters, Hardy discovered and in-
> dulged an unconscious and even reluctant sympathy with the de-
> moniacal creature he had initially conceived.[22]

This 'transfiguration' of Eustacia 'from satanic antagonist to romantic
protagonist'[23] was accompanied, moreover, by a 'revolution in the basic
form of *The Return of the Native*:

the little world of pastoral Wessex was widened to take in, among other things, the more comprehensive world of classical Greece.[24]

It is this first transfiguration that accounts for some of the anomalies of the text – the imperative need to accommodate characters and incidents that might have been at home in a rural comedy to the demands and expectations of a world of classical drama. Paterson draws our attention to the difficulties Hardy found with these transitions: it is very hard to make people of such humble origins assume 'tragic' and 'classical' status and frequently, for example, Clym just seems no more than wooden and *gauche* whereas Eustacia's outrages against the gods just seem at times like the tantrums of a spoilt child.

These changes were dramatic enough but they pale in comparison with those that take place between the serial edition published in *Belgravia* in January 1878 and the first edition of November 1878. The major change here is the *implication of Clym more closely into the episode of the closed door and thereby providing the source of the terrible and disproportionate sense of guilt over his mother's death that afflicts him towards the end of the novel.*[25] There had been no trace of this implication in the manuscript and in the serial edition Clym had not been at home at the moment when Eustacia shuts the door against Mrs. Yeobright. Clym's unconscious presence and its grievous consequences for his mental state are late interpolations at the time of the first edition:

> Clym's involvement in his mother's death and, in effect, the elaboration of the mother–son motif were not decided upon until after Book Fourth had been written in its entirety.[26]

In other words what to the modern reader must seem like the most blatant expression of an excessive Oedipal attachment[27] – that of Clym to the figure of his dead mother – and the most classic of Oedipal rivalries – that between Mrs Yeobright and Eustacia for the possession of Clym – are late intrusions into and, such is the intensity of the feeling generated, appropriations of a narrative that has already suffered an earlier transposition from a rustic to a heroic register. Paterson clearly recognizes the excess and the gratuitousness of this Oedipal invasion:

> At the same time, there is in Clym's guilty implication in his mother's death a strong element of the accidental and the improvised. It has, after all, no necessary relationship to Eustacia's death, generates an almost gratuitous pathos, and to this extent has less to do with the

novel itself than with the personal emotion of the author. It illus-
trates once again what could happen to the artistic integrity of the
book whenever the phantasmal image of Clym Yeobright dominated
its field of vision.[28]

A little later he writes:

> It is clear, certainly, that where the spectral image of Clym Yeobright
> was concerned, his imagination operated independently of artistic
> purpose and hence expressed itself in the inferior form of fantasy.
> Hardy indulged his feeling for his hero at the expense of his responsi-
> bility to the novel. Thus, if the marriage of Clym and Eustacia im-
> presses us as violent and perverse, it is because it was dictated less by
> their necessities as characters than by the necessities of the author
> himself.[29]

There is every evidence that in the bitter rivalry of Mrs Yeobright and
Eustacia and in Clym's tormented reaction to his mother's death Hardy
has allowed into the novel a whole clutch of emotions that he no longer
has under control.

Given Hardy's notorious reticence about the details of his personal life
it is never possible to say with absolute certainty what features of the
works are autobiographical or not but there is a good deal of circumstan-
tial evidence to suggest that in the later chapters of *The Return of the
Native*, in the account of the hero's abandonment of his chosen profession, in his return to his maternal roots, in the rivalry between
Mrs Yeobright and Eustacia and in his division between the two of
them, Hardy is importing into his fiction in barely disguised form many
of the tensions he is experiencing in his own life, particularly the tensions
that existed between his powerful mother, Jemima Hardy, and his wife
Emma, as well as the increasing friction that began to exist between Hardy
and Emma herself. Millgate's account of this period in Hardy's life and its
relevance to *The Return of the Native* is curiously ambivalent if not self-
contradictory. He first comments on the rivalry of Jemima and Emma:

> She and Emma never liked or trusted each other, and in later years a
> mutual antagonism flourished on the basis of real or imagined
> slights...[30]

and then goes on to retail the circumstances surrounding the composition of *The Return of the Native* and comments:

Because the personal connection was so direct and obvious, it seems almost inconceivable that Hardy would consciously have allowed the narrative to fall into autobiographical patterns. Yet the story is that of an idealistic and gifted young man who abandons the professional goals set for him by his ambitious and strong minded mother, becomes distracted from both practical and idealistic ambitions by his infatuation with a free-spirited woman unexpectedly encountered in a wild and lonely place, and subsequently endures – having largely provoked – the social and perhaps sexual frustrations of his disappointed wife and the bitter hostility which springs up between his wife and his mother.[31]

In spite of quite happily acknowledging that Mrs. Yeobright is 'based' on Hardy's mother[32] Millgate's logic here is quite bizarre – as it is again a little later when he writes:

Of all the 'autobiographical' elements in *The Return of the Native*, the one that in the end that remains the most fascinating derives from Hardy's use of his narrative not to recreate his own past experiences but rather *to explore in hypothetical terms a road he had not taken* [my italics, D.M.] – and in so doing, to see more plainly, and perhaps justify to himself, the course he had in fact chosen to follow. Clym's decision to reject his profession and return to the heath was quite distinct from the direction of Hardy's life since he had finally given up architecture, and while he perhaps made some of Clym's mistakes (notably in marrying Emma/Eustacia) he had not taken the false step of trying to go home again.[33]

On the contrary, the novel seems to echo *exactly* Hardy's own choices and experiences – this, after all is what the passage is saying in spite of itself: the rejection of his profession, the impetuous marriage, the return home – including the catastrophic introduction of his wife to his mother. Despite his many protestations against identifying him with his novels' characters (most notorious being the identification with Jude) Hardy was the most self-engrossed and most self-centred of authors and he himself declared that Clym was his favourite character – and no character betrays that self-engrossment and self-centredness, almost beyond self-understanding or self-analysis, more than Clym. Clym's self-reproach and his self-immolation towards the end of the novel are clearly pathological – shades here, even, of Hitchcock's *Psycho*:

Moreover, it had become a religion with him to preserve in good condition all that had lapsed from his mother's hands to his own...

(p. 409)

His mother's old chair was opposite: it had been sat in that evening by those who had scarcely remembered that it ever was hers. But to Clym she was almost a presence there, now as always. Whatever she was in other people's memories, in his she was always the sublime saint whose radiance even his tenderness for Eustacia could not obscure. But his heart was heavy: that mother had *not* crowned him in the day of his espousals and in the day of the gladness of his heart. And events had borne out the accuracy of her judgement, and proved the devotedness of her care. He should have heeded her for Eustacia's sake even more than for his own. 'It was all my fault,' he whispered. 'O, my mother, my mother! would to God that I could live my life again, and endure for you what you endured for me!'

(p. 473)

It seems to me that there can be little argument but that into the latter stages of the novel there is a massive importation of a mother fixation and an Oedipal guilt that is not only paralysing for Clym but is barely within the control of the author himself. It is not the last time that we shall come across, to use Paterson's significant term, *phantasmal* material deriving from traumatic events in Hardy's own life entering into and taking over the organization of his work. Here, in *The Return of the Native*, the Mrs. Yeobright/Clym Yeobright relationship becomes such a model of the Oedipal impasse that D. H. Lawrence can draw on it for his depiction of the similar relationship that obtains between Mrs. Morel and Paul Morel in *Sons and Lovers* – though, fortunately, it might be thought, for him, Lawrence had the benefit of Frieda's familiarity with the work of Freud to help him bring this material under control. *Sons and Lovers*, in many ways, can be seen as the analysis and 'working through' of *The Return of the Native*.

It is here that we can return to *Anti-Oedipus* for it seems to me that in Deleuze and Guattari's onslaught on the Oedipus complex we have an astonishingly precise account of the impasse arrived at at the end of *The Return of the Native*. The movement between territorial, despotic and capitalist formations that was earlier traced in the *narrative themes* of the novel – Clym divided between the Heath and Paris, Eustacia torn between a territorial fetishism, the longing for a heroic lover and the need for money – can now be seen to characterize the *series of strata* laid down in the course of the composition of the work from the Ur-text of 1877 to the Uniform Edition of 1895. We have seen how the Ur-novel was described by Paterson as a primarily rural and magical work embued with the kind of folkloric material we might expect of a *territorial forma-tion* (Thomasin and Susan Nunsuch's fetishism seem to be survivals from that strata). As the result of the 'bowdlerization' and 'revaluation' prompted by what Paterson himself terms a censorship of '*despotic* [my italics, D.M.] completeness' this early rustic work was completely revamped as a powerful romantic tragedy with *classical, mythical* and *heroic* overtones where the would-be models are Prometheus, Oedipus, Hamlet and Lear – that is by a second, imperious, strata wholly incom-mensurate with the first, modest, local and provincial, tale. The *territor-ial*, we might say, has been wholly subsumed and over-coded by themes prompted by a *despotic* code. Then, late in the day, at the time of the revision of the text for the Uniform Edition of 1895 this second strata is itself supplanted and catastrophically thrown out of kilter by the erup-tion into the text of a body of *Oedipal* material there is every evidence the author does not control. *Territorial, Despotic, Oedipal*: the strata of *The Return of the Native* would almost seem to be designed to illustrate the argument of *Anti-Oedipus* which might be summarized as the cata-strophic supplanting of an unconscious conceived of as a field of *mo-lecular* production (what, after all, is the Heath?) by the *dramatis personae* of a tawdry theatre centred on *molar* identities (Daddy, Mummy and poor little Me – in the case of Clym just Mummy and poor little Me).

It is only now that we have all the strata of the novel in place that we can begin to give a full account of the curiously quixotic and mercurial role of Diggory Venn, the Reddleman. There is, it must be said, very little that need be added to what Paterson has to say about him:

> The instability of the reddleman as a character-image is ultimately traceable to fluctuations in the conception of the novel over which, as we have seen, the author had no control... Diggory Venn repre-sents, then, a rough and almost forcible compromise between three essentially incompatible conceptions: the rude countryman, the le-gendary reddleman, and the solid citizen–husband.[34]
> The image of Diggory Venn represents a complex, then, of three clearly inrreconcilable elements: the yokel, the reddleman, and the ordinary citizen.[35]

I am not sure that all the correlations are quite as straightforward as Paterson makes them out to be: the 'legendary reddleman' seems to me to be just as much at home in a *territorial* formation as the 'yokel' and this leaves his compatibility with the second, *despotic* or *heroic/romantic* strata rather open to question – unless one is prepared to accord him, as Paterson does at one point, the status of 'romantic outcast'[36] or that of a *deus ex machina* which would fit in with the aspiration to classical form. Nevertheless it is quite clear that the dislocations of his character and the arbitrariness of the transitions that he makes from the one to the other has a lot to do with the archeological stratifications of the work's composition. Certainly his reversion to the condition of a comfortable bourgeois at the end of the novel is in keeping with the *domestic* focus of the later episodes – after the *rural/territorial* and the *despotic/heroic*. Moreover it is perhaps worth noting that in his metamorphosing from reddleman to gentleman dairy farmer, in turning from the flows of the heath to the fluctuations of the market – 'Yes, I am given up body and soul to the making of money. Money is all my dream.' (p. 458) – from the intensities of the *territorial* to the abstractions of the *capitalist* machine, Venn is in so many ways anticipating the opening moves of *The Mayor of Casterbridge*.

We cannot, however, end there. I do think that the Oedipal baggage at the end of the novel throws the whole thing off course but I am not sure that this is Hardy's last word. Clym, at the end, is unquestionably terminally damaged, pathetic rather than even sympathetic in his christological, sermon-on-the-mount, ramblings. That Hardy knows this is all rather pathetic is perhaps indicated by the rather obtuse text he gives Clym for his last sermon:

> 'And the king rose up to meet her, and bowed himself unto her, and sat down on his thrown, and caused a seat to be set for the king's mother; and she sat on his right hand. Then she said, I desire one small petition of thee: I pray thee say me not nay. And the king said unto her, Ask on, my mother, for I will not say thee nay.'
>
> (p. 474)

The text comes from I Kings 2 vv. 19–20 and it recounts how Basheba, Solomon's mother, asks that Adonijah, Solomon's elder brother, be given Abishag the Shunamnite, the late King David's last paramour, as a wife. Solomon quickly divines that this is a power-stratagem on Adonijah's part, an immediate threat to himself, and within four verses Adonijah is dead – executed by Solomon's express command. So the text by no means testifies to a son's acquiescence to a mother's request:

rather the opposite – that a mother's wishes should be treated with no less suspicion and circumspection than those of anyone else.

In fact, even earlier, at the very moment when the Oedipal crisis is given, however fortuitously, its name, there is the suggestion that the purely domestic tragedy, for all its immediate intensity, dwindles into insignificance against the background of the transcending heath. Clym has just been told by Johnny Nunsuch of his mother's last words: 'Cast off by my son!':

> ... Yeobright went forth from the little dwelling. The pupils of his eyes, fixed steadfastly on blankness, were vaguely lit with an icy shine; his mouth has passed into the phase more or less imaginatively rendered in studies of Oedipus. The strangest deeds were possible to his mood. But they were not possible in this situation. Instead of there being before him the pale face of Eustacia, and masculine shape unknown, there was only the imperturbable countenance of the heath, which having defied the cataclysmal onslaught of centuries, reduced to insignificance by its seamed and antique features the wildest turmoil of a single man.
>
> (p. 388)

Inevitably, then, we must return to the Heath. Here we need to recall the almost visceral allure of the heath for Clym:

> Clym had been so interwoven with the heath in his boyhood that hardly anybody could look upon it without thinking of him.... If anyone knew the heath well it was Clym. He was permeated with its scenes, with its substance, and with its odours. He might be said to be its product.
>
> (pp. 226 & 231)

The language here – 'interwoven', 'permeated' – so much suggests an organic bond that one cannot but regard the heath as a kind of womb, or indeed *placenta*,[37] of which Clym is indeed the 'product'. Significantly, again in a passage we have already quoted, Clym is later described lying in a 'nest of vivid green':

> The ferny vegetation around him, though so abundant, was quite uniform: it was a grove of machine-made foliage, a world of green triangles with saw-edges, and not a single flower. The air was warm with a vaporous warmth, and the stillness was unbroken. Lizards, grass-hoppers, and ants were the only living things to be beheld.

The scene seemed to belong to the ancient world of the carboniferous period, when the forms of plants were few, and of the fern kind; when there was neither bud nor blossom, nothing but a monotonous extent of leafage, amid which no bird sang.

(p. 264)

Here we have to abandon the facile identification of the heath with the womb: this is so much more and so much more positive. Clym's *return to the native land*, seen simply negatively, is undoubtedly regressive and back to the womb, but it is so much more than that for here we can see him entering into animal and mineral constellations way beyond out normal perceptions. So much so that we can argue that the climax of the novel comes not with the death of Eustacia and Wildeve nor with the death of Mrs. Yeobright nor with Clym's preaching at the end but with the glimpse of Clym reduced to being no more than a furze cutter, girt with the accoutrements of his trade,[38] absorbed and lost in the miracle of the heath like Matheson's *Incredible Shrinking Man*:[39]

His daily life was of a curious microscopic sort, his whole world being limited to a circuit of a few feet from his person. His familiars were creeping and winged things, and they seemed to enroll him in their band. Bees hummed around his ears with an intimate air, and tugged at the heath and furze-flowers at his side in such numbers as to weigh them down to the sod. The strange amber-coloured butterflies which Egdon produced, and which were never seen elsewhere, quivered in the breath of his lips, alighted upon his bowed back, and sported with the glittering point of his hook as he flourished it up and down. Tribes of emerald-green grasshoppers leaped over his feet, falling awkwardly on their backs, heads, or hips, like unskilful acrobats, as chance might rule; or engaged themselves in noisy flirtations under the fern-fronds with silent ones of homely hue. Huge flies, ignorant of larders and wire-netting, and quite in a savage state, buzzed about him without knowing that he was a man. In and out of the fern-dells snakes glided in their most brilliant blue and yellow guise, it being the season immediately following the shedding of their old skins, when their colours are brightest. Litters of young rabbits came out from their forms to sun themselves upon hillocks, the hot beams blazing through the delicate tissues of each thin-fleshed ear, and firing it to a blood-red transparency in which the veins could be seen. None of them feared him.

(p. 312)

Clym's abandonment of the 'flashy business' (p. 233) 'whose sole concern was the especial symbols of self-indulgence and vainglory' (p. 227) was in many ways a break down and a commitment to what Deleuze and Guattari would call a schizophrenic *line of flight*[40] – but there was no reason why this line of flight had to end in the catatonia that afflicts Clym at the end of the novel. R. D. Laing describes the schizophrenic journey in terms that cannot but remind us of the passages we have just quoted:

> This journey is experienced as going further 'in', as going back through one's personal life, in and back and through and beyond into the experience of all mankind, of the primal man, of Adam and perhaps even further into the being of animals, vegetables and minerals.[41]

For Laing this journey is not so much the symptom of an illness as the natural means of cure:

> Can we not see that *this voyage is not what we need to be cured of, but that it is itself a natural way of healing our own appalling state of alienation called normality.*[42] (Italics in the original)

This surely is borne out by the novel: in the above account of Clym amidst the heath we sense an extraordinary happiness, a complete dissolution of the self (so different from the pathetic self-engrossed creature at the end of the novel), an experience of an almost cosmic transcendence – pitched over almost into the ineffable with his poignant song, significantly entitled *Le point du jour* – Daybreak. Indeed, though it is now *dawn* and not *twilight* there is a sense here of a return to the inaugural moment of the text: a return to the *originating origin*, the *originary phantasm*.

This is the point – as Laing is at pains to convey: it is not the schizophrenic journey, *the return of the native*, that leads to break down and catatonic withdrawal *but the interruption of the journey*. Deleuze and Guattari write:

> Everything changes depending on whether we call psychosis the process itself [that is the schizophrenic journey], or on the contrary, the interruption of the process.[43]

and Laing speaks of the '*forme frustre* of a potentially *natural* process.'[44] Clym's tragedy is that his journey 'in' and 'beyond', his schizophrenic line of flight, is *interrupted* and *blocked* by, first, Eustacia and, secondly, his mother. Even from the beginning Clym senses that Eustacia is a mistake: 'I almost wish you had not had that party,' (p. 219) he tells his mother referring to the occasion of his first meeting with Eustacia. While Clym is in flight into the heath, Eustacia is in flight away from it: they are on diametrically opposed paths and their marriage cannot but terminate in stalemate (an ominously accurate term here) and impasse. Mrs. Yeobright similarly blocks the line of flight primarily by giving a *molar, personalist* (if I may put it that way) construction to his dilemma. The claim of Mrs. Yeobright on Clym is the classic Oedipal ploy: Oedipus gives desire a molar representation which distracts it like a lure from its real objective, the molecular intensities of the *body without organs* of the great maternal Heath.[45] Deleuze and Guattari speak of the fate that so often attends the line of flight: it either breaks through

> Or it strikes a wall, rebounds off it, and falls back into the most miserably arranged territorialities of the modern world as simulacra of the preceding planes, getting caught up in the asylum aggregate of paranoia and schizophrenia as clinical entities, in the artificial aggregates of societies established by perversion, in the familial aggregate of Oedipal neuroses.[46]

This seems to be what the *interrupted return* results in for Clym: reduced to clinical psychosis, trapped in a perverse marriage, and overwhelmed by Oedipal guilt – all three curiously distorted travesties or *simulacra* of the regimes traversed by the novel: the *body without organs* of the heath, the demand for a grand passion, the domestic compromise of the close. It is almost as if the flight heralded by the notion of the *return of the native* is hobbled by the very apparatus assembled to describe it so that 'novel' and 'return' are inherently inimical to one another. I think this was always Hardy's problem and accounts for much of the flimsily disguised paranoia and schizophrenia that hover about his novel-writing from beginning to end.[47]

3
The Exploding Body of *The Mayor of Casterbridge*

There is a good deal to be said for the view shared by two of Hardy's biographers that, in the words of the one:

> *The Mayor* is Hardy's most tightly and economically plotted novel.[1]

and in those of the other:

> [*The Mayor of Casterbridge*] remains the best plotted and the most dramatic of his works.[2]

and there is something rather predictable in the fact that *The Mayor* should have been the first of Hardy's texts to have been selected for inclusion in a school curriculum set by an examination board.[3] Compared with many of Hardy's other novels with their unfortunate tendency to raise questions about sexual behaviour and morality *The Mayor*, as a friend with a teenage daughter has remarked, is 'safe' – one could let one's servants read it. Moreover it is gratifyingly 'teachable' – all those temptingly available and easily framed questions on 'character' and 'fate' or on structure and plot, or on background and myth.[4] On the whole, the critics have not let us down with their essays on Henchard and Elizabeth-Jane, the Corn Laws and the comparisons to be drawn with *Oedipus* and *Lear*, *Julius Caesar* and *Othello*.

What emerges as at stake in this last concern is the level of historical specificity at which the novel should be read. On the one hand there is the uncompromising and more sociologically orientated view of Douglas Brown for whom *The Mayor of Casterbridge* is unquestionably a novel set in the 1840s and intricately concerned with the condition of agriculture on the eve of the Repeal of the Corn Laws[5] and for whom 'the analogies between *The Mayor* and Greek drama' are little more than literary flummery.[6] On the other hand there is, what we might call, the more 'literary' view propounded by critics of Brown such as Gregor and Maxwell,[7] and perhaps most forcefully presented by John Paterson, that *The Mayor of Casterbridge* should be regarded primarily as a work of almost classic tragic form for which the contingencies of history are no more than a convenient filling:

> To describe the dominating motive of the novel as therefore realistic, however, would be not only to underestimate, but also to leave largely unexplained, the great vitality that it ultimately generates. It would be to ignore the fact that its realistic data are in the end assimilated and controlled by the tragic form, and that it is this form and not the content, not its fidelity to the data of social history, that finally accounts for its perennial power.[8]

To my mind this potentially endlessly diverting debate between round-heads and cavaliers, or between the infantry and the cavalry, has been brought to a wonderfully elegant end in the Marxist – Althusserian and Machereyan – account of the text by Michael Valdéz Moses who argues that the interweaving of realistic materials and classical models is part and parcel of Hardy's ideological 'sleight-of-hand' whereby the real historical, and intractable, contradictions of the mid-nineteenth century are glossed and 'resolved' at the imaginative level by the imposition of classical forms:

> In Marxist terms one could regard the superimposition of the story of Oedipus on that of Henchard as an ideological feint, an attempt to mask the contradictions in bourgeois existence Hardy had uncovered by overlaying them with the aura of Greek myth. . . . All this would suggest Hardy's complicity in perpetuating a reigning ideological dogma; though his novel actually reveals the contradictions that riddle bourgeois existence, he succeeds in making that form of economic life palatable to his middle-class readers by assimilating it to the prestigious patterns of traditional Greek myth and tragedy.[9]

Nevertheless, he is careful to add that

> The very lack of structural integrity in the novel can be said to reveal the fissure between the idealised portrait of the bourgeois – elevated to tragic status by the myth background – and the sordid economic

and political realities out of which this self-destructive career emerges.[10]

In other words the structural disturbances of the text – Moses draws particular attention to the rather messy ending: the 'second exile' cheapening the effect of the first – call into question and lay bare the ideological ambitions of the novel as a whole and to this extent the novel can be read as a subtle form of what is, in effect, a pre-emptive self-critique. This is, indeed, an elegant solution. Nevertheless I am tempted to wonder – all the more so when my attention is drawn, as it has been, to other more enigmatic and less immediately obvious disturbances in the text – whether its very elegance is not just one more strategy of closure that would pre-empt a more searching critical analysis.

I think it helps if we return to the question of the specificity of the historical and political conjuncture that the text addresses and here I will begin by pitching my analysis somewhere between the concrete particularity of Douglas Brown and the trans-historical generic claims of John Paterson – at a level which one might call, for the moment, 'anthropological.' In other words rather than situating the text in relation to a specific moment which might be labelled '1846' and speak of a shift between 'heroic' and 'domestic' capitalism or between 'agrarian' and 'finance' capital we locate it instead at the moment of the confrontation between, in the terms afforded by *Anti-Oedipus*, a 'territorial' regime and its codings and a 'despotic' regime and its overcodings and all that that entails in terms of new systems of signification, new systems of gender relations, and the inevitable fall-out that this overcoding provokes in terms of the emergence of new threats and marginalities.

That the principal drama of the novel depicts the over-coding and supplanting of an agrarian, rural, territorial regime by an imperial, centralized, impersonal administrative order is figured in the very topography of Casterbridge itself. The town's imperial heritage is everywhere evident:

> Casterbridge announced old Rome in every street, alley, and precinct. It looked Roman, bespoke the art of Rome, concealed dead men of Rome.
>
> (p. 140)[11]

Its geometrical, arbitrary, shape squats uncompromisingly amidst its rural hinterland:

Casterbridge, as has been hinted, was a place deposited in the block upon a corn-field. There was no suburb in the modern sense, or transitional intermixture of town and down. It stood, with regard to the wide fertile land adjoining, clean-cut and distinct, like a chess board on a green table-cloth.

(p. 162)

The great opening scene of the novel – the wife-sale at Weydon-Priors – offers us, as in an overture, the major themes of the text. Out of the landscape emerges the dust-bestrewn Henchard and his wife and child. Henchard himself at this stage, hung about with his rustic tools, more 'an anthropological object' than 'a man of character.'[12] The furmity tent, the furmity woman, and the furmity itself – a kind of primitive, albeit nutritive, biotic soup – are like a last enclave of a doomed territorial regime, residual and already corrupted from within by the insidious presence of alcohol. Once intoxicated, Henchard, a kind of 'drunken king',[13] indulges himself with a bout of cantankerous bragging such as he has done many times before without any dire consequences – but this time, suddenly and unexpectedly, a new force intervenes from without, the sailor Newson – the name itself suggestive of a new order – and changes the whole complexion of the game with his 'five crisp pieces of paper.' (p. 78) With the introduction of money the whole nature of the scene changes:

> The sight of real money in full amount, in answer to a challenge for the same till then deemed slightly hypothetical, had a great effect upon the spectators.... Up to this moment it could not positively have been asserted that the man, in spite of his tantalizing declaration, was really in earnest.... But with the demand and response of real cash the jolly frivolity of the scene departed. A lurid colour seemed to fill the tent, and change the aspect of all within.

(p. 78)

The over-reaching vainglory and self-estimation of Henchard has already destabilized the territorial regime from within and renders it helpless to resist the swift *coup* of a new order from without – Newson here a harbinger of all that is to come later in the form of Farfrae.

The sale of his wife is one of the many moments of 'disseverance' that Henchard will experience in the course of the novel. It is a radical disavowal of his autochthonous roots and the great oath that follows to foreswear all strong drink or alcoholic liquor is another massive act of self-repression and self-denial.[14] The tragedy of Henchard is that for him the establishment of character, even of identity itself, always entails the institution of a certain lack and experience of loss without ever fully escaping the allure and the strength of all that his been denied and disavowed. For all his assumption of despotic status Henchard can never shake himself free from his territorial roots. The repressed, the territorial, in the figure of the haggish furmity woman, will return.

The extent to which Henchard remains marked by his own origins and the difference this makes for between him and Farfrae is consistently made clear in the comparisons drawn between him and the latter. The terms of the struggle are set out again and again. Early on Henchard, for example, shows his awareness of the differences between them:

> In my business, 'tis true that strength and bustle build up a firm. But judgement and knowledge are what keep it established. Unluckily I am bad at science, Farfrae; bad at figures – a rule 'o thumb sort of man. You are just the reverse – I can see that.
>
> (p. 117)

Later we are told, as Farfrae's influence gains apace:

> The old crude viva voce system of Henchard, in which everything depended on his memory, and bargains were made by the tongue alone, was swept away. Letters and ledgers took the place of 'I'll do't,' and 'you shall hae't,' and, as in all such cases of advance, the rugged picturesqueness of the old method disappeared with its inconveniences.
>
> (p. 160)

The townsfolk note the nature of the change:

> Where would his business be if it were not for this young fellow? 'Twas verily Fortune sent him to Henchard. His accounts were like a bramblewood when Mr. Farfrae came. He used to reckon his sacks by chalk strokes all in a row like garden-palings, measure his ricks by stretching his arms, weigh his trusses by a lift, judge his hay by a chaw, and settle the price with a curse. But now this accomplished young man does it all by ciphering and mensuration.
>
> (p. 177)

and, at the last, we are told

scales and steelyards began to be busy where guess-work had formerly
been the rule.

(p. 295)

This steady eclipse of an order based upon the evaluative eye, the taste
and texture of its produce, generous approximation and brusque bluster
and its being overtaken and overcoded by exact measurement, abstract
quantities and impersonal transactions – this obliteration of one order
by another – is poignantly symbolized in the repainting of the gates of
the corn-store:

> A smear of decisive lead-coloured paint had been laid on to obliterate
> Henchard's name, though its letters dimly loomed through like ships
> in a fog. Over these, in fresh white, spread the name of Farfrae.
>
> (p. 294)

It is always in the context of such an epochal and titanic struggle between
the old order and the new, the territorial and the despotic, that the
struggle between the two main protagonists of the novel must be seen.
On the one hand we have in the figure of Henchard – former hay-trusser,
fetishistic, credulous, intensely passionate – the bewildered, almost
tragic, avatar of a primitive territorial order, while, on the other, we
have, in the figure of Farfrae – the fair complexioned, coldly calculating,
scientifically innovative stranger from afar – the smooth-tongued,[15] op-
portunistically sentimental but, when necessary, chillingly ruthless ad-
venturer/conqueror/despot.[16] Deleuze cites *The Genealogy of Morals*:

> Some pack of blond beasts of prey, a conqueror and a master race
> which, organized for war and with the ability to organize, unhesitat-
> ingly lays its claws upon a populace perhaps tremendously superior
> in numbers but still formless.... In some ways that is incomprehen-
> sible to me they have pushed right into the capital...[17]

What we have here is the very origin of the State:

> It is exactly in this way that Marx defines Asiatic production: a higher
> unit of the State establishes itself on the foundations of the rural
> communities... The full body of the socius has ceased to be the
> earth, it has become the body of the despot, the despot himself or
> his god.... in place of the territorial machine, there is the 'mega-
> machine' of the state.[18]

The almost total incompatibility of temperament and conduct – an incompatibility rooted in the incompatibility of two quite distinct social regimes – that divides Henchard and Farfrae is clearly and dramatically illustrated in the two episodes that lead to their initial break with each other. The first centres on the treatment of Abel Whittle (pp. 167 ff.). Henchard has become impatient at Abel's frequent lateness for work and threatens to 'mortify his flesh ... ' When Abel is once again late for work Henchard personally rouses him from bed and marches him through the streets without breeches. Farfrae is scandalized by this behaviour and risks Henchard's displeasure by publicly saying so and by insisting that Abel be allowed to dress himself properly. Henchard is furious and counters Farfrae's charge that he has been tyrannical:

> "Tis not tyrannical!' murmured Henchard, like a sullen boy. 'It is to make him remember!'
>
> (p. 170)

It is characteristic of a territorial formation to associate memory with pain, to operate via a 'mnemotechnics,' that require 'blood, torture and sacrifice ... to create a memory'.[19] At first sight Farfrae's more 'humane' treatment seems far more kindly and even far more effective. It makes, in some ways for greater efficiency. Abel himself testifies to this later in the book when Farfrae's more enlightened practices have finally taken over:

> We work harder, but we bain't made afeard now. It was fear made my few poor hairs so thin! No busting out, no slamming of doors, no meddling with yer eternal soul and all that; and though 'tis a shilling a week less I'm the richer man; for what's all the world if yer mind is always in a larry, Miss Henchet?
>
> (p. 295)

The treatment is unquestionably less harsh – but the exploitation is the greater – more work for less money. What has gone along with the constant 'larry' is also a certain amount of benevolence and generosity. Under the regime of Henchard the rough justice had been offset by unlooked for kindness:

> During the day Farfrae learnt from the men that Henchard had kept Abel's old mother in coals and snuff all the previous winter. ...
>
> (p. 170)

In the end it is this 'deeper' memory of the body, of harshness and of kindness, that prevails. It is Abel who follows the broken Henchard into exile:

> 'You see he was kind-like to mother when she wer here below, though 'a was rough to me.... He was kind-like to mother when she wer here below, sending her the best ship-coal, and hardly any ashes from it at all; and taties, and such-like that were very needful to her.'
>
> (p. 408).

The second episode which so dramatically differentiates Henchard's whole conception of the social order from Farfrae's is that in which each sets about organizing the 'celebration of a national event,' (pp. 173 ff.). Henchard's instinctive penchant is for the spectacular and gratuitous, a no-expense-spared outdoor jamboree reminiscent of the primitive institution of potlach:

> He advertised about the town, in long posters of a pink colour, that games of all sorts would take place here; and set to work a little battalion of men under his own eye. They erected greasy-poles for climbing, with smoked hams and local cheese at the top. They placed hurdles in rows for jumping over; across the river they laid a slippery pole, with a live pig of the neighbourhood tied at the other end, to become the property of the man who could walk over and get it. There were also provided wheelbarrows for racing, donkeys for the same, a stage for boxing, wrestling, and drawing blood generally; sacks for jumping in. Moreover, not forgetting his principles, Henchard had provided a mammoth tea, of which everybody who lived in the borough was invited to take part without payment.
>
> (pp. 174–5)

The emphasis here is clearly on (predominantly masculine) skill, prowess, brutality and festive cruelty – 'drawing blood generally,' – as well as an almost aggressive, belligerent, generosity.

Farfrae's scheme is more canny and more calculated, ostensibly less spectacular and from the outside 'unattractive.' (p. 175). But his 'enclosure' – 'the pavilion as he called it' – provides an 'interior' (p. 176) protected from the elements, a private, privileged space for a stringed band and dancing. Farfrae himself, first to Henchard's disgust and then to his chagrin, is the focus of attention – particularly that of the ladies. And what galls most: he has charged for admission at so much a head – a

kind of embryonic poll tax. As near as could have been possible Farfrae
has created something like a miniature court, or even petty fiefdom, or
state, with himself the beheld of all the beholders. As the storm lashes
Henchard's primitive spectacle to shreds, the young Sun King dances
into the night.

This account of the principal drama of the novel in terms of the over-
coding of a territorial regime, represented by Henchard, by a despotic
regime represented by Farfrae, however 'new' the terminology might
appear to be, hardly takes us very far. Hardy's reading of Comte, for
example, would have made him familiar with the distinction between
'fetishistic' and 'monotheistic' social formations and there can be little
doubt that Hardy was fully aware of the Comtean scheme of *The Mayor.*
What makes the further reading of Hardy's work alongside that of
Deleuze and Guattari worthwhile, however, is the almost uncanny precision with which Hardy seems to anticipate a number of the more
abstruse features of the Deleuzian and Guattarian model. Two major
areas of complexity concern *writing* and *incest*, first as separate, but then
as intimately linked, issues. Deleuze and Guattari's own discussion of
this relationship between, on the one hand, the establishment of a
linguistics of the signifier and, on the other, the *despotic over-coding of
alliance and filiation*, is possibly one of the densest and least penetrable
sections of their *Anti-Oedipus.*

In *Anti-Oedipus* Deleuze and Guattari develop an elaborate distinction
between what they there describe as 'territorial' and 'barbarian' (or
'despotic' or 'imperial') systems of representation (in *A Thousand Plateaux* these differences are seen in terms of 'pre-signifying' and 'signifying' semiotic systems[20]). The key to the differences between the two
systems lies in the changed relationship between what they term the
'*voice*' and '*graphism*' i.e. between *speech* and '*marking/writing*' – often on
the body. Their most concise account of the change they are attempting
to describe is the following summary of the work of Leroi-Gourhan:

> primitive societies are oral not because they lack a graphic system but
> because, on the contrary, the graphic system in these societies is
> independent of the voice; it marks signs on the body that respond
> to the voice, react to the voice, but that are autonomous and do not
> align themselves on it. In return, barbarian civilizations are written,
> not because the voice has been lost, but because the graphic system
> has lost its independence and its particular dimensions, has aligned
> itself on the voice and become subordinated to the voice, enabling it
> to extract from the voice a deterritorialized abstract flux that it

retains and makes reverberate in the linear code of writing. In short, graphism in one and the same movement begins to depend on the voice, and induces a mute voice from on high or from the beyond, a voice that begins to depend on the graphism. It is by subordinating itself to the voice that writing supplants it.[21]

What this means is that in 'territorial' or 'primitive' formations there is not the intimate bond between *speech* and *writing* as there is in the 'barbarian' or 'despotic' system that introduces and depends upon the *phonetic signifier* as its sole support of signification. In territorial formations voice and gesture, speech and writing/marking enjoy a relative autonomy linked only by a connotative resonance which can only be remarked and enjoyed by the presence of the third organ (after mouth and hand) – the witnessing and appreciative eye. The three together – the intoning voice, the marking hand, and the witnessing eye – constitute what Deleuze and Guattari call the 'magic triangle' of territorial representation. It is just such a plurilinear, multifaceted system of communication that we find, early in the novel, to be characteristic of the market-folk of Casterbridge:

> The yeomen, farmers, dairymen, and townsfolk, who came to transact business in these ancient streets, spoke in other ways than by articulation. Not to hear the words of your interlocutor in metropolitan centres is to know nothing of his meaning. Here the face, the arms, the hat, the stick, the body throughout spoke equally with the tongue. To express satisfaction the Casterbridge marketman added to his utterance a broadening of the cheeks, a crevicing of the eyes, a throwing back of the shoulders, which was intelligible from the other end of the street. If he wondered, though all Henchard's carts and wagons were rattling past him, you knew it from perceiving the inside of his crimson mouth, and a target-like circling of his eyes. Deliberation caused sundry attacks on the moss of adjoining walls with the end of his stick, a change of his hat from the horizontal to the less so; a sense of tediousness announced itself in a lowering of the person by spreading the knees to a lozenged-shaped aperture and contorting the arms.
>
> (p. 130)

Here, clearly, 'forms of corporeality, gesturality, rhythm, dance and rite coexist heterogeneously with the vocal form.'[22]

With the advent of the Despot and 'writing' in the ordinary sense of the term – that is a system of signification based upon the phonetic alphabet – the 'magic triangle' of the territorial formation is totally crushed. The hand no longer *marks* bodies but subjects itself to *transcribing the voice* of the Despot; the voice itself no longer *sings* or *intones* but allows itself to be *dictated to by the script it recites*; and the eye no longer *sees* but merely *reads*. Writing, at one and the same time becomes *subservient* to the voice – as the authority it merely records – and *dictates* to the voice how it should speak – as in the invocations of 'correctness of pronunciation', for example. All linguistics of the phonetic signifier – that is Saussurian linguistics[23] – denote conquest and overcoding, appropriation and deterritorialization – a deterritorialization of the voice which loses its autonomous register and a deterritorialization of the mark and the trace by their deprivation of sense. It is only with the advent of an Imperial or Despotic order that the *local markings* (which that new order cannot read) are *appropriated* to record an order from a *voice elsewhere* and that the *local voice* (which, again, the new order cannot understand – as in *Heart of Darkness* it is the screech of the jungle) is *appropriated* to read only the marks *already appropriated* by that *alien voice* and to conform itself to what that *alien voice* declares to be 'proper'.

This 'imperial' origin of the phonetic signifier is perhaps nowhere more clearly illustrated than by what might well be taken as the paradigmatic, as well as the earliest, example: the formation of the Greek phonetic alphabet from non-phonetic Phoenician signs – a process of appropriation and deterritorialization precursive to a truly global conquest:

> The decisive point, however, came considerably later, when the Greeks took over the so-called Phoenician alphabet. With the signs came the Phoenician names of the letters, so that perfectly good Semitic words – *aleph*, an ox, *bet*, a house – were turned into Greek nonsense syllables, *alpha*, *beta*, and so on.... Equipped with this remarkable new invention, the Greeks could now record everything imaginable, from the owner's name scratched on a clay jug to a book-length poem like the Iliad.[24]

Throughout *The Mayor of Casterbridge* Henchard is represented as someone for whom the intricacies of the written word are always a source of unease when not of downright awe. We are told early on that he finds 'penmanship a tantalizing art' (p. 146) and, later, he confesses that 'I am a poor fool with a pen.' (p. 201). There is even the suggestion that writing rather repels him, as if it were a form of defilement:

Henchard himself was mentally and physically unfit for grubbing subtleties from soiled paper...

(p. 146)

It is, of course, one of the principal differences between Henchard and Farfrae that the latter is totally at home with written records, accounts, balance sheets and so forth – it is no coincidence that his first contact with Henchard is through a scribbled note. On the other hand it might almost be said that nothing so much contributes to Henchard's downfall as do acts of writing. First there is Susan's posthumous note that devastatingly reveals to him the secret of Elizabeth-Jane's birth and later there is the bundle of Lucetta's letters. It is Henchard's unfamiliarity with the skills and protocols of writing that result in his letting these letters fall into the hands of Jopp:

The pen and all its relations being awkward tools in Henchard's hands he had affixed the seals without an impression, it never occurring to him that the efficacy of such a fastening depended on this. Jopp was far less of a tyro...

(p. 327)

Henchard's clumsiness exploited by Jopp's dexterity provides the Mixen Lane lumpen with all the ammunition they require for mounting the skimmington ride that precipitates Lucetta's death.

The character, however, for whom the issue of literacy – that is of conforming to the protocols of the phonetic alphabet and the order of the signifier in general – is most critical is Elizabeth-Jane. Again and again we are made aware of how difficult Elizabeth-Jane finds the task of educating herself, of making herself able to read and write and speak 'properly' – that is, to wean herself of her natural inclination to speak in dialect and to break herself to the disciplines of formal grammar. 'One grievous failing of Elizabeth's', we are told, 'was her occasional pretty and picturesque use of dialect words – those terrible marks of the beast to the truly genteel.' (p. 200). For Henchard, the paranoiac parvenu, these lapses by Elizabeth-Jane are intolerable and it is he that spurs her to ever greater efforts:

The sharp reprimand was not lost upon her, and in time it came to pass that for 'fay' she said 'succeed'; and that she no longer spoke of 'dumbledores' but of 'humble bees'; no longer said of young men and women that they 'walked together' but that they were 'engaged'; that she grew to talk of 'greggles' as 'wild-hyacinths'; that when she had not slept she did not quaintly tell the servants next morning that she had been 'hag-rid', but that she has 'suffered from indigestion.'

(p. 200)

We see here, very clearly, the over-coding of dialect words (on the whole wonderfully expressive and sensuously evocative – 'fay', 'dumbledores', 'greggles') by a largely latinate/classical – indeed, imperial – vocabulary: 'succeed', 'engaged', 'wild-hyacinths', 'suffered from indigestion'. But it is not just a take-over of one vocabulary by another that I sense here: 'dumbledores' and, perhaps especially, 'greggles' seem to me like little sound sculptures rather than names or classifications, little autonomous sound bites: dental, labial, gutteral and – with 'fay' – frictive. For the dialect speaker they have a 'meaning' but they also offer – rather like the Phoenician alphabet referred to by Finlay – a basic set of phonetic elements that could be used to construct an alphabet. Other components might be found in 'jowned' (p. 201) and 'leery' (p. 206) – as well as the already mentioned 'hag-rid'. So that we already have the following:

D – dumbledore

F – fay

G – greggle

H – hag

J – jowned

L – leery

Add the consonants and we have here a third of an alphabet! This is only an exercise but one can see how phonetic appropriation renders the original words/sounds 'senseless' and 'quaint'.[25]

It is not just the use of dialect words that gives Elizabeth-Jane problems: her hand-writing also leaves much to be desired:

She started the pen in an elphantine march across the sheet. It was a splendid round, bold hand of her own conception.... [she] produced a line of chain-shot and sand-bags.

(p. 201)

Such an idiosyncratic set of marks falls far short of what Henchard deems to be 'proper young girl['s]' writing.

What the whole 'writing lesson' at the beginning of Chapter twenty (pp. 200–1) indicates is that Elizabeth-Jane finds herself at the dividing line between territorial and despotic representation. Of the territorial regime she retains the relative autonomy of sound and mark – of dialect and graphism – whereas what she aspires to master is the conflation of sound and script – the 'proper' grammar – of the despotic order, the order of the signifier. That this entails a self-inscription in the imperial regime is only underlined by her determination, 'incited by the Roman characteristics of the town she lived in' (p. 203), to learn Latin.

Elizabeth-Jane's role in the novel is far more ambivalent than is generally recognized. On the one hand it would be easy to regard her as someone co-opted and inscribed within a patriarchic/despotic order – as when Henchard more or less forces her to take his name:

> She got a piece of paper, and bending over the fender wrote at his dictation words which he had evidently got by heart from some advertisement or other – words to the effect that she, the writer, hitherto known as Elizabeth-Jane Newson, was going to call herself Elizabeth-Jane Henchard forthwith.
>
> (p. 194)

But this is to ignore the extent to which, throughout the text, Elizabeth-Jane seems to be complicit in this process. Earlier, for example, she has literally tried to write herself into Farfrae's discourse:

> The next day was windy – so windy that walking in the garden she picked up a portion of the draft of a letter on business in Donald Farfrae's writing, which had flown over the wall from the office. The useless scrap she took indoors, and began to copy the calligraphy, which she much admired. The letter began 'Dear Sir', and presently writing on a loose slip 'Elizabeth-Jane', she laid the latter on 'Sir', making the phrase 'Dear Elizabeth-Jane.'
>
> (p. 182)

Indeed, this is something we will have to return to – Elizabeth-Jane's complicity within and collusion with the patriarchal order of which she appears to be both the object to be obtained and the victim to be exploited, both apologist and critic, alibi and scapegoat.

In an important sense, however, any discussion as to whether Elizabeth-Jane is an accomplice or a victim of the patriarchal order instituted by the Despot is handicapped by its precipitancy. It addresses a state of things that has already happened, or is assumed to have happened, which requires a prior interrogation: who, or, indeed, what, is 'Elizabeth-Jane'? Surely the most dramatic revelation in the novel is that Elizabeth-Jane is not Elizabeth-Jane and that Henchard's 'daughter' is *not* his 'daughter'. What the Elizabeth-Jane/Elizabeth-Jane dilemma suggests is the essential precariousness of the relationship between names and bodies, *sema* and *soma*, signifier and signified. In a sense this volatile relationship between bodies and names is reminiscent of the purely connotative resonance of voice and graphism in territorial representation. They are not 'fixed' one upon the other in a one to one bi-univocal relationship. 'Sister', 'mother', 'daughter' can slide on and off a specific body as a series of provisional affective intensities. There is no necessary coincidence of person and name, of *soma* and *sema*, of signified and signifier. It is only within the severe regime of the despotic sign – the Saussurian regime of the differential and arbitrary sign – that the signifier is required to fix its signified. If this condition is not satisfied the whole system collapses. In this situation, as the novel makes all too clear, Elizabeth-Jane's name pre-exists her: she is not the object designated by her signifier but its effect. This arbitrariness and indifference and pre-eminence of the signifier is embedded in the title of the novel: who is the Mayor of Casterbridge? Henchard? Farfrae? It is the irony of Lucetta's note to Henchard when she responds to the rhetorical question as to how long she will stay in Casterbridge:

> That depends upon another; and he is a man, and a merchant, and a Mayor. . . .

> (p. 218)

The names designate nobody: they may be occupied by Henchard or by Farfrae – or by Dr. Chalkfield. This is the very characteristic of the signifying order:

> The statement survives its object, the name survives its owner.[26]

Elizabeth-Jane's insight is never more keen than when she senses that

> her experience had consisted less in a series of pure disappointments than in a series of substitutions.

> (p. 250)

She is, after all – or before all – the substitute of herself, a signifier for another signifier in the closed circle of signification.

It is interesting, at this point, to compare and contrast Elizabeth-Jane's role and function in the text with that of Lucette/Lucetta Sueur/Templeman. There is a certain symmetry to their roles: both have a craving for respectability and whilst, for Elizabeth-Jane this requires that she abandons her use of dialect words, for Lucetta this requires that she bury her shady past in Jersey and, to that end, she must avoid any betrayal of the fact that she is completely fluent in French (p. 223). But in almost all other aspects the two are diametrical opposites. On the one hand Elizabeth-Jane finds a name awaiting her, whereas Lucette/Lucetta Sueur/ Templeman has almost an embarrassment of names to be forgotten. Schematically we might say that whereas Elizabeth-Jane's ambition is to be inscribed in the signifying order, Lucetta's 'Protean' (p. 246) propensities threaten to scramble it. While Elizabeth-Jane has to learn to write, Lucetta's major preoccupation as the story progresses is to destroy a whole bundle of her previous scribblings. Assuming, just for a moment, a rather crude chronological perspective, it is almost as if Elizabeth-Jane is coming from the past of a territorial, or pre-signifying order to find a place in a signifying regime of signs, while Lucetta is almost returning from the future of a post-and a-signifying regime of scrambled codes and nomadic deterritorializations to re-establish a lost legitimacy. Sea-side resorts are always slightly suspect, alien, artificial, places in Hardy's work and Jersey is by far the most exotic locale he ever makes use of. Lucetta's parentage, too, is more than a little suspect – her father 'some harum-scarum military officer' (p. 149) (we are reminded of Eustacia Vye) and she describes her own early life:

> As a girl I lived about in garrison towns and elsewhere with my father, till I was quite flighty and unsettled.
>
> (p. 222)

If a territorial, pre-signifying regime is characterized by pre-personal and trans-personal affective intensities, and the despotic signifying regime by molar/discrete identitities, then the post-signifying and a-signifying regime must be characterized as one of hectic simulations and schizoid instabilities. Lucette/Lucetta Sueur/Templeman *is* unstable: not only do we sense her acute sense of insecurity, but the very play of her names threatens to deconstruct her identity. Lucette/Lucetta – as well as her boarding house residence in Jersey – suggest the demi-monde, while Sueur (homophonic with 'sewer')/Templeman suggest a schizophrenic self-division between depths and heights, the mundane and the divine, abasement and transcendence. Throughout the novel we see her adopting roles – dressing up (p. 238 – 'But settling upon new clothes is so trying,' said Lucetta, 'You are that person' (pointing to one of the arrangements) 'or you are that totally different person' (pointing to the other), 'for the whole of the coming spring.') and dressing down – as when she goes to beg Henchard to return her letters. Unlike Elizabeth-Jane, who reads, Lucetta whiles away her time with card-tricks (p. 222) which are, in a sense, a reduction of the status of the pack both from functions of divination (telling fortunes – which might find a place in a territorial regime) and of regal hierarchization (Ace, King, Queen, Knave and the rest that one can associate with a Despotic regime) to meaning-less – that is a-signifying – presdigitations. Fittingly Lucetta herself is described in this very same scene as a kind of playing-card figure (p. 223 – '... the inverted face of Lucetta Templeman whose large lustrous eyes had such an odd effect upside down.') – again indicative of her rather sad, even tawdry, *passe-partout* status.

In Deleuze and Guattari the institution of the despotic order and a regime of signs based on the bi-univocity of the signifier/signified rela-tionship is intimately bound up with the emergence of the familial form of the incest taboo.

Drawing on the work of Luc de Heusch, Deleuze and Guattari describe how the Despot must commit a 'double incest', once with the 'mother' and once with the 'sister'.[27] 'Incest' with the 'mother' ties up the filiative line of biological descent while 'incest' with the 'sister' ties up lateral alliances. Endogamy (marriage within the group) and exogamy (mar-riage without the group) are thus both knotted, as it were, in the despot's 'double incest'. It is by this means that the Despot overcodes filiation and alliance.

> Incest goes by twos: the hero is always sitting astride two groups, the one where he leaves to find his sister, the other where he returns to find his mother again. The purpose of this double incest is not to produce a flow, but to overcode all the existing flows, and to ensure that no intrinsic code, no underlying code escapes the overcoding of the despotic machine; hence it is by virtue of his sterility that he guarantees the general fecundity. The marriage with the sister is on the outside, it is the wilderness ordeal, it expresses the spatial diver-gence from the primitive machine; it provides the old alliances with an outcome; it founds the new alliance by effecting a generalized appropriation of all the alliance debts. The marriage with the mother is the return to the tribe; it expresses the temporal divergence from the primitive regime (the difference between the generations); it

constitutes the direct filiation that results from the new alliance, by effecting a generalised accumulation of filiative stock. Both marriages are essential to the overcoding, as the two ends of a tie for the despotic knot.[28]

Now it seems to me that, despite the fact that neither Elizabeth-Jane nor Lucetta are actually his 'mother' or 'sister', the two marriages of Farfrae in *The Mayor of Casterbridge* conform very much to this pattern.[29] His first marriage, to Lucetta, takes place outside the tribe/town at Port Bredy; the second, to Elizabeth-Jane takes place inside the tribe/town itself. With the first marriage the despot, Farfrae, in effect ties up exogamous alliances while, with the second, he ties up endogenous filiation. But that is only a secondary effect of this double incest for what is important is not so much the marriage with the 'sister' and the 'mother' as the elaborate mythical – which is what this double marriage is – operation that *constitutes* the 'mother' and 'the sister' *for the first time*. The effect of the royal or despotic incest then is to establish the discernibility of the mother and the sister as discrete persons – as privileged but prohibited spouses – as against a more generalized and extensive dispersal of the affectivities of mothering and sistering in more 'primitive', indeed possibly more complex, social formations which might involve a whole range of taboos regarding maternal uncles, second and third cousins, discriminations of tribal lines and locations.

In thus constituting the mother and the sister as discernible persons and molar entities as opposed to affective intensities and prepersonal dispersals the double incest of the despot performs a similar operation to that of the institution of the regime of the signifier: it weds the signifier to the signified in an arbitrary and indissoluble embrace of bi-univocity:

> What made incest impossible – namely that at times we had the appellations (mother, sister) but not the persons or bodies, while at other times we had the bodies, but the appellations disappeared from view as soon as we broke through the prohibitions they bore – has ceased to exist. Incest becomes possible in the wedding of kinship bodies and family appellations, in the union of the signifier with its signified.... In incest it is the signifier that makes love with its signifieds.[30]

I think it is now possible to understand for the first time the strange game or 'tease' Hardy plays with the relationship of Henchard and Elizabeth-Jane. More than one critic has spoken of Henchard's

'unconscious incestuous love for Elizabeth-Jane'. In fact there is absolutely no evidence for such an allegation in the text.[31] Any incest
between Henchard and Elizabeth-Jane is impossible for the reasons
Deleuze and Guattari give: on the one hand Elizabeth-Jane is not Elizabeth-Jane (i.e. not his daughter – we have the appellation but not the
body) and therefore there can be no taboo on any relationship between
them; on the other hand Elizabeth-Jane is his daughter (i.e. we have the
appellation and the body) and while he regards her as such any suggestion of sexual attraction does not arise. Neither Elizabeth-Jane (the
stigma of her illegitimacy) nor Lucetta (her shady past) can be said to
have legitimate names or identities until they are married to the despotic figure of Farfrae. It is at this point that we can perhaps recognize
the sheer brilliance – in more senses than one – of the strategically
placed seed-drill at the centre of the novel:

> It was the new fashioned agricultural implement called a horse-drill,
> till then unknown in its modern shape, in this part of the country,
> where the venerable seed-lip was still used for sowing as in the days of
> the Heptarchy. Its arrival created about as much sensation in the
> corn-market as a flying machine would create at Charing Cross.
> The farmers crowded round it, women drew near it, children crept
> under and into it. The machine was painted in bright hues of green,
> yellow, and red, and it resembled as a whole a compound of hornet,
> grass-hopper, and shrimp, magnified enormously. Or it might have
> been likened to an upright musical instrument with the front gone.
> That is how it struck Lucetta. 'Why, it is a sort of agricultural piano.'
> she said.
>
> (p. 238)

While Henchard pours his scorn upon this monstrous contraption a
voice can be heard coming from within – Farfrae singing one of his
sentimental ballads – and he emerges to rebut him:

> 'Stupid? O no!' said Farfrae gravely. 'It will revolutionize sowing heer-
> about! No more sowers flinging their seed about broadcast, so that
> some falls by the wayside and some among thorns, and all that. Each
> grain will go straight to its intended place, and nowhere else what-
> ever!'
>   'Then the romance of the sower is gone for good,' observed Eliza-
> beth-Jane.
>
> (p. 240)

Lucetta's notion that 'it is a sort of agricultural piano' is a pretty shrewd one and one suspects that she has in mind something more like a pianola with its winding machinery and perforated paper rolls – in fact something rather like a glorified writing machine or ticker-tape puncher. For what this machine represents, strikingly, is the despotic writing machine itself, animated, like the signifier, by a ghostly voice from afar. There is a studied ambiguity in this machine putting an end to careless and haphazard 'broadcasting' – Henchard's *viva voce* regime is gone for good. Moreover, showing the affinity between, on the one hand, the despotic signifying system that depends upon an exact alignment of signifier and signified and, on the other, the strict deployment of rules of affiliation and alliance centred upon the incest taboo, the seed-drill operates, too, as a form of genetic policing – indeed a seed *drill*: 'Each grain will go to its intended place, and nowhere else whatever.' Indeed, to the extent that the whole novel works to achieve its own kind of genetic policing the seed-drill offers us a perfect metaphor of the work as a whole.

If there is anything that grates in this scene it is surely Elizabeth-Jane's rather too prim and pat rejoinder to Farfrae's effusion concerning the merits of the seed-drill: 'The romance of the sower is gone for good.' This is disturbing for if there is a policing consciousness in the novel it is surely that of Elizabeth-Jane whose obsession with 'respectablity' and 'niceness' has frequently been commented on and whose alliance with the point of view of Hardy himself has just as frequently been noted. That she is a totally new kind of female consciousness in Hardy's work becomes evident if one compares her with what Havelock Ellis has to say of the earlier heroines in an article he wrote on the eve of publication of *The Mayor*:

> Mr. Hardy's way of regarding women is peculiar and difficult to define, not because it is not a perfectly defensible way, but because it is in a great way new. It is, as we have already noted, far removed from a method, adapted by many distinguished novelists, in which women are considered as moral forces, centripetal tendencies providentially adapted to balance the centrifugal tendencies of men; being, indeed, almost the polar opposite to that view.[32]

Elizabeth-Jane is precisely the kind of 'centripetal' 'moral force' or consciousness off-setting the centrifugal tendencies of the male consciousnesses in the text that Ellis is describing here. Millgate speaks of her as 'the nearest approach to the distinctly Hardyan point of view'[33] and another critic, Robert Langbaum, describes her as a 'new kind of heroine',[34] as 'Hardy's nearest approach so far to a Jamesian central intelligence',[35] and adds that '[t]hrough much of the book she acts as surrogate for the author.'[36] Again and again we are made aware of Elizabeth-Jane's position as 'that silent observing woman' (p. 182), as 'this discerning silent witch (p. 243).... surveying.... from the chrystalline sphere of a straightforward mind.' (p. 250). This 'dumb, deep-feeling, great-eyed creature' (p. 204) at times seems herself to be trapped within the keep of her own mind – her 'inner chamber of ideas' (p. 166) – interrogating herself on the riddle of life:

> and all this while the subtle-souled girl asking herself why she was born, why sitting in a room, and blinking at the candle; why things around her had taken the shape they wore in preference to every other possible shape. Why they stared at her so helplessly, as if waiting for the touch of some wand that should release them from terrestrial constraint; what that chaos called conscious-ness, which spun in her at this moment like a top, tended to, and began in. Her eyes fell together; she was awake, yet she was asleep.
>
> (p. 189)

I do find this quite moving but I am still made uneasy by the trivial patness of the 'romance of the sower' quote as I had been by what we have recorded earlier of Elizabeth-Jane's readiness to inscribe herself within the patriarchal order. This 'articulation of herself in the available codes' may be closely 'identified with the way Hardy saw himself as a writer'[37] but there is a good deal of evidence that this identification is not as complete as it at first appears and that Elizabeth-Jane's claims to be the moral consciousness of the text are undermined by the frequent tendency of that consciousness to indulge in uncharitable excess. Hardy himself remarks:

> Any suspicion of impropriety was to Elizabeth-Jane like a red rag to a bull. Her craving for correctness of procedure was, indeed, almost vicious.
>
> (p. 289)

and there is, indeed, something vicious in her silent admonitions to Lucetta later – whose only crime at this stage seems to be no more than absolute adoration of her husband:

full of her reading [we are significantly told], she [EJ] cited Rosalind's exclamation: 'Mistress, know yourself; down on your knees and thank heaven for a good man's love.'

(p. 309)

In a complex and interesting discussion of the novel Marjorie Garson has already spoken of the 'somewhat blurred and ambiguous... treatment of Elizabeth-Jane's various excellencies' and has begun to question the extent to which Hardy's identification with the point of view of Elizabeth-Jane is at odds with 'the text's more generous and liberal social notions.'[38] Garson, too, draws attention to Elizabeth-Jane's 'terrible sense of propriety', 'ruthless prissiness' and 'paranoid sobriety'[39] and has noted how 'Elizabeth-Jane always lines up with the Father... and with the patriarchal order'[40] – indeed to such an extent that she can speak of the 'ventriloquism' of the closing paragraphs of the text where Elizabeth-Jane seems little more than a mouthpiece for the Hardyan 'philosophy'.[41] Garson's conclusion seems to be that while the text as a whole suggests that there is something rather strident, if not hysterical (these are my words, not Garson's), about Elizabeth-Jane's sense of propriety Hardy is too frightened of what it stands in place of – the threat of female power: an 'instinctive terror of the woman who castrates and kills'[42] – to abandon her. Indeed there is a sense here not so much of an author protecting his character as a character protecting her author.

If there is a threat to the world of the novel and to the world of Casterbridge that, it must be remembered, is here being constituted for the first time,[43] then, in the first instance, it must be from the amalgam of forces represented by Mixen Lane and the Skimmington Ride. Much has already been written about Mixen Lane both as a sociological phenomenon (a 'degenerate space'[44]) and as a narrative *topos* – what Suzanne Keen calls a 'narrative annex' – that is a narrative area adjacent to the main plot where significant and sometimes major plot changes are engineered.[45] Hardy's description of Mixen Lane is memorable:

Though the upper part of Durnover was mainly composed of a curious congeries of barns and farmsteads, there was a less picturesque side to the parish. This was Mixen Lane, now in great part pulled down.

Mixen Lane was the Adullam of all the surrounding villages. It was the hiding place of those who were in distress, and in debt, and in trouble of every kind. Farm-labourers and other peasants, who combined a little poaching with their farming, and a little brawling and bibbing with their poaching, found themselves sooner or later in

Mixen Lane. Rural mechanics too idle to mechanize, rural servants too rebellious to serve, drifted or were forced into Mixen Lane.

... Vice ran freely in and out certain doors of the neighbourhood; recklessness dwelt under the roof with the crooked chimney; shame in some bow-windows; theft (in times of privation) in the thatched and mud-walled houses by the sallows. Even slaughter had not been altogether unknown here. In a block of cottages up an alley there might have been erected an altar to disease in years gone by. Such was Mixen in the times when Henchard and Farfrae were Mayors.

...

Yet amid so much that was bad needy respectability also found a home. Under some of the roofs abode pure and virtuous souls whose presence there was due to the iron hand of necessity, and to that alone. Families from decayed villages – families of that once bulky, but now nearly extinct, section of village society called 'liviers', or lifeholders – copyholders and others, whose roof-trees had fallen for some reason or other, compelling them to quite the rural spot that had been their home for generations – came here, unless they chose to lie under a hedge by the wayside.

(pp. 328–30)

It has been noted more than once that this description of the composition of Mixen Lane is little short of a direct transcription of Hardy's earlier essay on 'The Dorsetshire Labourer' where his anger at the changes taking place in the countryside is patent:

The changes which are so increasingly discernible in village life by no means originate entirely with the agricultural unrest. A depopulation is going on which in some quarters is truly alarming. ... The occupants who formed the backbone of the village life have to seek refuge in the boroughs. This process, which is designated by statisticians as 'the tendency of the rural population towards the large towns,' is really the tendency of water to flow uphill when forced. ... This system is much to be deplored, for every one of those banished people imbibes a sworn enmity to the existing order of things, and not a few of them, far from becoming merely honest Radicals, degenerate into Anarchists, waiters on chance, to whom danger to the State, the town – nay, the street they live in, is a welcomed opportunity.[46]

Mixen – the word means 'dunghill'[47] – is the sink or sump where the seething mass of all those deracinated and deterritorialized by shifts in

modes of production or change of regimes gather and resent and con-
spire. Its primary condition is its volatility consisting, as it does, of a
dangerous mixture of both archaic and residual and emergent and
embryonically revolutionary forces.[48]

All that having been said, it has not, as far as I have been able
to discover, been remarked sufficiently the extent to which the Skimmington Ride, which is the most manifest expression of the threat
represented by Mixen Lane, is primarily planned and urged and
executed by *women*: the extraordinarily powerful triumvirate (if the
inappropriateness of the term be allowed) of Nance Mockridge, Mother
Cuxsom and Mrs Goodenough, the old furmity hag. Once
again, following on Carlyle and Dickens, the prime fear provoked by
revolution is the fear of women on the march – John Paterson, at one
point, significantly refers to Nance Mockridge as 'the local Mme
Lafarge'.[49]

In what is already something of a 'classic' study of *The Mayor of Casterbridge* Elaine Showalter interprets the wife-sale of the opening as Henchard's divorce of 'his own "feminine" self'.[50] She goes on to argue that
what the plot then retails is the series of experiences of 'unmanning'
(the return of the furmity woman, the meeting with Lucetta in the Ring
['he was unmanned' p. 324], the fight with Farfrae ['Its (Henchard's
attitude) womanliness sat tragically on the figure of so stern a piece of
virility.' p. 348]), that results in Henchard's rediscovering his 'feminine'
self. This redemption is expressed most obviously in his discovery of his
love for and need of Elizabeth-Jane.

In many ways Henchard seems to behave like the classic paranoiac.[51]
His suppression of his 'feminine' self – indeed the repudiation of
his whole affective life – coupled with his love-hate relationship with
Farfrae betrays all the symptoms of a repressed passive homosexuality.
The hiatus of eighteen or so years between the opening scene
and the return of Susan and Elizabeth-Jane – the twenty-one years of
abstention of his oath – are a remarkable instance of an attempt to
live virtually without a body.[52] The one lapse, of course, being the affair
with Lucetta in Jersey – but even then the text makes it plain that
Henchard was more the passive object of Lucetta's machinations than
the active predator. Indeed, all the evidence is that Henchard is, indeed,
a 'woman hater' (p. 148). The coincidental return of Susan and Elizabeth-Jane and the arrival on the scene of Farfrae seem to mark the lifting
of the repression and the unconscious flowering of a powerful homosexual libido: Farfrae attracts Henchard in a way the latter barely com-
prehends:

'To be sure, to be sure, how that fellow does draw me!' he had said to himself. 'I suppose 'tis because I'm so lonely. I'd have given him a third share in the business to have stayed!'

(p. 125)

or, at least, won't acknowledge:

'You can see that it isn't all selfishness that makes me press 'ee.... Some selfishness perhaps there is, but there is more; it isn't for me to repeat what.'

(p. 132)

Henchard's insistence that Farfrae reminds him of his, Henchard's, brother is quite preposterous when we recall how unlike the two are: it is a self deluding explanation for the attraction Henchard feels for Farfrae (p. 117). The subsequent rivalry and sense of persecution that Henchard comes to feel in relation to Farfrae is a classic instance of the two strategies of *defence* and *projection* that Freud attributes to Schreber's paranoia: a *defence* against a repressed passive homosexuality,[53] and the *projection* outwards of what is repressed from within. Farfrae, who was 'at one time loved and honoured,' becomes 'the person who is now hated and feared for being a persecutor'.[54] It is at this point that Henchard's experience of 'unmanning' becomes susceptible of a quite different interpretation to that placed upon it by Showalter. Schreber, too, enjoyed fantasies of 'being transformed into a woman'[55] but this was in order to makes himself available to the 'rays of God'[56] – that is, it was to allow him to acquiesce in the passive 'feminine' role provided it was accorded divine sanction. The 'becoming woman' in this case is not the rediscovery of a feminine side but a *strategy by means of which women are excluded altogether*:

Dr Schreber may have formed a phantasy that if he were a woman he would manage the business of having children more successfully [than a woman could] ...[57]

It was precisely such a challenge to the whole Deleuze and Guattarian notion of 'becoming woman' that formed the radical thrust of Alice Jardine's argument in her by now notorious article 'Women in Limbo':

Is it not possible that the process of 'becoming woman' is but a new variation of an old allegory for the process of women becoming obsolete? There would remain only her simulacrum: a female figure caught in a whirling sea of male configurations. A silent, mutable, head-less, desire-less, spatial surface necessary only for *His* metamorphosis?[58]

This seems to me to describe not only the ambition of the text but also the predicament of Elizabeth-Jane at the end – mutable, head-less (recall her 'ventriloquism') and 'desire-less': 'happiness was but the occasional episode in a general drama of pain' (p. 411) – let's not gloss this as wisdom or stoicism (and if we do they are not hers anyway) – and very much a spatial surface for masculine inscription – as we have seen.

Marjorie Garson has brilliantly linked the 'unusually controlled'[59] nature of *The Mayor of Casterbridge* to the occlusion of the feminine and, more particularly, the *female body* from the text:

There is no sense here of sexy texture, no rustling of silky skirts.... Female bodies in *The Mayor of Casterbridge* neither expand to decentre the man's story nor open to expose male fantasy of penetration and control. Their containment is an aspect of the novel's tragic decorum and one of the reasons that *The Mayor of Casterbridge* has no compelling female character.[60]

For Garson the erotic presence that is denied the female body is displaced instead onto the body of the town, Casterbridge, itself. Throughout the text a whole battery of images and metaphors ascribe to Casterbridge propensities to bulge, burst, overspill, pack, breach, overhang, thrust, transgress and generally confound and permeate boundaries:

The old-fashioned fronts of these houses, which had older than old-fashioned backs, rose sheer from the pavement, into which the box-windows protruded like bastions, necessitating a pleasing *chassez–déchassez* movement to the time-pressed pedestrian at every few yards.... In addition to these fixed obstacles which spoke so cheerfully of unrestraint as to boundaries, movables occupied the path to a perplexing extent.... Moreover every shop pitched out half its contents upon the trestles and boxes on the kerb, extending the display each week a little further into the roadway.... Horses for sale were tied in rows, their forelegs on the pavement, their hind legs in the street.... (I)n an eastern purlieu called Durnover. Here wheat-ricks overhung the old Roman street, and thrust their eaves against the church tower...

(pp. 128–9 & 162)

'If there is a deeply imagined body in this text,' Garson writes, 'it is the body of Casterbridge itself...The town is eroticised: the bees and the seeds which penetrate it pollinate it, and whispering skirts rustle here only in the timid leaves.... Casterbridge displaces and diminishes the individual female characters...'[61] This eroticizing and feminizing of the body of the town itself considerably modifies and even contradicts our first sense of the town as an implacably severe and symmetrical imperial structure. It alerts us to a tension, that runs throughout the novel, between control and discipline, on the one hand, and the exuberant potential of the female body on the other.

There is a sense disseminated (to use an appropriate metaphor) throughout the text not of the woman as an agency of castration and death[62] but of the sheer physical energy and potential and *excess* of the female body. It is this that has to be controlled and contained. Elizabeth-Jane, we are told, even when enjoying unexpected affluence,

> refrained from *bursting* out like a water-flower that spring and clothing herself in *puffings* and knick-knacks, as most of the Casterbridge girls would have done in her circumstances. (p. 158) [the emphasis mine DM]

Later we are told of her fear of '*blossom(ing)* too gaudily the moment she had become possessed of money' (p. 166) [again my emphasis, DM] and when Lucetta tells her of her marriage to Farfrae there is, again, another powerful image of blockage:

> 'Let me think of it alone,' said the girl quickly, *corking up* the turmoil of her feelings with grand control. (p. 290 – my emphasis, DM)

Earlier there is the telling image of the evidently powerful Mrs. Stannidge of *The Three Mariners* remaining 'as fixed in the arm-chair as if she had been *melted* into it when in a *liquid* state.' (p. 112 – my emphasis, DM)

What is emerging from all these images, and others, is the fear of the woman as a fluid, mobile, eruptive and dynamic body. It is no accident that the old furmity woman, Mrs Goodenough, is first associated with her famous brew and its characteristically swollen grains:

> the mixture of corn in the grain, flour, milk, raisins, currants, and what not, that composed the antiquated slop in which she dealt...was nourishing, and as proper a food as could be obtained within the four seas; though, to those not accustomed to it, the grains of wheat

swollen as large as lemon-pips . . . might have had a deterrent effect at
first.

(p. 73)

and then with urinating shamelessly against the wall of the church.
Even the plague of 'unpincipled bread' (p. 97) is the result of 'growed
wheat' (ibid.) – that is of wheat germinating and sprouting before its
time. Nance Mockridge, herself, when we first meet her is described as
virtually bursting out of her clothes –

> In an open space before the church walked a woman with her gown-
> sleeves rolled up so high that the edge of her under linen was visible,
> and her skirt tucked up through her pocket hole.
>
> (p. 97)

It is this attire and her brazen stance that earned her Paterson's 'the local
Mme Lafarge' sobriquet. Here her threatening energy is expressed in her
pulling pieces of bread off the loaf from under her arm and pressing them
on one and all – an image of forceful distribution.[63] And, Mrs Cuxsom –
the third of the triumvirate we left organizing the Skimmington ride – is
not only a woman of considerable 'tonnage' (p. 155) – clearly a buxom
Mrs Cuxsom – but also comes of a line of famously fertile women:

> '[Her mother] were rewarded by the Agricultural Society for having
> begot the greatest number of healthy children without parish assist-
> ance, and other virtuous marvels.'
>
> (p. 155)

It is this wariness in the text of powerful, fluid, generative women that
accounts to a considerable extent for the shabby treatment meted out to
Lucetta.

It is extraordinary the extent to which critics seem prepared to go
along with Hardy's calumniation of Lucetta. For many this is achieved
by adopting a particular interpretation of the description of the 'ghastly'
mask that figures as a keystone to the arch framing the rather shady rear
door Elizabeth-Jane discovers behind High Place Hall:

> To her surprise she found herself in one of the little used alleys of the
> town. Looking round at the door which had given her egress, by the
> light of the solitary lamp fixed in the alley, she saw it was arched and
> old – older even than the house itself. The door was studded, and the

keystone was a mask. Originally the mask had exhibited a comic leer, as could still be discerned; but generations of Casterbridge boys had thrown stones at the mask, aiming at its open mouth; and the blows thereon had chipped off the lips and jaws as if they had been eaten away by disease. The appearance was so ghastly by the weakly lamp-glimmer that she could not bear to look at it – the first unpleasant feature of her visit.

The position of the queer old door and the odd presence of the leering mask suggested one thing above all others as appertaining to the mansion's history – intrigue. By the alley it had been possible to come unseen from all sorts of quarters of the town – the old play-house, the old bull-stake, the old cock-pit, the pool wherein nameless infants had been used to disappear. High Place Hall could boast of its conveniences undoubtedly.

(pp. 211–21)

Both Marjorie Garson and Suzanne Keen have chosen to see the mask as imputing to Lucetta a sordidness ('intrigue') and corruption ('disease') – which associate her with the sexual profligacy and deviancy of Mixen Lane. The former regards the 'ghastly' mask as emblematic of Lucetta's

'ghastly' body and hints at the kind of corruption Hardy cannot make explicit.[64]

while the latter – quite mistakenly – has the door itself open directly onto Mixen Lane.[65]

There may be some justification for this association and perhaps it is what Hardy intended. Nevertheless it seems to me that the mask is open to an alternative interpretation that relates it much more intimately to the context in which it appears – that is of the description of High Place Hall.[66] The *leitmotif* of this description has clearly been announced in the adage that 'Blood built it, and Wealth enjoys it.' (p. 211) What follows is an account of a neo-classical *Palladian* building – that is of a building that clearly embodies the imperial and enlightened pretensions of the town – which is nevertheless revealed to be founded on an 'older' structure associated with public and collective spectacles of pain and death: the bating of bears tied to a stake and of cocks fighting in the ring – as well as with the murder of innocence: 'the pool wherein nameless infants had been used to disappear.' In this interpretation the distorted features of the mask would not so much indicate the consequences of disease as the effects produced by pain and torture – that is by those very rituals and institutions that form the necessary but bloody basis of the despotic order.

To return to Lucetta: rather than ghastly and syphilitic – Garson's innuendo is plain[67] – there is every evidence in the text that Lucetta enjoys boisterous good health (that Elizabeth-Jane might find her a little jaded is only to be expected from such a sour-puss). Lucetta doesn't just go for a walk she 'bound(s) along the road' (p. 277) or 'trots' (p. 286). When Elizabeth-Jane comes to see her she 'bound(s) up like a spring on hearing the door open' (p. 221) and when Farfrae comes in when she is expecting Henchard she 'jump(s) up' and '(flings) back the curtain' (p. 228). Her notes to Henchard are sprightly and witty (ok, flirtatious too) and she is spontaneously very kind to Elizabeth-Jane when she first overhears her crying in the churchyard. We have already noted how much brighter her comment on the drilling machine is than that of Elizabeth-Jane. She dotes fondly on Farfrae after marriage and at the end she is already pregnant. In short the 'Protean', flexible, probably 'flexuous' at some point to employ Hardy's favourite adjective, but certainly mobile, impetuous, spontaneous, energetic, *fluid* and, above all, *fertile* Lucetta embodies – yes, embodies – just the kind of female power that the text has been at such pains to constrain. Lucetta *Sueur – suer*: to sweat – 'represents' that very 'mechanics of fluidity' – to employ Irigaray's phrase[68] which the megamachine of the despotic order and its system of representation – the order pre-eminently celebrated in *The Mayor of Casterbridge* – cannot accommodate.

Critics seem to want to get rid of Lucetta almost as quickly and unproblematically as does the text. '(The erotic Lucetta is, compared to the other major characters, too trivial to command much sympathy.)' writes Robert Langbaum.[69] Even Garson can write:

> Lucetta is a peculiarly disposable character, discarded as easily as her effigy, which – unlike Henchard's – never turns up to haunt the story with a specular *frisson*.[70]

Au contraire: the quotation from Garson has a footnote attached to the word character and when one turns to it one reads the following:

> At an early stage of the composition Hardy had Henchard burn Lucetta's photograph: 'there's an end of her and here goes her picture. Burns it up flame creeps up face etc.' See Winfield, 'The Manuscript of Hardy's *Mayor of Casterbridge*' (1973), p. 87.[71]

Here is a clue to another reading of the 'ghastly' (p. 212) mask of High Place Hall – *not of a syphilitic face but of a face in agony being consumed by flames.* The displacement is not from Mixen Lane but from that other narrative 'annex' of the text, the Ring. The schoolboys throwing stones at the mask in High Place Hall (p. 212) are the very same that would normally have been playing cricket in the Ring (p. 141) – that other site in the text of age coeval with the door at the rear of High Place Hall (p. 211: 'old – older than the house itself.'). They are not playing there, we have been told earlier, because of bad memories and strange haunt-ings of gladiatorial combats watched by Hadrian's legions – but above all because of the 'ghastly'[72] story of the nineteen-year-old Mary Channing who was burned there in 1705 in front of a baying mob of 10,000 spectators, including the architect of St Pauls' Cathedral, Sir Christopher Wren[73] – the pre-eminent exponent in England of that very *Palladian* architecture that fronts High Place Hall!

The trial and execution of Mary Channing obsessed Hardy. The fullest account is to be found in the 1706 tract *Serious Admonitions to Youth, in a Short Account of the Life, Trial, Condemnation and Execution of Mrs. Mary Channing who, for Poisoning her Husband, was Burnt at Dorchester… With Practical Reflections.*[74] Mary Channing, née Brooks, was born in Dorches-ter in May 1687 and was brought up with considerable indulgence by her doting parents who encouraged her to sing and dance. By her mid-teens she had attracted a considerable circle of admirers for the favour-ites among whom she bought generous presents with money stolen from her parents. In order to impose some sort of restraint on her, her parents decided to marry her off at the age of seventeen to Thomas Channing, a local shopkeeper. Despite being allowed by her husband still to entertain a large circle of dubious friends Mary soon became bored with married life and, it is alleged, just thirteen weeks after the wedding, caused the death of her husband by mixing mercury with his bowl of rice. Mary was arrested and sent to trial and found guilty but because she was pregnant the execution was delayed until 21 March 1706. She gave birth to her child in prison and was so struck down subsequently by fever that she wished to die. At the time of her execu-tion she was just nineteen years old.

The details of her execution by being burnt at the stake are truly horrific – those very details, alas, that clearly had a macabre attraction for Hardy. There is a first account in *The Mayor of Casterbridge* when he accounts for the sinister associations of the Ring:

> Apart from the sanguinary nature of the games originally played therein [in its capacity as a Roman amphitheatre], such incidents

attached to its past as these: that in 1705 a woman who had murdered her husband was half-strangled and then burnt there in the presence of ten thousand spectators. Tradition reports that at a certain stage of the burning her heart burst and leapt out of her body, to the terror of them all, and that not one of those ten thousand people ever cared particularly for hot roast after that.

(p. 141)

The attempted humour of the last clause seems to me to be particularly distasteful.

He gives a slightly more detailed account of the execution, quoting from the *Serious Admonition* tract, in his description of Maumbury Ring in *The Times* of 9 October 1908:

She was conveyed from the gaol in a cart 'by her father's and husband's house,' so that the course of the procession must have been up High-East-street as far as the Bow, thence down South-street and up the straight old Roman road to the Ring beside it. 'When fixed to the stake she justified her innocence to the very last, and left the world with a courage seldom found in her sex. She being first strangled, the fire was kindled about five in the afternoon, and in the sight of many thousands she was consumed to ashes.' There is nothing to show that she was dead before the burning began, and from the use of the word 'strangled' and not 'hanged,' it would seem that she was merely rendered insensible before the fire was lit. An ancestor of the present writer who witnessed the scene, has handed down the information that 'her heart leapt out' during the burning, and other curious details that cannot be printed here.[75]

Yet a further account is to be found pasted into his *Memoranda Notebook* in 1919:

Jan. 25th. Mr Prideaux tells me more details of the death of Mary Channing (burnt for the poisoning of her husband, [not proven]) in 1705, in Maumbury Ring, Dorchester. They were told him by old Mr. – – , a direct descendant of one who was a witness of the execution. He said that after she had been strangled & the burning had commenced, she recovered consciousness [owing to the pain from the flames probably] & and writhed and shrieked. One of the constables thrust a swab into her mouth to stop her cries, & the milk from her bosoms (she had lately given birth to a child) squirted out in their faces 'and made 'em jump back.[76]

Gittings reports that even late into his life Hardy had to be almost forcibly restrained from regaling an audience that included a fifteen-year-old girl with the lurid details of the execution.[77] Finally there are two poems by Hardy that refer to Mary Channing: the first *The Mock Wife* directly, the second, *The Bride-Night Fire*, a very funny dialect poem, rather more indirectly. In the *The Mock Wife* Thomas Channing, on his deathbed and unaware of Mary's part in his demise and that she is in prison, calls for her to embrace him for one last time. Unable to produce Mary herself his friends persuade a 'buxom' young lady to assume the role of a 'mock-wife' and take her place so that Thomas can die happy. In *The Bride-Night Fire* the lively young Barbree is forced to marry old Tranter Sweatley and so lose her true love Tim Tankens. On the wedding night the bride seems resigned to her fate:

> But to eyes that had seen her in tide-times of weal,
> Like the white cloud o' smoke, the red battlefield's vail,
>   That look spak' of havoc behind.[78]

When Tranter Sweatley goes to his 'linhay' for one last jug of wine, so the story has it (and this is the one Barbree is sticking to), 'the candle-snoff kindled some chaff from his grain' and the whole house burned down around him leaving our Barbree free to marry Tim – though not without incurring the communal rebuke of a 'skimmity-ride'.

The execution of Mary Channing was truly awful and deserves a similar place in the English hall of infamy to that which Damien's execution in 1757 holds in the history of France. Mary Channing might be one more of those 'infamous men' (sic) that Michel Foucault excavates from the period 1660–1760 as mute victims of the exercise of despotic power[79] – those

> anomalous minor individuals whose various transgressions thrust them into a direct corporeal encounter with the machineries of power.[80]

Mary Channing is the corpse missing from the field of power that Henchard intuits as he walks along the banks of the Froom:

> Above the cliff, and behind the river, rose a pile of buildings, and in the front of the pile a square mass cut into the sky. It was like a pedestal lacking its statue. This missing feature, without which the

design remained incomplete, was, in truth, the corpse of a man; for the square mass formed the base of the gallows, the extensive buildings at the back being the county gaol. In the meadow where Henchard now walked the mob were wont to gather whenever an execution took place, and there to the tune of the roaring weir they stood and watched the spectacle.

(p. 198)

Without the tortured exploding body of Mary Channing the Despotic order instituted in *The Mayor of Casterbridge* lacks all credibility, is missing an integral part and condition of its structure:

> In the darkest region of the political field the condemned man represents the symmetrical, inverted figure of the king.[81]

It is only when we begin to recognize that the trauma that lies behind *The Mayor of Casterbridge*, the sufficient reason that motivates the malaise that afflicts Casterbridge and the guilt that assails Henchard, is not the celebrated wife-sale[82] that opens the text but the collective murder of a nineteen year old who had dared to threaten the institutions of the civic order, that we can begin to understand many of the resonances of the text.

When Marjorie Garson, for example, speaks of 'the too-penetrable, too-flexible woman [that has] to be cast out', or of 'the expansive potential of the female body', or that

> Sex and death are linked in the too-penetrable body of the woman, the woman with a 'past', the woman with a skeleton in her closet.[83]

or when she speaks of the *corps morcelé*[84] represented by the mask at High Place Hall I cannot but feel that the power, the *excess* and *urgency*, of her language derives not from the evidence of the actual text itself that she cites but from an unconscious awareness of the phantasmatic[85] horror that lies behind it. In another article in the same *New Casebook* collection Julian Wolfreys recounts at length his sense that '*The Mayor of Casterbridge* is haunted.'[86] He speaks of 'a certain spectral revenance', 'a spectral movement' and goes on to speak of Hardy's 'haunted art'.[87] Wolfreys then complains that

> Despite these tantalising apparitions of critical acknowledgement of the spectral, however, no critic of Hardy, to my knowledge, has

offered an extended analysis of the spectral in *The Mayor of Caster-bridge*.[88]

Sadly, in spite of a mincing invocation of the shades of Freud, Hillis-Miller, Derrida and Deleuze, Wolfreys himself does not seem to get much further and concludes seemingly rather more baffled than when he began:

> In addition, who is haunted precisely? Is it Casterbridge? Is it Hench-ard? Or is it Hardy himself, who, having returned home to Dorchester in 1883, to build himself a home – Max Gate – with the help of his family – in his home begins to be haunted in the very moment of being at home? What causes Hardy to dig into local archives, seeking stories of wife-sales, even as the laying of foundations for Max Gate reveals the bones of the long dead? What returns for Hardy, even as Hardy returns?[89]

Both Garson and Wolfreys seem dimly aware of a horror that dare not speak its name. It is only John Paterson, in the article on the 'tragic' status of *The Mayor* that I have already referred to, who seems to have had some inkling of the sheer trauma inflicted upon Casterbridge/Dorchester by the terrible event of 1705:

> Like its maimed and guilt-haunted ruler, then, Casterbridge is demor-alized and disabled by its grisly past.[90]

But Paterson, too, seems to determined to stifle his own intuition when he adds the following footnote:

> This not to suggest that as a 'cause' of the city's demoralization, the criminality of its past operates on the same level as the criminality of its chief magistrate. It enters the novel only at the level of reference and allusion and not at the level of action and to this extent serves no more than a symbolic function. The city's gruesome history acts, in short, less as a direct cause of its discomposure than as an analogy with the history of Michael Henchard.[91]

This is not only obscene – the appalling execution of Mary Channing as no more than a *symbol* of the criminality of Henchard???? – but demon-strates a totally inadequate notion of 'causality'. The causality of an obsession or the causality of a trauma – whether that that afflicts a person or a town – does not work on the basis of a simple mechanical linkage of 'cause and effect' but on the principle of a random distribution of effects that echo and repeat each other ungoverned by considerations of identity or similarity. While one might just make a case for some similarities between the giddy youth and tragic deaths of Mary Channing and Lucetta – not least their 'writhing' and 'shrieking' – what is more to the point is that the exploded – bursting, excreting, squirting, indeed *phallic* – body of Mary Channing is spread across the text as if the latter were some kind of rebus – or like the aftermath of a suicide bomb.

We have already looked at Marjorie Garson's account of the swollen, bursting, packed, overspilling, thrusting body of Casterbridge itself and this grossness indeed seems to hang about the eves and crevices and sills of the town like the lumps of flesh of a *corps morcelé*. This propensity of the town to swell and burst seems to have determined also the names of its most distinguished citizens among whom we have not just Grower (p. 283), but Bulge (p. 225) and, most astonishingly of all, Blowbody! (p. 355) That Henchard's crime might have been far more sinister than a mere-wife-sale – indeed, that it might have involved torture and sadistic mutilation – is hinted at in Nance Mockridge's astonishing suspicion that 'There is a bluebeardy look about 'en; and 'twil out in time.' (p. 156) And, indeed, there is more than a trace of sadistic humour in his reading of Lucetta's letters to Farfrae in her, Lucetta's, hearing. And is not the public burning of Mary Channing not just one more example, albeit an extreme one, of the 'memnotechnics of power' that we have earlier seen exercised on the body of Abe Whittle?

But where the exploding, excreting, fluid, fertile body of the executed woman most evidently returns to exact a terrible revenge against the State that has condemned her is in that triumvirate that we have seen organizing the Skimmington Ride, for each of them – Nance Mockridge, Mother Cuxsom and Mrs Goodenough – is an avatar or surrogate of Mary Channing. We have already commented on the bursting body and revolutionary posture of Nance Mockridge. In addition, however, the name 'Nance' is generic for a 'whore' or 'prostitute' which is no doubt how Mary Channing would have been described, but, more importantly, surely in the name 'Mockridge' we have an echo of that 'buxom' 'Mockwife' who has stood in for Mary Channing in the poem of that name. That Mother 'Cuxsom' is an echo of the 'buxom' of the same poem goes without saying. The old furmity woman's, Mrs Goodenough's, excretory pissing against the wall of the church seems to me to be the most magnificent gesture of female defiance – and truly worthy of Mary Channing whose only recorded utterance I have been able to trace is 'Kiss my arse!'[92] Finally, in the 'sweat' of Lucetta *Sueur* is there not a trace, too, of that other barely disguised version of Mary Channing, sweet Barbree *Sweatley* of *The Bride-Night Fire*?

No, I do not believe that I have proved beyond all reasonable doubt that it is Mary Channing that haunts *The Mayor of Casterbridge* but I truly believe that it is so. Moreover – to recall at this point our opening debate as to the specificity of the historical reference of the text versus its status as tragedy: I believe that it is only by recalling that specific event – the execution of 1705 – which was a State event of spectacular cruelty, that we can restore at all a tragic status to *The Mayor of Casterbridge*. Again, to recall our opening remarks, 'controlled' it may be but 'safe' *The Mayor of Casterbridge* is certainly not: indeed it is the most dangerous of Hardy's novels for it reveals an obsession that does him no credit at all.

On this last point there has been some discussion as to the psychology that informs the work. Millgate argues that Henchard

> is perhaps Hardy's most remarkable exercise in characterization, the richly and sympathetically imagined embodiment of those qualities of ambition, authority, vigour, violence, and sexual aggressiveness which Hardy knows to be lacking in himself . . . [93]

Seymour-Smith bridles somewhat at this slur and argues that 'Tom' had 'as much authority . . . vigour . . . and 'sexual aggression' as anyone else.'[94] A little earlier, however, he has had his own stab as to what perhaps lies behind the spectral distress of the novel. *A propos* of the wife-sale, for example, he wonders

> Did Tom feel that he, too, in some way 'sold', sacrificed his own wife in moving to Dorchester, in order to fulfil *his* destiny.[95]

Part of the story at this stage is that it is at precisely this period that Hardy and Emma finally accepted that they were to remain childless and that the differences between them began to grow at an alarming rate. It is from this period that his poem *He Abjures Love* is dated[96] and it seems to me that there is an intimate connexion between these events and the move to Dorchester and the writing of *The Mayor of Casterbridge*. Earlier we remarked that Lucetta's note declaring that her future depends on 'a man, and a merchant, and a Mayor' (p. 218 – and see above p. 64) is quite arbitrary in so far as any referent is concerned: that it might apply equally to Henchard, Farfrae or Chalkfield – or, indeed, to Hardy himself for in creating Casterbridge and instituting Wessex itself Hardy, too, in effect, is establishing himself as 'a man, and a merchant[97] and a Mayor' – and if not a Mayor, exactly, certainly as a Justice of the Peace as he became for the Borough of Dorchester in 1884.[98] What Seymour-Smith is suggesting is that the price of this 'mayoralty' was something like the sale or, worse, *sacrifice* of his wife. He imputes to Hardy

> a dark premonition...that by coming to live in the only place in which he felt he could fulfil himself creatively, his birthplace, he was sacrificing Emma and his love for her – and hers for him. *That same intuition had already seen her against a signpost, looking as if crucified.*[99]

His allusion is to the astonishingly moving and quite hauntingly pre-monitory poem *Near Lanivet, 1872*:

> There was a stunted handpost just on the crest,
>   Only a few feet high:
> She was tired, and we stopped in the twilight time for her rest,
>   At the crossways close thereby.
> She leant back, being so weary, against its stem,
>   And laid her arms on its own,
> Each open palm stretched out to each end of them,
>   Her sad face sideways thrown.
> Her white clothed-form at this dim-light cease of day
>   Made her look like one crucified
> In my gaze at her from the midst of the dusty way,
>   And hurriedly 'Don't,' I cried.
> I do not think she heard. Loosing thence she said
>   As she stepped forth ready to go,
> 'I am rested now. – Something strange came into my head;
>   I wish I had not leant so.
> And wordless we moved onward down from the hill
>   In the west cloud's murked obscure,
> And looking back we could see the handpost still
>   In the solitude of the moor.
> 'It struck her too,' I thought, for as if afraid
>   She breathed as we trailed;
> Till she said, 'I did not think how 'twould look in the shade,
>   When I leant there like one nailed.'
> I, lightly: 'There's nothing in it. For *you*, anyhow!'
>   – 'O I know there is not,' said she...
> 'Yet I wonder....If no one is bodily crucified now,

In spirit one may be!'
And we dragged on and on, while we seemed to see
In the running of Time's far glass
Her crucified, as she had wondered if she might be
Some day. – Alas, alas!

Whether it was a burning at the stake in 1705 or a crucifixion at a cross-roads near Nanivet in 1872 or simply the decision in or about 1883–84 that his wife was no longer integral to the project whereby he would guarantee himself a heritage, all the evidence is that *The Mayor of Caster-bridge* is haunted by an appalling sacrifice.

4
Tess of the d'Urbervilles: 'a becoming woman'

Tess of the d'Urbervilles is both exemplary and anomalous with regard to our basic scheme of territorial, despotic and capitalist social formations. Whereas each of the other three novels tends to confine itself either to one regime – as in *The Return* and in *Jude* – or, at most, to the conflict between two regimes – as in *The Mayor* – in this novel it is the fate of the heroine to traverse not just one, not two, but *all* the regimes from the 'territorial' backwater of Marlott through the benign but nevertheless structurally 'despotic' regime of Talbothays[1] and the harsh featureless 'capitalist' desert of Flintcomb Ash to the 'artificial', 'reterritorialized' exotic sea-side resort of Sandbourne.

That Tess's tragedy stems in part from her being caught between a number of different social regimes is probably one of the common-places of critical accounts of the novel and the passages where Tess's education and training differ from her mother's are well known:

> Mrs. Durbeyfield spoke the dialect; her daughter, who had passed the Sixth Standard in the National School under a London-trained mistress, spoke two languages; the dialect at home, more or less; ordinary English abroad and to persons of quality.[2] (p. 58)
>
> Between the mother, with her fast-perishing lumber of superstitions, folk-lore, dialect and orally transmitted ballads, and the daughter, with her trained National teachings and Standard knowledge under an infinitely Revised Code, there was a gap of two hundred years as ordinarily understood. When they were together the Jacobean and Victorian ages were juxtaposed. (p. 61)

There has, however, been a tendency to see Tess as caught between essentially *two* different regimes – usually the traditional and the modern world – and we have already suggested that the novel in fact covers a far greater variety of quite distinct social formations. It seems to me, for example, that this is the principal shortcoming of Jacques Lecercle's earlier 'Deleuze and Guattarian' reading of the novel. Lecercle writes:

> I will try to show that the contradiction which lies at the bottom of the novel is that between two languages and two cultures, between Tess's dialect and the dominant language in her world, the Queen's English.[3] In the novel, as in Tess, two cultures and two languages clash: this violence is at the unstable centre of Tess's world.[4]

Lecercle conflates too quickly the roles played by Alec and Angel in regarding them both as simply speakers of 'the voice of history – the Queen's English, the voice of education . . .' in contrast with the 'voice of folk-lore (the dialect, of course . . .)'.[5] What this fails to recognize is that, in Deleuze and Guattarian terms, Alec and Angel can be seen to be operating within two quite different regimes of signs – and the fact that these are two quite different regimes accounts for much of the oppressive power of the novel, for the sense that Tess is caught between the upper and the nether mill-stones of two incompatible but equally coercive forms of control.

One of the principal differences between *Anti-Oedipus* and *A Thousand Plateaux* is the reorganization and reformulation of the differences between territorial, despotic and capitalist systems of representation in terms of a whole new typology of 'regimes of signs' which only in part corresponds with the earlier series.[6]

Deleuze and Guattari now list four principal regimes of signs: a 'pre-signifying regime' (which corresponds very closely to the system of representation of a 'territorial formation'); a 'signifying regime' (which corresponds more or less to the system of 'despotic' representation); a 'counter-signifying regime' (which corresponds to a nomadic social machine described elsewhere in *A Thousand Plateaux*); and a 'post-signifying regime' which does not correspond, as one might have expected, with the 'capitalist' model of representation, but with the 'despotic' order in different mode.

Here I want to concentrate – as, in fact, do Deleuze and Guattari – on the second and fourth of these regimes – the 'signifying' and 'post-signifying' regimes. These constitute, on the one hand, 'a paranoid-interpretative ideal regime of signifiance' and, on the other, 'a passional, post-signifying subjective regime.' 'We are trying,' they say to make a distinction between a paranoid, signifying despotic regime of signs and a passional or subjective, post-signifying authoritarian regime. Authoritarian is assuredly not the same as despotic, passional is not the same as paranoid, and subjective is not the same as signifying.[7]

Some idea of the kind of distinction they are trying to establish can be gathered from the three or four examples they give of the different regimes: on the one hand the paranoid despotic-signifying regime of the Egyptian Pharaoh as opposed to the passional-authoritarian regime of the Hebrews; the Machiavellian political manoeuvring of the Shakespearian Henries contrasted with the passionate malignity and treacheries of Richard III; the irresponsible – dare we say 'cavalier'? – statecraft of the Stuarts compared to the passional and authoritarian commitment of Cromwell. Already it is perhaps possible to anticipate in part what light this distinction between the two regimes might cast on the nature of the power relationships set up within *Tess of the d'Urbervilles* that are centred respectively on Alec and Angel.

What lies behind Deleuze and Guattari's concept of the despotic-signifying regime is the essential ambiguity of the Saussurian notion of the *sign* – where, on the one hand, the sign is made up of a *signifier* and a *signified* (an *acoustic image* and a *concept*), while, on the other hand, the *signified* is only the *signifier* for another *signifier*. The imperialism or despotism of this regime lies in that vertical dimension of the *signifier* as the expression of a *signified* – i.e. of a transcendental *meaning* or *idea* that is *outside* the play of *signifiers* – and which offers itself as kind of guarantor of the intelligibility of a *signified* which in fact is no more than the extrapolated *effect* of a relay between one *signifier* and another *signifier*. The system is paranoid in its very essence for it is always afraid that a *signifier* might escape it, call the bluff of the transcendental *signified* which has no status but what the play of the *signifier* can impart to it.[8]

The despotic-signifying regime consists of six principal elements:

1. A centre of signification centred on the body or face of the despot.[9]
2. A series of circles emerging from that centre consisting of sets of signs that always refer back to the centre.
3. A body of interpreting priests who are always on the watch to ensure that any new sign that enters the circles are linked back to the despotic centre.
4. A group of hysterical adulants who are always ready to jump from circle to circle reinforcing and refurbishing the resonance of the system.

5. Whatever cannot be accommodated within the system is projected onto a scapegoat figure who is then driven out along what must be deemed a negative line of flight.
6. The whole system is held together by trickery and deceit.[10]

Deleuze and Guattari summarize the system as follows:

> The complete system, then, consists of the paranoid face or body of the despot-god in the signifying centre of the temple; the interpreting priests who continually recharge the signified in the temple, transforming it into signifier; the hysterical crowd of people outside, clumped in tight circles, who jump from one circle to another; the faceless, depressive scapegoat emanating from the centre, chosen, treated and adorned by the priests, cutting across the circles in its headlong flight into the desert.[11]

In *Tess* it is Alec d'Urberville who occupies the (usurped) role of the despot in a despotic-signifying regime which exploits the d'Urbervilles' genealogy (a set of signifiers lying in wait for her) first to ensnare Tess and then to do his best to cut off all avenues of escape even while Tess herself must become inevitably the scapegoat figure that bears all the excess that such a regime cannot accommodate. The initial gesture of the system is the incorporative move taken by the 'interpreting priest' Parson Tringham, 'the antiquary of Stagfoot Lane.' (p. 43). In this scheme of things Kingsbere-sub-Greenhill with its 'rows and rows of vaults (and) effigies under Purbeck-marble canopies' (p. 45) occupies the place of a central court and point of reference – even when Tess has least reason for acknowledging the connection, her move to Talbothays is in part influenced by its proximity to Kingsbere (p. 156). Ominously, too, the ancestral line is associated with distinctive *facial* traits. Even before meeting Alec, Tess has associated the d'Urbervilles with a *face*:

> She had dreamed of an aged and dignified face, the sublimation of all the d'Urberville lineaments, furrowed with incarnate memories representing in hieroglyphic the centuries of her family's and England's glory.
>
> (p. 79)

And there are the two grim ancestral portraits that greet them on their doomed wedding night at Wellbridge (pp. 283–4).

But it is Alec himself who is introduced primarily as a *face*:

He had an almost swarthy complexion, with full lips, badly moulded, though red and smooth, above which was a well-groomed black moustache with curled points, though his age could not be more than three- or four-and-twenty. Despite the touches of barbarism in his contours, there was a singular force in the gentleman's face, and in his bold rolling eye.

(p. 79)

The *grand guignol* or pantomime excess of this description is of precisely the kind that has earned Hardy a reputation for stylistic ungainliness: on the other hand if what Hardy is offering is an iconic delineation of a specific power-structure – indeed what we have here seems more like a mask than a face – then it seems to me that the caricatural excess does not come amiss.

What we sense in the text is the ever-widening circles of Alec's power as Tess vainly strives to outstrip it. Parson Tringham is not the only figure that wittingly or unwittingly serves this power structure. The other figure who serves to bind Tess into the power structure that emanates from Alec is the loathsome Farmer Groby, who at several important junctures in the text almost seems to emerge from the ground to confront Tess again with her past, to refer her back to her original disgrace. (Alec himself also performs similar moves from time to time: his emergence beside Tess at her garden bon-fire (p. 431); his rising, Dracula-like, from the tomb in Kingsbere Church towards the end (p. 449) – Deleuze and Guattari speak of the habit dead signifiers have of returning from the dead to reclaim the living.)[12]

But the system is kept going, too, by another figure who fills the role of Deleuze and Guattari's 'hysterical crowd' that keeps bolstering the regime even while in thrall to it. This is the part played by Tess's mother, Joan Durbeyfield who, almost as much as Parson Tringham, is responsible for setting the whole diabolical thing in motion with her 'grand projick' (p. 64) of sending Tess off to claim kinship with the d'Urbervilles at Trantridge. Throughout it is Joan's economies with truth and subterfuges and deceit that are as great a factor in Tess's destruction at the hands of Alec as is any other. From beginning to end Alec has no more willing aider and abetter in his treachery and deceit than Joan Durbeyfield: to this extent she embodies the very *trickery* that is endemic to the despotic signifying system.

Finally, the last element in the system – the figure of the *scapegoat*. Such, of course, is Tess herself who at times seems to be atoning not only for her own past but also for the crimes of her ancestors (p. 119). Tess herself seems to recognize her place in the economy of such a regime:

> 'Now punish me!' she said, turning up her eyes to him with the hopeless defiance of the sparrow's gaze before its captor twists its neck. 'Whip me, crush me; you need not mind those people under the rick! I shall not cry out. Once victim, always the victim – that's the law!'
>
> (p. 411)

It is characteristic of the despotic regime that the scapegoat figure should regard its relation to the whole as one of negation and exclusion.

We can contrast this despotic signifying regime with the authoritarian, post-signifying, passional regime point by point:

1. Instead of a centre of signification there is a 'point of subjectivation' which is something like an interpellative call or address which becomes an '*idée fixe*'. Now the face turns away – in fact there is a double turning away – and the central role is now taken by the Voice.
2. Instead of a series of circles there is now the detachment of a packet of signs – like the Ark of the Covenant – and a serial line of flight.
3. There are no signifier-signifier links but a relationship between the subject of enunciation (*sujet d'énonciation*) and the subject of the statement (*sujet d'énoncé*) so that the discourse of the former insinuates itself into the discourse of the latter.
4. Instead of a chorus of adulants furbishing the system, the subject of the statement (*sujet d'énoncé*) *internalizes* the references and becomes self monitoring and self-legislating.
5. Instead of the negative line of flight of the despotic signifying system the scapegoat figure now embraces the line of flight as a positive proceeding, an existence under reprieve by way of atonement.
6. Finally, rather than *trickery*, the whole system is characterized by *betrayal*.[13]

Deleuze and Guattari describe it as follows:

> There is no longer a centre of signifiance connecting to expanding circles or an expanding spiral, but a point of subjectification constituting the point of the line. There is no longer any signifier–signified

relation, but a subject of enunciation (*sujet d'énonciation*) issuing from the point of subjectification and a subject of the statement (*sujet d'énoncé*) in a determinable relation to the first subject. There is no longer a sign-to-sign circularity, but a linear proceeding into which the sign is swept via subjects (*s'engouffre à travers les sujets*).... The point of subjectification is the origin of the passional line of the post-signifying regime. The point of subjectification can be anything. It must only display the following characteristic traits of the subjective semiotic: the double turning away, betrayal, and existence under reprieve.[14]

No matter in what order we take them every one of these characteristics are to be found illustrated in Angel's relationship with Tess. Significantly Angel first emerges at Talbothays as a 'voice' from behind a dun cow (p. 169):

> Angel Clare rises out of the past not altogether as a distinct figure, but as an appreciative voice...
>
> (p. 169)

Almost his first effect upon Tess is to supplant her own voice so that we are told again and again:

> her natural quickness, and her admiration for him, [had] led her to pick up his vocabulary, his accent, and fragments of his knowledge, to a surprising extent.
>
> (p. 238)

or that

> His influence over her had been so marked that she had caught his manner and habits, his speeches and phrases, his likings and aversions.
>
> (p. 270)

So much so that later Alec can not only congratulate her on her 'good English' (p. 389) but so complete is her recall of Angel's language and thought patterns even when she does not understand what they mean ('her acute memory for the letter of Angel's remarks, even when she did not comprehend their spirit' (p. 400)) that Alec is also able quite easily to appropriate their original meaning for his own ends. (pp. 403 and 410). In fact so completely have the utterances of the 'subject of enunciation' (*sujet d'énonciation*) become internalized by the 'subject of the statement' (*sujet d'énoncé*) that the self-restraint Tess imposes on herself by observance of Angel's injunctions results in an almost complete paralysis of her own will:

> Thus her silence of docility was misinterpreted. How much it really said if he had really understood! – that she adhered with literal exactness to orders which he had given and forgotten; that despite her natural fearlessness she asserted no rights, admitted his judgment to be in every respect the true one, and bent her head dumbly thereto.
>
> (p. 421)

It is characteristic of this new passional and authoritarian regime that the role in it that compares to Groby in the despotic signifying regime is assumed by the itinerant sign-painter originally employed by the Rev. Clare. His comma-punctuated injunctions –

THY, DAMNATION, SLUMBERETH, NOT.

(p. 128)

THOU, SHALT, NOT, COMMIT –

(p. 129)

– break up the signfying order and turn the words into interpellative cajoling admonishments – from being simply sentences, we might say, they become *sentences* in the legal sense of the term.

Perhaps the saddest moment in the book – saddest because no more than a heartbeat away from what might have been a happy resolution – is that in which Angel and Tess separate after the catastrophic honeymoon at Wellbridge. Their farewell has an almost ritual quality. Angel enjoins Tess:

> But until I come to you it will be better that you should not try to come to me.

And Tess 'simply repeat(s) after him his own words':

> Until you come to me I must not try to come to you?
>
> (p. 324)

Alec then hands Tess a small 'packet containing a fairly good sum of money' and then the two turn away from each other:

The fly moved up the hill, and Clare watched it go with an unpre-
meditated hope that Tess would look out of the window for one
moment. But that she never thought of doing, would not have
ventured to do, lying in a half-dead faint inside. (p. 325)

Here, in the tacit contract that she will not seek him out, and the double
turning away, is what Deleuze and Guattari describe as the 'point of
subjectification' – the subjecting of the *sujet d'énoncé* to the *sujet d'énonciation*. The little detached packet of signs, which Angel has given to her,
Tess comes to regard with an almost religious devotion as if they were
the very Ark of the Covenant:

She could not bear to let them go. Angel had put them into her hand,
had obtained them bright and new from his bank for her; his touch had
consecrated them to souvenirs of himself – they appeared to have had
as yet no other history than such as was created by his and her own
experience – and to disperse them was like giving away relics.

(p. 347)

There is indeed something almost fetishistic in Tess's regard for her
'idolized husband' (p. 181):

At first she seemed to regard Angel Clare as an intelligence rather
than as a man....

(p. 181)

There was hardly a touch of earth in her love for Clare. To her sublime
trustfulness he was all that goodness could be – knew all that a guide,
philosopher, and friend should know. She thought every line in the
contour of his person the perfection of masculine beauty, his soul the
soul of a saint, his intellect that of a seer.

(p. 257)

Even at the end when

Worn and unhandsome as he had become, it was plain that she did
not discern the least fault in his appearance. To her he was, as of old,
all that was perfection, personally and mentally. He was still her
Antinous, her Apollo even...

(p. 475)

The point of subjectification, the double turning away,[15] the detached
packet of signs, the fetishistic idolization, the internal assumption of the

judgements passed upon her, the commitment to an existence under reprieve, the 'stagnation' (p. 346) of an infinite postponement waiting for a husband who may never return – in many ways a punishment, indeed a betrayal, more cruel than death itself – all these are constituents of a passional, conscience-driven regime quite other than that which had first made Tess the victim of the casually irresponsible despot of the signifying regime, Alec.

Both regimes are equally coercive but in different ways. Alec's is a regime of overt mastery –

'Remember, my lady, I was your master once! I will be your master again. If you are any man's wife you are mine!'

(p. 412)[16]

and even Tess finds herself acknowledging this deep down:

It was not her husband, she had said. Yet a consciousness that in a physical sense this man alone was her husband seemed to weigh on her more and more.

(p. 442)

whereas Angel's power is perhaps more dangerous and more insidious for he seems to work his way into her very mind and take up residence there. The one seems to embody the very *idea* of power, whereas the other seems to appeal to an emotional and imaginative *ideal*. The first seems to wish to reduce Tess to the objective status of an instrument of pleasure; the second de-realises her by elevating her to the status of a visionary deity – 'He called her Artemis, Demeter' (p. 187) – :

he was, in truth, more spiritual than animal.... Though not cold-natured, he was rather bright than hot – less Byronic than Shelleyan; could love desperately, but with a love more especially inclined to the imaginative and ethereal; it was a fastidious emotion which could jealously guard the loved one against his very self.

(p. 257)

It must remain a moot point as to which of the two causes Tess the greater distress: the irresponsible sensualist who exploits her naïveté, or the lamentably limited puritan who cannot cope with her past; the cynically amoral rake who at least takes care of her mother and brothers and sisters and dresses her in cashmere (p. 465), or the morbidly self-engrossed idealist who is disturbed by her very sexuality.

I want to consider, now, to what extent Deleuze's account of the distinctive features of sadism and masochism which is to be found in his much earlier *Présentation de Sacher-Masoch*[17] anticipates many of the features of the despotic-signifying and authoritarian-post-signifying regimes we have just discussed. Deleuze begins by recalling that the Middle Ages distinguished two kinds of 'diabolisme' or perversion: the one due to *possession*, the other which stemmed from a *pact* or *alliance*.[18] From this initial distinction a whole set of others ensues. The sadist, for example, tends to address his victims by way of 'instructions' while the masochist is inclined to be more 'persuasive', addressing the woman who is to administer his punishment more as an educator than either as a master or even as a potential victim[19] – and this because it is an essential feature of the masochistic scenario or fantasy that the masochist first *educate* the person who is to act as his tormentor. The two perversions share common elements, but these elements are articulated in totally different ways. Both the sadist and the masochist are involved in relations of power and pain but whereas the sadist treats his victims with an ill-disguised contempt as if administering pain in accordance with some scheme of higher reason, the masochist's pain becomes only a fantastically orchestrated subterfuge whereby he can indulge a forbidden desire. Contrasted with the cold reason of the sadist is the imaginative fantasizing of the masochist. While the sadist seems bent on destroying the world in conformity with some *idea* of absolute mastery, the masochist disavows the reality of the world in conformity with an arrested and fetishized *ideal*. The sadist tends to operate by imperatives and haste as if everything must be indulged in at once, whereas the masochist seems to operate by stretching things out, by postponement and suspension – as if the intensity of the pleasure is relative to the pain of the delay. To achieve these quite distinctive ends the sadist acts by planning anarchic *institutions* that make a mockery of the law – a perfect brothel, for example – whereas the masochist seems to achieve his ends by a *contract* – the contract that is part and parcel of his training of his tormentor – which subverts the law by parodying it to excess. For the masochist the very pleasure forbidden by the law becomes the reward of an exaggerated compliance that reverses the causal relation of guilt and pleasure: the punishment designed to forestall or prohibit an erection becomes the very means of provoking it.[20]

Now, I am not suggesting that either Alec is a sadist, or Angel a masochist – though the degree to which the latter implements virtually the whole of what Deleuze calls the 'properly masochistic constellation' – 'disavowal, suspense, waiting, fetishism, fantasy [*and* the contract]'[21] – suggests that the charge would not be wholly unfounded – but I believe it is the case that there is at least a tendency on the part of both of them to incline towards these two extremes: Alec's mastery and 'instructions' (how to whistle, for example), Angel's reverence and concern to educate (the 'lords and ladies' episode, for example) the woman who will become the source of his own distress; Alec's predilection for speed and promptness, Angel's inclination to delay and adjournment; Alec's instrumental exploitation, Angel's idealization and fetishization – above all, perhaps, Alec's *negation* of Tess's very existence in his relegation of her to an instrument of pleasure contrasted with Angel's brutal *disavowal* of her sexual identity when she confesses her past to him.

But what is perhaps most significant about what we might call, after Deleuze, the sadist and masochist 'constellations' and where, perhaps, they contribute most to the overall thematic structure of *Tess of the d'Urbervilles*, is that both of them can be seen as indictments and mockeries of the pretensions of the notion of a moral law. In his essay on Sacher-Masoch Deleuze writes:

> There has ever been only one way to think about the law and that is by means of a comic mode made of irony and humour.[22]

For Deleuze the comic potential of the sadistic and the masochistic modes derives from the fact that they are, respectively, ironic and humorous reversals of the (Oedipal) origins of the law: the sadist reverses the law by returning to and reversing its origin in the *negation* of an identity with the father – the sadist *negates* the *negation* by in fact *inflating* the identification with the father; the masochist, on the other hand, reverses the law in his own way by getting around the consequences of the law which are derived from the *disavowal* of the desire for the mother – the masochist *disavows* the *disavowal* and jubilantly *celebrates* a triumphant rebirth in the arms of the mother denied him. In both cases there is a reversal of the very sublimation and desexualization that first produced the law via the simultaneous *constitution* and *prohibition* of both its *subject* and its *object* – the father and aggression, the mother and desire.[23] At the same time this return to the prohibited identification with the father and the repressed desire for the mother entails a *resexualization* of those very figures that are only made possible – that is constituted as discrete identities – as a result of a *desexualization*: it is the *impossibility* – the absolute *unseizability* – of this moment, for it is the very border between *desexualization* and *resexualization*, that accounts for the opposite strategies of the sadist and the masochist: the sadist tries to hit the moment by sheer speed of thought, while the masochist endeavours to arrest it by means of imagination and fantasy. The sadist and the masochist endeavour to have it both ways: on the one hand they want to reverse the constitutive sublimations of the law and thereby enjoy the anarchic and non-differentiated intensities of unbridled instincts while on the other they wish to hang on to the identifications and differentiations that can only be precipitates of this border experience.

The sadistic and masochistic latencies of the text, then, are part and parcel of what I think we need to be prepared to recognize as a macabre but, nevertheless, in many ways, almost a *comic* exasperation with the stupidity of a moral order that would seek to harness, shackle, condemn and destroy Tess. There are several moments when this note of exasperated laughter can be heard in the text: two familiar ones are the mocking close:

> 'Justice' was done, and the President of the Immortals, in Aeschylan phrase, had ended his sport with Tess. And the d'Urberville knights and dames slept in their tombs unknowing.
>
> (p. 489)

and the almost hectoring commentary that follows upon Tess's seduction/rape in The Chase:

> But, might some say, where was Tess's guardian angel? where was the providence of her simple faith? Perhaps, like that other god of whom the ironical Tishbite spoke, he was talking, or he was pursuing, or he was in [sic] a journey, or he was sleeping and not to be awaked. (p. 119)

But there are others: there is the gleam of the setting sunlight on the shoes of the forlorn body of Prince being hauled back to Marlott which conjures up an oddly comic vision at this point (p. 72); or again the strangely dissonant note mentioning the fact that the jar that held the flowers on Sorrow's grave was emblazoned with the words 'Keelwell's Marmalade' (p. 148). Indeed there is often something exuberantly comic about Alec's behaviour like some early Joker figure while there is a terribly barbed humour in Angel's final stealing away with his deceased wife's sister on his arm. Grotesque as the suggestion might be, is there not a suspicion, here, that the plight of Tess might be, in the end, not unlike that which Wilde feared was courted by Dickens' Little Nell: less a tragedy than a farce which would leave all those without a heart of stone reduced to helpless laughter?

Let us return now to that 'border' between sexualization and desexualization, between sublimation and desublimation, that Deleuze posits as the *impossible* object of both the sadist and the masochistic project – *impossible* because it marks the very moment of a passage or *leap* between a desire, at the point where it is barely distinguishable from pure animal *need*, in a condition of optimal heterogeneity, and a desire harnessed to discrete drives and identities; between an untrammelled disposability of maximal flux and the domestic economy of the Oedipal regime – whether it be institutionally despotic and signifying or contractually authoritarian and passional. It is an impossible moment to *think*, even though it is the very moment in which *thought* itself is born: *before* it there is only physiological *need*; while *after* it, there are indeed distinguishable subjects and objects, but *between* the two – in the impossible hiatus – is the sheer *nebula* of human and non-human potential – the infinity of 'incompossible'[24] affects and identities glimpsed only in the moments of an absolute intensity akin to self-annihilation and death. And this is the point for it is precisely this *border experience* which Tess 'represents' – 'represents' between inverted commas because essentially *unrepresentable* for it is essentially a moment of *becoming*, of *being in-between*, of radical *anomaly*. It is the moment that at various stages in his work Deleuze associates with the 'phantasm',[25] the 'Death Instinct', with 'repetition' and the 'Eternal Return' for it is the jubilant moment of passage between the heterogeneity and multiplicity of affective intensities and the constitution of fixed and molar identities. It is, in a strange way – and I want to capture some of the magical ambiguity of the term for Tess herself – the very *Eve* of identity.

In the course of the foregoing I have summarized three configurations of the various power-structures that prevail in *Tess of the d'Urbervilles*: the first was the typology of social formations – territorial, despotic, capitalist and 'post'-capitalist regimes; the second was the distinction between the despotic signifying system and the authoritarian post-signifying system; the third drew on the difference between the sadist and the masochist perversions of the law. Now, each of these configurations allows us to venture what I think are important new interpretations of Hardy's notoriously provocative description of Tess as a 'pure woman'.

The first of these derives from Tess's essentially *nomadic* relation to the regimes that she traverses: Tess can be seen to *migrate* from regime to regime, whether we consider *regime* in the *geographical* or the *psychic* register, without becoming captured or enmeshed in any of them – in this sense she is quite unlike Eustacia Vye who quite simply becomes swallowed up in the gaps between the regimes she attempts to traverse.

It is this status of Tess as a *residual* and *nomadic* subject that allows us to appropriate for her the terms Deleuze and Guattari use to designate such a peripheral subjectivity – a *'celibate machine'*:

> The question becomes: what does the celibate machine pro-
> duce?... The answer would seem to be intensive qualities... in their
> pure state, to a point that is almost unbearable – a celibate misery and
> glory experienced to the fullest, like a cry suspended between life
> and death, an intense feeling of transition, states of pure naked
> intensity stripped of all shape and form.[26]

It is this 'celibate', 'migratory', 'nomadic' – Deleuze and Guattari would add 'schizophrenic' – experience of intense transitions and becomings that gives Tess a first transcendence for which the word 'pure' is no more and no less than apposite.

It was Tess's anomolous position with regard to both the *despotic signifying* and *authoritarian passional* regimes that led me to consider attributing to her a second 'transcendence' or 'purity' by associating her with Deleuze and Guattari's notion of 'The War Machine.' As figures epitomising, respectively, the despotic signifying and the authoritarian post-signifying regimes Alec and Angel can quite easily be assimilated to the two major poles of power that Deleuze and Guattari identify at the beginning of their essay on 'The War Machine':

> George Dumézil.... has shown that political sovereignty, or domin-
> ation, has two heads: the magician-king and the jurist priest. Rex and
> flamen, raj and Brahman, Romulus and Numa, Varuna and Mitra, the
> despot and the legislator, the binder and the organiser.[27]

The War Machine, however, is to be found at neither pole:

> As for the war machine in itself, it seems to be irreducible to the State
> apparatus, to be outside its sovereignty and prior to its law: it comes
> from elsewhere.... Rather it is like a pure and immeasurable multi-
> plicity, the pack, an irruption of the ephemeral and the power of
> metamorphosis. *It unties the bond just as it betrays the pact.*[28]

The war machine is a pure *anomaly*, irreducible to either pole: it comes from without; it operates with incredible speeds and slownesses – not in terms of geographical displacements but in terms of affects and inten-sities: even when immobile the war machine may be operating at intense speed, and even when in flight it may be in a condition of total rest. It is like the Japanese wrestler: one moment moving with incredible slowness, the next at lightning speed.[29] The War Machine operates more like 'Go' than 'Chess': instead of set pieces and protocols, it operates by multiplicities, by groupings and encompassings, by insinuations, and infiltrations.

Tess is such an *anomaly* (p. 135), conjuring away and confounding those very apparatuses that would appropriate her. We have to be prepared to imagine a Sumo Tess: it is only so that the vexed question of her so-called passivity can be resolved. Tess is never passive – even in stasis she reverberates with speed – the moment one is lulled she strikes like a viper – as when she strikes Alec with her field glove (p. 411) or in those many other moments when she flares up. What distinguishes the war machine from the molar and majoritarian identifications of the state is its capacity for flight, for metamorphosis, for minoritarian becomings[30] – becoming animal and becoming imperceptible: this is what Tess moves through – she unties the bond (with Alec) and betrays the pact (with Angel); she is in perpetual and precipitate flight. Tess increasingly becomes animal-like in her being hunted, as she seeks for indiscernibility:[31]

> and there was something of the habitude of the wild animal in the unreflecting instinct with which she rambled on – disconnecting herself little by little from her eventful past at every step, obliterating her identity. . . .
>
> (p. 349)
>
> She also, by a felicitous thought, took a handkerchief from her bundle and tied it round her face under her bonnet, covering her chin and half her cheeks and temples, as if she were suffering from toothache. Then with her little scissors, by the aid of a pocket looking glass, she mercilessly nipped her eyebrows off, and thus assured against aggressive admiration she went on her uneven way.
>
> (p. 354)

Here is a second sense of 'purity' – a propensity to slip away, to disburden oneself of identity, to become indiscernible, to go 'unnoticed',[32] a constellation of affects, out-manoeuvring and for ever eluding the constellations of power that would bear down upon one. This might seem just perverse in that Tess, at the end, seems to be totally destroyed by Alec and Angel but I think this is to misread the novel. Tess's outburst against Alec –

'My God! I could knock you out of the gig! Did it ever strike you that what every woman says some women may feel?'

(p. 125)

is often cited as evidence of Tess's vigorous demand that she be taken to mean what she says. Why should we refuse to accept that she means what she says at the end when she walks towards her captors and simply says 'I am ready' (p. 487)? Nietzsche remarks somewhere that tragedy is only sad for the spectators – not for those who are the tragic protagonists.[33] To sit snivelling over Tess's 'unhappy end' is to refuse once more to accept that she means what she says and to endeavour once again to re-inscribe her within our fantasies of her. The 'tragic' – in the sense of 'sad' – reading of the novel only once again denies Tess her autonomy, her eccentricity, her lack of compromise with – her *non-adulteration* by – the apparatuses of capture that lie in wait for her. What we have in the pure intensity of Tess's trajectory is nothing less than the luminous path of a savage anomaly.[34]

And finally, I want to return to that non-apprehensible, unseizable *border* or *becoming* that we located as the impossible object of the sadist and masochist projects. In a recent and important essay Peter Widdowson has sought to de-essentialize Tess and relativise her into a 'series of seemings' and in so doing construe the novel as a 'post-modernist' deconstruction of the 'bourgeois-humanist (patriarchal and realist) notion of the unified and unitary human subject'.[35] My own feeling is that this is perhaps a too negative and reactive an account of what is Hardy's far more *positive* achievement – the nature of which is testified to in the quotations from Deleuze and Guattari with which I have prefaced this study.[36] This is the creation of what Deleuze calls here a 'subjectless individuation...these clusters of sensations' and which he associates elsewhere in a series of provocative formulations with *'becoming woman, becoming animal, becoming imperceptible.'*[37] What Deleuze and Guattari have in mind by these phrases are those atomizings and dissolutions of molar identities in processes of affective becomings that are like maximal dispersals of intensities prior to and on the very edge of identificatory purchase and arrest. Tess is such a molecular *becoming* – such a *becoming woman*: the English 'becoming' has a fitness here way beyond its merely translating the French 'devenir'. Throughout the text Tess is hardly ever presented as a simple unitary subject: again and again she is presented as either a composite (pp. 52, 140, 232) or as part of group or a collective (pp. 136, 161, 167, 243). The little group she forms with Izzy, Marian and Retty at Talbothays is frequently presented as a collective identity, a group of 'four' (pp. 200, 201, 215) or a 'bevy' (pp. 139, 199, 204) so that there is a sense that identity itself is something like 'a little group' (*une groupuscule*).[38] There is also, again and again, a sense of her being atomized or dissolved into the landscape or the atmosphere around her: like the field-woman Hardy describes she becomes a 'portion of the field; she has somehow lost her own margin' (p. 137) or 'natural processes' become 'a part of her own story' (p. 134). Time and again we sense that Tess, or Tess and Angel, are virtually being molecularized into the mist that surrounds them:

> Minute diamonds of moisture from the mist hung, too, upon Tess's eyelashes, and drops upon her hair like seed pearls. (p. 188)
> Upon this river-brink they lingered till the fog began to close round them – which was early in the evening at this time of the year – settling on the lashes of her eyes, where it rested like crystals, and on his brows and hair.
>
> (p. 259)

There is something more than mere 'pathetic fallacies' or 'soft-focus' voyeurism or a vague pantheism going on in these passages for they are part of a much more sustained 'impressionist' or even 'pointillist' technique – something like the 'mad late-Turner' style Hardy admired so much – which atomizes and molecularizes the scenes in the novel: all those fogs and mists and hazes (pp. 106, 123, 136 187, 230), the pollenization of sound (p. 179) or of light (p. 258), the spurts of sap in shoots (p. 187), the collective thrusts of seasons (p. 207) which seem to dissolve the boundaries of the human and the non-human, the animal and the vegetable, the material and the spiritual worlds so as to constitute an almost Spinozist composite nature stretching from the infinitesimally small to the infinitely great.[39] In such a commingling of the natural and the human worlds character and setting become inextricably fused the one into the other to produce what Deleuze and Guattari call '*haecce-ities*'[40] – a 'haecceity' being a kind of experiential space-time event – like Lorca's 'five in the afternoon' or Lewis Caroll's 'tea-time':

> There is a mode of individuation very different from that of a person, thing, or substance. We reserve the name *haecceity* for it.[41]

It is this notion of a *haecceity* that allows us now to reconfigure the trajectory of Tess that we traced at the beginning of this essay in terms of an affective mapping which Deleuze himself derives from Spinoza.

Spinoza asks what a body can do[42] and Deleuze paraphrases his reply in terms of longitude and latitude:

> We call the longitude of any body the set of relations of speed and slowness, of rest and movement, of particles that compose it.... We call latitude the mass of affects that fills a body at any moment, that is to say the intensive state of an anonymous force (force of existence, the power to be affected). And so we establish the cartography of a body.[43]

What this gives us is a radically new understanding of the nature of what might be meant by the notion of a 'pure woman'. Deleuze and Guattari write:

> Doubtless, the girl becomes a woman in the molar or organic sense. But conversely, becoming-woman or the molecular woman is the girl herself. The girl is certainly not defined by virginity; she is defined by a relation of movement and rest, speed and slowness, by a combination of atoms, an emission of particles; haecceity.[44]

Tess is 'pure' not because of some prurient notion of virginity but because she is a magnificent testimony to what a body can do – through her speeds and slownesses, through her affective capacity for love and to be loved, for her molecular sympathies and intensities, for her enormous capacity for life. In fact I am not at all sure that our tears for Tess at the end are tears of sorrow, but rather tears at the sheer joy of Tess's inhuman power of goodness. In a sense what *Tess of the d'Urbervilles* seems to establish in the end is an *ethics* that provides a grid of affective and intensive co-ordinates that casts a net of reference far wider than the power structures, the social formations, the regimes of signs and the configurations of desire – that is those several normative and perverse *moralities* (but which is which?) – that have provided its narrative armature.[45]

5
Tess: the Phantasmatic Capture

In the previous chapter I have looked at the ways in which Tess might be said to have been threatened by a number of 'captures' – (a) by a series of social structures (territorial, despotic, capitalist); (b) by two quite different regimes of signs (despotic signifying, authoritarian passional); or (c) by two quite different configurations of desire (sadistic, masochistic) – all of which she manages to skirt and transcend in her nomadic line of flight. Nevertheless I have left undiscussed what is without doubt the most powerful strategy of capture of all and one the provides the novel with its major structural scheme. This is what I want to call the 'phantasmatic capture' of Tess because it is a capture that can be best described in terms of the model of the 'phantasm' first elaborated in their seminal paper of 1964 – 'Fantasme originaire, fantasmes des origines, origine du fantasme'[1] (translated into English in 1968 as 'Fantasy and the origins of sexuality'[2]) – by Jean Laplanche and J.-B. Pontalis and later developed by Deleuze in his *Logique du sens* of 1969.

In their retracing of the genealogy and the vicissitudes of the notion of the phantasm in Freud's work Laplanche and Pontalis show how fantasy and phantasms had always been of importance to Breuer and Freud but that the concept began to assume a particular significance at the moment when Freud found it necessary to revise his early 'seduction theory'. This was the theory that a trauma was caused when the memory of what had been an earlier sexual assault on a child by an adult – that is at a time when the child was neither physiologically nor mentally equipped to comprehend or deal with such an assault – was triggered by the associations provoked by a later – that is post-pubertal – event which, in turn, provoked a pathogenic response. What was, and remained, of major significance in this early theory was its insight into the reasons why repression arose chiefly in relation to human sexuality and this because of the temporality established between the 'too early' of the infantile assault and the 'too late' of the post-pubertal reactivation. Famously, in 1897 Freud announced that he was abandoning this theory and replaced it instead with a theory of endogenous infantile sexual development for which the so-called 'scenes of seduction' were no more than fantasy disguises. The reasons he gave for this change were: first, that he had found it impossible to trace any 'real' seduction in his patient's past and, in any case, there was no real 'index of reality' in the unconscious; secondly, such was the frequency with which his patients reported these 'seductions' he feared that, if they were indeed true, the number of guilty parental figures or closet paedophiles that would have had to exist in Viennese society at the time would have exceeded statistical probability) At about the same time, however, Freud 'discovered' the Oedipal phantasm/fantasy, first in his own self analysis and then as a quasi-universal determinant in the aetiology of human desire and sexuality and, closely associated with the Oedipal phantasm, a number of other standard or typical phantasms such as those of the 'primal scene' and 'castration' as well as the phantasm or fantasy of 'seduction' itself. It was these that Freud described as 'original' or 'originary' phantasms as they seemed to be always related to events concerned with the 'origination' of the human. In a long and important footnote Laplanche and Pontalis write:

> If we ask ourselves what these phantasms of origins mean to us, we find ourselves at another level of interpretation. We see then how it can be said of them that not only are they part of the symbolic order, but that they *translate* [*traduisent*: the English translation translates this important word as *represent*], via the mediation of an imaginary scenario which claims a purchase on it, the inscription [Fr: *insertion*] of the most radically constitutive symbolic order on the real of the body. What does the primal scene mean for us? The link between the biological fact of conception (and of birth) and the symbolic fact of filiation, between the naked act [*acte sauvage*] of coitus and the existence of the triad of mother–infant–father. In the phantasms of castration the real–symbolic link is even more obvious. Let us add, as far as the [phantasm] of seduction is concerned, that it is not only, as we have already shown, because he had found a number of real acts of seduction that Freud was able to make of the phantasm a scientific theory, so discovering via this detour the function itself of the phantasm; it is also because he wanted to account for, in terms of an origin, the advent of sexuality to the human being.[3]

Freud was still perplexed as to the 'origins' of these 'scenes of origins' and for a time toyed with two possibilities: one was proposed by Jung and this is that such scenes were in effect no more than retrospective constructions by the patient from his or her later vantage point – Freud was quick to reject this suggestion. The second was the notion of 'phylogenetic memories' i.e. that these scenes of origin derived from events long in the past of the race or species and handed down by some form of genetic memory. What finally made this 'phylogenetic' theory untenable was the presence in so many of the recorded dreams or phantasms of incidental details of events that could only have had a contingent and not a purely transcendent origin – such as the presence, in a phantasm of the primal scene, of the small noise (*petit bruit*) that had first triggered it: in other words the origin of the phantasm of origin was to be found in the phantasm of origin itself. It was this role of *sound*, of *bruit*, that led Freud closest to his final formulation of the nature and role of the phantasm. 'Phantasms are produced,' Laplanche and Pontalis quote from Freud, 'by an unconscious combination of things lived and things heard' and this 'heard' must not be confined to raw sound but to

> – the history, or legends, of parents, grand-parents, ancestors; the *lore* [*dit*] or the *noise* [*bruit*] of the family, this spoken or secret discourse, previous to the subject, into which it must come or to which it must have recourse.[4]

It is in this conjunction of the *lived* [*vecu*] and the *heard* [*entendu*] that we have the very essence of the phantasm and it is only here that Freud finally manages to articulate the endogenous and the biological body and its instincts on the inherited schema of a society and its culture. The phantasm or fantasy is not a simple disguise or expression of an infantile sexuality, nor is it a transcendentally archetypal scheme with its origins in a mythical past.[5] What occurs in the phantasm is the implantation of the world of human meaning and all that that entails in terms of desire, sexuality, gender, and social status on a body hitherto driven by little else than pre-programmed biological need. In the phantasm the whole chorus of family legends, cultural traditions, folk-tales, gossip, myths, hover around the neonate and unco-ordinated body with its pulsations, rhythms, imbibings, excretions, thrusts and recoils and seek to order, mark, inscribe, claim and articulate it.

There are two final remarks to be made about this implantation of the human and the cultural on the purely biological. The first is that this is not a simple, 'one-off', punctual inscription which 'takes' at once, but rather a doubled, or delayed, inscription which, as we have seen, Freud had already located in the original 'seduction theory': the effect of the inscription is always a delayed effect, an after-effect, a phenomenon for which Freud coined the term *Nachträglichkeit* and which Laplanche has chosen to translate as *afterwardsness*.[6] As with the theory of seduction it always takes time for the subject to arrive through processes of both mental and physiological maturation at an understanding or a realization – even an unconscious one – of the significance of the original event. *The time of the phantasm – of what I take to be a 'phantasmatic capture' – is the 'between', the 'Nachträglichkeit', of the event and this afterward realization.* The second remark that requires to be made is that these phantasmatic scenarios – whether the typical ones associated with the primal scene, seduction and castration – or the more heterogeneous ones deriving from familial or cultural lore – are not so much conscious and deliberate impositions as *unconscious* transmissions and implicatings of the parents' own unconscious phantasms and fantasies – as when, for example, the mother, when washing and changing her new born child, unwittingly passes on her own unconscious sexual needs and longings.[7]

Even taken as a mass of heterogeneous conjectures rather than as a coherent theory there is much in this material that suggests a proximity to the problematics of *Tess of the d'Urbervilles*. There is the very early association of the phantasmatic event with a hypnagogic or 'second state': not a few commentators have remarked upon the fact that at almost every crucial event in her life Tess seems to be in a state of reverie or trance – the death of Prince, the rape or seduction in the Chase, the exhaustion provoked by the threshing machine, her arrest at Stonehenge – even, if not above all, the murder of Alec which is committed in something like a state of transport or compulsion. But there is much also that suggests that the novel as a whole is written as though the narrator himself is in some kind of trance or second state: there is a mesmeric *drive* – the psychoanalytical *zwang*, or compulsion – about the whole thing compared, for example, with the clumsy manipulations of, say, *The Woodlanders* that precedes it or the calculated plotting of *Jude* that follows it. Indeed, at times, there seems to be something drunken or drug induced about the instabilities and sheer vertigo of the narrative point of view where within the space of a few lines we move from soaring over-head shots to sudden macro-like close-ups, from the aerial views of a Tess as a fly on a billiard cloth to the witnessing of a tear running down her cheek.

Secondly, Freud's original 'seduction theory' – his abandonment of which has been the object of much criticism – might almost have been arrived at as a result of reading *Tess* or with *Tess* in mind for Tess, too, clearly, is the victim of a 'too early' sexual aggression which is remedied only 'too late' by an explosive understanding 'after the event' (*Nachträglichkeit*) – and it is pertinent to recall here the early title proposed for the novel: *Too Late Beloved*. In many ways the whole novel is but one long case-history of the traumatic consequences of an act of predatory and precocious seduction.[8]

But, just as Freud found himself dissatisfied with the very primitive nature of the seduction theory, the novel, too, is not content with such reductiveness. It is not just that the whole scene of Tess's seduction is draped in ambiguity (no 'index of reality', perhaps, recalling Freud's problems with the seduction theory) as to the relative parts played in it of violence and complicity: Hardy, like Freud, goes on to consider the role of other, more transcendent determinations, indeed of other 'originary' scenes. Prior to the 'seduction scene' itself the novel has already offered us at least two other phantasmatic scenes that depict determining events in the establishing of the existential fate and sexual identity of Tess. The first – the carousel in Rollivers – albeit in a randomized form, contains all the elements of a 'primal scene' while the second – the death of Prince – not only proleptically anticipates the violence of the later rape/seduction but can also be taken to constitute a brutal act of castration.

As a 'primal scene' – 'a large bedroom upstairs, the window of which was thickly curtained with a great woollen shawl' (p. 63)[9] – Rollivers is characteristically associated with what is furtive and secret and while on this occasion Tess herself is not in some state of reverie nevertheless the setting as a whole is steeped in fug, alcoholic transport and dissolved identities:

> The stage of mental comfort to which they had arrived at this hour was one wherein their souls expanded beyond their skins, and spread their personalities warmly through the room. In the process the chamber and its furniture grew more and more dignified and luxurious; the shawl hanging at the window took upon itself the richness of tapestry; the brass handles of the chest of drawers were as golden knockers; and the carved bed-posts seemed to have some kinship with the magnificent pillars of Solomon's temple.
>
> (pp. 63–4)

Dominating this phantasmatic scenario is the 'gaunt four-post bed' where the revellers, among them the inebriated Durbeyfield and his wife, sit and sprawl. It is here, literally, *that the 'secret' (p. 64) 'grand projick' (ibid.) that will determine Tess's existence is conceived* – the plan of sending her to 'claim kin' with the rich d'Urbervilles (p. 65). Typical of the shifting positions that subjectivity might occupy in the phantasmatic scenario here the 'lying in wait' (*être aux écoutes*) position that Freud always associates with the primal scene is metonymically occupied by 'little Abraham' who from under the bedstead overhears and blurts out the primary effect of such a scene – the announcement of a filiation:[10]

> 'Yes; and we'll all claim kin!' said Abraham brightly from under the bedstead. 'And we'll all go and see her when Tess has gone to live with her; and we'll ride in her coach and wear black clothes!'
>
> (p. 65)

It is this scene that Tess's entrance interrupts (*interruption* another characteristic of the phantasm of the primal scene) and brings to a close but by this time, albeit as yet unknown to her, its unconscious effects – its *enigmatic signifiers*[11] – have already been registered and her fate determined.

The phantasmatic nature of the second episode, the death of Prince, could hardly be more evident. Significantly, just at a moment when Tess finds herself drawn into discussing, with little Abraham, her place in the universe she finds herself falling 'more deeply into reverie than ever' as the passing hedges become 'attached to fantastic scenes outside reality' (p. 70).

> Then, examining the mesh of events in her own life, she seemed to see the vanity of her father's pride; the gentlemanly suitor awaiting herself in her mother's fancy; to see him as a grimacing personage, laughing at her poverty, and her shrouded knightly ancestry. Everything grew more and more extravagant, and she no longer knew how time passed. A sudden jerk shook her in her seat, and Tess awoke from the sleep into which she, too, had fallen.
>
> . . . A hollow groan, unlike anything she had ever heard in her life, came from the front, followed by a shout of 'Hoi there!'
>
> . . . Something terrible had happened . . .
>
> . . . The morning mailcart, with its two noiseless wheels, speeding along these lanes like an arrow, as it always did, had driven into her slow and unlighted equipage. The pointed shaft of the cart had entered the breast of the unhappy Prince like a sword, and from the wound his life's blood was spouting in a stream, and falling with a hiss into the road.
>
> (pp. 70–1)

This is possibly the most powerfully phantasmatic moment in the book and, significantly, it is prefaced by the recollection of *parental* fantasies:[12] her father's 'pride' and her mother's 'fancy'. The whole episode is powerfully over-determined. Typically the phantasm is announced by a terrible *sound* or '*bruit*' – 'A hollow groan, unlike anything she had heard' – and an interpellation: 'Hoi there!'[13] The symbolism of the passage hardly warrants commentary. There is first the cruel demolition of Tess's assumption of the masculine and paternal position – her replacement of her father on this fateful journey. The death of Prince is the death of her own 'princely' ambitions, a kind of call to heel, how dare you!, this isn't for *girls* – an inapellable act of mutilation, of castration. At the same time the penetrating shaft of the mail (male?) cart is a dreadful act of violation and rape. Mary Jacobus has shown, for example, in her study of the manuscripts of *Tess*, that this scene was originally clearly meant to anticipate the later rape or seduction by Alec:

> ... Tess's last thoughts before dropping off and waking to find Prince impaled by the oncoming mail coach are of the young man [i.e. Alec] 'whose gig was part of his body'.[14]

There is a sense, too, that the terrible wound and the massive flow of blood which 'splashed [Tess] from face to skirt with crimson drops' (p. 71) is like a sudden menstrual flow which drains both Tess and the scene as a whole:

> The atmosphere turned pale ... the lane showed all its white features, and Tess showed hers, still whiter. (ibid.)

And, finally, the culminating effect of the episode on Tess herself is that she henceforth 'regard[s] herself in the light of a murderess' (p. 73) – a role she is, of course, doomed to duly assume with the killing of Alec. Penny Boumelha rightly connects the two scenes – the two events that bracket all phantasmatic captures – speaking of

> ... an image-chain linking Tess's experiences from the death of Prince to her final penetrative act of retaliation ...[15]

The convulsive outpouring of Tess's 'dirge' (pp. 469–70) is like a haemorrhaging conflation of the 'hollow groan' and the spilt blood of the earlier scene which are taken up again – typical of the echoes and reduplications of phantasmic structures – in the 'Drip, drip, drip' and the scarlet blot on the white ceiling (p. 471). And yet I wonder whether even this dreadful act fully exorcises the trauma of this shattering violation. Just before Tess dozes off we hear of 'the occasional heave of the wind' that 'became the sigh of some immense sad soul, coterminous with the universe in space, and with history in time' (p. 70) and we do not hear this cosmic voice again until the fleeing Tess and Angel reach Stonehenge:

> The wind, playing upon the edifice, produced a booming tune, like the note of some gigantic one-stringed harp.
>
> (p. 483)

It is almost as if Tess can never find peace, never find herself 'at home' (p. 484), never truly be set free, until the penetrating shaft of the mail-cart is redeemed by the 'vast erection' (p. 483) of the Temple of the Winds.

Confronted by what he found to be the frequency and typicality of the originary phantasms – of the primal scene, castration and seduction – Freud, we have seen, was, for a time, himself, seduced by the notion that they were due to a 'phylogenetic' heritage deriving from some traumatic event in the past and borne onwards by a kind of race memory. And there is, indeed, some suggestion that Hardy too ascribed a kind of phylogenetic origin to the phantasms that capture and victimise Tess as when he conjectures on the reponsibility of Tess's own forbears for her present plight:

> One may, indeed, admit the possibility of a retribution lurking in the present catastrophe. Doubtless some of Tess d'Urbeville's mailed ancestors rollicking home from a fray had dealt the same measure even more ruthlessly towards peasant girls of their time.
>
> (p. 119)[16]

Nevertheless, despite the almost classic exemplarity of the phantasms we have just described there is too much evidence in the text that Tess is not just fashioned by these more 'transcendent' schema but rather by a whole host of other voices, other legends and other discourses. Few characters can be so much the focus of a chorus of rumours, of ascriptions, of hopes, of fears, of religious, gender, mythical and eschatological identifications both from within and from without the text. From within the text there is produced a Tess who, in addition to the stereotypical roles foisted upon her by Alec and Angel, is the culmination of a whole folk tradition, of anonymous voices, tales, auguries, legends –

> Like all the cottagers in Blackmoor Vale, Tess was steeped in fancies
> and prefigurative superstitions...
>
> (p. 84)

and it is astonishing the amount of lore that bears upon her from the Cerealia and the *Compleat Fortune-Teller* to local gossip about ne'er do wells like Jack Dollop and the celebratory verses of the book of Proverbs and the *Song of Songs*. Tess might complain about having not been exposed to the experience of the novels that ladies will have read (p. 131) but she, herself, is saturated by culture, legend and tradition. The rather melodramatic and somewhat cumbersome introduction of the legend of the 'd'Urberville coach' does no more than underline this weight of prescripted and prescriptive determinations.

As far as models found outside the text are concerned, Penny Boumelha has remarked that 'Tess brings together for the first time the "types" of women that have frequently been counterposed in the earlier work' and that, more generally, 'it is possible to find in Tess the shadow of innumerable cultural archetypes (Patient Griselda, the scapegoat, the highborn lady in disguise)'[17] – and one has only to leaf through some of the more scholarly accounts of *Tess* to find your Eves, Scarlet Women, Penelopes, Persephones, Saint Theresas (of course) and Madonnas. Peter Widdowson has already shrewdly drawn attention to the ways in which Tess's

> 'character' seems to be composed entirely of other people's images of
> her.... Tess is composed of all the 'object images' the novel defines
> her as, primarily deriving from male lookers, including the narrator/
> Hardy and us as readers in our collusion with those images....[18]

For Widdowson this is part of Hardy's mischievous 'dismantling of the bourgeois-humanist (patriarchal and realist) notion of the unified and unitary subject' so that, in the end

> Tess *has no character at all*: she is only what others (most especially the
> author) construct her as; and so she is herself merely a 'series of
> seemings' or 'impressions'.[19]

I think Widdowson is absolutely correct in what he identifies as a kind of 'phenomenological' account of Tess but I am reluctant to go to the extreme of concluding that as a result Tess '*has no character at all*'. Rather, what seems to be happening is that, in *Tess*, Hardy seems to be working with a wholly new conception of what is entailed in the 'construction' of a 'character' or of a 'consciousness' – a conception that finds parallels in the psychoanalytical notion of the phantasm where the human becomes human – acquires character and conscious-ness – when the accumulated and consorted *bruit* or *dit* – the *lore* – of the tradition or the culture becomes accreted around and inscribed on the blank surface of the physiological body. This, after all, is precisely the notion invoked in the famously prurient comment that follows on the catastrophic event in The Chase:

> Why it was that upon this beautiful feminine tissue, sensitive as gossamer, and practically blank as snow as yet [earlier Tess has been described as 'a mere vessel of emotion untinctured by experience' p. 51], there should have been traced such a coarse pattern as it was doomed to receive.
>
> (p. 119)

In a sense what Tess becomes is a kind of 'phenomenological pal-impsest' – or, to recall another favourite image of Freud for the unconscious, a 'magic writing block'[20] – of all that she unconsciously registers of what has been said or thought about her, of all that has anticipated and been brought to bear upon her, of all the phantasmatic events that she has passed though. What this means is that Tess becomes something like an 'expressive digest', or 'phenomenological prism' of the world into which she has been born – a world not just of material conditions but of a host of pre-existing roles, attributes and singularities. I think this accords well, in fact, with what we sense of her luminous presence. Much has been made of Tess as the object of voyeuristic fantasy but much less has been said of the degree to which we see the world through her. Indeed at times in the course of the text Tess seems to function like an 'expressive cursor' or like one of those ruler magnify-ing glasses that come with miniaturised editions of the Complete Oxford Dictionary. Again and again we sense that the world only comes into being, or achieves true intensity, through Tess's conscious-ness of it. 'At times,' we are told, 'her whimsical fancy would intensify natural processes around her till they seemed part of her own story. Rather they became part of it; for the world is only a psychological phenomenon and what they seemed they were.' (p. 134) Later we find Angel musing:

Upon her sensations the whole world depended to Tess; through her existence all her fellow creatures existed to her. The universe itself only came into being for Tess on the particular day in the particular year in which she was born.

(p. 214)

More than conveying something of Tess's subjectivity I think this tells us a great deal about the ontological status of her world. Tess becomes something like the Leibnizian 'singular substance' or 'monad' that plays such an enormous part in Deleuze's thinking about the nature and status of what he calls a 'transcendental' consciousness.[21] The classic passages are to be found in Leibniz's early *Discourse on Metaphysics*:

Moreover, each [singular] substance is like a whole world, and like a mirror of God, or indeed the whole universe, which each expresses in its own fashion.... For it expresses, albeit confusedly, everything which happens in the universe, past, present, and future.[22]

and the much later *Principles of Nature and Grace*:

The beauty of the universe could be seen in each individual soul, if we could only unfold all that is enfolded in it, and which will become perceptible only as it develops over time ... Every soul knows infinity, knows everything, but confusedly.... Only God has a distinct knowledge of everything.[23]

Perhaps this invocation of a 'Leibnizian phenomenology' is Deleuze's richest and most subtle contribution to the theory of the phantasm, but it is not the only one. One of the strengths of this theory is its relegation of the notion of the discrete individual and the subjecting of it to a whole host of pre-individual and trans-individual determinations and singularities but this meta-physical level requires an equally complex model of biological and organic pre-individual singularities to match it. This Deleuze finds in Gilbert Simondon's extraordinarily idiosyncratic and provocative *L'individu et sa genèse physico-biologique*.[24]

Simondon's work is far too complex to summarize adequately here and in what follows I have merely attempted to extrapolate a number of the notions which contribute to the theory of the phantasm and which, therefore, cast some further light on the dynamics of *Tess*.

Simondon begins his work by rejecting all theories of individuation – of the genesis of the individual – which fail to recognize that the individual is born out of a *pre-individual reality*, a *meta-stable equilibrium*, a *sur-fusion* and *sur-saturation* of quantic energies and flows which are *more than a unity, more than an identity*. The individual emerges from this pre-individual matrix by means of a process of *partial resolution* that produces both the individual and his (thereby impoverished) environment. The model for this process is that of crystallization in liquids which evolves by means of successive *phases* or *resolutions* or *precipitations* of conditions of *stable equilibrium* out of the original ambient *meta-stable* solution. Until the process is exhausted each act of precipitation or individuation cannot but remain partial, bringing with it a kind of reservoir or *neotenic cache* of as-yet non-resolved, non-precipitated *pre-individual* potentialities which will be available for later resolutions and precipitations:

> one might conjecture that the [process of] individuation does not exhaust the whole of the pre-individual reality, and that an order [*régime*] of metastability is not merely negotiated [*entretenu*] by the individual, but carried by him, so that the constituted individual transports with him a certain charge associated with the preindividual reality, imbued [*animée*] with all the potentials that characterise [such a reality].... This preindividual nature that remains associated with the individual is a source of future metastable states from which might emerge new individuations.[25]

The crystallization model is adequate only for processes of purely *physical* individuation where growth is merely on the outside, on the surface, and relatively abrupt, quickly achieved. For the *living* organization there has to be also an *internal* process of growth which consists, strangely enough, of a *slowing down (ralentissement)*[26] of the purely physical process so that there is now a *permanent* process of *individuation*, a continual *resonance* set up between moments of equilibrium and disequilibrium, a perpetual process of *individuation by the individual* – so that the individual seems to be endlessly emerging from him or herself, from his or her own internal reserves, like a reverse Russian Doll. After the *physical* and the *vital* there is the development of the *psychic* and the *collective* and perhaps what is most political about Simondon's model is that for him the emergence of the *psychic* and the *collective* are closely associated, for the *psychic* comes from a 'new plunge into the preindividual reality' [*une nouvelle plongé dans la réalité préindividuelle*][27] and this 'new plunge' reveals that the *pre*-individual is also a *trans*-individual – that the *psychic* cannot be resolved at the level of the individual but only at the level of the collective.[28] The ethic that emerges from all this and one that is found again and again throughout Deleuze's work, is one that is measured by the *amplitude* of the *resonance* set up across the *preindividual* and *transindividual* fields that the individual traverses. One can see here how Simondon's ethic of transindividuality and the collective which emerges from a 'physico-biologic genesis' hooks up with the metaphysical ambition of Leibniz's *Monadology* where ultimately each individual monad expresses the City of God.[29]

If we now return to *Tess*, it is not too much to say that, once we shed the prejudice which makes us concentrate exclusively on the already consti-tuted individual, we become increasingly aware that what much of the text recounts is the process of the *individuation* of Tess out of a matrix of trans-individual and pre-individual groupings and collectivities. One of the recurrent movements of *Tess* is the establishment of over-saturated fields and subsequent processes of discrimination and selection, of ex-trapolation and precipitation. Early in the text, for example, in the ac-count of the Cerealia procession, we are made aware of Tess as part of a larger grouping of individuals scarcely distinguishable from each other and it is Angel's misfortune not to be able to discriminate among them (p. 54). When he looks back at the dancing we get a vision of almost a Brownian dance of molecules with one, Tess, standing apart:

> He had not yet overtaken his brothers, but he paused to get breath, and looked back. He could see the figures of the girls in the green enclosure whirling about as they had whirled when he was among them. They seemed to have quite forgotten him already.
>
> All of them, except, perhaps, one. This white shape stood apart by the hedge alone.
>
> (p. 54)

Again and again in the course of the text we find this process whereby Tess has to be differentiated out from the 'bevy' (pp. 139, 199, 236) or the groups of girls (pp. 136, 138, 161, 167, 204, 214–15, 243) that constitute an accompanying entourage or vicinity. What in each case the accom-panying group or entourage seems to suggest is the presence of a hinter-land of as-yet untapped energies and resources so that at each crisis Tess seems to have at her command hitherto unexpended energies rather like some kind of neotenic cache. From early in the text we are made aware of Tess's almost dangerous excess of vital and untapped energy:

> Phases of her childhood lurked in her aspect still. As she walked along today, for all her bouncing handsome womanliness, you could some-

time see her twelfth year in her cheeks, of her ninth sparkling from her eyes; and even her fifth would flit over the curves of her mouth now and then.

(p. 52)

She had an attribute which amounted to a disadvantage just now...It was a luxuriance of aspect, a fullness of growth, which made her appear more of a woman than she really was.

(p. 82)

There was, it might be said, the energy of her mother's unexpended family, as well as the natural energy of Tess's years, rekindled after the experience which had so overwhelmed her at the time...

(p. 158)

A particularly fine spring came round, and the stir of germination was almost audible in the buds; it moved her, as it moved the wild animals, and made her passionate to go...and some spirit within her rose automatically as the sap in the twigs. It was unexpended youth, surging up anew after its temporary check, and bringing with it hope, and the invincible instinct towards self-delight.

(pp. 150–1)

And it is this sense of immense reserves that accounts for the extraordinary feats of physical endurance that Tess survives in the course of her wanderings.

The spectacle of an individuation taking place or emerging against a *sur-fused* and *sur-saturated* background is nowhere better shown than in the famous garden scene:

The outskirt of the garden in which Tess found herself had been uncultivated for some years, and was no damp and rank with juicy grass which sent up mists of pollen at a touch; and with tall blooming weeds emitting offensive smells – weeds whose red and yellow and purple hues formed a polychrome as dazzling as that of cultivated flowers. She went stealthily as a cat through this profusion of growth, gathering cuckoo-spittle on her skirts, cracking snails that were underfoot, staining her hands with thistle-milk and slug-slime, and rubbing off upon her naked arms sticky blights which, though now snow-white on the apple-tree trunks, made madder stains on her skin; thus she drew quite near to Clare, still unobserved of him.

Tess was conscious of neither time nor space. The exaltation which she had described as being producible at will by gazing at a star, came now without any determination of her; she undulated upon the thin notes of the second-hand harp, and their harmonies passed like breezes through her, bringing tears to her eyes. The floating pollen seemed to be his notes made visible, and the dampness of the garden the weeping of the garden's sensibility. Though near nightfall, the rank-smelling weed-flowers glowed as if they would not close for intentness, and the waves of colour mixed with the waves of sound.

(pp. 178–9)

Here, in this quasi-phantasmatic scene – *Tess was conscious of neither time nor space* – we witness an extraordinary commingling of the richly sensuous and organic on the one hand – the juices of the garden drenching and infusing Tess with a rich sensuality – and the metaphysical precipitated into the material world on the other:

> ... she undulated upon the thin notes of the second-hand harp, and their harmonies passed like breezes through her, bringing tears to her eyes. The floating pollen seemed to be his notes made visible, and the dampness of the garden the weeping of the garden's sensibility.

Perhaps nowhere else has such a marriage of what I have referred to above as the 'phenomenological residue' of the cultural world – *his notes made visible* – and the 'neotenic cache' of exorbitant, natural, organic profusion been so magnificently achieved.

The phantasm might well be a universal *given* but this does not mean that there is a universal *content*, for each culture will have its own 'originary' and 'originating' phantasms.[30] Nevertheless in each case it can be safely assumed that that phantasmic structure will entail an orientation and a politics since the whole function of the phantasm is to integrate the subject into what is, in effect, the *symbolic* order of the tribe. That the 'nuclear complex', Oedipus, enshrines a specific kind of patriarchal or despotic power hardly requires comment. In *Tess* the specific politics of the various phantasmatic structures to which Tess is subject is strikingly revealed in the powerfully resonant breakfast scene that occurs early in her stay at Talbothays:

> The early mornings were still sufficiently cool to render a fire acceptable in the large room where they breakfasted; and by Mrs Crick's orders, who held that he was too genteel to mess at their table, it was Angel Clare's custom to sit in the yawning chimney-corner during the meal ... The light from the long, wide, mullioned window opposite shone in upon his nook, and assisted by a secondary light of cold

blue quality that shone down the chimney, enabled him to read there easily whenever disposed to do so. Between Clare and the window was the table at which his companions sat, their munching profiles rising sharp against the panes.... For several days after Tess's arrival Clare, sitting abstractedly reading from some book, periodical or piece of music just come by post, hardly noticed she was present at table. She talked so little, and the other maids talked so much, that the babble did not strike him as possessing a new note, and he was ever in the habit of neglecting the particulars of an outward scene for the general impression. One day, however, when he had been con-ning one of his music-scores, and by force of imagination was hearing the tune in his head, he lapsed into listlessness, and the music-sheet rolled to the hearth.... The conversation at the table mixed in with his phantasmal orchestra till he thought: 'What a fluty voice one of those milk-maids has! I suppose it is the new one.'

Clare looked round upon her, seated with the others.

(p. 175)

Again there is the mood of 'abstraction' and 'listlessness' characteristic of reverie[31] which turns the whole tableau into a phantasmal scenario with a clearly delineated power structure. Angel's position is peculiarly priv-ileged for he sits in his chimney-corner like the lone gaoler at the centre of a mini-panopticon while the milk-maids themselves sit conveniently ranged and profiled against the mullion window. Once again we can see Tess being selected and extrapolated out of the 'babble' of an environing group so that her 'fluty voice' can be accommodated within a 'phantas-mal orchestra':[32] the process whereby the subject is phantasmatically integrated into the 'score' of a patriarchal order could hardly be clearer.

The movement here from 'babble' to 'phantasmal orchestra', from a position of relative anonymity to a place in a socially accredited sym-bolic order is, in fact, no more than the movement of the text as a whole. What is astonishing about this structure is that it is not just present in isolated incidents and episodes but writ large across the body of the book. It is astonishing, for example, how very many people have seized upon the garden episode – indeed as I have done above – for one reason or another while completely failing to see that this is but one episode of a carefully constructed series which begins with the Cerealia episode and climaxes twice in the unconsummated wedding night at Wellbridge and the murder of Alec in Sandbourne. It is at this point that it becomes necessary to consider what becomes of the model of the phantasm when, as occurs in Deleuze's *Logique du sens*, to it is added

Melanie Klein's accounts of the paranoid-schizoid, depressive and Oedipal 'positions'.[33]

So far we have talked about the 'double time' of the phantasm – the
phenomenon described by Freud's *Nachträglichkeit* (see above) – and the
place of the phantasm at the meeting point of the *vecu* and the *entendu*,
the *lived* and the *heard*, the *body* and *culture*, the *neotenic cache* and the
phenomenological residue. Earlier, however, I have touched, too, on the
difference between the 'deeper' genetic *phantasm* and the 'lighter', more
'superficial' *fantasy*.[34] It is to this matter of the different 'levels' of the
phantasm that I must now turn.

We have already noted that Laplanche and Freud saw an essential
affinity between the *phantasm* of the depths and the *fantasy* of the
surface, between the *phantasm* regarded as the very *kernel* of the unconscious and the *fantasy* as it emerges in *day-dreams* and *secondary elabor-
ations*. Nevertheless there remain important differences: principal
amongst these is the fact that whereas the *day-dream* or *fantasy* tends
to be anchored in a subject and to conform to acceptable syntactic rules,
the *phantasm* or *deeper structure* tends to lack any secure subject positions
or even syntactical coherence:

> At the pole of the day dream, the scene is essentially in the first
> person, the place of the subject marked and invariable. The organiza-
> tion is stabilized by the secondary revision, ballasted by the 'self': the
> subject, one might say, lives his reverie. The pole of the originary
> phantasm, on the contrary, is characterized by an absence of subjec-
> tivization along with the presence of the subject *in* the scene ...
>
> 'A father seduces a daughter', such might be for example the sum-
> marized formulation of the phantasm of seduction. The mark of the
> primary process is not here the absence of organization, as one
> sometimes says, but the particular character of the structure: it is a
> scenario with multiple entrances, in which nothing says that the
> subject will find its place in the first instance in the term *daughter*;
> one might find it locate itself just as well in *father* or in *seduces*.[35]

This decentred or dispersed subjectivity of the originary phantasm is one
of its most characteristic features and I have had occasion to appeal to it
in a number of my earlier remarks.[36] Deleuze, however, wants to extend
the stratifications of the phantasm and the account of the evolution of
consciousness that it offers to a much deeper level. For Deleuze, 'everything begins in the abyss'[37] – that is the 'theatre of terror', or naked *bruit*,
of Melanie Klein's schizo-paranoid position where the unconscious is

the site of a frenzied *melée* of 'internal partial objects, introjected and projected, alimentary and excremental, poisonous and persecutory, explosive and toxic'.[38] These splittings and conflicts are characteristic of the early oral-anal phase where the child's destructive and aggressive instincts (avatars of the primary death drive) are turned on its first objects – chief amongst these the mother's body and particularly the breast – in phantasized attacks. These first objects of conflicting moods of love and hate, are shredded into consumable (oral) and expulsable (anal) bits or *effigies*[39] and this in turn leads to feelings of anxiety and persecution.[40] To this succeeds the 'depressive position' centred now not on the *partial* objects of the paranoid phase but on the 'project-ive identification' with an introjected *complete* 'Good Object' on high.[41] As supreme eminence, or *idol*, the Good Object on high combines both parental figures and becomes then a prototype of the *superego* and as such a bearer of the *voice* of tradition.[42] At the same time this aloof-ness and *hauteur* of the Good Object is manifested in its tendency to turn away and withdraw itself, to retire into impassivity. The Good Object is essentially a 'lost' or 'virtual' object: never so much found as refound.[43] So, while this marks an important stage in psychic integra-tion there is nevertheless the danger that excessive identification with the Good Object might lead to feelings of inferiority and inadequacy and the turning away of the Good Object to feelings of frustration and guilt.[44] The positions often overlap or coincide with each other so that there can be violent manic-depressive mood swings when it is felt that the complete Good Object is threatened by the aggressive partial objects or the aggressive partial objects are rebuked by the complete Good Object.

After the partial objects of the *depths* and the Good Object on *high* there begins to emerge, along a completely different axis, an *erotogenic surface* spreading out from the mucous orifices of the body.[45] This extrapolation of a surface out of the preceding depths is in part facili-tated by the aerial perspective of the Good Object on high whose exalted perspective smoothes over and flattens out the faults and declivities of the schizo-paranoid body like a patchwork of fields beneath the wing of a plane.[46] After the *subversion* of the depths and the *conversion* of the heights comes the *erotic perversion* of the surface:

Our sexual body is like a Harlequin's cloak.[47]

While each of these surface zones enjoys its own mode of satisfaction and pleasure afforded by the hallucinatory *image* appropriate to it (the thumb for sucking, for example) a more important task remains to be achieved which is the suturing and linking of these partial surfaces into a whole. It is this that is achieved by the *phallus*, the privileged *image* of the genital zone but which has also experienced the fragmentation of the depths and the eminence of the heights. It is to the phallus that is enjoined the supreme task of integrating the partial local drives of the sexual body as well as conjuring the threats from the schizoid paranoid depths and the prohibitive aloofness of the depressive heights. It is this that constitutes the reparative and redemptive ambition – the eminently good intentions – of the Oedipal moment.[48]

Why then, asks Deleuze, does everything go so wrong?[49] Primarily Oedipus is the tragedy of an impossible symbiosis. In the first place the phallus mistakenly models its role on that of the *idol* that is the Good Object on high now conceived of as an amalgam of both parents, of the beneficent breast of the mother and the potent phallus of the father. Secondly there is the ambition to make whole the mother wounded by the aggressions of the partial objects from the depths and to bring back, to make present, the ideal father whose very essence is his having turned away. It is the utopian ambition of this triangular and undifferentiated, incestuous embrace of child/mother/father that the Oedipal moment, with its scenario of castration and disavowal, fractures and sublimates.[50] It is here that, in Deleuze's broader scheme, the *phantasm* proper occurs – that is that shift from the biological to the social domain, from the purely biological and physiological order to the structure of human relationships.[51] What the phantasm marks and effects is a massive leap (*saut*)[52] from an order which is primarily physiological to a domain where it is primarily the mental that prevails. It is this that makes the phantasm central to the twin processes of desexualization and sublimation[53] and to the establishment of a domain where something like consciousness and thought is at last possible. What the phantasm here constitutes is a kind of double screen or invisible membrane across which the physio-biological genesis of the individual reverberates at last with its phenomenological heritage.[54]

If we now return to *Tess* it is striking to note in how measured a way Hardy's account of what we might call the 'growth of Tess's consciousness' is mapped out in a series of tableaux that correspond very closely with the Kleinian and Deleuzian stages we have just described.[55] I have already drawn attention to the almost spawn-like aspect of the Cerealia dance where each white figure is wrapped in its little nimbus – 'each had a private little sun for her soul to bask in' (p. 50) – and where each seems to await germination by the 'peeled willow wand' (p. 50) that it carries, and where Tess's red ribbon seems more than anything like the scarlet filament in a yoke. This scene, nevertheless, is little more than prefatory and it is in a second episode where I think the first Kleinian position can be located. This is the dance at Chaseborough:

> When she came close and looked in she beheld indistinct forms racing up and down to the figure of the dance, the silence of their footfalls arising from their being overshoe in 'scroff' – that is to say the powdery residuum from the storage of peat and other products, the stirring of which by their turbulent feet created the nebulosity that involved the scene. Through this floating, fusty *débris* of peat and hay, mixed with the perspirations and warmth of dancers, and forming together a sort of vegeto-human pollen, the muted fiddles feebly pushed their notes, in marked contrast to the spirit with which the measure was trodden out. They coughed as they danced, and laughed as they coughed. Of the rushing couples there could barely be discerned more that the high lights – the indistinctness shaping them to satyrs clasping nymphs – a multiplicity of Pans whirling a multiplicity of Syrinxes; Lotis attempting to elude Priapus, and always failing.
>
> (p. 107)

What we seem to have here is less a dance between humans than some riotous *mélée* indulged in by an indiscriminate heap of coupling organs and partial objects indifferent as to questions of identity and personal responsibility. The gathering as a whole – a 'vegeto-human pollen' – is scarcely above the level of the organic *débris* or 'scroff' that lies around it. Indeed the onomatopoeic 'scroff' suggests that we are barely above the level of brute noise (*bruit*). The notes might gloss the 'Pans', 'Syrinxes', 'Lotis's' and 'Priapus's' as 'classical deities' but their very 'multiplicity' suggests much more an unrestrained *débauche* on the part of sundry genitalia. It is like a witches' dance of effigies and fetishes. The 'Pans', 'Syrinxes', 'Lotis's' and 'Priapus's' recall the oral-sadistic and cannibalistic desires of Klein's schizoid-paranoid position where the fragmented objects in their introjective and projective to-ing and fro-ing ring the changes on paranoia and persecution. The increasing state of intoxication caused by bad beer enjoyed by these creatures recalls the part played in this 'position' by the phantasized incorporation of poisons and toxins.

This, I am suggesting, is the 'objective correlative' of Tess's state of consciousness at the time of the fateful visit to Chaseborough and it is significant that it is immediately followed by the 'paranoid-persecutory' row between Tess and Car and Nancy Darch (p. 110) – triggered in a sense by the toxic 'treacle' that runs down Car Darch's back. Car Darch's rolling on the ground to rub off the treacle is like a schizophrenic fretting and loss of surface.[56] This, in turn, provokes Tess, uncharacteristically and ill-advisedly we might think, to use abusive – that is willfully penetrative – language:

> ...and if I had known you was of that sort, I wouldn't have so let myself down as to come with such a whorage as this is!
>
> (p. 112)[57]

The only escape from the dangers of this situation is a sudden change of elevation, a leap from the depths to the heights, from the schizo-paranoid to the depressive position: at this particular conjuncture it is the fortuitously passing Alec, momentarily in the position of the Good Object, who miraculously carries her off:

> 'Neatly done, was it not, dear Tess?' he said by and by.
>
> (p. 114)

Alec, of course, is not the Good Object – this is the position pre-eminently commanded by Angel Clare; but it is important to appreciate that in many ways Alec is a kind of double or mirror image of the Good Object, Angel, and so presents that measure of instability and ambiguity that always haunts the Good Object: that it can be the object of both love and hate, of both devotion and frustration; the source of both encouragement and prohibition, of both adoration and fear. That Alec and Angel are in many ways doubles one of the other, or two sides of a single figure, accounts for the careful way in which Hardy makes sure that we draw parallels between them: Alec's strawberry picking echoed in Angel's black-berrying, Alec's 'what a crumby girl' echoed in Angel's 'what a fresh and virginal daughter of nature', Alec's flash gig echoed in the night ride to the railway terminal – and so on. Morever the risk that the Good Object on high might always succumb to the schizoid depths is made evident in the several moments in the text where Alec and Angel virtually assume their opposite poles: Alec in becoming an itinerant preacher (even at one point contemplating going to India as a missionary!), Angel in his overtures to Izzy Huett (p. 343).

Far from facilitating Tess's escape from the depths Alec's role is rather one more instance of that intrusive violation and damage characteristic of the schizoid-paranoid position. The psychic set-back is marked by a return to base, to Marlott, and its accompanying burden of distress illustrated by the birth and death of Sorrow. It is from Marlott that Tess must set out again and heal herself. Nothing describes this process of healing and binding better than the account of the harvesting:

> Her binding proceeds with clock-like monotony. From the sheaf last finished she draws a handful of ears, patting their tips with her left palm to bring them even. Then stooping low she moves forward, gathering the corn with both hands against her knees, and pushing her left gloved hand under the bundle to meet the right on the other side, holding the corn in an embrace like that of a lover. She brings the ends of the bond together, and kneels on the sheaf while she ties it, beating back her skirts now and then when lifted by the breeze. A bit of her naked arm is visible between the buff yellow of the gauntlet and the sleeve of her gown; and as the day wears on its feminine smoothness becomes scarified by the stubble, and bleeds.
>
> (p. 138)

There is almost an immediate transition here from the perfervid dance at Chaseborough where the 'scroff' of that scene has become the 'stubble' here which still has the potentiality to score and scar Tess's delicate flesh. But the overall tendency is towards the binding (Freud)[58] and progressive integrating (Klein) of recalcitrant partialities and there is a clear invitation to see in this harvesting an act of love. The figure here, at this point still anonymous, offers again the space for archetypal inscriptions – the solitary reaper, Ruth ('living as a stranger and an alien here' p. 139), and, chief of all, Eros whose chief purpose, Freud insists, is that of 'uniting and binding'.[59] Although Tess is then singled out for special mention it is once again one of those occasions when she is extrapolated from an environing group that suggests more trans- or pre-individual, and collective forces – Tess's experience here reminding us of Simondon's *'nouvelle plongé dans la réalité préindividuelle'* that we have discussed earlier:

> The movements of the other women were more or less similar to Tess's, the whole bevy of them drawing together like dancers in a quadrille at the completion of a sheaf by each, everyone placing her sheaf on end against those of the rest, till a shock, or 'stitch' as it was here called, of ten or a dozen was formed.
>
> (p. 139)

What is being described here is the slow marshalling and careful distribution of all those forces and energies that have hitherto held such anarchic sway in the depths and the preparing them for the advent of the new and beneficent Good Object on high.

It is Angel who most clearly represents this Good Object: at his very first appearance at Talbothays his role is announced by two striking characteristics: firstly he is announced preeminently as a Voice, and secondly he is revealed to be someone whom we have met before – that is someone who has already been Lost. A third characteristic appears very shortly: his association with Height – not only does he live in the attic above the girls, but Tess soon grows fearful of his 'Andean altitude' (p. 181).

With the emergence of the Good Object we move from the *bruit* of the depths to the *voice* from on high.[60] The voice becomes the voice of the super-ego and the voice that carries the authority of tradition:

> Freud insisted on the acoustic origin of the super-ego . . . the voice of the family that bears the tradition.[61]

As the epitome of the Good Object Angel is teacher and counselor, scholar and protector. Tess is peculiarly appreciative, for example, after the experience with Alec, of his chivalrous respect both for her and the other milk-maids (p. 257). Her regard for him is little short of idolatrous and recalls that extremity of attitude with regard to good and bad objects reported by Melanie Klein:[62]

> There was hardly a touch of earth in her love for Clare. To her sublime trustfulness he was all that goodness could be – knew all that a guide, philosopher, and friend should know. She thought every line in the contour of his person the perfection of masculine beauty, his soul the soul of a saint, his intellect that of a seer.
>
> (p. 257)

Angel, significantly, is not the Good Object that is simply found but the Good Object that is *re-found after having been lost*:

> The Good Object is by nature a lost object: that is to say it only shows itself and appears from the very first as lost, as *having been lost*.[63]

In a sense this accounts for Tess's tragic and excessive idealization of him for he has all the allure of a lost and virtual ideal, the chance of an impossible recuperation. To speak of him even casually as her 'Prince Charming' is to remind ourselves, too, that Tess's whole tragedy stems from the loss of a 'Prince'. Angel is endowed with patriarchal and heroic associations: he is compared with Peter the Great and accredited with ambitions to become 'an American or Australian Abraham' (p. 181) and there is even the suggestion, in the progression of his training from farm to farm, of the seven labours of Hercules, Hercules 'the peace-maker and surveyor of surfaces'.[64] From his lofty vantage it is Angel as the Good Object who effects discriminations and distributions – as when, for example, he 'ranges' the cattle in accordance with what he knows of the partialities of the milk-maidens (p. 177) or in his growing awareness of the inadequacy of his imaginary personification of country folk as 'the pitiable dummy known as Hodge':

> The typical and unvarying Hodge ceased to exist. He had been disin-
> tegrated into a number of varied fellow creatures...
>
> (p. 173)

This task of selection and discrimination is one that Angel then moves on to assume in relation to the milkmaids themselves. We have already seen this happening in the breakfast scene at Talbothays and, to some extent, in the garden scene – where Tess is extrapolated from the world around her. But the garden scene now requires a further comment which places it more clearly in the sequence that runs from the schizo-paranoid depths to Oedipus for what we have here is clearly that consti-tution of the patchwork surface of sexuality Deleuze has compared to a Harlequin's cloak – after the binding of the partial objects and the encounter with the Good Object, the constitution of a surface:

> She went stealthily as a cat through this profusion of growth, gathering cuckoo-spittle on her skirts, cracking snails that were underfoot, staining her hands with thistle-milk and slug-slime, and rubbing off upon her naked arms sticky blights which, though now snow-white on the apple-tree trunks, made madder stains on her skin...
>
> (p. 179)

Tess's body is being erotically 'painted' here as effectively as it is by the voyeuristic gaze that accompanies her throughout the novel. The con-stitution of the erotic surface seems to prime the body for the subse-quent burgeoning of an untrammelled sexuality such as that endured by the girls in their sleeping quarters – again there is a stress on the transpersonal and collective:

> The air of the sleeping chamber seemed to palpitate with the hopeless passion of the girls. They writhed feverishly under the oppressiveness of an emotion thrust upon them by cruel Nature's law – an emotion which they had neither expected or desired.... The differences which distinguished them as individuals were abstracted by this passion, and each was but portion of one organism called sex.
>
> (p. 204)

Again, Angel, as the Good Object, has had his part to play in the provocation of the turmoil experienced by the girls and their evident frustration but in a sense it has here been aggravated by his prior exercise of a choice and an adjudication. In the astonishingly beautiful wading scene (pp. 199–203) the turbulence has been given an orientation and a set by a rampant phallic mastery.[65]

The wading scene is too long to quote at any length but I am sure it will be recalled. The four girls, on the way to Mellstock Church in their Sunday best, are confronted by a flooded roadway that bars their way. While debating what to do Angel Clare turns up in his long wading boots and carries each of them, one by one, along the flooded stretch and deposits them safely on the further side, making sure to keep Tess to last: 'Three Leahs to get one Rachel.' (p. 202) It is a scene of such sexual and erotic charge that it upset some of the earlier readers of the book and at one stage Hardy had Angel, rather than carry each of the girls in his arms, wheel them along the stream in a wheel-barrow!

There are number of details that are worth noting. There is first the collective plight of the four girls:

> The rosy-cheeked, bright-eyed, quartet looked so charming in their light summer attire, clinging to the roadside bank like pigeons on a roof-slope ... Their gauzy skirts had brushed up from the grass innumerable flies and butterflies which, unable to escape, remained caged in the transparent tissue as in an aviary.
>
> (p. 200)

The flimsy, gauzy skirts recall to some extent the superficial colours of the Harlequin's cape while the trapped flies and butterflies are like the residual presence of the partial objects of the schizoid-paranoid depths – and the four hang like pigeons on a roof-slope – suspended on high:

depths, surface, heights all resumed at this critical conjuncture. And at this very moment, right on cue, along strides Angel like a veritable Jolly Green Giant:

> His aspect was probably as un-Sabbatarian a one as a dogmatic parson's son often presented; his attire being his dairy clothes, long wading boots, a cabbage-leaf inside his hat to keep his head cool, with a thistlespud to finish him off.
>
> (p. 200)

Angel could hardly look more like a phallic fertility figure and the episode climaxes in a moment of blissful fulfillment:

> 'I did not expect such an event to-day.'
> 'Nor I.... The water came up so sudden.'
> That the rise in the water was what she understood him to refer to, the state of her breathing belied. Clare stood still and inclined his face towards hers.
> 'O Tessy!' He exclaimed.
> The girl's cheeks burned to the breeze, and she could not look into his eyes for her emotion.
>
> (p. 203)

It is at this point that the final selection of Tess is made: the 'sousing' (p. 201) tread along the stream is like a parting of the tides of polymorphous perversity and the charting of a genital (and Oedipal) destiny.

The alert reader, however, will already have begun to sense the extraordinarily fragile and precarious nature of this relationship. This not merely because of what we are told of Tess's own misgivings nor because of what we perceive to be Angel's excessive idealization of Tess, but because the essentially critical evolution of the romance is set against a background of other critical thresholds so that there is throughout a perpetual sense of being on edge, of the risk of failure, of falling back. The whole sojourn at Talbothays is set against a background of milk production that involves a number of critical strata that have to be successfully broached and traversed from the need to weed out the clusters of garlic in the meadows (pp. 185ff) and the ranging of cattle for the milk-maids (p. 177–8), through the waiting for the butter to 'come' in the churn (p. 189), and the need to judge absolutely precisely the depth to which a skimming ladle should be immersed (pp. 186, 231, 233), to the wringing of cheese whey (p. 205) and the degree of dilution the milk might undergo before it reaches its consumers in the city (p. 251). Once again the larger scene – the sequence of critical thresholds involved in the production of butter, cheese, milk – churning, skimming, wringing – offer a kind of 'objective correlative' to the critical thresholds crossed in Tess's mental and spiritual trajectory so that we, as readers, strangely share her anxieties and apprehensions. For the most part the crossing of the several thresholds, like the 'binding' in the earlier harvesting scene, mark a gain in discrimination and refinement, ever greater degrees of consistency. Nevertheless there is a significant shift when reference is made to the fact that the milk that reaches the city is likely to be subject to dilution and watering down. This is significant for it suggests that the process whereby the milk has been produced to achieve an optimum product has now crested and that what has followed has been the beginning of a kind of counter-movement and adulteration – as if the process is about to shift into reverse. From this moment onwards – that is the moment of the journey to the railway terminal which marks the climaxing of one social regime, dominated by the rural economy and the production of milk, and its encounter with quite another one, dominated by steam and the city – there is more and more the sense of a regime not enjoying an increasing consistency but, rather, an increasing instability and fragmentation: the water-weeds are being cut and allowed to drift down the river (p. 244), the water meadows are being 'taken up' ready for winter irrigation (p. 258) – already earlier there has been 'the breaking-up the masses of curd before putting them into vats' (p. 239). In other words, whether we are talking about the evolution of Tess's consciousness or of Talbothays as a *socius* – that is as a socio-economic structure – there are on the one hand a whole series of processes which lead to greater stratification and compaction while on the other there are others at work undermining these very processes threatening them with subversion and disintegration.[66] It is this threat from beneath, from the depths, that constantly gnaws at Tess and her love for Angel:

> She walked in brightness, but she knew that in the background those shapes of darkness were always spread. [She knew that they were waiting like wolves just outside the circumscribing light, but she had long spells of power to keep them in hungry subjection there.] They might be receding, of they might be approaching, one or the other, a little every day.[67] (p. 260 – I have reordered the sequence slightly).

Where everything goes wrong, where the whole house of cards collapses, is the catastrophic wedding night at Wellbridge. Here, at the very moment when there should be a final passage beyond the schizoid-paranoiac threats of the persecutory depths and an escape from the manic-depressive moods endured in the shadow of an uncritically worshipped ideal Good Object, there is, instead, a calamitous failure. It is the Oedipal threshold and Angel fails to cross it. Tess, confronted with Angel's confession can accommodate the loss of the ideal; Angel, faced with Tess's revelation that she is not ideal, but flawed and vulnerable, just cannot cope: his repudiation of her is a massive act of disavowal and a refusal to transcend the Oedipal moment. Ironically at the very centre of a novel so structured around the mechanics of the phantasm there is a complete failure of that translation which the phantasm is supposed to facilitate. Angel falls short and instead of coming to terms with Tess's sexual identity and abandoning his own idealistic zealotry – the two necessary conditions of the phantasmal leap of sublimation – he plunges back into the depths of psychosis. No more compelling illustration of the Lacanian adage that 'what is foreclosed in the symbolic [here it should be glossed as what is not accommodated/translated[68] within the phantasm] returns in the real in hallucinatory form'[69] could be found than the night-walking episode that follows Angel's denial of Tess. In this most moving episode we have the phantasmic structure of the whole relationship dramatically shown in negative form – as Tess fully recognizes:

> Ah! now she knew what he was dreaming of – that Sunday morning when he had borne her along through the water with the other dairymaids...
>
> (p. 319)

> Opposite the spot to which he had brought her was such a general confluence, and the river was proportionately voluminous and deep. Across it was a narrow foot-bridge; but now the autumn flood had washed the handrail away, leaving the bare plank only, which lying a few inches above the speeding current, formed a giddy pathway for even steady heads...he now mounted the plank, and sliding one foot forward, advanced along it ... The swift stream raced and gyrated under them, tossing, distorting, and splitting the moon's reflected face. Spots of froth travelled past, and intercepted weeds waved behind the piles.
>
> (p. 319)

The swirling schizoid-paranoid depths, the Good Object precariously balanced above them, and the narrow, fragile line between the two the traversal of which is so fraught with danger.[70] And in this reversal of the phantasm Angel is bearing Tess towards death.

The whole question of the relationship between the phantasm and the death drive or the death instinct – and, indeed, what is the death drive or instinct? – is an extraordinarily complex one and what follows should be regarded as little more than conjecture or speculation rather than any attempt to come to any conclusion.

The first step is to clarify the relationship between *instincts*, the *phantasm* and *drives*. Throughout his work both as a theorist and as a translator of Freud's work Laplanche has laboured to recall that there are *two* words in German, *Instinkt* and *Trieb*, that have too readily been translated into French and English by the *one* term, *instinct*[71] whereas what is required are *two* terms: *instinct* and *pulsion* in French; *instinct* and *drive* in English. By *instinct* we are to understand those hard, pre-wired, behavioural traits that belong to the purely biological and animal domain whereas by *drive* we are to understand those more mercurial aspects of human behaviour that can remain quite arbitrary with regard to their origins and aims – whence the vagaries and vicissitudes of human sexuality compared with the mere functionality of reproduction. In a sense we can understand from what we have already said about the phantasm that it is the phantasm itself that mediates between *instincts* and *drives*, or is responsible for the *translation* of the one into the other. Nevertheless, this too, is inadequate for at one point Freud himself, when asking himself whether something comparable to *instincts* could be found in humans, came to the conclusion that such an equivalent was to be found in the *phantasm* itself.[72] I now intend to take this a step further and propose that the distinction between *life drives* and *death drives* can to a certain extent be established in accordance with the orientation and direction with which the phantasm is traversed: when the traversal entails increasing integration and consistency then we are in the presence of the life drives; when the reverse is the case, when the movement is backward and retrograde from the heights to the depths with increasing disintegration and lack of consistency, then we are in the presence of the death drive. It is not just that: the death drive comes not just from a regression back to a stage or a position previously transcended but *the carrying back to that previous position attitudes and experiences and knowledges gained at the more 'advanced' levels*. The death drive is a carrying back of all that is distinctly human towards the domain of biology and the instincts. It is a diabolical reversion of *drive* to *instinct*. The very phrase: the *death/instinct* – is

emblematic of this reversion as we link the distinctively human experience of death with the distinctly biological domain of instinct.[73]

As a *topos* Flintcomb-Ash is clearly intended as an anti-type to those of
Marlott and Talbothays: instead of the heliotropic idyll of the harvesting
at Marlott and the opulent lushness of Talbothays, Flintcomb-Ash presents a 'starve-acre' (p. 360) aspect and all the evidence is that we are in a
totally new, much harsher, regime of 'paynight', 'work-folk', 'wages' and
'female field labour' (p. 359). Rather than activities of binding and
integration we are here confronted with a whole series of activities
dedicated to hacking, slicing, cutting, threshing, breaking down. The
harshness and the bleakness are evident from the scene of Tess and
Marian's swede-hacking:

> The swede field in which she and her companion were set hacking
> was a stretch of a hundred odd acres, in one patch, on the highest
> ground on the farm, rising above stony lanchets or lynchets – the
> outcrop of siliceous veins in the chalk formation, composed of
> myriads of loose white flints in bulbous, cusped and phallic sha-
> pes... the whole field was in colour a desolate drab; it was a complex-
> ion without features, as if a face, from chin to brow, should be only an
> expanse of skin. The sky wore, in another colour, the same likeness: a
> white vacuity of countenance with the lineaments gone. So these two
> upper and nether visages confronted each other all day long, the
> white face looking down on the brown face, and the brown face
> looking up at the white face, without anything standing between
> them but the two girls crawling over the surface of the former like
> flies.
>
> (p. 360)

It is a nightmarish setting – the two blank faces confronting each other –
dehumanized, dephantasmatized. The scattered bulbous, phallic shapes
that have Marian later shrieking with obscene laughter recall the priapic
partial objects amongst the 'scroff' of the dancing scene at Chaseborough. Whole objects here are being reduced to partial objects, the
phantasmic processes are in reverse – even flagged by the reversal here
of Car Darch's name to Dark Car who with her Amazonian sister assists
at the reed-pulling, another process entailing cutting, crunching, and
fragmentation as the refuse of 'pull-tails' mounts around them (p. 368).

The whole Flintcomb-Ash episode reaches its climax, or nadir perhaps, in the great threshing scene:

Close under the eaves of the stack, and as yet barely visible, was the red tyrant that the women had come to serve – a timber-framed construction, with straps and wheels appertaining – the threshing-machine which, whilst it was going, kept up a despotic demand upon the endurance of their muscles and nerves.

A little way off there was another indistinct figure: this one black, with a sustained hiss that spoke of strength very much in reserve. The long chimney running up beside an ash-tree, and the warmth which radiated from the spot, explained without the necessity of much daylight that here was the engine which was to act as *primum mobile* of this little world. By the engine stood a dark motionless being, a sooty and grimy embodiment of tallness, in a sort of trance, with a heap of coals by his side: it was the engine-man. The isolation of his manner and colour lent him the appearance of a creature from Tophet, who had strayed into the pellucid smokelessness of the region of yellow grain and pale soil, with which he had nothing in common, to amaze and to discompose its aborigines.

What he looked he felt. He was in the agricultural world, but not of it. He served fire and smoke; these denizens of the fields served vegetation, weather, frost, and sun...The long strap which ran from the driving-wheel of his engine to the red thresher under the rick was the sole tie-line between agriculture and him.

(pp. 404–5)

The whole episode is rightly celebrated for it is rich in drama and symbolism – most obviously that of a clash between two socio-economic orders as a primarily agricultural and rural order can be seen to be succumbing to the harsh discipline of a relentless and unforgiving industrial machine. But the threshing machine and its driving steam engine and its dark attendant represent much more than that for here we are at the very mouth of hell itself. The steam engine itself is presented, strikingly, as pure *drive* – it has no other connexion to the world around it. The threshing machine, on the other hand, is little other than a gigantic maw, a massive digestive organ, gulping down the sheaves and spewing forth *faeces* like a 'buzzing red glutton' (p. 413): the machine itself seems to return us to the anal-oral abyss of the schizoid-paranoid depths – figured again in the last moments of the whole process:

The time for the rat-catching arrived at last, and the hunt began. The creatures had crept downwards with the subsidence of the rick till they were all together at the bottom, and being now uncovered from their last refuge they ran across the open ground in all directions, a loud shriek from the by-this-time half-tipsy Marian informing her companions that one of the rats had invaded her person.... The rat was at last dislodged, and amid the barking of dogs, masculine shouts, feminine screams, oaths, stampings, and confusion as of Pandemonium, Tess untied her last sheaf; the drum slowed, the whizzing ceased, and she stepped from the machine to the ground.

(p. 415)

With the untying of the sheaves a massive process of destratification is going on and there is a whole sense of all semblance of order or even simple human dignity being discomposed and reduced to pure animality, to the naked aggression of the death drive.

Not surprisingly this whole reversed traversal of the phantasm from a moment of failed sublimation to a point where *drive* again aligns itself with pure animal *instinct* – the very process we have identified with the *death drive* – can be traced again in the career of Alec once he reappears in the novel. Taking up the structure of the narrative where it has been left by the failure of Angel our first glimpse of the returned Alec is as a *travesty of the Good Object*:

To think of what emanated from that countenance when she saw it last, and to behold it now!... There was the same handsome unpleasantness of mien, but now he wore neatly trimmed old-fashioned whiskers, the sable moustache having disappeared; and his dress was half-clerical, a modification which had changed his expression sufficiently to abstract the dandyism of his features, and to hinder for a second her belief in his identity.

It was less a reform than a transfiguration...

...The lineaments, as such, seemed to complain. They had been diverted from their hereditary connotation to signify impressions for which nature did not intend them. Strange that their very elevation was a misapplication, that to raise seemed to falsify.

(pp. 383–4)

From what he tells us Alec's conversion has been in large part due to an 'Oedipal' conversion prompted by the death of his mother and a meeting with the elder Clare who has had the courage to put him in his place. I think that for a brief period of time we sympathize with Alec's good intentions[74] but such is the 'ghastly *bizarrerie*' (p. 383) of the transformation and the rather 'jolly' way Alec talks about it we are not too surprised when he begins to revert to type: the phantasmatic *translation* has not taken. From the moment that he meets with Tess again all Alec's good intentions are of no avail and in the latter part of the novel we see him assume a variety of roles which have increasingly ominous associations with the devil and death itself. At times Alec recalls the Malign Genius of Descartes – and there is much about him that is highly entertaining as when, for example, he appears before Tess across her garden bonfire dressed as Satan himself:

> 'A jester might say this is just like Paradise. You are Eve, and I am the Other One come to tempt you in the disguise of an inferior animal.'
>
> (p. 431)

It is Alec's obsession with Tess, the *idée fixe*, that marks the reversion to *drive* and with that reversion a *drive to death* as his machinations become more devious and peremptory. A little after the scene in the garden we have another glimpse of Alex 'in a white mackintosh . . . riding down the street' and tapping at the lattice window of Tess's cottage (p. 437): it is a quintessentially folkloric image of Death the Pale Rider calling for a soul. Finally there is the remarkable incident in the church at Kingsbere where Alec springs, Dracula like, from an altar-tomb to clasp the fainting Tess (p. 449). It is, in a sense, at this very moment, the end of the penultimate section of the novel, that Death, in the figure here of Alec, at last manages to claim Tess as its own. The next time we, and Angel, meet Tess she has more or less become a zombie:

> . . . his original Tess had spiritually ceased to recognize the body before him as hers – allowing it to drift, like a corpse upon the current, in a direction dissociated from its living will.
>
> (p.467)

Angel, meanwhile, has pursued his own journey into death and beyond, his sojourn in Brazil taking the place of the classical *topos* of the descent into the world of the afterlife and the purchase of wisdom through confronting great men from the past. Here that role is fulfilled by the 'large-minded stranger' whom he meets on his travels and whose message is 'sublimated by his death' (p. 422). Up to a point this 'sublimation' makes up for the 'failed leap' of the Wellbridge moment: it is like a moment of therapy and *afterward* working through. I say 'up to a point' for there is never any sense that the returned Angel is much more than a *revenant*, again zombie like in his dogged tramp to find the lost Tess and hardly rising at all to any grasp of her final sacrifice.

Tess's killing of Alec brings the phantasmatic capture of the text to an end. In killing Alec she closes the 'image-chain linking [her] experiences from the death of Prince to her final penetrative act of retaliation...'[75] and exorcises her early violation in the Chase. The killing of Alec also closes the tragically unfinished business of the Wellbridge wedding night of which this is another phantasmatic reworking and recapitulation. Mrs Brooks spying through the key-hole reminds us of that 'lying in wait' (*être aux écoutes*), as well as the *'petit bruit'* of the 'rustle' that disturbs her, that often flag the primal scene; the dispersed and strangely disembodied mockery of the Wellbridge scene ('The fire in the grate looked impish – demoniacally funny...The fender grinned idly...' p. 297) is now concentrated in the bitter taunting of Alec (p. 475). As in the earlier scene Tess is richly bedecked and a meal is waiting but unlike the earlier scene when Tess's confession is passed over in silence we are now allowed to hear the outpouring of her tortured soul: it comes forth halting like a primal scream (p. 469) – perhaps the only time in the text we hear Tess's own voice not inhibited by the protocols of others. And in the killing of Alec Tess, too, finally traverses the phantasm in driving at the heart of the loss that was its primary source and origin. But in killing Alec she is also killing that drive which has inhumanly possessed her and drained the life blood from her. The killing of Alec is the killing of Death itself.

'Traversing the phantasm': I think we have to be careful with this notion and perhaps as with so many other concepts it might benefit from being pluralized: 'traversals' of the phantasm. There is, for example, the normative traversal that putatively leads to a successful 'resolving' of the Oedipus complex and sublimation; there is the traversal that might lead downwards and backwards to the drive and death; there is the traversal that seeks the heart of the phantasm – the absence that sets it in motion – and seeks to absent that absence. It is this that Slavoj Zizek designates as the only 'authentic act' and one that is properly catastrophic for in that act the subject destroys the phantasmatic ground of his or her own subjectivity and the act can only lead to '*aphanasis*, self erasure'.[76] It is this that Zizek characterizes as the ultimately 'ethical' act: 'Even I don't know how I was able to do it, it just happened!'[77] For Deleuze such a 'catastrophic' traversal in which the subject achieves a moment of acephalous self transcendence is that which lifts it out of the prison of the phantasm and into the domain of the Eternal Return.[78]

And then there is the traversal that yet remains to be undertaken. There is still the final scene:

> The prospect from this summit was almost unlimited. In the valley beneath lay the city they had just left, its more prominent buildings showing as in an isometric drawing – among them the broad cathedral tower, with its Norman windows and immense length of aisle and nave, the spires of St. Thomas's, the pinnacled tower of the College, and, more to the right, the tower and gables of the ancient hospice, where to this day the pilgrim may receive his dole of bread and ale. Behind the city swept the rotund upland of St. Catherine's Hill; further off, landscape beyond landscape, till the horizon was lost in the radiance of the sun hanging above it.
>
> Against these far stretches of country rose, in front of the other city edifices, a large red-brick building, with level gray roofs, and rows of short barred windows bespeaking captivity, the whole contrasting greatly by its formalism with the quaint irregularities of the Gothic erections. It was somewhat disguised from the road in passing it by yews and evergreen oaks, but it was visible from up here. The wicket from which the pair had lately emerged was in the wall of this structure. From the middle of the building an ugly flat-topped octagonal tower ascended against the east horizon, and viewed from this spot, on its shady side and against the light, it seemed the one blot on the city's beauty. Yet it was with this blot, and not with the beauty, that the two gazers were concerned.
>
> Upon the cornice of the tower a tall staff was fixed. Their eyes were riveted on it. A few minutes after the hour had struck something moved slowly up the staff, and extended upon the breeze. It was a black flag.
>
> (p. 489)

I am not the first to observe the extent to which this scene echoes another to be found early in the *Life*:

> An unusual incident occurred during his pupillage at Hick's which though it had nothing to do wide his own life, was dramatic enough to have mention. One summer morning at Bockhampton, just before he sat down to breakfast, he remembered that a man was to be hanged at eight o'clock at Dorchester. He took up the big brass telescope that had been handed on in the family, and hastened to a hill on the heath a quarter of a mile from the house, whence he looked towards the town.

The sun behind his back shone straight on the white stone façade of the gaol, the gallows upon it, and the form of the murderer in white fustian, the executioner and officials in dark clothing and the crowd below being invisible at this distance of nearly three miles. At the moment of his placing the glass to his eye the white figure dropped downwards, and the faint note of the town struck eight.

The whole thing had been so sudden that the glass nearly fell from Hardy's hands. He seemed alone on the heath with the hanged man, and crept homeward wishing he had not been so curious. It was the second and last execution he witnessed, the first having been that of a woman two or three years earlier, when he stood close to the gallows.[79]

Perhaps what is most striking about this account is the information that this is the *second* hanging that he has witnessed, the first having been that of a woman – a Martha Brown – two or three years earlier. Robert Gittings prints the following account, evidently by Hardy himself, of this first hanging taken from *The Sketch* of 2 November 1904:

Mr Neil Munro tells a curious story of the origin of Mr Hardy's 'Tess'. When Hardy was a boy he used to come into Dorchester to school, and he made the acquaintance of a woman there who, with her husband, kept an inn. She was beautiful, good and kind, but married to a dissipated scoundrel who was unfaithful to her. One day she discovered her husband under circumstances which roused her passion so that she stabbed him with a knife and killed him. She was tried, convicted, and condemned to execution. Young Hardy, with another boy, came into Dorchester and witnessed the execution from a tree that overlooked the yard in which the gallows was placed. He never forgot the rustle of the thin black gown the woman was wearing as she was led forth by the warders. A penetrating rain was falling; the white cap was no sooner over the woman's head than it clung to her features, and the noose was put round the neck of what looked like a marble statue. Hardy looked at the scene with the strange illusion of its being unreal, and was brought to his complete senses when the drop fell with a thud and his companion on a lower branch of the tree fell fainting to the ground. The tragedy haunted Hardy, and, at last. provided the emotional inspiration and source of the matter for 'Tess of the d'Urbervilles'.[80]

The erotic charge of this first hanging and Hardy's evident arousal by it is clear – it reads like a 'snuff' movie – and it was something that was to remain with him more or less for the rest of his life. What at first sight might appear to be no more than a rather morbid erotic *fantasy* when it becomes the subject of obsessive repetitions and insistence then clearly it shifts to the status of an 'orginary *phantasm*'. In a sense the phantasmic capture that holds Tess throughout the novel is Hardy's own originary phantasm – hence the voyeurism of the text and the sheer *drive* with which it is written. It is all too easy to sneer or even condemn the extent to which in *Tess* Hardy is clearly indulging himself but there is surely also the sense that he is in many ways endeavouring to take the whole thing out and have a long look at it, work it through, traverse it. The end of *Tess* suggests that he has not yet let go of it, though the question is clearly being raised as to what will become of Hardy's imaginative world if and when the phantasm that has held it together is finally abandoned.

6
Retranslating *Jude the Obscure* I

Let us recall our basic scheme as it is set out in *Anti-Oedipus*:

> The prime function incumbent upon the socius has always been to codify the flows of desire, to inscribe them, to record them, to see to it that no flow exists that is not properly dammed up, channeled, regulated. When the primitive *territorial machine* proved inadequate to the task, the *despotic machine* set up a kind of overcoding system. But the *capitalist machine* ... finds itself in a totally new situation: it is faced with the task of decoding and deterritorializing the flows.[1]

In previous chapters we have examined these processes of *coding*, *overcoding* and *decoding*, of *territorializing* and *deterritorrializing*, in relation to the dynamics of the Heath in *Return of the Native*, to the power-struggles delineated in *The Mayor of Casterbridge*, and to the succession of regimes traversed by Tess in *Tess of the d'Urbervilles*. With *Jude* we sense, almost at once, that something catastrophic has happened:

> Old as it was, however, the well-shaft was probably the only relic of the local history that remained absolutely unchanged. Many of the thatched and dormered dwelling-houses had been pulled down of late years, and many trees felled on the green. Above all, the original church, hump-backed, wood-turreted, and quaintly hipped, had been taken down, and either cracked up into heaps of road-metal in the lane, or utilized as pig-sty walls, garden seats, guard-stones to fences, and rockeries in the flower-beds of the neighbourhood.
>
> (p. 50)[2]
>
> The brown surface of the field went right up towards the sky all round.... The fresh harrow-lines seemed to stretch like channellings

in a piece of new corduroy, lending a meanly utilitarian air to the expanse, taking away its gradations, and depriving it of all history beyond that of the few recent months, though to every clod and stone there really attached associations enough and to spare – echoes of songs from ancient harvest-days, of spoken words, of sturdy deeds. Every inch of ground had been the site, first and last, of energy, gaiety, horse-play, bickerings, weariness. Groups of gleaners had squatted in the sun on every square yard. Lone-matches that has populated the adjoining hamlet had been made up there between reaping and carrying. Under the hedge which divided the field from a distant plantation girls had given themselves to lovers who would not turn their heads to look at them by the next harvest; and in that ancient cornfield many a man had made love-promises to a woman at whose voice he had trembled by the next seed-time after fulfilling them in the church adjoining. But this neither Jude nor the rooks around him considered. For them it was a lonely place, possessing, in the one view, only the quality of a work-ground, and in the other that of a granary to feed in.

(p. 53)

There is a terrible air of desolation about the opening description of Marygreen and there is a deep sense of a heritage exhausted or erased. Like the 'obliterated graves' of the churchyard now 'commemorated by eighteenpenny cast-iron crosses warranted to last five years' (p. 50) it is a world that has lost its originally sacred codings and has succumbed instead to meanly utilitarian and wholly desacralized registrations and inscriptions. In *Jude* the richly sensuous shearing scenes of *Far From the Madding Crowd* and the luxuriant lushness of Talbothays are a world away and, indeed, the whole of Wessex itself seems to be sliding off the rim of the world. The great highways and ridgeways – like the Icknield Street – are now over-grown and abandoned (pp. 59, 190 & 357) and one of the dominant markers of this shift in mapping is the repeated insistence on the fact that the great roads have given way to the sprawl of the new railways, that a totally new axiomatic prevails – indeed there is almost a sense that in order to follow the journeyings of the principal characters nothing would be more helpful than a railway timetable.[3] And much of this wandering seems aimless and disoriented – 'a cat's cradle of futile journeyings' as one earlier critic has described it[4] – and the repeated locations 'at' – At Marygreen, At Christminster, At Melchester – suggests no more than tangential contact, a 'nomadic' passing through rather than any permanent stay (see p. 379). *Jude* is a novel of a loss of markings and mappings, of a scrambling of codings, of missing *ciphers*, of apocryphal compilations – like the *brochure* of juggled and shuffled New Testament books proposed by Sue (p. 206) – of massive processes of marginalization and deterritorialization and, consequentially, of exile and anomie.

It's not just the *world* of *Jude* that seems to have become unhinged: much of the writing itself seems to be peculiarly slack and uncontrolled – clumsy, even – so that even sympathetic readers find it lacking in taste and acceptability.[5] There is not just the occasional stylistic blemish that is to be found throughout Hardy's work – such as the account of Arabella's first reaction to Jude:

> She saw that he had singled her out from the three, as a woman is singled out in such cases, for no reasoned purpose of further acquaintance, but in commonplace obedience to conjunctive orders from headquarters, unconsciously received by unfortunate young men when the last intention of their lives is to be occupied with the feminine.
>
> (p. 81)

but more the arched contrivance of much of the dialogue between Sue and Jude with its 'sermony' hectoring (pp. 323–5) and bandying of quotation and counter-quotation as if they were, as an early reviewer remarked, College Extension students. Sue, at times reminds us of what was once said of Jane Austen's Fanny Price: she speaks either with the voice of the school-girl or the voice of the school-teacher.[6] Nowhere is this too mannered style more clearly evident than in the notorious exchange between Sue and Jude immediately after the death of the children:

> 'And I was just making my baby darling a new frock; and now I shall never see him in it, and never talk to him any more! ... My eyes are so swollen that I can scarcely see; and yet little more than a year ago I called myself happy! We went about loving each other too much – indulging ourselves to utter selfishness with each other! We said – do you remember? – that we would make a virtue of joy. I said it was Nature's intention, Nature's law and *raison d'être* that we should be joyful in what instincts she afforded us – instincts which civilization had taken upon itself to thwart. What dreadful things I said! And now Fate has given us this stab in the back for being such fools as to take Nature at her word!'

She sank into a quiet contemplation, till she said, 'It is best, perhaps that they should be gone. – Yes – I see it is! Better that they should be plucked fresh than stay to wither away miserably!'

'Yes,' replied Jude. 'Some say that the elders should rejoice when their children die in infancy.'

'But they don't know!...O my babies, my babies....

Again Sue looked at the hanging little frock and at the socks and shoes....What ought to be done?' She stared at Jude, and tightly held his hand.

'Nothing can be done,' he replied. 'Things are as they are, and will be brought to their destined issue.'

She paused. 'Yes! Who said that?' she asked heavily.

'It comes in the chorus of the *Agamemnon*. It has been in my mind continually since this happened.'

'My poor Jude – how you've missed everything! – you more than I, for I did get you! To think you should know that by your unassisted reading, and yet be in poverty and despair!'

(p. 413)

John Goode has already spoken of the latter part of this dialogue as being in the 'worst possible taste'[7] and John Hughes has described the entire episode as 'unbelievable: incredible in the first sense, unbearable in the other.'[8] It begins movingly enough with an acute sense of loss when Sue speaks of 'just making my baby darling a new frock: and now I shall never see him in it...' but then shifts into a kind of fey reverie of their past –

and yet little more than a year ago I called myself happy! We went about indulging ourselves to utter selfishness with each other. We said – do you remember? – that we would make a virtue of joy. I said it was Nature's intention, Nature's law and *raison d'être* that we should be joyful in what instincts she afforded us – instincts which civilization had taken upon itself to thwart.

Not only is this surely self-deluding – it is hard to believe that the pair ever gave way to utter self-indulgence or were ever completely happy together given the strain of their sexual relationship[9] – it is embarrassingly arch and self-conscious, very typical of Sue's propensity to construct a winning image of herself.[10]

Sue then reverts to the pathetic mode but now it has a stagy, histrionic, edge to it:

She sank into a quiet contemplation, till she said, 'It is best, perhaps that they should be gone. – Yes – I see it is! Better that they should be plucked fresh than stay to wither away miserably!'

which is then matched by Jude's platitudinous, quite dreadful,

Some say that the elders should rejoice when their children die in infancy...

Then we have once again the touching anguish of Sue's 'O my babies, my babies' and her forlorn asking what is to be done, only to be met this time with Jude's 'abysmally bathetic'[11] quotation from *Agamemnon* and her astonishingly and patronizingly complimenting him on it. A few pages later Arabella is sneered at for 'seeming utterly unable to reach the ideal of a catastrophic manner' (p. 423) but one must wonder whether what is recorded here is any more satisfactory.

What is the effect of all this? I think it is to make us feel profoundly uneasy and bewildered, confronted with a body of ill-sorted and ill-matched material for which nobody seems to want to accept responsibility. There is a sense of being abandoned to one's own devices by an author who has absolutely no concern for us or even, perhaps, for what he is writing.[12] There is the same sense of carelessness or lack of clear authorial control again on those occasions when the confusion of free-indirect and direct speech is such that it is almost impossible to make out who is speaking. A good example is to be found in the account of Sue's reflections during her convalescence after the loss of the children:

Vague and quaint imaginings had haunted Sue in the days when her intellect scintillated like a star, that the world resembled a stanza or melody composed in a dream; it was wonderfully excellent to the half-aroused intelligence, but hopelessly absurd at the full waking; that the First Cause worked automatically like a somnambulist, and not reflectively like a sage; that at the framing of the terrestrial conditions there never seem to have been contemplated such a development of emotional perceptiveness among creatures subject to those conditions as that reached by thinking and educated humanity. But affliction makes opposing forces loom anthropomorphous; and those ideas were now exchanged for a sense of Jude and herself fleeing from a persecutor.

(p. 417)

Here, in the classic realist text, we would expect to have Sue's thoughts reported in a free-indirect speech by an omniscient author, but, instead, we sense that the ruminations on the First Cause and the plight of a 'thinking and educated humanity' are directly reported expressions of Hardy's own reflections so that by the end of the passage we have no idea whose thoughts are whose.[13]

Then there is that 'pointless trick' described by Christine Brooke-Rose: the 'pretended unknown' – those moments when the narrator seems to be introducing an unknown character when it is clear that the character is known and expected as when Sue's visit to Jude's work-place is re-counted as follows:

> On an afternoon at this time a young girl entered the stone mason's yard with some hesitation, and lifting her skirts to avoid dragging them in the white dust, crossed to the office . . .
>
> (pp. 146–7)

which effects a kind of 'pseudo-exclusion of readers'.[14] It occurs again when Jude is waiting for Sue to arrive to attend Aunt Drusilla's funeral:

> There was a long time to wait, even now, till he would know if she arrived. He did wait, however, and at last a small hired vehicle pulled up at the bottom of the hill, and a person alighted, the conveyance going back, while the passenger began ascending the hill.
>
> (p. 269)

It is as if, at such moments, Hardy cancels the tacit contract, the shared purview that has been established between writer and reader and returns, instead, to a kind of fresh start where identities already established have to be re-established, re-negotiated. There is, again, a sense that any authorial umbrella covering the text might have has no room under it for the reader. It is almost as if the novelist has abandoned all responsibility and refuses to be held to account for his own work.[15] The text itself, and the reader too, have been orphaned.

This sense of being left to one's own devices by a narrator who is offering us a body of material not completely worked over and endowed with a final shape, is experienced elsewhere in the novel. Not so much, perhaps, in the famous anthology of quotations with which Hardy first describes Christminster – though there is a definite sense of Trivial Pursuit about the whole exercise – or even the quite overwhelming use of allusion in the novel[16] as in the wholesale and completely unmediated 'dumping' of what we know to have been Hardy's own reading record (what C. H. Sissons calls appositely 'the furniture of Hardy's own mind'[17]) as the record of Jude and Sue's own intellectual odyssey:

> I have read two books of the Iliad, besides being pretty familiar with passages such as the speech of Phoenix in the ninth book, the fight of Hector and Ajax in the fourteenth, the appearance of Achilles unarmed and his heavy armour in the eighteenth, and the funeral games in the twenty-third. I have also done some Hesiod, a little scrap of Thucidides, and a lot of the Greek Testament....
>
> (pp. 78–9)

> I have had advantages. I don't know Latin and Greek though I know the grammars of those tongues. But I know most of the Greek and Latin Classics through translations, and other books too. I read Lemprière, Catullus, Martial, Juvenal, Lucian, Stern, De Foe, Smollet, Fielding, Shakespeare, the Bible, and other such; and found that all interest in the unwholesome part of those books ended with its mystery.
>
> (p. 201)[18]

As with the quotations swapped by Jude and Sue, or the Christminster extracts, or the many epigraphs scattered throughout the novel, or the fragments of Latin and Greek, or even the little games with changes of font – 𝔄𝔏𝔏𝔈𝔏𝔘𝔍𝔄, Η ΚΑΙΝΗ ΛΙΑΘΗΚΗ – even the little pointing hand accompanying the 'Thither J.F.' (p. 120) – there seems to be something wholly undigested about this material – non-metabolized, unworked, untranslated, – so that such signifiers remain detached from any signified: they become, in effect, de-signified signfiers.[19] Both Christine Brooke-Rose and John Hughes have remarked on the extent to which the novelist seems to be treating his very material, his very medium, as little better than awkward *impedimenta* which, like Phillotson's household bits and pieces and the luggage Jude and Sue seem to haul around with them throughout the novel, keeps getting in everyone's way.[20] It comes as no surprise, therefore, that the figure of Little Father Time, himself little more, at first sight, than an item of luggage, should be regarded as 'very hard to swallow'[21] – again the metaphor of indigestibility. The same metaphor is to be found again when John Goode declares the novel 'simply not fit for consumption'.[22] Similarly a number of commentators have remarked that for all the 'cleverness' of their talk there is little sense that either Sue or Jude have in any real sense *learned* anything from their experience, made any of the knowledge their *own*[23] – i.e. have not properly digested it. Take Jude's climactic speech at Christminster, for example, where if Jude has learnt anything at all one would expect to see some evidence of it. It is too long to quote at length and I suspect that it is recalled as more 'militant' and 'subversive' than, in fact, a close reading shows it to be – what this reveals is confusion, a good deal of self pity, an overall vagueness and a smattering of 'preacherly' piety – exemplified in the concluding lines:

> I perceive there is something wrong in our social formulas: what it is can only be discovered by men or women with greater insight that mine, – if indeed, they ever discover it – at least in our time. 'For who knoweth what is a good man in this life? – and who can tell a man what shall be after him under the sun?'
>
> (p. 399)

This is pretty inadequate, if not simply pathetic, as a diagnosis at this stage of the narration – indeed offering little more insight into either his own or the more general social situation than his drunken recitation of the Nicene Creed earlier in the novel (pp. 172–3) – a scene which, incidentally, as marking his former exit from Christminster, clearly structurally complements the present one that marks his return.

It is ironic and paradoxical, then, that this most under-worked and ill-disciplined of texts is, nevertheless, that very text which is most obviously and most notoriously the one most dominated by the author's sense of design.[24] This was evident even to Hardy's earliest readers as we learn from his response to a review by Edmund Gosse:

> Your review is the most discriminating that has yet appeared. It required an artist to see that the plot is almost geometrically constructed...[25]
> Of course the book is all contrasts – or was meant to be in its original conception. Alas, what a miserable accomplishment it is, when I compare it with what I meant to make it! – e.g., Sue & her heathen gods set against Jude's reading the Greek Testt; Christminster academical, Chr in the slums; Jude the saint, Jude the sinner; Sue the Pagan, Sue the saint; marriage, no marriage; &c. &c.[26]

Elsewhere he speaks of the 'rectangular' lines of the story and the 'quadrille' that must necessarily follow from the 'involutions of four lives'.[27] There are many occasions when we sense the sheer contrivance of the work: the symmetries of the stories of the two main protagonists, the number of coincidental and fortuitous encounters, the rather ungainly doubling of characters with required interlocutors (Phillotson with Gillingham, Arabella with Amy), the heavy-handed symbolism (of the shorn Samson, or the rabbit 'gin', for example), and so on and so forth. There is, too, the whole polemical dimension of the text – the interventions in the current debates on education and marriage and the accompanying issues of class and gender – which gained the novel much of its original notoriety and which continues to attract a disproportionate amount of critical attention.

It is time that an attempt is made to account for the radical ambiguity of a text that, as we have seen, on the one hand seems to register a loss of mappings and of discipline while on the other it reintroduces the most rigorous structural symmetry and a studiedly provocative polemical programme. First, and perhaps most importantly, we need to note the extent to which this 'schizophrenic' tendency of the text *mimics* or *enacts* at its own level the very 'schizophrenia' of the capitalist social formation: that is not just the propensity of that formation (as recorded at the beginning of this chapter) to effect deterritorializations and scramble all codings but also the avidity and promptness with which it sets about instituting counteractive strategies of *reterritorialization* and *reaxiomatization*:

> . . . there is the twofold movement of decoding and deterritorializing flows on the one hand, and their violent and artificial reterritorialization on the other.[28]
> It axiomatizes with one hand what it decodes with the other.[29]
> The flows are decoded *and* axiomatised by capitalism at the same time.[30]
> Civilized modern societies are defined by processes of decoding and deterritorialization. But *what they deterritorialize with one hand, they reterritorialize with the other.*[31]

In other words, to use a notion that was central to the theoretical work of Lucien Goldmann, the structure of *Jude the Obscure* is *structurally homologous* with the contradictory and conflicting tendencies prevailing in capitalism itself. The crisis registered by *Jude the Obscure* is thus much wider and more radical than those crises centred on marriage and education and on class and gender that figure so prominently in the novel. While these might indeed be symptomatic of the more general crisis, I can't help feeling that they do little more here than furnish the novel (as, indeed, Hardy suggests) with a polemical programme required primarily as a structural necessity – what the Russian Formalists would have called a 'motivation of the device':

> The marriage laws being used in great part as the tragic machinery of the tale...The difficulties...of acquiring knowledge in letters without pecuniary means were used in the same way...(Preface pp. 41 & 42)

Even so – and this is the second point that follows upon consideration of the more *general* social context – I do not think we have yet satisfactorily located precisely where that crisis is marked in Hardy's own *personal* – psychological and professional – trajectory. What has prompted this dramatic abandonment of what in *Tess* is still a profoundly romantic and encompassing vision of the world and the adoption instead of a narrative strategy heavily dependent upon geometrical contrasts and polemical provocation?[32]

We ended our discussion of *Tess of the d'Urbervilles* by remarking how much in thrall Hardy seemed to remain, even after the processes of 'dephantasmatization' described in *Tess*, to his own 'originary phantasm' or 'primal scene' centred on the lost object of the hanged woman and we wondered at the time what would happen to Hardy's novelistic universe once that originary phantasm was abandoned. To even begin to answer this question and understand its implications for *Jude the Obscure* we need to turn briefly to the text that was wholly contemporary with it: *The Well-Beloved*.

7
Traversing *The Well-Beloved*

For Tracy Ryan

I can think of no other text by Hardy that produces such violently opposed reactions as does *The Well-Beloved*.[1] Perhaps the most unrestrained of the earlier responses is that of Katherine Mansfield:

> 5th June, 1918. p.114. Last night . . . I read THE WELL-BELOVED by Thomas Hardy. It really is APPALLINGLY BAD, SIMPLY ROTTEN – withered, bony and pretentious. This is very distressing. I thought it was going to be such a find and hugged it home from the library as though I were a girl of fifteen. Of course, I wouldn't say this about it to another human being except you – c'est entendu. The style is so PREPOSTEROUS, too . . .[2]

while its most distinguished admirer was probably Marcel Proust who not only saw in the novel something of the *essence* of Hardy's work – what he terms its 'stonemason's geometry' – but was quite happy to acknowledge his indebtedness to it for its treatment of time and erotic reminiscence.[3] More recently there has been, on the one hand, the extraordinarily subtle reading of the novel by Hillis Miller as a meditation on the function of repetition in the domains of love and artistic creation and for whom the novel is 'one of the most important nineteenth-century novels about art,'[4] while, on the other, there is the virulently hostile reading by Patricia Ingham who seems to regard the text as little more than a chauvinistic/misogynistic tract and all suggestion that the text might be concerned with spiritual or aesthetic issues is little more than special pleading.[5]

The story is preposterous enough. It tells how a sculptor, Jocelyn Pierston, the son of a quarry owner on the Isle of Slingers (Portland Bill), driven by the fantasy of an ideal woman he calls the Well-Beloved, becomes engaged, at twenty years of age, to his cousin Avice Caro but betrays her to elope with Marcia Bencomb, the daughter of one of his father's business rivals. The affair (in the original *The Pursuit of the Well-Beloved* they actually marry) with Marcia doesn't work out and she leaves him in something of a tiff and goes to live abroad (echoes here of Arabella). Pierston, in the meantime, has a successful career as a sculptor – his sculptures themselves sublimated and compulsively repeated celebrations of the Well-Beloved – and becomes a Royal Academician. At the age of forty, after a brief fascination with a society lady, a Mrs. Pine-Avon, Pierston is called back to the Isle of Slingers by news of the death of his first love, Avice. At her funeral he sees her daughter, Ann, who so resembles her mother that Pierston insists on calling her Avice and with whom he proceeds to fall hopelessly in love. This infatuation is also doomed to failure – in part because the second Avice is a congenital flirt and, in any case, already married. Nevertheless, she is fond enough of Pierston and shrewd enough to recognize the eligibility that his wealth confers upon him to attempt to engineer *twenty years later* his marriage to *her* daughter, Avice the third. This, too fails to materialize partly because Pierston is too old (though, again, in the original *Pursuit* Pierston does briefly marry her – indeed bigamously so, for his first wife, Marcia, is still alive) but mainly because the third Avice is already deeply in love with her former French teacher, Henri Leverre, who turns out to be the long-lost Marcia's step-son. At this stage Pierston more or less has a complete breakdown only to be nursed back to something like health by a returned Marcia whom he finally marries.

The principal theme of the story, however, is ostensibly the series of repeated loves for the three Avices over a period of some forty years – it is this that aggravates some critics who simply think that Hardy is indulging an old man's fantasies – and it cannot but be admitted that there is probably an element of truth in that. Pierston, however, accounts for these repetitious loves by explaining, as he does to his friend Somers, that in every instance he is not so much in love with any of the particular women but in love with the capricious 'wraith' or 'spirit', the Well-Beloved, which seems to migrate from figure to figure but which nevertheless holds him, Pierston, compellingly in thrall. As long as the Well-Beloved 'occupies' a particular woman Pierston is 'in love' with that woman but, inevitably, the wraith moves on and the former embodiment is reduced to an empty shell.[6] Ingham sees this as nakedly exploitative:

... it represents a partially successful attempt to appropriate them as unitary woman despite their difference.... He (Pierston) resolves his problem about their identity by a violent decision that they are the same.[7]

but this is to ignore totally the fact that Pierston regards his allegiance to the 'Goddess', the 'Platonic' Well-Beloved, as little more than a curse and disaster. Moreover Pierston is not just the victim of the obsession that compels him but, as often as not, the victim of the very women on whom one might regard him as preying. Apart from the first Avice with whom in fact, he realizes, he is *not* in love but to whom he becomes engaged and then betrays, Pierston is subsequently given a decidedly peremptory brush-off by Marcia while the second Avice not only turns out to be a mirror image of himself – that is one for whom the 'Well-Beloved' moves from man to man just as it does from woman to woman for Pierston – but also quite deliberately manipulates what she knows about his affective proclivities to promote the match with the third Avice. In between, in the case of the fragrant Mrs. Pine-Avon, it is she, the woman, who first rejects – even treats shabbily – Pierston. Moreover Pierston cuts an increasingly pathetic, even tragic, figure as he senses the emotional arrest entailed by the enslavement to the Well-Beloved:

His record moved on with the years, his sentiments stood still.

(p. 65)

When was it to end – this curse of his heart not ageing while his frame moved naturally onward?

(p. 95)

But what could only have been treated as a folly by outsiders was almost a sorrow to him.

(p. 111)

So that, towards the end

His life seemed no longer a professional man's experience, but a ghost story.... He desired to sleep away his tendencies, to make something happen which would put an end to his bondage to beauty in the ideal.

(p. 140)

and there is something truly horrific – reminiscent of Wilde's *Dorian Grey* – in the sixty-year-old Pierston's glimpse of himself in a mirror:

As he sat thus thinking, and the daylight increased, he discerned, a short distance before him, a movement of something ghostly. His position was facing the window, and he found by chance the looking glass had swung itself vertical, so that what he now saw was his own shape. The recognition startled him. The person he appeared was too grievously far, chronologically, in advance of the person he felt himself to be.

(p. 121)

The story, in effect, comes to a close when, in the course of the breakdown provoked by the farce of the elopement of the third Avice with Henri Leverre and the death of the second Avice, Pierston finds that in one and the same moment he has lost his aesthetic sense and escaped from the enthrallment to the Well-Beloved:

The artistic sense had left him, and he could no longer attach a definite sentiment to images of beauty recalled from the past. (p. 145) '... The fever has killed a faculty which has, after all, brought me my greatest sorrows, if a few little pleasures.... The curse is removed.'

(p. 148)

For Hillis Miller the whole novel tells the story of a fantastic bewitchment and a subsequent experience of disenchantment and demystification.[8] He has explored at length Pierston's 'fantastic' capture and the compulsion to repeat that manifests itself both in Pierston's art and his insistence on loving the 'same' woman through three generations – indeed not just these three women for the Well-Beloved has embodied itself briefly and fitfully in any number of women – its primary characteristics, indeed, being its mobility and unpredictablity. Nevertheless I fear that Hillis Miller's reading – encouraged to some extent by what I think are Pierston's own (and, perhaps, Hardy's) mistaken attempts to come to terms with the nature of the fantastic capture – suffers greatly from a wholly inadequate appreciation of the truly radical and constitutive – what I want to call 'genetic' – function of what he, Hillis Miller, describes as 'fantasy' and what I have preferred to call the 'phantasm'.[9]

In the first place Hillis Miller seems to be prepared to accept two interpretations of the figure of the Well-Beloved – as Platonic ideal[10] and as a narcissistic self[11] – which receive, it is true, some measure of support from the text itself. As far as the 'Platonic' ideal is concerned there is the concessionary allusion in the Preface of 1912 where Hardy describes Pierston as a fantast...but whom others may see only as one that gave objective continuity and a name to a delicate dream which in vaguer form is more or less common to all men, and is by no means new to Platonic philosophers.

(p. xxii)

while in the body of the narrative itself we have Pierston's own attempts to account for his obsession, in this instance, with the second Avice:

Beyond the mere pretty island girl (to the world) is, in my eye, the Idea, in Platonic phraseology – the essence and epitome of all that is desirable in this existence.

(p. 77)

This is all very well as far as it goes but its very conventionality hardly accounts for the driven intensity of the narrative and it fails completely to come to terms at all with what we shall find later to be the *contingent* source of the obsession with the Well-Beloved.

The notion, on the other hand, that the Well-Beloved is in some sense himself derives from a passage that Hillis Miller chooses to quote at the head of his essay:

He was subject to gigantic fantasies still. In spite of himself, the sight of the new moon, as representing one who, by her so-called inconstancy, acted up to his own idea of a migratory Well-Beloved, made him feel as his wraith in a changed sex had suddenly looked over the horizon at him. In a crowd secretly, or in solitude boldly, he had often bowed the knee three times to this sisterly divinity on her first appearance monthly, and directed a kiss towards her shining shape.

(p. xi and p. 109)

And it is around this notion of the Well-Beloved as the missing 'self' – 'his wraith in a changed sex' – that Hillis Miller develops his whole interpretation of *The Well-Beloved*. For Hillis Miller given that the Well-Beloved is the 'self' or, at least, as in the text, embodied in closely consanguineous figures, any consummation of a relationship with one of these figures would be tantamount to an act of *incest* and hence the object of *taboo*: it is this that requires the 'failure' of all of Pierston's relationships. Moreover, since the Well-Beloved marks a desire constituted by *lack* within the subject, any embrace of any of the avatars of this *lack* 'would be for Jocelyn to discover that the source of his bubbling creativity is an absence, not a fecundating power.'[12] For Hillis Miller this *lack*, – this 'emptiness' or 'impotence' – accounts for the 'failure of his sculpture and . . . the failure of his loving.'[13] Finally, though I am not at all sure of the logic of this next move, the compulsive repetitions of the narrative indicate both a fear of death and a fear that death is 'impossible to obtain.'[14] It is possibly at this point that the confusions of Hillis Miller's account, which had had a certain plausibility, become evident when, for example, he astonishingly interprets the 'repetition compulsion' as an *inhibition* of the death wish whereas for Freud it is the 'repetition compulsion' itself which first drew the death wish or instinct to his attention.[15] Even more astonishingly Hillis Miller then goes on to make the claim that

> The ultimate grimness of the human condition in *The Well-Beloved*, as in Hardy's work generally, is not the universality of death but the fact that it might be impossible to die.[16]

On the contrary, what seems to be the most salient and even tragic note of *The Well-Beloved* is not the impossibility of death but the impossibility of *life* – see the quotations above: 'His record moved on with the years, his sentiments stood still . . . ' (p. 65), and so on.

Hillis Miller's error is to found his interpretation on a notion of fantasy and repetition catastrophically centred upon total identities (self and other) and real repetitions of the 'same'. He is absolutely right when he describes the self as constituted by a lack[17] but it is not the lack of another 'self' that can be supplied

> by joining [one]self to a beloved of the opposite sex. The beloved is goddess, mother, mistress, sister, mirroring counterpart, all in one, the lover's wraith in a changed sex.[18]

but rather the *lack of a virtual* or *lost partial object* which can ever only be lost or virtual and whose very essence is to be *partial* rather than *whole*, *nomadic* rather than *static*, *different* rather than the *same*.[19] It is this loss of the *partial* or *virtual object* – the Lacanian *objet petit a* in all its manifold avatars – that institutes desire and marks the shift from the biological to the human: sometimes it is felt as the loss of that which is more the self than the self itself; at others its proximity provokes a horror at the return of that *real* the occlusion of which is the condition of desire. It is this lambent instability and ambiguity that, it seems to me, Hardy is at pains to describe albeit with inadequate theoretical tools (whence the flirta-

tions with 'Platonic' and 'narcissistic' – 'his wraith in a changed sex' –
interpretations[20]) in his attempts to describe the nature of the Well-
Beloved. He gives a long list of the different guises that the Well-Beloved
has adopted (p. 34) and concludes:

> She was a blonde, a brunette, tall, *petite, svelte*, straight-featured, full,
> curvilinear. Only one quality remained unalterable: the instability of
> tenure. In Börne's phrase, nothing was permanent in her but change.
>
> (p. 35)

Far from moving from the *same* to the *same*, from *identity* to *identity* the
Well-Beloved moves from the *different* to the *different*: the whole, as is
noted several times, is a *masquerade*:

> He knew that he loved the masquerading creature wherever he found
> her, whether with blue eyes, black eyes, or brown; whether present-
> ing herself as tall, fragile, or plump. She was never in two places at
> once; but hitherto she had never been in one place long. (p. 8)
>
> Four times she masqueraded as a brunette, twice as a pale-haired
> creature, and two or three times under a complexion neither light
> nor dark. Sometimes she was a tall, fine girl, but more often, I think,
> she preferred to slip into the skin of a lithe airy being, of no great
> stature.
>
> (p. 25)
>
> That liquid sparkle of her eye, that lingual music, that turn of her head,
> how well he knew it all, despite the many superficial changes, and how
> instantly he would recognize it under whatever complexion, contour,
> accent, height, or carriage that it might choose to masquerade.
>
> (p. 40)

What these accounts of what we might call 'phantasmatic visitations'
reveal are several major characteristics of the kind of *repetition* that is
involved. Firstly, it is not a repetition of the same by the same, but of a
difference by a difference. Secondly the repetitions are not from *whole* to
whole but from *partial* to *partial*, from *trait* to *trait*: it is such an obsession
with *partialities* and *traits* that accounts for the role played by fetishism
in the aetiology of desire. Thirdly, the movement from repetition to
repetition, from visitation to visitation, is marked by a high degree of
mobility and unpredictability – so much so that – and this might constitute a 'fourthly' – at the limit, it becomes clear that the *visitant* – the
Well-Beloved – is *never* present, but always else-where, in a perpetual

state of adjacency – like a 'will-o'-the-wisp' (or 'Jill o' the wisp' as Pierston describes it in the text (p. 43)). Fifthly, this perpetual adjacency reveals the fact that the very object that drives these repetitions – the Well-Beloved *itself* (if that is not a contradiction in terms) – is always a *lost* or *virtual object* – never actually *there*, always *lacking at its proper place* as Lacan characterizes it in his seminar on Poe's *Purloined Letter*.[21] Deleuze neatly sums up this double-movement of *masquerade* (what he calls *disguise*) and *displacement*:

> Repetition only constitutes itself by means of and within *processes of disguise* (*déguisements*) that affect the terms and the relations of the series in reality; but this is so because it depends on the virtual object as an immanent instance whose distinctive feature is in the first place *displacement*. [emphasis in the original][22]

This means that from the very beginning there has never been any 'Well-Beloved' or lost or virtual object *that had once been there and been lost*: it has always already been lost, the first time is always a second time – once again the phenomenon of *Nachträglichkeit* we discussed at length in the chapter on *Tess*. There has never been a 'first' Avice of which the 'second' Avice is a repetition: the 'first' Avice was already a repetition and endowed with all the ineffable *radiance*[23] of that *originating reminiscence* or *originary phantasm*:

> The soul of Avice – the only woman he had *never* [Hardy's emphasis] loved of those who had loved him – surrounded him like a firmament... He loved the woman dead and inaccessible as he had never loved her in life... Yet the absurdity did not make his grief the less: and the consciousness of the intrinsic, almost radiant, purity of this new-sprung affection for a flown spirit forbade him to check it. The flesh was absent altogether; it was love rarefied and refined to it highest attar. He had felt nothing like it before.
>
> (pp. 51–2)

Moreover we will gain some measure of the allure of this 'first' Avice and the hold she has over both Pierston and Hardy himself if we consider for a moment the curiously heightened – indeed, hypnotic if not hypnagogic – account of the *translation*[24] of the corpse of the first Avice into the resurrected body of the second – which *translation*, in effect, marks the real origin of the text to the extent that it most strikingly describes that opening up of a resonance between a past and a present which is the very mark of the phantasm and therefore of the obsession with the Well-Beloved:

> Against the stretch of water, where a school of mackerel twinkled in the afternoon light, was defined, in addition to the distant lighthouse, a church with its tower, standing about a quarter of a mile off, near the edge of the cliff. The churchyard gravestones could be seen in profile against the same vast spread of watery babble and unrest.
>
> Among the graves moved the form of a man clothed in a white sheet, which the wind blew and flapped coldly now and then. Near him moved six men bearing a long box, and two or three persons in black followed. The coffin, with its twelve legs, crawled across the isle, while around and beneath it the flashing lights from the sea and the school of mackerel were reflected; a fishing-boat, far out in the Channel, being momentarily discernible under the coffin also.
>
> The procession wandered round to a particular corner, and halted, and paused there a long while in the wind, the sea behind them, the surplice of the priest still blowing. Jocelyn stood with his hat off: he was present, though he was a quarter of a mile off; and he seemed to hear the words that were being said, though nothing but the wind was audible.
>
> He instinctively knew it was none other than Avice whom he was seeing interred; *his* Avice, as he now began to presumptuously call her.
> . . .
> The lispings of the sea beneath the cliffs were all the sounds that reached him, for the quarries were silent now. How long he sat there lonely and thinking he did not know. Neither did he know, though he felt drowsy, whether inexpectant sadness – that gentle soporific – lulled him into a short sleep, so that he lost count of time and consciousness of incident. But during some minute or minutes he seemed to see Avice Caro herself, bending over and then withdrawing from her grave in the light of the moon.
>
> She seemed not a year older, not a digit less slender, not a line more angular than when he had parted from her twenty years earlier, in the lane hard by. A renascent reasoning on the impossibility of such a phenomenon as this being more than a dream-fancy roused him with a start from his heaviness.
>
> 'I must have been asleep,' he said.
>
> (pp. 55–56)

Now, what this strangely hallucinatory scene – 'he lost count of time and consciousness' – in its deep structure seems to me to recall once again is that traumatic experience of having witnessed a hanging which has been posited as the 'originary phantasm' providing 'the emotional inspiration and some of the matter for *Tess of the d'Urbervilles*.'[25] It is worth recalling it again here both as it occurs in the *Life* and with interpolations from other accounts of the same event to be found in Gittings:

> An unusual incident occurred daring his pupillage at Hicks's which, though it had nothing to do with his own life, was dramatic enough to have mention. One summer morning at Bockhampton, just before he sat down to breakfast, he remembered that a man was to be hanged at eight o'clock at Dorchester. He took up the big brass telescope that had been handed on in the family, and hastened to a hill on the heath a quarter of a mile from the house, whence he looked towards the town. The sun behind his back shone straight on the white stone façade of the gaols the gallows upon it, and the form of the murderer in white fustian, the executioner and officials in dark clothing and the crowd below being invisible at this distance of nearly three miles. At the moment of his emplacing the glass to his eye the white figure dropped downwards, and the faint note of the town clock struck eight. The whole thing had been so sudden that the glass nearly fell from Hardy's hands. He seemed alone on the heath with the hanged man, and crept homeward wishing he had not been so curious. It was the second and last execution he witnessed, the first having been that of a woman two or three years earlier, when he stood close to the gallows.[26]

He never forgot the rustle of the thin black gown the woman was wearing as she was led forth by the warders. A penetrating rain was falling; the white cap was no sooner over the woman's head than it clung to her features, and the noose was put round the neck of what looked like a marble statue. He was so close that he could actually see her features through the rain-damp cloth over her face. Hardy looked at the scene with the strange illusion of its being unreal.

He wrote in his eighties, in words whose unconscious tone is barely credible, 'what a fine figure she showed against the sky as she hung in the misty rain, and how the tight black silk gown set off her shape as she wheeled half round and back', after Calcraft had tied her dress close to her body.

Years later, he himself repeated the story...he emphasized again the weird effect of the woman's features showing through the execution hood.... Hardy 'never forgot the rustle of the thin black gown the woman was wearing'.... There can be hardly any doubt that hanging, and particularly the hanging of a woman, had some sort of sexual meaning for Hardy, which remained powerfully in his thoughts to the end of his life. This account hints that it supplied at least part of the emotional power of his best-known novel.[27]

There is no space here for an exhaustive comparison of the two scenes but I hope there are sufficient details in common, albeit *displaced* in relation to each other characteristic, as we have seen, of phantasmatic repetition, to establish that the scene in *The Well-Beloved* is the 'same' as that recounted in the *Life* and the biography:

Life/Biography	*The Well-Beloved*
Distance: ¼ mile	Distance: ¼ mile
bright light	twinkling light
gallows	light-house, tower
murderer in white fustian	man clothed in a white sheet
executioner and officials in dark clothing	two or three persons in black
the rustle of the thin black gown	the surplice of the priest still blowing
strange illusion of its being unreal	drowsy...loss of consciousness
alone on the heath with the dead man	both in and out of the scene – 'present though a quarter of a mile off'
	hearing/not hearing

What is remarkable about this scene is that it not only provides the clue to the temporality of the novel and its pattern of repetitions through time (more properly, perhaps, *out* of time) but also an outline (precisely that) sketch of the stratified *topography* of the novel – that is of tier upon tier of geological and sculptured form emerging from the 'babble and the unrest' and the 'lispings' of the sea and climaxing in the image of the suspended body. It was precisely this stratified topography of *The Well-Beloved* that, as we remarked above, led Proust to applaud it for its exemplary status in Hardy's *œuvre*.[28] For what the juxtapositioning of the *originary scenes* of the *Life* and *The Well-Beloved* clearly allow us to see is the deep complicity between the stratifications of the island and their culmination in the sculptures produced by the academician. That there is an umbilical link between the quarries worked by the father on the island and the artistic production of the son in London is hinted at more than once (see pp. 39 and 139) and it is perhaps worth recalling that in his progress from the one to the other – from the schizoid depths of the quarries to the sculpted heads of the Good Object (the Well-Beloved in all its forms) – Jocelyn has had to serve his necessary apprenticeship at the aggressive and reparative positions:

> This son is doen great things in London as a' image carver; and I can mind when, as a boy, 'a first took to carving soldiers out o' bits o' stwone from the soft-bed of his father's quarries; and then 'a made a set o' stwonen chess-men, and so 'a got on.
>
> (p. 12)[29]

At all levels it is the phantasmatic structure that prevails – for if the reverie in the grave-yard marks the *erotic* resurrection of the 'original' Avice then the sculpted busts in the London studio are *aesthetic* replicas of the ghastly features of the hanged woman:

> A penetrating rain was falling; the white cap was no sooner over the woman's head than it clung to her features, and the noose was put round the neck of *what looked like a marble statue.* [my emphasis] He was so close that he could actually see her features through the rain-damp cloth over her face.

It is at this point that we need take in charge our own prurience and hypocrisy for it is all too easy to find ourselves condemning this macabre obsession with the figure of the hanged woman. Undoubtedly there is something profoundly disturbing about it but it is sheer nonsense to think that somehow we *choose* our phantasms; rather the contrary: we become what our phantasms cause us to be. In this sense Hillis Miller is absolutely right to suggest that the writer is less the *author* than the *function* of his tale.[30] Where Hillis Miller is wrong, however, is in his insistence that the phantasmatic obsession that drives the text is the source of its 'impotence' and 'infecundity' and 'failure'.[31] On the contrary, no matter how delimitating and debilitating it might be – no matter in what *lack* or *lost* or *virtual* object it is grounded – the *originary phantasm* is the generative matrix of what makes us human and the source, therefore, of all that we can become and of what we can achieve. Moreover this phantasmatic drive is at the *opposite pole* to the 'Platonic' fantasy – indeed, of the very *fantasy* that has disguised the *phantasmatic* genesis of the text: as Hardy wickedly (or perhaps unconsciously) indicates by the epigraph which prefaces his fable –

One shape of many names

– the Well-Beloved is not so much a *heavenly* principle from on high as a *daemonic* force from below: the 'One shape of many forms' 'refers not to an ideal beloved as in Hardy's novel, but to the 'Spirit of evil'.[32] The philosophy that informs *The Well-Beloved* is a profoundly anti-Platonic one whereby the aesthetic or even the erotic object emerges as a *simulacrum* or *effect* of a brew of forces lying in the depths. Indeed there is an uncanny parody of this daemonic production from the depths in the glimpse of the 'presence' cast up by the seas about the isle:

> It was a presence – an imaginary shape or essence from the human multitude lying below: those who had gone down in vessels of war, East Indiamen, barges, brigs, and ships of the Armada – select people, common, debased, whose interests and hopes had been as wide asunder as the poles, but who had rolled each other to oneness on that restless sea-bed. There could almost be felt the brush of their huge composite ghost as it ran as a shapeless figure over the isle, shrieking for some good god who would disunite it again.
>
> (pp. 10–11)

The haunting power of this image derives in large part from its being a composite derived from a populous history rather than from the fantasies of a solitary subject and from the fact that it seethes still with a schizoid, self-annihilating energy. In the text itself it is the allure of the Race – that cauldron of conflicting and unpredictable currents that lie just off the island – that tempts Jocelyn to his death at the end of *The Pursuit of the Well-Beloved*. The allure of the Race is that ever present allure of the schizo-paranoid depths we looked at in the chapter on *Tess*: it is the possibility of destroying the self, of demolishing or deconstructing, that is, that phantasmatic structure of which the self is no more than a function-effect. It is this that is marked by the break-down of

Pierston towards the end of the story – his loss of a faculty that had become a curse, the loss of both his artistic and his erotic identities – and which is theatrically encapsulated in the 'dephantasmatization' of the Well-Beloved in the unmasking of Marcia:

> The cruel morning rays... showed in their full bareness, unenriched by addition, undisguised by the arts of colour and shade, the thin remains of what had once been Marcia's majestic bloom. She stood the image and superscription of Age – an old woman, pale and shrivelled, her forehead ploughed, her cheek hollow, her hair white as snow. To this the face that he once kissed had been brought by the raspings, chisellings, scourgings, bakings, freezings of forty invidious years – by the thinkings of more than half a lifetime.
>
> (p. 147)

In the text itself this is depicted as an incredibly brave episode on the part of Marcia but it is also incredibly brave of Hardy for here, if ever, he is bringing, Samson-like, his own phantasm down about his ears. The brilliant invocation of the activities associated with quarrying to describe the very collapse of the phantasmatic stratifications is a masterly laying bare of the very device that Proust has acclaimed as central to Hardy's work. And in the unveiling of Marcia, Hardy, with almost steely nerve, unwinds the rain-damp cloth that had clung to the features of the hanged woman and that had made her look like a marble statue and stares instead at the horror and the reality beneath. For this is the risk that is run when the phantasm is thus traversed – the re-emergence of the real occluded by the phantasm in all its abjectness and unlovely functionality:

> His business was, among the kindred undertakings which followed the extinction of the Well-Beloved and other ideals, to advance a scheme for the closing of the old natural fountains in the Street of Wells, because of their possible contamination, and supplying the townlet with water from pipes, a scheme that was carried out at his expense, as is well known. He was also engaged in acquiring some old moss-grown, mullioned Elizabethan cottages, for the purpose of pulling them down because they were damp; which he afterwards did, and built new ones with hollow walls, and full of ventilators.
>
> (p. 151)

It is difficult not to recognize here an anticipation or a recall of the description of Marygreen – with its 'obliterated graves' and 'eighteenpenny cast iron crosses' – that opens *Jude the Obscure*. Moreover what the close of *The Well-Beloved* clearly implies is that with the loss of the inspirational afflatus of the phantasm there can remain recourse only to a narrative which is 'machine made' and 'geometrical' (p.149) – the very characteristics we have already seen ascribed to the dephantasmatized world of *Jude*.

8
Retranslating *Jude the Obscure* II

What our detour through, or traversal of, *The Well-Beloved* surely allows us to propose as a premise to all that follows is that what we have in *Jude the Obscure* is a 'dephantasmatized' world – or, rather, that in *Jude* what we find is a world in the very process of dephantasmatization: it has yet to reach the apodictic condition that prevails at the end of *The Well-Beloved*. For if Christminster represents anything it is the ruin of a dream and that dream is, once again, that originary scene which we have seen so obsessing and driving and tormenting Hardy in these late novels. For Christminster is nothing less than one more transcription or translation or repetition of what we have more or less established as Hardy's 'originary phantasm' – the hanging witnessed from Bockhampton. For ease of reference I quote the by now familiar passage again:

> An unusual incident occurred during his pupillage at Hick's which though it had nothing to do wide his own life, was dramatic enough to have mention. One summer morning at Bockhampton, just before he sat down to breakfast, he remembered that a man was to be hanged at eight o'clock at Dorchester. He took up the big brass telescope that had been handed on in the family, and hastened to a hill on the heath a quarter of a mile from the house, whence he looked towards the town. The sun behind his back shone straight on the white stone façade of the gaol, the gallows upon it, and the form of the murderer in white fustian, the executioner and officials in dark clothing and the crowd below being invisible at this distance of nearly three miles. At the moment of his placing the glass to his eye the white figure dropped downwards, and the faint note of the town struck eight.

The whole thing had been so sudden that the glass nearly fell from Hardy's hands. He seemed alone on the heath with the hanged man, and crept homeward wishing he had not been so curious. It was the second and last execution he witnessed, the first having been that of a woman two or three years earlier, when he stood close to the gallows.[1]

To begin with the young Jude chooses as his vantage point to peer at the fabulous city the Brown House which we learn in the course of the text to be again linked with a *hanging* and to be enigmatically associated already with the history of his family.[2] It is towards evening when he climbs the ladder against the Brown House:

He then seated himself again, and waited. In the course of ten or fifteen minutes the thinning mist dissolved altogether from the northern horizon, as it had already done elsewhere, and about a quarter of an hour before the time of sunset the westward clouds parted, the sun's position being partially uncovered, and the beams streaming out in visible lines between two bars of slaty cloud. The boy immediately looked back in the old direction.

Some way within the limits of the stretch of landscape, points of light like the topaz gleamed. The air increased in transparency with the lapse of minutes, till the topaz points showed themselves to be the vanes, windows, wet roof slates, and other shining spots upon the spires, domes, freestone-work, and varied outlines that were faintly revealed. It was Christminster, unquestionably; either directly seen, or miraged in the peculiar atmosphere. The spectator gazed on and on till the windows and vanes lost their shine, going out almost suddenly like extinguished candles. The vague city became veiled in mist. Turning to the west, he saw that the sun had disappeared. The foreground of the scene had grown funereally dark, and near objects put on the hues and shapes of chimaeras.

(p. 61)

He repeats the adventure a few days later:

It was not late when he arrived at the place of outlook, only just after dusk; but a black north-east sky, accompanied by a wind from the same quarter, made the occasion dark enough. He was rewarded; but what he saw was not the lamps in rows, as he had half expected. No individual light was visible, only a halo or glow-fog over-arching the place against the black heavens behind it, making the light and the city seem distant but a mile or so.

He set himself to wonder on the exact point in the glow where the schoolmaster might be – he who never communicated with anybody at Marygreen now; who was as if dead to them here. In the glow he seemed to see Phillotson promenading at ease, like one of the forms in Nebuchadnezzar's furnace...

He had become entirely lost to his bodily situation during this mental leap...

(pp. 62–3)

Again it is not a matter of one to one correspondence of details between the two scenes but rather the over-all effect of them being in some sense the 'same'. There are some suggestive common features: the angle of light is very much the same with the sun behind the boy's back in both scenes even though in the one it is the morning light while in the second it is the evening sun. In the first the light falls on the 'white stone façade' of the prison while in the second it lights up the 'topaz points' or 'shining spots' – vanes, windows, wet slates, freestone work – of Christminster. The 'quarter of a mile' of the first scene becomes the 'quarter of an hour' in the second. Both scenes seem to end 'suddenly' – the first with the drop of the hanged man, the second with the lights 'going out almost suddenly, like extinguished candles' and both scenes close on a sense of guilt and foreboding. What is also common to the two scenes is the mesmeric compulsion of the first and the visionary, 'second state', again hypnagogic, effect of the second – its quality of 'mirage' or 'halo'. And the second scene is not just a repetition of the first scene but is itself repeated – a sure sign of its compulsive allure. But what is even more remarkable and what to a great extent confirms that the Christminster vision is a repetition of the original traumatic witnessing of the hanged woman is that in the original manuscript the second paragraph of the account of Jude's second glimpse of Christminster that we have quoted above *it is Sue, not Phillotson, who figures in the vision of Nebuchadnezzar's furnace*. The corrected passage reads as follows:

He set <u>himself</u> to wonder~~ing~~ <u>on</u> the exact point in the glow where ~~his cousin~~ <u>the schoolmaster</u> might be; ~~she~~ <u>he</u> who never communicated with ~~his branch of the~~ family <u>anybody at Marygreen now,</u> <u>who</u> was as if dead to them here. In the glow he seemed to see ~~her soul standing~~, <u>Phillotson</u> promenading at ease like one of the forms in Nebuchadnezzar's furnace.[3]

If the Christminster vision originally included the (subsequently *re-pressed*) figure of a ('dead to them') Sue Bridehead then it is even more clearly yet another manifestation of the originary phantasm and this must account for the sheer *radiance*[4] bestowed upon it by the jewelled imagery – the 'topaz points' – of the first glimpse above and which, in turn, recalls the apocalyptic vision of the Heavenly Jerusalem in Revelations:

18   And the building of the wall of it was *of* jasper: and the city *was* pure gold, like unto clear glass.
19   And the foundations of the wall of the city *were* garnished with all manner of precious stones. The first foundation *was* jasper; the second, sapphire; the third, a chalcedony; the fourth, an emerald;
20   The fifth, sardonyx; the sixth, sardius; the seventh, chrysolyte; the eighth, beryl; the ninth, a topaz; the tenth, a chrysoprasus; the eleventh, a jacynth; the twelfth, an amethyst.[5]

What needs to be recalled now with respect to this vision of Christminster which Jude at once associates with the 'new Jerusalem' (p. 62) is the increasingly impoverished representations to which the city becomes subject in the course of the novel. There is first the three-dimensional model of Jerusalem of the itinerant exhibition which Sue and her pupils and Jude visit in Christminster (p. 155). This, in turn, becomes the two-dimensional drawing of the same sketched by Sue back in her class-room (p. 157).[6] Then, much later in the text, on the occasion of the visit to the Great Wessex Agricultural Show at Stoke-Barehills we are shown the 'Model of Cardinal College, Christminster; by J. Fawley and S. F. M. Bridehead' (p. 363) – that is of but one part of the city as a whole – and then, finally, there are the rather pathetic 'Christminster Cakes' (pp. 382–3) sold by Sue at the Spring Fair at Kennetbridge and which are 'unceremoniously munch[ed]' by Arabella. There is every suggestion here that the phantasm has been subjected to the reverse of the trajectory we have ascribed to it in our discussion of *Tess*: instead of emerging from the oral-anal depths via the linking of partial objects and the evolving of symbolic objects (at the level of the constitution of an erotogenetic surface) and of parental images (at the Oedipal level[7]) here we have regressed from a radiant epiphany back through the imagistic and the symbolic, back through partial objects to an oral annihilation: Christminster/the 'new Jerusalem' is literally munched into non-existence.[8] This reversal of trajectory from phantasmatic climax to oral aggression is that very reversal of the drive we have associated with the Death Instinct[9] – it is this that drives and structures the text as a whole.

The progressive attenuation or corruption of the phantasm can be spotted in two other moments in the text. The first occurs when Jude re-encounters Arabella serving behind a bar in a public house in Christminster:

> Feeling tired, and having nothing more to do till the train left, Jude sat down on one of the sofas. At the back of the barmaids rose bevel-edged mirrors, with glass shelves running along their front, on which stood precious liquids that Jude did not know the name of, in bottles of topaz, sapphire, ruby and amathyst. The moment was enlivened by the entrance of some customers into the next compartment, and the starting of the mechanical tell-tale of moneys received, which emitted a ting-ting every time a coin was put in.
>
> The barmaid attending to this compartment was invisible to Jude's direct glance, though a reflection of her back was occasionally caught by his eyes. He had only observed this listlessly, when she turned her face for a moment to the glass to set her hair tidy. Then he was amazed to distinguish that the face was Arabella's.
>
> (p. 236)

The 'topaz points' of Christminster as well as the bejewelled radiance of the Heavenly Jerusalem are clearly echoed in the 'bottles of topaz, sapphire, ruby and amathyst' and the 'ting-ting' of the till recalls the town clock striking eight of the original hanging scene. But what is interesting is that here even this debased phantasm still serves as a mode of mediation between Jude and Arabella. Indeed, isn't it the case that much of the pain of the text and of the relations between the various couples, particularly of Jude and Sue and of Sue and Phillotson, is that they are too utterly close to one another,[10] too much nerve-end against nerve-end – hence the resort to sills (p. 265) or mirrors (p. 315) or photos or notes as modes of buffering and mediation.

The final glimpse of what is by now a vestigial phantasm comes with the great disillusionment Jude experiences when he seeks out the writer of a greatly loved hymn anticipating 'what a man of sympathies he must be', what a 'man of soul' or 'perfect adviser' – i.e. Jude's search once again for 'someone', for an 'Other',[11] who might give a meaningful structure to his world – only to discover that the musician has abandoned music for marketing wine:

> He handed Jude an advertisement list of several pages in booklet shape, ornamentally margined with a red line, in which were set

forth the various clarets, champagnes, ports, sherries, and other wines with which he purposed to initiate his new venture.

(p. 254)

The list of variously coloured wines recall the brilliant bottles of the Christminster pub as these have recalled the 'topaz points' of the Heavenly Jerusalem: it is a bitter and sardonic and bleakly humorous joke that the radiance of the phantasm has degenerated to the status of a wine merchant's fly-sheet.

We are now in a better position to understand why Hardy depicts Christminster in the rather strange way that he does – by means of offering us a whole set of unassimilated and, in some cases, as Patricia Ingham has noted, mis-matched, quotations:

> The most extended attempt to annex Christminster learning appears in the voice of the spectres haunting the city that Jude imagines on his first night there. The emptiness of the assumed appropriation is evidenced by the fact that many of them are merely indirectly described and remain lifelessly unevocative; those quoted are not names but periphrastically alluded to.... The reader encounters, despite the coherence, of individual passages, an incoherent totality: a boy's anthology of purple passages, 'learning' perhaps in a literal sense, 'touchstones', a kaleidoscope.[12]

What these unassimilated pieces become are little more than the fragments of a non-incorporated tradition, as much miscellaneous *débris* as the 'traceries, mullions, transoms, shafts, pinnacles and battlements standing on the bankers half-worked, or waiting to be removed' (p. 131) for there is no longer any *structure* – there is no longer the *phantasmatic structure* – wherein they might become – to use Ingham's terms – 'annexed' or 'appropriated.'

In describing the structure and function of the phantasm in the chapter on *Tess* we drew attention to its following characteristics. The two principal structural characteristics of the phantasm that concerned us most in that chapter were its *temporal* aspect – the *afterward* effect of *Nachträglichkeit* – and its *stratifications* that linked the oral-anal depths with the heights associated with the Good Object and Oedipal intentionality.[13] But prior to all these and at the very heart of the phantasm was its function as the *interface* between the biological/physiological body and the accumulated wisdom – *dit* or *rumeur* – of the tribe – of the traditions and institutions of the symbolic order – precisely the fragmented remnants of which we see in the Christminster quotes. We drew particular attention to the role played in that articulation of the *body* on *meaning* of *translation*:

> We see then how it can be said of them [phantasms] that not only are they part of the symbolic order, but that they *translate* [*traduisent*], via the mediation of an imaginary scenario which seeks to get a purchase on it, the inscription [Fr. *insertion*] of the most radically constitutive symbolic order on the real of the body.[14]

Here the notion of *translation* is almost incidental – so much so that, as we remarked at the time, it does not even appear in the English version of the text – but in Laplanche's later work it comes to assume an almost pre-eminent significance. This stems in large part from an astonishing passage in Freud's correspondence with Fliess where Freud suggests that it might be possible to regard 'repression' as a 'failure of translation'.

> As you know, I am working on the assumption that our psychic mechanism has come into being by a process of stratification: the material present in the form of memory traces being subjected from time to time to a *rearrangement* in accordance with fresh circumstances – to a *retranscription* . . .
>
> I should like to emphasize the fact that the successive registrations represent the psychic achievement of successive epochs of life. At the boundary between two such epochs a translation of the psychic material must take place. I explain the psychoneuroses by supposing that this translation has not taken place in the case of some material, which has certain consequences . . .
>
> A failure of translation – that is what is clinically known as 'repression'.[15] (emphasis in the original)

From this Laplanche derives one of the principal theses of his later work: that 'The human being is, and will go on being, a *self-translating* and self-theorizing being.'[16] [my emphasis, D.M.]. For Laplanche, phantasmatic inscriptions derive from fragments of unconscious or half-conscious reveries directed at the child, almost as a primal act of seduction, by the parental world that attends to its needs. It is the task of the child to decipher and translate these unconscious communications so that they become conscious and cease to be the encysted memory traces that lead to later pathological conditions. It is the failure of such processes of translation that lead to the depositing in the unconscious non-metabolized and non-translated *designified signfiers* – i.e. those messages which remain un-interpreted and devoid of meaning. Indeed, these *engimatic signifiers* are not so much *deposited in* the unconscious as they in fact, *constitute* the unconscious. The first translations, moreover, may not always be successful: they may be *mis-translations* and it then becomes the task of an analyst to offer his patient the opportunity to undertake a *de-translation* of these earlier *mis-translations*. One can readily see how consciousness, iteslf, becomes a constant process of *de-translation* and *re-translation* of these *enigmatic signifiers*.[17]

We can now see that it is the attenuation and non-availability of this phantasmatic structure which explains so much of what we have earlier complained of as the 'unassimilated', 'undigested', 'non-metabolized' features of the text. *For the phantasmatic structure is that very device that supplies the novel itself with its internal 'kitchen' or digestive apparatus.* It is, in effect, what we are more usually inclined to call the author's informing *ideology* or *world view*: that set of unconscious presuppositions and assumptions – the whole *a priori apparatus* – with which he approaches the world as a whole. It is the lack of this phantasmatic structure that ensures that 𝕬𝕷𝕷𝕰𝕷𝕌𝕵𝕬𝕳, Η ΚΑΙΝΗ ΛΙΑΘΗΚΗ, the pointing hand – as well as the occasional passages in Latin and Greek, and the anthology of non-annexed or non-appropriated quotations – remain there on the page as inert and unmetabolized – as *untranslated* – *enigmatic signifiers*. Curiously, but significantly, from very early on Jude has associated the Christminster 'phantasm' (what he calls appropriately here 'ecstasy or vision') with *translation*:

> Ever since his first ecstasy or vision of Christminster and its possibilities, Jude had meditated much and curiously on the probable sort of process that was involved in turning the expressions of one language into those of another.
>
> (p. 71)

The phantasm, in other words, is that very *'secret cipher'* (p. 71), that *'law of transmutation'* (ibid.), which Jude vainly expected from his early grammars and the lack of which at the psychic or social level cannot be compensated for by any amount of industry. It is this that accounts for the huge weight of *impedimenta* and *luggage* in the text – and amongst the *impedimenta* and *luggage* we can include the much paraded but so inadequately digested knowledge accrued by Jude and Sue. With the failure of the phantasmatic structure there is the failure, too, of all socialisation and mediation so that consciousness and the world no longer relate to each other than in modes of what Shakespeare's Ulysses calls, when warning of what might be entailed by the collapse of what we might call *the feudal phantasm* or the *feudal symbolic order*, 'mere oppugnancy'.[18]

It is precisely this world of obtuse and recalcitrant objects and of blind and unmediated collisions consequent upon the loss of the phantasm and the symbolic order that Deleuze has elsewhere characterized, in discussing Michel Tournier's *Vendredi: ou les limbes du Pacifique,*[19] as '*un monde sans Autrui*'.[20] Tournier's novel, as its title suggests, is a long meditation on the theme of the *robinsonade* which, for Deleuze, amounts to asking 'what becomes of a man alone, *sans Autrui?*'[21] Deleuze's discussion of the notion of *Autrui* is long and complex and I am not at all sure in the end that it is very successful. Central to it is the concern that we should not regard *Autrui* simply as the *other person* but rather as an *a priori structure* antecedent to the various *autruis – other persons: you for me, me for you* – that effectuate it:

> Thus *Autrui a priori* as an absolute structure founds the relativity of others (*autruis*) as terms effecting the structure in each field.[22]
> We must therefore distinguish *Autrui a priori*, which designates that structure, from *cet autrui-ci* (this one here), *cet autrui-là* (that one there), which designate the real terms effectuating that structure in such and such a field.[23]

In other words *Autrui a priori* is a kind of *super-* or *meta-autrui*, a tacit epistemological or even ontological framework that determines that we should see the world in terms of selves and others, or of subject and object, or of male and female, or even in terms of alive and dead.[24] At times it is tempting to regard Deleuze's *Autrui* as rather like the Berkeleyan God who is always about in the quad[25] – that is if, as Berkeley maintained, *being is being perceived* (*esse est percipi*) the only thing that guarantees that things stay as they are when there is no-one around to see them is the presence of an all-seeing God. *Autrui*, like Berkeley's God, keeps things in their places when we are not around to see them; without *Autrui* – without this benevolent overseer – 'material objects would have a jerky life, suddenly leaping into being when we looked at them ...'[26] On the other hand Deleuze tends to bestow on *Autrui* a Leibnizian 'expressivity' – the expressivity of a *possible world*[27] – the world as a whole, in terms of Leibnizian phenomenology, made up of such constitutive expressive *autruis*[28] or *monads*, so that *Autrui* comes to represent in many ways the phenomenological world of social meaning.[29] To this extent, then, *Autrui* provides a principle of security and discipline, a sense of social cohesion.[30] Understood as such, Deleuze's *Autrui a-priori* – and particularly when one notes that in a curiously quiet aside Deleuze remarks on the peculiar affinity of *Autrui* with *language*,[31] – increasingly comes to resemble the Lacanian Symbolic Order: indeed Lacan's account of the distinction between the *other* and the *Other* (*autre/ Autre*) is totally compatible with that which Deleuze postulates between *autrui* and *Autrui a priori*:

> However, the meaning of 'the Other as another subject' is strictly secondary to the meaning of 'the Other as symbolic order'; . . . It is thus only possible to speak of the Other *as a subject* in a secondary sense, in the sense that a subject may occupy this position and thereby 'embody' the Other for another subject.[32]

If it is legitimate, therefore, to identify Deleuze's *Autrui* with the Symbolic Order and to see in the latter the Lacanian equivalent of Laplanche and Pontalis's *fantasme* – to the extent that, like the *fantasme*, it marks the break with the instinctive and the biological and the initiation into the world of drives and the social – then it is possible to consider all that Deleuze (and Tournier) have to say about what follows upon the collapse of the structure of *Autrui* as true, too, of any collapse of the phantasm.

The first effect of the loss of *Autrui*/Other/phantasm is one that we have already drawn attention to: a loss of all ontological security, a loss of all those mediations that position things and persons in relation to each other – subject in relation to object, male in relation to female – with the result that everything just seems to collide (*se cogner*) with everything else in naked confrontation.[33] The second effect is that everything that would otherwise have been processed by and *produced by* the intervention of the phantasmatic or symbolic order is now left excluded and un-treated – that process of exclusion to which Lacan has given the name *foreclusion*.[34] For Laplanche the equivalent term for this act of exclusion – for this failure to allow something into consciousness – is, as we have seen, '*a failure of translation*'[35] or of '*metabolization*'[36] and it is this that constitutes the unconscious. For both Deleuze and Tournier the initial result of the collapse of the phantasmatic and the symbolic is the threat of total disorientation and psychotic paralysis, held at bay – and this is the second result – only by a resort to a feverish commitment to activity and control: in *Vendredi* Robinson only escapes the allure of a psychotic collapse or neurotic regression by committing himself to an activity of administration and reglamentation that becomes a bizarre travesty of the rituals of colonialism.[37] Now, it seems to me that in many ways Hardy's commitment to the severe structural control that he has admitted to in the composition of *Jude* is akin to that same pathological resort to *administration* and *control* in the face of the panic induced by the collapse of the social and psychic scaffolding of the phantasmatic and symbolic orders. Moreover, once again the structure of the text indicates something of the nature of the world it is describing: power in *Jude* seems to stem less from some central disciplinary power than from local administrative controls and pressures: snooping landladies and unsympathetic landlords, school boards, the gossip of neighbours, landlords, train timetables, marriage licences, college rules, Artizans' Mutual Improvement Societies. Perhaps this is why Jude, in his forlorn speech at Christminster, cannot 'discover' what is wrong with the social formulas (p. 399): we have moved from a society of central and assignable disciplines to a society of ubiquitous and anonymous control.[38]

It is time, now, to consider more closely just what are the consequences of the failures of *translation* and *metabolization* that follow upon the collapse of the phantasmatic and symbolic structure of Hardy's narrative world. We have already talked at length of the unassimilated and undigested materials of the text and the many failures of translation that leave quotations, epigraphs, Greek and Latin phrases, guide-book material, dumped syllabuses, various allusions and *sententiae* – such as Jude's inopportune remarks in the death scene – raw and unappropriated, designified signifiers. What in fact is being held in abeyance by this wholesale incapacity to assimilate is not just a cerebral learning – quite the contrary: Jude and Sue 'learn' a lot – but *the psychic and initiatory inscriptions and differentiations that produce us as human beings – those that produce our sexuality, our gender, our vital state.*[39] It is this that constitutes Jude and Sue's tragedy: from beginning to end they remain unsexed, ungendered, unalive. It is this that requires that when Jude first comes across sexuality it comes in the 'untreated', 'naked', purely animal form of a pig's pizzle – i.e. in the form of a repulsive 'real', unsublimated by phantasmatic translation. It is this that accounts for the impossibility of Jude and Sue's relationship: as a couple they are paralysed by being non-differentiated, not sufficiently gendered, not sufficiently separated, while Sue's epicene androgynity hardly reaches to the condition, even, of a pre-sexual sexuality. Perhaps this suggests a deeper reason for the anxiety prompted by the sight of the marriage registration form:

'Names and surnames of the parties' – (they were to be parties now, not lovers, she thought). 'Condition' – (a horrid idea) – 'Rank or Occupation' – 'Age' – 'Dwelling at' – 'Length of Residence' – 'Church or Builing in which the Marriage is to be solemnized' 'District and County in which the Parties respectively dwell'.

(p. 348)

These are merely the formal equivalents of the positionalities relative to sexuality, gender and vital state supplied by phantasmatic initiation and the refusal to encounter it explains why the two are unalive from the start and seem drawn, vampire-like, to a mortuarial world of tombstones, graveyards, churches, carved and painted inscriptions, hymns and effigies.

It is here, perhaps, that we should contrast Jude and Sue's impasse with Arabella's redoubtable capacity for survival for if there is any figure in the text that demonstrates an astonishing gift for *self-translation* it is surely her. From her early dimple-making and hair-extensions to her opportunistic seduction of Physician Vilbert what Arabella Donn-Fawley-Donn-Bartlett-Donn-Fawley-Vilbert clearly rejoices in is a remarkable capacity for adapting herself to a variety of roles. She rings the changes on her marital state as easily as she mixes cocktails – her canny conducting of Jude 'through the varieties of spirituous delect-ation' (p. 453) shows all the skills of an initiate and there is a trace here of a too-late (for Jude) traversal of the phantasm we have already seen reduced to a wine-list. There can be no question but that, as Bayley has observed, Arabella makes Jude a far better sexual partner than does Sue. Nor is it an indication of shallowness that Arabella can so easily swap gin for grace in her brief flirtation with non-conformism after the death of Bartlett for there is in Arabella a residual sense of the ritual quality of life's important events. Even the pig-killing, for Arabella, again as Bayley has observed, has a ritual quality about it – the day of abstinence, the boiling of the water, the concern that the right knife be chosen, the care that the cut should not be too deep – none of which Jude has a clue about in his stark confrontation of the brute fact of killing.[40] Arabella, moreover, seems able to cope far better than Jude or Sue with the transition from a traditional rural world with its lore and customary ways to a modern world of commerce and sharp practice.

Baudrillard's 'symbolic exchange' is not the same as Lacan's 'symbolic order' and he differentiates it from the notion of the 'phantasm' (which he sees as a merely subjective, psychological compensation for the loss of the symbolic) but he is talking about the same thing as the collapse of the symbolic and of the phantasmatic (in the Laplanche and Pontalis sense of the term[41]) structure when he claims that what is not subjected to symbolic exchange returns to invest the real. For Baudrillard the primary exclusion has been that of 'the dead and of death'[42] and this 'extradition' of death as a symbolic event simply means that death is now everywhere:

> Pursued and censured everywhere, death springs up everywhere again.[43]

Foreclosed in the social death returns in hallucinatory form in the real. For Deleuze and Guattari this universalization of death stems from that very decoding of codes – the Deleuze and Guattarian equivalent of Baudrillard's 'extradition from the symbolic' – with which we began this account of *Jude*:

> At the same time as death is decoded, it loses its relationship with a model and an experience, and becomes an instinct.... There where the codes are undone, the death instinct takes hold of the repressive apparatus and begins to direct the circulation of the libido. One might then believe in liberated desires, but ones that, like cadavers, feed on images. Death is not desired, but what is desired is dead, already dead: images. Everything labours in death, everything wishes for death.[44]

Deleuze goes on to remark that the only modern myth is that of *zombies*: Jude and Sue are zombies – they take further the fate that we have seen befalling Angel and Tess towards the end of *Tess of the d'Urbervilles*. Deprived of the experience and model of death that the phantasm – like any initiatory event – affords they are left pursuing images and images which are dead. The Christminster they tread is itself more like an underworld of the dead than a City of Light or a Heavenly Jerusalem, a necropolis. Baudrillard's

> The cemetery no longer exists because modern cities have entirely taken over their function: they are ghost towns, cities of death.[45]

might have had Jude's early encounter with Christminster in mind.

If anyone in the text expresses this threat of a universal death instinct it is, of course, Little Father Time:

> 'The doctor says there are such boys springing up amongst us – boys of a sort unknown in the last generation – the outcome of new views

of life. They seem to see all its terrors before they have the staying power to resist them. He says it is the beginning of the coming universal wish not to live.'

(p. 411)

Little Father Time erupts into the text like an avenging angel and an inapellable fate. His 'mechanical creep' and devastating literalness (p. 344) give him the automaton characteristics of a zombie – there is much about him that reminds us of a miniature Frankenstein Monster. But Little Father Time is much more than the simple hallucinatory return of a death that has been extradited from the symbolic, for Little Father Time is the return of *all* that the phantasmatic collapse of the text has failed to accommodate or to translate. Little Father Time's exclusion from the phantasmatic and symbolic orders[46] has begun with his not being baptised (the non-baptism like the aborted marriage ceremony for Jude and Sue signalling a failure of phantasmatic/symbolic registration) and we have already commented on his indigestibility. As a figure Little Father Time is, indeed, onerously overloaded. Hardy introduces him to us with almost unseemly clumsiness (a clumsiness that we have seen to characterize the work as a whole) as the 'key' to the text (p. 342) – thus patly assuming that role of the *cipher* sought from the beginning – and, at his death we are told movingly:

The boy's face expressed the whole tale of their situation. On that little shape had converged all the inauspiciousness and shadow which had darkened the first union of Jude, and all the accidents, mistakes, fears, errors of the last. He was their nodal point, their focus, their expression in a single term. For the rashness of those parents he had groaned, for their ill-assortment he had quaked, and for the misfortunes of these he had died.

(p. 411)

To the extent that Little Father Time here expresses the whole of their tale – 'His face is like the tragic mask of Melpomene.' (p. 347) – he is the return of that expressive *Autrui* we have seen to be singularly lacking from the world of Jude and Sue – indeed, in many ways, Little Father Time is not just the return of an absent *Autrui* but, we sense too, that he is in part the return of the absent *Author*. Tragic though its consequences are it is Little Father Time who finally assumes some kind of responsibility for the world in which he finds himself. Indeed, compared to the sheer stupid bloody-mindedness of Jude wanting to watch the parades and the flustered, half-baked truths of Sue on the facts of life, Little Father Time's taking upon himself the responsibility for himself and his brother and sister is little short of heroic. More than that, in a curious way Little Father Time in many ways supplies the text with the very masculinity and femininity that Jude and Sue so clearly lack. Little Father Time is – as many who have read the text must have thought (even if they haven't said it out loud) – a 'little prick':

> ... an enslaved and dwarfed Divinity
>
> (pp. 342–3)

and as much a disturbing eruption into the text as the pig's pizzle – the hallucinatory return of the unaccommodated real. His distraught weeping at the news of a new baby, on the other hand, in its agitation and depth of concern is movingly maternal. Indeed, to the extent that Little Father Time may be said to represent *all* – here the masculine and the feminine, as well as everything else – that is excluded by the failure of the phantasmatic and symbolic orders he offers us an almost wickedly appropriate image of the Lacanian *lamella* which Lacan invites us to consider, with the introduction of a jokey neologism which seems designed for Little Father Time, as a sort of *'hommelette'*.[47] For Lacan the *lamella* is all that mess of heterogeneity prior to the processing by the symbolic order that is the very condition of our humanity and so can represent here all that has been excluded by the collapse and the failure of the phantasm.

Little Father Time is not just the return of unaccommodated drives: he is also the return of all the undigested *meanings* of the text – the return of all the *de-signified* and *enigmatic signifiers* that bestrew the narrative – not least, perhaps, that admonishing pointing finger.[48] He is the return too of the Biblical wrath and the Classical fate encoded, like traces of Alien DNA,[49] in the early fragments of Gothic and Greek script. In Little Father Time – his very name itself a de-signified signifier, it is *not* his name – we have encapsulated that very cultural heritage bowdlerized by the Christminster quotes – a heritage that, abused, like Chronos, will wreak vengeance on its children. Little Father Time in *Jude* functions like the paternal metaphor – Oedipus – and hence as the voice of Symbolic Order. It is this that accounts for his startling authority, his peremptoriness, his absoluteness, for what the return of these unaccommodated and untranslated and enigmatic signfiers is is the emergence of the *super-ego* and the *categorical imperative*.[50] Little Father Time is the unknown persecutor that Sue so dreadfully fears at the end:

'There is something external to us which says, "You shan't!" First it said, "You shan't learn!" Then it said, "You shan't labour!" Now it says, "You shan't love!"'

(p. 412)

The awful finality of this prohibitive voice comes, of course, from its very unconsciousness, from its raw and untranslated exclusion from the phantasmatic and symbolic orders. The dreadful hanging of the two younger children and the suicide of Little Father Time himself are like the *obscene obverse* of the originary phantasm – the Bockhampton hanging – the *real* that the phantasmatic structure is designed first to translate and then to occlude.

What makes the whole thing even more tragic and pathetic is that Hardy shows that the original trauma need not have remained quite so encysted and unresolved – might otherwise have been digested – metabolized and translated. He does this through the aged widow Mrs Edlin who brings to the text memories of earlier and more serene regimes:

He hardly expected she would come; but she did, bringing singular presents, in the form of apples, jam, brass snuffers, an ancient pewter dish, a warming pan, an enormous bag of goose-feathers towards a bed. She was allotted the spare room in Jude's house, whither she retired early, and where they could hear her through the ceiling below, honestly saying the Lord's Prayer in a loud voice, as the Rubric directed.

(p. 349)

If there is a voice of sanity in the text it is surely hers:[51] it is she who poo-poos Jude and Sue's excessive squeamishness about getting married –

Nobody thought o' being afeard o' matrimony in my time, nor of much else but a cannon-ball or empty cupboard.

(p. 395)

and, again, it is she that bluntly tells Phillotson that his remarriage to Sue is wrong:

The truth's the truth.

(p. 344)

Here, in her arrival to be a witness to Jude and Sue's wedding, she comes bearing the fruits and the *regalia* (how distant are these 'brass snuffers', 'pewter dish' and 'warming pan' from the sundry *impedimenta* that clutter up the world of *Jude*!) of a distant territorial formation (we are reminded here of the festive peasant world of *The Return of the Native*) while, with her Lord's Prayer uttered scrupulously in conformity with the Rubric, she shows her deference to a despotic order with its procedures and over-codings. But what is more important is that Mrs Edlin almost casually *traverses the originary phantasm* and shows how so easily it might have been exorcized and demystified. Again Mrs Edlin gives voice to a past – the story associated with the Brown House, the site of the originary phantasm.

It is a story that has been buried or, at least, consigned to half-truth and innuendo by Aunt Drusilla and so become encysted as an enigmatic signifier – as something not understood, not digested and therefore malignant and festering:

> 'Your father and mother couldn't get on together, and they parted. It was coming home from Alfredston market, when you were a baby – on the hill by the Brown House barn – when they had their last difference, and took leave from one another for the last time. Your mother soon afterwards died – she drowned herself, in short, and your mother went away with you to South Wessex, and never came here any more . . . '
>
> 'Where did father and mother part – by the Brown House did you say?'
>
> . . . 'A little further on – where the road to Fenworth branches off, and the handpost stands. A gibbet once stood there not onconnected with our story. But let that be.'
>
> (p. 116)

Earlier we have associated the Brown House with the originary phantasm but here we see that that, too, might have been a mask for *another* even more primary *primal* scene – the sight of the parents quarrelling and separating so typical of phantasms and fantasies of the *primal scene*. And that this is again a *phantasm* rather than an ultimately *real* event is suggested by that origin again being pushed even further back: 'A gibbet once stood there not onconnected with our history. But let that be.' The story remains half-finished, incomplete, repressed ready to become an unconscious *enigmatic signifier*: Aunt Drusilla's unconscious passes on into the unconscious of Jude – and of Sue, for she had earlier been responsible for her too – with all the fatal persistence and immortality of a germ plasm, for this is where much of their dread of sexuality and marriage comes from.

It is this story that Mrs Edlin retells and *retranslates*:

'But things happened to thwart 'em, and if everything wasn't vitty
they were upset. No doubt that's how he that the tale is told of came
to do what 'a did – if he *were* one of your family.'

'What was that?' said Jude.

'Well – that tale, ye know; he that was gibbeted just on the brow of
the hill by the Brown House-not far from the milestone between
Marygreen and Adfredston, where the other road branches off. But
Lord, 'twas in my grandfather's time; and it medn' have been one of
your folk at all.'

'I know where the gibbet is said to have stood, very well,'
murmured Jude. 'But I never heard of this. What – did this man –
my ancestor and Sue's – kill his wife?'

'Twer not that exactly. She ran away from him, with their child, to
her friends; and while she was there the child died. He wanted the
body, to bury it where his people lay, but she wouldn't give it up. Her
husband then came in the night with a cart, and broke into the house
to steal the coffin away; but he was catched, and beings obstinate,
wouldn't tell what he broke in for. They brought it in burglary, and
that's why he was hanged and gibbeted on Brown House Hill. His wife
went mad after he was dead. But it medn' be true that he belonged to
ye more than to me.'

(pp. 349–50)

Like the various versions of the originary phantasm that we have looked
at this story is the 'same' and 'not the same' as Aunt Drusilla's which we
can now see was already a repetition of a much older story going back at
least to the time of Mrs Edlin's grandfather – back and back we go until it
is clear that *these are not real histories but folk myths*: 'O, it is only a tale,'
said Sue cheeringly' – and, for once, briefly, correctly. It might not even
be their own family: it might be Mrs Edlin's but she, clearly, is losing no
sleep over it, for by her telling she has exorcised its exclusively private
and guilt-inducing secrecy – returned it to the public domain – and at
one and the same time *de-translated and re-translated* it.

Sue and Jude, of course, have to insist on reclaiming the tale for
themselves: rather than accepting Mrs Edlin's retranslation of the familial
myth into an anodyne folk-tale they have to insist on their own translation of it into the awful language of classical (the house of Atreus) and Old
Testament (the house of Jeroboam (p. 350)) doom. Here, moreover, it is
significant that Mrs Edlin's easy and matter-of-fact demystification of the

originary phantasm is at once cancelled by Little Father Time – he whose
very existence as an *enigmatic signifier* depends on Mrs Edlin's account
never being brought to light – restoring to it its prohibitive effects:

'If I was you, mother, I wouldn't marry father!'

(p. 350)

The blight that Mrs Edlin's 'exhilarating tradition' (p. 350) might have
lifted just tightens its hold and leads to the tragic *denouement*.

The ending of *Jude* is terrible: nothing can palliate the horror of Sue's
final surrender – it's a violation worse than rape and it's like one of those
moments, like Gloucester's blinding, that you feel just shouldn't be
allowed on stage. Nevertheless, what has prepared Sue for this ultimate
self-immolation is an earlier capitulation which takes place on the floor
of St. Silas':

> High overhead, above the chancel steps, Jude could discern a huge,
> solidly constructed Latin cross – as large, probably, as the original it
> was designed to commemorate. It seemed to be suspended in the air
> by invisible wires; it was set with large jewels, which faintly glim-
> mered in some weak ray caught from outside, as the cross swayed to
> and fro in a silent and scarcely perceptible motion. Underneath,
> upon the floor, lay what appeared to be a heap of black clothes, and
> from this was repeated the sobbing that he had heard before. It was
> Sue's form, prostrate on the paving.

(p. 425)

Here, again, scrambled but in some ways distilled to its erotic essence, is
the Bockhampton phantasm. Again there is the gibbet – now the heavy
swaying cross, the swaying metonymically displaced from the hanging
body; here again is the same radiant jewelled atmosphere, the slanting
highlights; and on the floor the abject pitiable woman, sobbing in her
damp, black clothes. It is a complex and compelling compendium of
fetishization, homoerotic longing, narcissism, sadism, masochistic identification and transvestism. It is a dangerously revelatory image of the
dark but seductive fascination that lies at the heart of Hardy's fiction.

The scene of Jude's death is equally revelatory:

> The window was still open to ventilate the room, and it being about
> noontide the clear air was motionless and quiet without. From a
> distance came voices; and an apparent noise of persons stamping.

'What's that?' murmured the old woman.

'Oh – that's the doctors in the Theatre, conferring Honorary degrees on the Duke of Hamptonshire and a lot more illustrious gents of that sort. It's Remembrance Week, you know. The cheers come from the young men.'

'Ay; young and strong-lunged! Not like our poor boy here.'

An occasional word, as from some one making a speech, floated from the open windows of the Theatre across to this quiet corner, at which there seemed to be a smile of some sort upon the marble features of Jude; while the old, superseded, Delphin editions of Virgil and Horace, and the dog-eared Greek Testament on the neighbouring shelf, and the few other volumes of the sort that he had not parted with, roughened with stone-dust where he had been in the habit of catching them up for a few minutes between his labours, seemed to pale to a sickly cast at the sounds. The bells struck out joyously; and their reverberations travelled around the bedroom.

(p. 490)

Here, too, is the phantasm: at its focal point the 'marble features of Jude' recalling the haunting image of the first hanging Hardy saw:

A penetrating rain was falling; the white cap was no sooner over the woman's head than it clung to her features, and the noose was put around the neck of what looked like a marble statue.[52]

Again there are the bells striking at the close of the passage and again we have all the majesty of a public ritual – but this time the perspective from which the phantasm is viewed, the position within which the point of view of the phantasm is located, has changed. Here we are with the dead man indifferent to the 'huzzahs!' of the crowd and the triumph of the 'illustrious gents'. Again we recall Foucault:

In the darkest region of the political field the condemned man represents the symmetrical, inverted figure of the king.[53]

Here the phantasmatic structure has shed all its radiance: no longer the 'topaz' points of the Heavenly Jerusalem but, instead, the 'old, superseded Delphin editions of Virgil and Horace, and the dog-eared Greek Testament', 'roughened with stone-dust'. The tomes for all the regal association that the 'Delphin' might bestow, have become tombs. It is the phantasm seen from the other side and the phantasm bereft of all investment – like the shells of those from whom the spirit of The Well-Beloved has fled. Jude lies a corpse in the sarcophagus of the dephantasmatized text.

Notes

Note on references to French and English material.

On the whole I have used available English translations from the French but, in a number of cases, I have felt more comfortable and more confident working from the original texts. In such cases I have quoted the French original first but in all cases I have added a reference to the corresponding passages in the available English translations in square brackets afterwards.

1 Introduction

1 Deleuze, G. and Guattari, F. *Anti-Oedipus* (London, Athlone Press, 1984), pp. 132–3
2 Deleuze, G. (with Claire Parnet) *Dialogues* (Paris, Flammarion, 1977), p. 51 [*Dialogues* trans. Hugh Tomlinson and Barbara Habberjam, London, Athlone Press, 1987 pp. 39–40].
3 There are one or two exceptions such as the essays by Jacques Lecercle on *Tess of the d'Urbervilles* and John Hughes on *Jude the Obscure* to which I refer below pp. 80 and 147–8.
4 Deleuze, G. and Guattari, F. *A Thousand Plateaux* (London, Athlone Press, 1987).
5 *Anti-Oedipus* p. 33: 'The prime function incumbent upon the socius [i.e. the social formation (D.M.)] has always been to codify the flows of desire, to inscribe them, to record them, to see that no flow exists that is not properly dammed up, channeled, regulated. When the primitive *territorial machine* proved inadequate to the task, the *despotic machine* set up a kind of over-coding system. But the *capitalist machine*, insofar as it was built on the ruins of a despotic State more or less removed in time, finds itself in a totally new situation: it is faced with the task of decoding and deterritorializing the flows.'
6 *Anti-Oedipus* pp. 141 and 222.
7 For a summary see ibid. p. 261.
8 *Anti-Oedipus* p. 337.
9 The commitment to milk production and the seasonal monitoring of the river-beds give the regime at Talbothays many of the characteristics of Karl Wittfogel's 'hydraulic' societies (see his *Oriental Despotism* New Haven, Connecticut, Yale University Press, 1957) that offers Deleuze and Guattari one of their principal sources for their model of a despotic formation. See *Anti-Oedipus* pp. 211 and 220 and *A Thousand Plateaux* p. 363.
10 This is a slight revision of the usual translation which reads: *It is at work everywhere* . . . The original French is *Ça fonctionne partout*. . . . (*L'Anti-Oedipe*

(Paris, Editions de minuit, 1972, p. 7). *Ça* can mean 'it is' but here Deleuze and Guattari have more in mind a plurality of forces, of flows, better expressed by *ça et là*, 'here and there' which is better conveyed by the plural.

11 *Anti-Oedipus* pp. 1 & 5.

12 *Anti-Oedipus*, p. 46.

13 ibid. p. 26.

14 ibid. p. 109.

15 ibid. p. 54.

16 ibid. p. 55.

17 ibid. p. 188.

18 ibid. p. 295.

19 ibid. p. 267.

20 ibid. pp. 60, 73, 110.

21 ibid. p. 73.

22 ibid. p. 357.

23 Ronald Bogue, for example, refers to the *body without organs* or *BwO* (this is the standard abbreviation) as Deleuze and Guattari's 'most elusive concept' (*Deleuze and Guattari* London, Routledge and Kegan Paul, 1989) p. 92. André Colombat, in his *Deleuze et la littérature* (Berne, Peter Lang, 1991) p. 189 confesses that the notion of the *BwO* 'nous est encore obscure' while Philip Goodchild, after attempting to explain the notion, has to admit that 'None of this seems immediately clear'. (*Deleuze and Guattari* London, Sage, 1996) p. 77.

24 *Antonin Artaud: Four Texts* Translated by Clayton Eshleman and Norman Glass (Los Angeles, Panjandrum Books, 1982) p. 79. See also *Logique du sens* (Paris, Éditions de Minuit, 1969) p. 108 [*Logic of Sense* trans. Mark Lester with Charles Stivale; ed. by Constantin V. Boundas, London: Athlone Press, 1989, p. 88] and *Anti-Oedipus* pp. 8–9.

25 See 'How do you make yourself a body without organs' in *A Thousand Plateaux* pp. 151–5.

26 Gregory Bateson *Steps to an Ecology of Mind* (New York, Ballantine Books, 1972) p. 113. *A Thousand Plateaux* p. 158. I am not sure that we have to go that far to find such *plateaux*: one has only to think of 'The Cold War'.

27 Deleuze *Spinoza: Practical Philosophy* trans. Robert Hurley (San Francisco, City Lights Books, 1988. See also *A Spinoza Reader. The* Ethics *and Other Works* Edited and translated by Edwin Curley (Princeton, N.J., Princeton U. P., 1994) pp. 152ff.

28 *Anti-Oedipus* p. 41. See also Brian Massumi *A User's Guide to Capitalism and Schizophrenia* (Cambridge, Mass., M.I.T., 1992) p. 68. Perhaps Deleuze and Guattari should have considered the child's first *stool*: it obviously gives the little chap enormous pleasure and as an avatar of the *body without organs* probably accounts for Coleridge speaking of 'defecating into pure transparency'.

29 See G. Deleuze *Dialogues* p. 96 [p. 78].

30 It has been put to me that it is likely that Hardy himself suffered a 'botched' or difficult afterbirth. See the *Life* p. 14: 'Had it not been for the common sense of the estimable woman who attended as monthly nurse, he might never have walked the earth. At his birth he was thrown aside as dead till

rescued by her as she exclaimed to the surgeon: "Dead! Stop a minute: he's alive enough, sure!"'

31 This has necessarily been a brief discussion of the *body without organs* though I hope it has offered some clarity. I will return to the notion in discussing *The Return of the Native* where I shall posit the Heath as a classic example of a *body without organs*, as the precarious frontier between the *molecular* and the *molar*. One more thing: as the frontier or interface between *need* and *desire* the *body without organs* has a clear affinity with the notion of the *phantasme* which I discuss below pp. 13–19.

32 ibid. p. 9.

33 ibid. p. 11.

34 ibid. p. 17.

35 ibid. p. 21.

36 See my *Partings Welded Together* London, Methuen & Co., 1987, pp. 85–9.

37 ibid. p. 141.

38 ibid. p. 148.

39 ibid. p. 148. For an example of such a nomadic figure consider the Reddleman in *The Return of the Native*. See below pp. 28–9.

40 *Partings Welded Together*, pp. 144–5. See my account below of the hair-cutting scene in *The Return of the Native* p. 30.

41 *Partings Welded Together*, p. 142.

42 ibid. p. 153.

43 Whence the suspicion in which are held intruders and reformers such as Wildeve and Clym in *The Return of the Native*. See below p. 33.

44 *Partings Welded Together*, p. 194

45 ibid. p. 140

46 ibid. p. 257

47 J. Laplanche and J.-B. Pontalis 'Fantasme originaire, fantasmes des origines, origine du fantasme' *Les temps modernes* vl. 19, jan–juin 1964. p. 1854 fn. 44 [p. 10 fn. 22]. English translation: 'Fantasy and the origins of sexuality', *The International Journal of Psychoanalysis* vol. 49, 1968. This translation was republished in *Formations of Fantasy* ed. Victor Burgin, James Donald and Kora Kaplin (London, Methuen, 1986). A revised edition (principally involving formatting) of the original essay was published by Hachette in 1985 and reprinted in the series 'Pluriel' in 1999. Throughout the following I have referred to the *Les temps modernes* version as it is the one that most closely correlates with the available translation and the translations are my own. References to the corresponding passages in the available English translation are added in square brackets.

48 ibid. pp. 1854–5 fn. 45 [trans. p. 11 fn 22].

49 See the quote above – 'If we ask ourselves what these phantasms of origins mean to us . . .'

50 See below pp. 99–101.

51 See especially his *New Foundations in Psychoanalysis* trans. David Macey (Oxford, Basil Blackwell, 1989), *Essays on Otherness* trans. John Fletcher (London, Routledge and Kegan Paul, 1999) and the essays collected in *Jean Laplanche: Seduction, Translation, Drives* ed. John Fletcher and Martin Stanton (London, Institute of Contemporary Arts, 1992).

52   On this last see especially his *Four Fundamental Concepts of Psychoanalysis* (London, Penguin, 1979) p. 273 and Slavoj Zizek *The Plague of Fantasies* (London, Verso, 1997) p. 33 and *The Ticklish Subject* (London, Verso, 1999) pp. 374–5.
53   Zizek in *The Plague of Fantasies* (p. 7) likens its function to that of the mythical Cartesian *pineal gland* that is supposed to link the body to the mind.
54   S. Freud 'Beyond The Pleasure Principle' in *Penguin Freud Library*, vol. XI *On Metapsychology* Penguin, 1984, pp. 283ff.
55   See *Seduction, Translation, Drives* p. 15
56   See Deleuze *Différence et Répétition* (Paris, Presses Universitaires de France, 1968) pp. 138–9 [*Difference and* Repetition trans. Paul Patton, London, Athlones Press, 1994, p. 105] and Laplanche *New Foundations in Psychoanalysis* p. 110. The Oedipal phantasm, for example, clearly has resonances with the primal scene and the phantasm of seduction. This expressive resonance of one phantasm with another affords us an indispensable key to an understanding of Leibniz's *Monadology*. See below my discussion of the *Monadology* and what I call a 'Leibnizian phenomenology' in the chapter on Tess and the phantasm.
57   See Pierre Klossowski *Nietzsche and the Vicious Circle* trans. Daniel W. Smith (London, Athlone Press, 1997) Ch. 3: 'The Experience of the eternal Return'. These quotations are from pp. 57–8.
58   'Fantasme originaire...' p. 1866 ['Fantasy...' p. 16].
59   For the two kinds of repetition see *Différence et Répétition* p. 32 [p. 20] and J. Hillis Miller *Fiction and Repetition* (Oxford, Basil Blackwell, 1982) Ch. I.
60   See Robert Gittings *Young Thomas Hardy* (London, Penguin, 1978) pp. 58–9.
61   Westport, Connecticut, Geenwood Press, 1963. Reprinted California, University of California Press, 1978.
62   See especially *Dialogues* p. 59 [p. 47]: 'One can never stress enough the damage that the phantasm has done to literature...'
63   First published in *Critique* No. 282 (1970) and published in English in *Language, Counter-memory, Practice* trans. Donald F. Bouchard and Sherry Simon; ed. Donald F. Bouchard (New York, Cornell University Press, 1977) pp. 165–96.
64   op. cit. p. 165.
65   op. cit. p. 180. For some reason the original has left out the question mark.
66   *A Thousand Plateaux* p. 154; *Mille plateaux* p. 188.
67   Foucault op. cit. p. 170. I think it is one of the catastrophic confusions of Deleuze and Guattari's work that they regard the notion of *fantasy* as a direct threat to the *body without organs*. This is because they (that is Deleuze *and* Guattari together – the Deleuze of *Logique du sens* and *Différence et Répétition* seems to me not only to have a perfectly adequate understanding of the notion of the *phantasme* but to be particularly committed to it) have a very inadequate understanding of the structure and function of what I have termed the *phantasme* (as opposed to *fantasy*). What Deleuze and Guattari fail to see is that the *body without organs* is the very site where the *phantasme* takes place. (See below p. 126.)
68   *Dialogues* p. 84.
69   See above p. 16.
70   *Dialogues* pp. 85–6.
71   See pp. 133–4; pp. 178–80.

72 A series clearly indebted to Melanie Klein. See especially her essay 'Notes on some schizoid mechanisms' in *The Selected Melanie Klein* ed. Juliet Mitchell (London, Penguin Books, 1986) pp. 176–200.
73 I have already explored the relationship between the *phantasm* and the *nation* elsewhere. See my 'Phantasm and Nation: Sarmiento's *Facundo*' in *New Comparison* No. 29 Spring 2000 pp. 5–26.
74 See below p. 178.

2 The Interrupted Return

1 Thomas Hardy *The Return of the Native* ed. George Woodcock (London, Penguin Books, 1978) pp. 53–4. All references to the text are to this edition.
2 Spinoza *The Ethics and Other Works* Ed. and trans. Edwin Curley (New Jersey, Princeton, 1994) pp. 57 & 198.
3 Martin Heidegger 'The Origin of the Work of Art' in *Poetry, Language, Thought* trans. and intro. by Albert Hofstadter (New York, Harper and Row, 1971) p. 46 & 49:

> Earth is that which comes forth and shelters. Earth, self-dependent, is effortless and untiring. Upon the earth and in it, historical man grounds his dwelling in the world, in setting up a world, the work sets forth the earth.... The setting up of a world and the setting forth of earth are two essential features in the work-being of the work.

4 For the notion that 'lying in wait' (*être aux écoutes*) is a necessary feature of the *originary phantasm* of the primal scene see Laplanche and Pontalis 'Fantasme originaire...' p. 1853 [p. 10].
5 For the notion of the *originary phantasm* see above Introduction pp. 13–19 and below pp. 108–11.
6 From D. H. Lawrence *Study of Thomas Hardy* Ed. Bruce Steele (London, Grafton Books, 1986) p. 21.
7 Deleuze, G. and Guattari, F. *Anti-Oedipus* (London, Athlone Press, 1984) pp. 141–2.
8 I sometimes like to think that what we have here is an anticipation of the celebrated 'magical realism' associated with writers such as Alejo Carpentier and García Márquez. Compare the passages quoted here with the following from Carpentier's inaugural 'magical realist' text *The Kingdom of the World* trans. Harriet de Onís (London, André Deutsch, 1990):

> To his surprise he discovered the secret life of strange species given to disguise, confusion and camouflage, protectors of the little armoured beings that avoid the pathways of the ants. His hand gathered anonymous seeds, sulphury capers, diminutive hot peppers; vines that wove nets among the stones; solitary bushes with furry leaves that sweated at night; sensitive plants that closed at the mere sound of the human voice; pods that burst at midday with the pop of a flea cracked under the nail; creepers that plaited themselves in slimy tangles from the sun.
>
> (p. 14)

9   See Otis B. Wheeler 'Four *Returns of the Native*' in *Nineteenth Century Fiction*
     (June, 1959) p. 34.
10   See the Introduction pp. 4, 7.
11   See above Introduction p. 10.
12   From the notes to the Penguin edition by George Woodcock p. 488.
13   See *Anti-Oedipus* p. 153:

> The primitive machine is not ignorant of exchange, commerce, and
> industry; it exorcises them, localizes them, cordons them off, encastes
> them, and maintains the merchant and the blacksmith in a subordinate
> position, so that the flows of exchange and the flows of production do
> not manage to break the codes in favor of their abstract or fictional
> quantities.

and above p. 11.
14   See Intoduction above pp. 12–13.
15   Compare this juxtapositioning with the juxtapositioning of the dicing scene
     note above p.32.
16   The writer may state here that the original conception of the story did not
     design a marriage between Thomasin and Venn. He was to have retained his
     isolated and weird character to the last, and to have disappeared mysteri-
     ously from the heath, nobody knowing whither – Thomasin remaining a
     widow. But certain circumstances of serial publication led to a change of
     intent.
       Readers can therefore choose between the endings, and those with an
     austere artistic code can assume the more consistent conclusion to be the
     true one. (p. 464 note)

17   Cf. *Anti-Oedipus* p. 281:

> The body without organs is like the cosmic egg, the *giant molecule*
> swarming with worms, bacilli, Lilliputian figures, animalcules, and hom-
> unculi, with their organization and their machines, minute strings, ropes,
> teeth, fingernails, levers and pulleys, catapults.... The two sides of the
> body without organs are, therefore, the side on which the mass phenom-
> enon and the paranoiac investment corresponding to it are organized on a
> microscopic scale, and on the other side on which, on a submicroscopic
> scale, the molecular phenomena and their schizophrenic investment are
> arranged. It is on the body without organs, as a pivot, as a frontier between
> the molar and the molecular, that the paranoiac-schizophrenia division is
> made.

18   *The Making of 'The Return of the Native'* (Westport, Connecticut, Greenwood
     Press, 1963. Reprinted California, University of California Press, 1978).
19   op.cit. pp. 4–6.
20   ibid. p. 17.
21   ibid. p. 17.
22   ibid. p. 29.
23   ibid. 29.

24 ibid. p. 30.
25 ibid. p. 67.
26 ibid. p. 69 note.
27 The notorious allusion to Oedipus in the text – 'his mouth had passed into the phase more or less imaginatively rendered in studies of Oedipus' (p. 388) – in fact did not appear until the Uniform Edition of 1895. Even then, of course, any link with Freud's 'Oedipus' would have had to be purely tele-pathic given that Freud himself did not come across the 'Oedipus complex' himself until 1896.
28 Paterson, op. cit. p. 75.
29 ibid. p. 131.
30 Michael Millgate *Thomas Hardy: a Biography* (Oxford, Oxford University Press, 1982) p. 186.
31 ibid. p. 200.
32 ibid. See also Robert Gittings *The Older Hardy* (Harmondsworth, Middlesex, Penguin Books, 1980) p. 25.
33 Millgate op.cit., p. 201.
34 Paterson op. cit. p. 59.
35 ibid. p. 49.
36 ibid. p. 49.
37 And so the prototypical *body without organs*. See above the Introduction p. 7.
38 Compare our association of the donning of gear with the *body without organs* in the Introduction p. 6.
39 See *A Thousand Plateaux* p. 279.
40 Deleuze and Guattari – Deleuze especially – again and again, associate Hardy with this obsession with a *line of flight*: see the two passages with which I prefaced my Introduction above p. 1.
41 R. D. Laing *The Politics of Experience* (London, Penguin Books, 1967) p.104. Cf *Anti-Oedipus* pp. 130ff.
42 ibid. p. 136.
43 *Anti-Oedipus* p. 130.
44 Laing op. cit. p. 102.
45 See *Anti-Oedipus* p. 162:

> Incest as it is prohibited (the form of discernible persons [i.e. son, mother DM]) is employed to repress incest as it is desired (the substance of the intense earth). The intensive germinal flow is the representative of desire; it is against this flow that the repression is directed. The extensive Oedipal figure is its displaced represented (*le représenté déplacé*), the lure or fake image, born of repression that comes to conceal desire.

See also pp. 172–3.
46 *Anti-Oedipus* p. 283
47 I didn't mention it at the time but I think it is significant that the song Clym sings on the Heath at his moment of climactic happiness is not only a *poem* but also in *French*: for a moment Hardy escapes from the constraints of *prose* and from his *mother* tongue. See Deleuze's discussion of Louis Wolfson's

'Le Schizo et les langues ou la phonétique chez le psychotique' (*Les temps modernes* no. 218, juillet, 1964) in *Logique du sens* p. 104.

3   The exploding body of *The Mayor of Casterbridge*

1   Martin Seymour Smith *Hardy* (London, Bloomsbury, 1994) p. 323.
2   Robert Gittings *The Older Hardy* (London, Penguin Books, 1980) p. 66.
3   Peter Widdowson *Hardy in History* (London, Routledge and Kegan Paul, 1989) p. 80. See also Marjorie Garson 'The Mayor of Casterbridge: the Bounds of Propriety.' in The Macmillan *New Casebook* on *The Mayor of Casterbridge* ed. Julian Wolfreys (London, Macmillan – now Palgrave Macmillan – 2000) p. 81.
4   See also the sample questions quoted by Widdowson pp. 85–6.
5   This argument for the historical specificity of the text receives massive support, of course, from Hardy's own prefatory note:

> Readers of the following story who have not yet arrived at middle age are asked to bear in mind that, in the days recalled by the tale, the home Corn Trade, on which so much of the action turns, had an importance that can hardly be realized by those accustomed to the sixpenny loaf of the present date, and to the present indifference of the public to harvest weather.
>
> The incidents narrated arise mainly out of three events, which chance to range themselves in order at about the intervals of time given, in the real history of the town called Casterbridge and the neighbouring country. They were the sale of a wife by her husband, the uncertain harvests which immediately preceded the repeal of the Corn Laws, and the visit of a Royal personage to the aforesaid part of England.
>
> (p. 67)

All references to the text are to the Penguin Edition edited by Martin Seymour Smith. (London, 1978).
6   Douglas Brown *The Mayor of Casterbridge* (London, Edward Arnold, 1962) pp. 38–43.
7   Ian Gregor *The Great Web: the Form of Hardy's Major Fiction* (London, Faber and Faber, 1974). J. C. Maxwell 'The "Sociological" Approach to *The Mayor of Casterbridge*.' *Imagined Worlds: Essays on Some English Novels and Novelists in Honour of John Butt*. Eds Maynard Mack and Ian Gregor (London, Methuen and Co., 1968).
8   John Paterson 'The Mayor of Casterbridge as Tragedy' in the Norton Critical Edition of *The Mayor of Casterbridge* Second Edition, ed. Phillip Mallett (New York and London, Norton, 2001) p. 359.
9   Michael Valdéz Moses 'Agon in the Market Place' in the Macmillan *New Casebook* p. 192.
10   ibid.
11   All references are to the Penguin Classics edition edited by Martin Seymour-Smith (London, Penguin Books, 1978).
12   John Goode *Thomas Hardy: the Offensive Truth* Basil Blackwell, Oxford, 1988, p. 79.

13 See Luc de Heusch *The Drunken King or The Origin of the State* Trans. Roy Ellis (Bloomington, Indiana University Press, 1982).
14 Deleuze speaks somewhere of alcohol as being 'the plant within us.'
15 *Anti-Oedipus* p. 196: 'The State [that is the Despot] operates by means of euphemisms.'
16 It is difficult not to think here that the prototype for the fair-haired, smooth-tongued, chillingly ruthless despot that comes from afar and enters into the very heart of the city is Hernando Cortéz, the Conqueror of Mexico.
17 *Anti-Oedipus* pp. 192 and 195. Nietzsche *On the Genealogy of Morals* ed. Walter Kaufman (New York, Vintage Books, 1969) pp. 86–7.
18 *Anti-Oedipus* p. 194.
19 G. Deleuze and F. Guattari *Anti-Oedipus* (London, Athlone Press, 1977) p. 171. See also Nietzsche *The Genealogy of Morals* p. 61.
20 For a discussion of this revised terminology see below the chapter on '*Tess*: a becoming woman'.
21 *Anti-Oedipus* p. 202.
22 G. Deleuze and F. Guattari *A Thousand Plateaux* (London, Athlone Press, 1987) p. 117.
23 *Anti-Oedipus* p. 207: 'Even when it speaks Swiss of American linguistics manipulates the shadow of Oriental despotism.'
24 Finlay, M. I. *The Ancient Greeks* (London, Chatto & Windus, 1963) p. 19; *Anti-Oedipus* p. 208.
25 In a curious way Hardy actually allows us, a little later in the novel, to experience this moment of linguistic expropriation. It comes with Constable Stubberd's reading of the transcription of the statements made by the old furmity woman, Mrs. Goodenough, at the time of her arrest:

> She said, 'Put away that dee lantern,' she says.
> 'Yes.'
> 'Says she, "Dost hear, old turmit head? Put away that dee lantern. I have floored fellows a dee sight finer-looking than a dee fool like thee, you son of a bee dee me if I haint,' she says.
>
> (p. 273–4)

When I first read this I thought the 'dees' and 'bees' were no more than strange, unfamiliar, dialect words and it is only when Henchard badgers Stubberd:

> Come – we don't want to hear any more of them cust dees and bees. Say the words out like a man, and don't be so modest, Stubberd; or else leave it alone!
>
> (p. 274)

that these 'words' became reduced to meaningless phonemes – like the *alpha* and *beta* in the quotation from Finlay above.
26 *A Thousand Plateaux* p. 113.
27 *Anti-Oedipus* p. 202.
28 ibid. p. 201.

29 De Heusch himself records that the roles of 'sister' and 'mother' are frequently simulated. What is important in what he calls this *'inceste sociologique'* is that the prescribed positions or functions are occupied. He also goes on to say that 'the very ambiguity of the symbolism of incest which cumulates in a veritable will to dissimulate renders any interpretation of the facts particularly difficult.' op. cit. p. 89.
30 *Anti-Oedipus* pp. 209–10.
31 Which is certainly not the case, as we shall see below, with the equally frequently alleged 'unconscious homosexual' love between Henchard and Farfrae.
32 Havelock Ellis 'Thomas Hardy's Novels' *Westminster Review,* LXIII, 1883 p. 358.
33 Millgate *Thomas Hardy: His Career as a Novelist* (London, Macmillan, 1994) p. 253.
34 Langbaum R. 'The minimization of sexuality in *The Mayor of Casterbridge'* in the Macmillan *New Casebook* p. 130.
35 ibid. p. 128.
36 ibid. p. 129.
37 I am shamelessly borrowing what John Goode has to say about Ethelberta in *The Hand of Ethelberta.* See John Goode *Thomas Hardy: the Offensive Truth* (Oxford, Basil Blackwell, 1988) p. 36.
38 Marjorie Garson *'The Mayor of Casterbridge:* the boundaries of propriety' in the Macmillan *New Casebook* p. 103. See also her *Hardy's Fables of Identity: Woman, Body, Text* (Oxford, Clarendon Press, 1991).
39 ibid. pp. 94–5.
40 ibid. p. 100.
41 ibid. p. 107. Ian Gregor describes her as Hardy's 'veiled narrator'. *The Great Web: the Form of Hardy's Fiction* (London, Faber and Faber, 1974) p. 124.
42 ibid. p. 103.
43 See Millgate's chapter on 'The Evolution of Wessex' in his *Thomas Hardy: His Career as a Novelist* pp. 235ff.
44 See William Greenslade 'Degenerate Spaces' in the Norton edition of *The Mayor of Casterbridge* pp. 414–24. See also the Appendix to Merryn Williams *Thomas Hardy and Rural England* (London, Macmillan, 1972).
45 Suzanne Keen 'Narrative Annexes: Mixen Lane' in the Norton edition of *The Mayor of Casterbridge* pp. 437–51.
46 'The Dorsetshire Labourer' in *Thomas Hardy's Personal Writings* ed. Harold Orel (London, Macmillan, 1967) pp. 188–9.
47 See Greenslade op. cit. p. 416.
48 Keen op. cit. p. 453.
49 Paterson op. cit. p. 357.
50 Elaine Showalter 'The unmanning of the Mayor of Casterbridge' in the Norton edition of *The Mayor of Casterbridge* p. 396.
51 See Sigmund Freud's discussion of the Schreber Case: *Pelican Freud Library 9: Case Histories II* (London, Penguin Books, 1979) pp. 131–223.
52 Compare Schreber: 'he lived for a long time without a stomach, without intestines, almost without lungs, with a torn oesophagus, without a bladder, and with shattered ribs, he used sometimes to swallow part of his own larynx with his food etc.' ibid. p. 147.

53 ibid. p. 132. The date of Schreber's first illness, by the way, is 1884: the year of composition of *The Mayor of Casterbridge*.
54 ibid. p. 175.
55 ibid. p. 147.
56 ibid.
57 ibid. 195.
58 Alice Jardine 'Women in Limbo: Deleuze and His Br(others) *SubStance* no. 44/5, (1984), p. 54.
59 Marjorie Garson 'The Bounds of Propriety' in the Macmillan *New Casebook* p. 81.
60 Garson, ibid. pp. 83. See also in the same volume Robert Langbaum's essay on 'The Minimization of Sexuality' pp. 116–31.
61 Garson, op. cit. pp. 83, 84, 86.
62 See note 40.
63 I risk suggesting here that there is more than a passing hint in this depiction of Nance Mockridge of the classic pose of a woman with a pitcher – the pitcher, of course, a symbol for the milk yielding breast.
64 p. 90.
65 Anyone familiar with the geography of either Casterbridge or Dorchester knows this is impossible. Unfortunately much of her argument depends upon this displacement.
66 To be scrupulously fair, Garson does contemplate this alternative which 'casts a more sinister light on her [Lucetta's] victimisers' (op. cit. p. 90) but she then seems to lose the thread of her argument largely due to her strange contention that Hardy wants the 'positive body' of the town to 'endorse' Henchard.
67 See also Keen op. cit. p. 446.
68 Luce Irigaray *This Sex Which Is Not One* (New York, Cornell University Press, 1985) p. 106.
69 Langbaum 'The Minimization of Sexuality' p. 130 – note his dismissive use of parenthesis: almost always a sign that something important is being left out!
70 Garson p. 90.
71 ibid. p. 113.
72 Hardy's term for the story as he recounts it in his description Maumbury Ring in *Hardy's Personal Writings* ed. Harold Orel (London, Macmillan, 1967).
73 See the Programme Notes to *White Mercury, Brown Rice* (see fn. 74).
74 Ben. Bragg, London, 1706 British Library Shelfmark: G.13957. More recent accounts, wholly dependent on the 1706 text, are to be found in 'The History of the Dorchester Gallows' Rev. S. E.V. Filleul in *Proceedings of the Dorset Natural History and Antiquarian Field Club* XXXII pp. 61–9 and in *Dorset Murders* Roger Guttridge (Wimborne, Dorset, Ensign Books, 1986) pp. 9–24. There is an interesting recent play on the trial of Mary Channing, arguing her innocence, by David James entitled *White Mercury, Brown Rice* (1995) (Dorchester County Library).
75 'Maumbury Ring' in *Thomas Hardy's Personal Writings* ed. Harold Orel (London, Macmillan, 1967) p. 230.
76 *The Personal Notebooks of Thomas Hardy* ed. Richard H. Taylor (London, Macmillan, 1978) p. 38.
77 Gittings *The Older Hardy* p. 273.

78   *The Oxford Authors: Thomas Hardy* ed. Samuel Hynes (Oxford, Oxford University Press, 1984) p. 28.
79   Michel Foucault 'The Life of Infamous Men' in *Michel Foucault: Power, Truth, Strategy* ed. M. Morris and P. Patton (Sydney, Feral, 1979) pp. 76–7.
80   Elizabeth Grosz *Volatile Bodies* (Bloomington, Indiana University Press, 1994) p. 139.
81   Michel Foucault *Discipline and Punishment* (London, Penguin Books, 1977) p. 29. See also Elizabeth Grosz op. cit. p. 151 'As the object of sovereign forms of justice, punishment and torture, the body is a frail and pathetic object capable of being broken, the converse of the king's body...'.
82   I am inclined to think that it is only a rather sheltered middle-class readership that would be truly shocked at the wife-sale. For the poor who could not afford divorce or annulment or whatever legal legerdemain the wealthy could resort to the 'sale' of a wife was a perfectly respectable way of formalizing a separation. See the accounts of various wife-sales in Appendix C of Norman Page's edition of *The Mayor of Casterbridge* (Ontario, Canada, Broadway Press, 1997) pp. 378–82.
83   Garson op. cit. pp. 91 & 109.
84   Garson p. 89.
85   For a more extensive account of what I mean here by 'phantasmatic' see my Introduction above pp. 13–19 and the chapter on *'Tess*: the Phantasmatic Capture' below.
86   Julian Wolfreys 'Haunting Casterbridge, or "the persistence of the unforeseen."' Macmillan *New Casebook* p. 153.
87   ibid. pp. 153, 155.
88   ibid. p. 155.
89   ibid. p 163.
90   John Paterson op. cit. p. 354.
91   ibid. p. 354 fn. 5.
92   *Serious Admonition* p. 42.
93   Millgate *Thomas Hardy: a Biography* (Oxford, Oxford University Press, 1982) p. 253.
94   Seymour Smith *Hardy* (London, Bloomsbury, 1994) p. 339.
95   ibid. 327.
96   Millgate *Biography* p. 238; Gittings *The Older Hardy* p. 164.
97   Hardy was quite aware of the value of 'Wessex' as a marketing asset. See Millgate *Thomas Hardy: His Career as a Novelist* p. 236.
98   Millgate ibid. p. 243.
99   Seymour-Smith p. 327 – my emphasis, D.M.

4   *Tess of the d'Urbervilles*: 'a becoming woman'

1   See note 9 of my Introduction:

   The commitment to milk production and the seasonal monitoring of the river-beds give the regime at Talbothays many of the characteristics of Karl Wittfogel's 'hydraulic' societies (see his *Oriental Despotism* New Haven,

Connecticut, Yale University Press, 1957) that offers Deleuze and Guattari one of their principal sources for their model of a despotic formation.

See *Anti-Oedipus* (London: Athlone Press, 1984) pp. 211 and 220 and *A Thousand Plateaux* (London: Athlone Press, 1987) p. 363.

2   All references are to the Penguin edition edited by David Skilton, London: Penguin Books, 1978.

3   Jacques Lecercle, 'The violence of style in *Tess of the d'Urbervilles*' in *Alternative Hardy* ed. Lance St. John Butler (London: Macmillan, 1989) p. 6.

4   ibid. p. 14.

5   ibid.

6   See the chapter 'Several regimes of signs' in *A Thousand Plateaux* pp. 111–48.

7   *A Thousand Plateaux* p. 121.

8   For a fuller account of all this see *Anti-Oedipus* p. 207: 'Even when it speaks Swiss or American linguistics manipulates the shadow of Oriental despotism.'

9   According to Deleuze and Guattari the *face* or, indeed, a *mask* is 'the Icon proper to the signifying regime.' (*A Thousand Plateaux p. 115.*) i.e. it supplements the bluff of the *signifier* in the absence of the *signified*.

10   See *A Thousand Plateaux* pp. 141–7.

11   ibid. p. 116.

12   ibid. p. 113.

13   See ibid. pp. 119–34.

14   ibid. pp. 127 and 129. I have also included, largely to indicate the greater elegance – *énonciation, énoncé* – of the argument in the original, a number of phrases from the French edition of *Mille Plateaux* (Paris: Éditions de Minuit, 1980) pp. 160 and 161.

15   The propensity of Tess to 'turn away' is quite consonant with her 'double effacement' with regard to both Angel's parents and her own family (p. 371).

16   cf. pp. 96 and 126: Alec's 'kiss of mastery'; Tess's: 'See how you've mastered me.'

17   Deleuze, G. *Présentation de Sacher-Masoch* (Paris: Éditions de minuit, 1967). English translation: *Coldness and Cruelty* trans. Jean McNeil, (New York: Zone Books, 1989). In what follows I have preferred to use the French edition and my first references are therefore to that. References to the corresponding passages in the English translation follow in square brackets.

18   *Présentation* p. 20 [pp. 20–1].

19   ibid. p. 19 [p. 19].

20   ibid. p. 78 [p. 88].

21   ibid. pp. 63 and 66. [pp. 72 and 75].

22   ibid. p. 75 [p. 86].

23   See the section entitled '*La loi, l'humeur et l'ironie*' in *Présentation de Sacher-Masoch* pp. 71–8. Chapter 7 in the English translation: 'Humour, irony and the law', pp. 81–90.

24   For the distinction between 'compossible' and 'incompossible' affects – indeed, worlds – see Deleuze's discussion of Leibniz's *Monadology* in *Logique du sens* (Paris, Éditions de Minuit) 1969 pp. 134ff [*Logic of Sense* trans. Mark Lester with Charles Stivale; ed. by Constantin V. Boundas (London: Athlone Press) 1989 pp. 111ff.].

204 *Thomas Hardy: Megamachines and Phantasms*

25 For a fuller account of the phantasm see the Introduction pp. 13–19 and the chapter '*Tess*: the Phantasmic Capture' below pp. 108–11; 123–6.
26 *Anti-Oedipus* p. 17.
27 *A Thousand Plateaux* p. 351.
28 ibid. p. 352. The italics are in the original.
29 ibid. p. 356.
30 For the distinction between 'majoritarian' and 'minoritarian' and their links with the distinction between 'molar' and 'molecular' structures see *A Thousand Plateaux* pp. 272–93. 'Molar' or 'majoritarian' figures or structures tend to be integrated and stabilised wholes in positions of domination and, to this extent, the apotheosis of the 'molar/majoritarian' pole is the 'white-man, adult-male' (*A Thousand Plateaux* p. 291). All those figures that refuse to subscribe to these structures of domination and which resist them either by falling short of them or by out-manoeuvring them are deemed to be 'molecular' or 'minoritarian.' 'In this sense women, children, but also animals, plants and molecules, are minoritarian.' (ibid.)
31 *A Thousand Plateaux* p. 396: As Virilio says, war in no way appears when man applies to man the relation of the *hunter* to the animal, but on the contrary when he captures the force of the *hunted* animal and enters an entirely new relation to man, that of war (enemy, no longer prey).
32 ibid. p. 279.
33 See Gilles Deleuze *Nietzsche and Philosophy* trans. Hugh Tomlinson, (London: Athlone Press, 1983), p. 18.
34 By these allusions both to the 'Shining Path' (*sendero luminoso*) guerilla movement in Peru and to Antonio Negri's great book on Spinoza – *The Savage Anomaly* trans. Michael Hardt, (Minneapolis and Oxford: University of Minnesota Press, 1991) – I make no apologies for associating Tess with a revolutionary tradition.
35 'Post-modernizing *Tess of the d'Urbervilles*' in *On Thomas Hardy*, Peter Widdowson, (London: Macmillan, 1998), p. 133.
36 See above p. 1.
37 See 'plateau' 10 in *A Thousand Plateaux* pp. 233ff.
38 *Anti-Oedipus* p. 362. See also p. 271: 'What is a girl, what is a group of girls?'.
39 For the *locus clasicus* see Spinoza *Ethics* (II,P13,L7,Scol.) ed. Edwin Curley, (Princeton: Princeton University Press 1994), p. 127. The extent to which Hardy was familiar with Spinoza's work is still a matter for conjecture (see the comments by Lennart A. Björk in his edition of *The Literary Notebooks of Thomas Hardy* (London: Macmillan, 1985), pp. 260–1) but I think a case can be made for a strong Spinozist influence in the composition of *Tess*.
40 *A Thousand Plateaux* p. 273.
41 ibid. p. 261.
42 Spinoza, *Ethics* (III,P2,Schol.) p.155.
43 Deleuze, G. *Spinoza, philosophie pratique* (Paris: Éditions de minuit, 1981), p. 171 [*Spinoza: Practical Philosophy* trans. Robert Hurley (San Francisco: City Lights Books, 1988) p. 127–8].
44 *A Thousand Plateaux* p. 276.
45 For the distinction between an '*ethology*' and a *morality* see *Spinoza, philosophie pratique* p. 168: 'The *Ethics* of Spinoza has nothing to do with a morality:

he conceived of it as an ethology, in other words as a composition of speeds and slownesses, of powers of affecting and being affected...' [p. 125].

5 *Tess*: the Phantasmatic Capture

1 *Les temps modernes* vol. 19 jan–juin, 1964 pp. 1833–68. A revised edition (principally involving formatting) of the original essay was published by Hachette in 1985 and reprinted in the series 'Pluriel' in 1999. Throughout the following I have referred to the *Les temps modernes* version as it is the one that most closely correlates with the available translation.

2 *The International Journal of Psychoanalysis* vol. 49, Pt 1, pp. 1–18. This translation was republished in *Formations of Fantasy* ed. Victor Burgin, James Donald and Cora Kaplin, Methuen, 1986. References to *The International Journal of Psychoanalysis* translation are offered in square brackets.

3 'Fantasme...' p. 1855 [p. 11].

4 ibid. p. 1854 [p. 11].

5 Laplanche and Pontalis are quite prepared to acknowledge that even the 'universality' of the Oedipal complex – the psychoanalytical phantasm *par excellence* – may be culturally relative. See 'Fantasme....' pp. 1852–4 fn 40 [p. 10 fn 20].

6 See John Fletcher's 'Introduction' to Jean Laplanche *Essays on Otherness* (London and New York: Routledge and Kegan Paul, 1999) pp. 1, 6–7, 10, 15–17, 51.

7 These unconscious transmissions, which are like 'mini-scenarios', are what Laplanche, in his later work, calls 'enigmatic signifiers'. See *New Foundations for Psychoanalysis* trans. David Macey (Oxford: Basil Blackwell, 1989) p. 126

8 'precocious seduction' becomes a key notion in Laplanche's later work. See *New Foundations* pp. 106ff.

9 All references to *Tess of the d'Urbervilles* are to the 1978 Penguin edition.

10 See above p. 94 footnote 5.

11 See footnote 7 above.

12 i.e. precisely examples of those 'enigmatic signifiers' we have referred to above.

13 The phantasm as a whole is an interpellative device: a placing of the subject by addressing it.

14 Mary Jacobus, 'Tess: the making of a pure woman', in *Tearing the Veil* ed. Susan Lipshitz, (London: Routledge and Kegan Paul, 1978) p. 82.

15 Penny Boumelha, '*Tess of the d'Urbervilles*: Sexual ideology and narrative form' in the New Casebook Series *Tess of the d'Urbervilles* ed. Peter Woodison (London: Macmillan, 1993) p. 47.

16 Angel, too, at the end wonders 'what obscure strain in the d'Urberville blood had led to this aberration.' p. 475. For a more sustained account of the Darwinian and Weismannian influences on *Tess* see P. Morton *The Vital Science: Biology and the Literary Imagination 1860–1900* (London: Allen & Unwin, 1984) pp. 194–211 and K. Ansell-Pearson *Germinal Life* (London, Routledge and Kegan Paul, 1999) pp. 189ff.

17 Penny Boumelha, p. 54.

18   Peter Widdowson, 'Postmodernizing *Tess of the d'Urbervilles*' in his *On Thomas Hardy* (London: Macmillan, 1998) pp. 117 & 122.
19   ibid. p. 132.
20   'Magic writing block' is my appropriation of the French version of what the standard English translations call the 'mystic writing pad'. See S. Freud, 'A note upon the "Mystic Writing Pad"', *The Penguin Freud Library* vol. 11 (London: Penguin Books, 1991) pp. 428–34. I first came across the phrase in J. Derrida's now classic essay 'La scène de l'écriture' in his *L'écriture et la différence* (Paris: du Seuil, 1967) [*Writing and Difference* London: Routledge and Kegan Paul, 1978].
21   See *Logique du sens* (Paris: Éditions de Minuit, 1969) pp. 133ff [*Logic of Sense* trans. Mark Lester with Charles Stivale; ed. by Constantin V. Boundas (London: Athlone Press, 1989) p. 109ff.] and, of course, the study on Leibniz, *Le Pli* (Paris: Éditions de minuit, 1988) [*The Fold* trans. Tom Conley (London: Athlone Press, 1993)].
22   Leibniz, *Discourse on Metaphysics* §9 in G. Leibniz, *Philosophical Texts* ed. R. S. Woolhouse and Richard Francks, (Oxford, Oxford University Press, 1998) p. 60.
23   Leibniz, *Principles of Nature and Grace* §13 in ibid. p. 264.
24   Gilbert Simondon, *L'Individu et sa genèse physio-biologique* (Paris: Presses Universitaires de France, 1964). A translation of the 'Introduction' to this study is to be found in *Incorporations* ed. Jonathan Carey and Sanford Kwinter, (New York: Zone Books, 1992) pp. 296–319. In all cases the translations from the French are mine.
25   Simondon, pp. 10–11 [p. 305].
26   ibid. p. 151 and p. 263.
27   ibid. 152.
28   ibid. p. 12 [p. 307].
29   Leibniz, *Monadology* §85, ed. Nicholas Rescher, (Pittsburgh, University of Pittsburgh Press, 1991) p. 281.
30   So the Oedipal structure itself might be only contingent. See the footnote to 'Fantasme originaire...' p. 1852 [p. 10]: 'In the perspective of structural anthropology one might see there [i.e. the Oedipal complex] *one of the modalities* of the law that founds interhuman exchanges, a law susceptible, according to the difference of cultures, of being embodied in other characters and in other forms, the prohibitive function of the law for example being filled by another agency than that of the father.' See also J. Laplanche *New Foundations for Psychoanalysis* David Macey, (Oxford: Basil Blackwell, 1989) p. 90: '...what we call the Oedipus complex is in a sense subject to contingency.' and p. 91: 'The sacrosanct universality of the Oedipus can be seen as one of the many solutions to a problem created by the situation in which adults and children relate to one another (and that is universal), and by the entry of the child into the adult universe.'
31   As in the Rollivers scene discussed above it is unimportant who 'has' the reverie. What is important are the positions allocated 'within' the reverie – *not which subject has the reverie, but where does the reverie have each subject.*
32   The fact that the orchestra here is described as 'phantasmal' is a happy, but nevertheless, illuminating coincidence.

33 G. Deleuze *Logique du sens* pp. 218ff [pp. 187ff]. For Melanie Klein see especially 'Notes on some schizoid mechanisms' in *The Selected Melanie Klein* ed. Juliet Michel, (London: Penguin Books, 1986) pp.176–200.
34 See Introduction p. 14–15.
35 'Fantasme originaire...' pp. 1860–1 [pp. 13–14].
36 As, for example, in my accounts of the scene at Rollivers' and the breakfast scene at Talbothays.
37 *Logique du sens* p. 219 [p. 188].
38 ibid. 218 [p.187].
39 This seems to me to be a better term than either Melanie Klein's *'imago'* or Deleuze's *'simulacre'* both of which lead to confusion. *'Effigy'* seems to me to convey better the fragmented, metonymic, relation of the partial objects to the whole.
40 See Melanie Klein, 'Notes on some schizoid mechanisms', in op. cit. pp. 176–7.
41 ibid. pp. 183–4.
42 *Logique du sens* p. 225 [p.193].
43 ibid. p. 222 [p. 191]. See also Melanie Klein, 'The psychogenesis of manic-depressive states' in op. cit. p. 118.
44 ibid. p. 178.
45 *Logique du sens* pp. 228–9 [pp. 196–7].
46 ibid. p. 230 [p. 198].
47 ibid. 229 [p. 197].
48 ibid. p. 236 [p. 202] 'We must imagine Oedipus not only innocent but full of zeal and good intentions.'
49 ibid. p. 239 [p. 205].
50 It is perhaps worth recalling the original expression of revulsion that this undifferentiated condition elicits from the man himself – Sophocles' Oedipus:

> Incestuous sin! Breeding where I was bred!
> Father, brother, and son; bride, wife and mother;
> Confounded in one monstrous matrimony!
> All human filthiness in one crime compounded!

Sophocles *The Theban Plays* trans. E. F. Watling (London: Penguin Books, 1948) p. 64.
51 see above p. 14, fn. 49.
52 ibid. p. 254 [p. 218].
53 ibid. p. 242 [p. 208]. See also Freud, 'The ego and the id', *Penguin Freud Library*, vol. XI, (London: Penguin Books, 1991) p. 386.
54 One can clearly recognize here the affinity of the *phantasm* with the *body without organs*. See the Introduction pp. 20–1.
55 This is why I think that those readings that argue that Tess has 'no character' are mistaken. I think it is possible to read *Tess* almost as Deleuze reads *Alice in Wonderland*: the whole text is an exploration of Tess's/Alice's consciousness: *Tess's Adventures in Wonderland?* See *Logique du sens* passim.
56 Car Darch's name, especially as we find it later in the text – Dark Car (p. 366) – clearly suggests an association with the death drive.

57   For the 'schizoid-paranoid' nature of obscenities see *Logique du sens* p. 287 [p. 246]: 'the obscene word figures rather the direct action of one body on another...'.

58   On 'binding' see also the article on 'Liaison' (binding) in J. Laplanche and J.-B. Pontalis, *Vocabulaire de Psychanalyse* (Paris: Presses Universitaires de France, 1967) pp. 221–4.

59   S. Freud *The Penguin Freud Library* vol. XI, (London: Penguin Books, 1991) p. 386.

60   *Logique du sens* p. 225 [p. 193].

61   ibid.

62   'The psychogenesis of manic-depressive states' in *The Selected Melanie Klein* p. 123.

63   *Logique du sens* p. 222 [p. 191].

64   ibid. p. 157 [p. 132]: For Deleuze, Hercules, like the phallus, has known the adventures of the depths and the heights and now bestrides the surface.

65   Here it is necessary to recall the task enjoined upon the phallus to 'sutur(e) and link' the partial surfaces of the Harlequin body into an integral whole. See above p. 126.

66   Students of Deleuze and Guattari will have surely noticed that in making so much of Deleuze's notion of the *phantasm* I seem to be ignoring the fact that in his later work – see the *Dialogues* with Claire Parnet, Flammarion, Paris, pp. 59–60 [*Dialogues* trans. Hugh Tomlinson and Barbara Habberjam, (London: Athlone Press, 1987) p. 47] – he seems to anathematize the concept. Well, maybe, but I remain convinced of its importance to Deleuze and that the *phantasm* plays an enormously important part in the whole apparatus of strata and stratification in *A Thousand Plateaux* (see especially the completely manic essay on '10,000 B.C.: The geology of morals' and the essay on 'Several Regimes of Signs') and in the notion of 'Autrui' (which I think is the *phantasm in all but name*) which first appears in the discussion of Michel Tournier's *Vendredi* in the appendix to *Logique du sens* and is taken up again as a model 'concept' in *Qu'est-ce que la philosophie?* Éditions de minuit, Paris, 1991, pp.21 ff. [*What is philosophy?* Verso, London, 1994, pp. 16 ff].

67   Cf. *Logique du sens* p. 222 [p. 190]: 'The body of a child is like a trench (*fosse*) full of introjected wild animals that strain to snap in the air at the Good Object....'.

68   See above p. 109 for the part played by translation in the phantasm – particularly at this Oedipal moment.

69   Quoted by Laplanche and Pontalis in 'Fantasme originaire...' p. 1849 fn 32 [p. 8 fn 16].

70   It is worth recalling that two of Tess's former companions who, as such, have 'tracked' Tess's trajectory, Marian and Retty, have already succumbed to the allure of the (schizoid-paranoiac) depths: Marian to drink, and Retty to an attempted suicide by drowning (p. 289). Izzy Huett, the third companion, does not suffer the same fate because she is taken further along in Tess's wake to the point where she almost passes the threshold that has thwarted Tess – when Angel invites her to go to Brazil with him.

71   See the relevant articles on 'Instinct' (*Instinkt/instinct*) and 'Pulsion' (*Trieb/drive*) in the *Vocabulaire de psychanalyse* pp. 203 & 359.

72   Laplanche and Pontalis 'Fantasme originaire....' p. 1861 [p. 14].

73 To detail adequately the sources for this paragraph would entail listing practically everything I have read for the past few years. The notion of 'traversing the fantasy' comes originally from Lacan's *Four Fundamental Concepts of Psychoanalysis* (London: Penguin Books, 1979) p. 273. It has been taken up recently by Slavoj Zizek – see especially his *The Plague of Fantasies* (London: Verso, 1999) pp. 30ff – and by a number of other commentators such as Yannis Stavrakakis *Lacan and the Political* (London: Routledge and Kegan Paul, 1999) and Jason Glynos *A Lacanian Approach to Ethics and Ideology*, Ph.D. thesis, University of Essex, 2000. While benefiting from their occasional insights I am not sure that my notion of 'traversing the fantasy/ phantasm' is the same as theirs. Other sources that have been of importance have been Deleuze's *Logique du sens* p. 258 [p. 222] and his remarks on the dangers of 'destratification' in *A Thousand Plateaux* pp. 270 & 284. There are debts, too, to Laplanche's *Life and Death in Psychoanalysis* (Baltimore: John Hopkins University Press, 1976) (see especially pp. 121–4) and his *New Foundations for Psychoanalysis* (Oxford: Basil Blackwell, 1989) pp. 141ff. Yet another source, perhaps surprisingly, is D. H. Lawrence's extraordinary essay of 1921 *Fantasia and the Unconscious*. Finally, in all conscience, I must declare a debt to *Startrek*! A recurrent theme of the series and one that emerges clearly in the first *Startrek* film and, I believe, the fifth, *The Voyage Home*, is that of an advanced probe that has been sent out years or even centuries earlier and which now returns as a death threat to the present unless it can be 'rehumanized' (or, in the case of *The Voyage Home*, 're-whale-ized') by re-establishing communication with it: i.e by rephantasmatizing it. For a classic literary example of the reversion to a death drive through a process of dephantasmatization, through a regressive traversal of the phantasm then consider Kurtz of *Heart of Darkness* or, indeed, Sophocles' Oedipus himself: from the pattern of social differentiation offered by his foster parents, Polybus and Meropé, Oedipus regresses to a state of incestuous non-differentiation.

74 For the importance of 'good intentions' in relation to the Oedipal moment see Deleuze *Logique du sens* p. 239 [p. 205]: 'for it is with the Oedipal complex that intention is born, the moral notion *par excellence*.'

75 See above p. 114.

76 Slavoj Zizek *The Ticklish Subject* (London: Verso, 1999) p. 374.

77 ibid. p. 375.

78 See *Logique du sens* pp. 280 and 256 [pp. 240 & 220].

79 *The Life of Thomas Hardy 1840–1928* (London: Macmillan, 1962) pp. 28–9.

80 Robert Gittings *The Young Thomas Hardy* (London: Penguin Books, 1978) pp. 58–9.

6 Retranslating *Jude the Obscure* I

1 Gilles Deleuze and Felix Guattari *Anti-Oedipus* (London: Athlone Press, 1984) p. 33.

2 All references to the text are to the Penguin Classics edition of 1985 edited and introduced by C. H. Sisson.

3   So when Jude invites Sue to go and sit in the Cathedral at Melchester she can retort: '... I'd rather sit in the railway station.... That's the centre of the town life now. The Cathedral has had its day.' (p. 187)

4   Geoffrey Thurley *The Psychology of Hardy's Novels* (Queensland: University of Queensland Press, 1975) p. 197.

5   Terry Eagleton has spoken of the text's 'unacceptability' ('Liberality and Order: the Criticism of John Bayley', *New Left Review*, 110 (1978), p. 39); John Goode of its 'incomprehensibility' (quoted by Christine Brooke-Rose, 'Ill Wit and Sick Tragedy: *Jude the Obscure*' in *Alternative Hardy* ed. Lance St. John Butler (Basingstoke: Macmillan, 1988) p. 39); John Hughes reports that 'many of Hardy's readers have found the novel unreadable' *Lines of Flight* (Sheffield: Sheffield Academic Press, 1997) p. 102. Hughes' essay is one of the few 'Deleuzian' readings of Hardy's work that I have encountered but while I found his close reading of particular passages sensitive and illuminating I am unable to come to terms with the positive and optimistic reading that he wrests from the 'untimeliness' of the text.

6   Cf. Marlene Springer *Hardy's Use of Illusion* (London: Macmillan, 1983) p. 163: 'Sue recites rather than responds.'

7   John Goode *Thomas Hardy: the Offensive Truth* (Oxford: Basil Blackwell, 1988) p. 139.

8   Hughes op. cit. p. 103.

9   Hence Hardy's wry irony earlier: 'That the twain were happy – between their times of sadness – was indubitable.' (p. 357)

10 cf. p. 368: 'Sue was always much affected at a picture of herself as an object of pity...'

11 Brooke-Rose op. cit. p. 28.

12 John Bayley seems to me to be reacting to the same sense of the reader being left to his or her own devices when he speaks of Hardy's 'repudiation' of his own text, of his 'diffidence' and 'withdrawal'. See *An Essay on Thomas Hardy* (Cambridge: Cambridge University Press, 1977) pp. 196–7. Indeed, recently I have begun to wonder whether the authorial stance of *Jude* is not looking forward to the sublime indifference that characterizes the Immanent Will in *The Dynasts*:

> *Spirit of the Years:*
> In the Foretime, even to the germ of Being,
>   Nothing appears of shape to indicate
> That cognizance has marshalled things terrene,
>   Or will (such is my thinking) in my span.
> Rather they show that, like a knitter drowsed,
> Whose fingers play in skilled unmindfulness,
>   The Will has woven with an absent heed
>   Since life first was; and ever will so weave.

The Dynasts (London: Macmillan, 1978) pp. 22–3.

13 Other examples have been commented on by John Goode (op. cit. p.139) and Christine Brooke-Rose op. cit. pp. 38ff. where she comments at length on Patricia Ingham's misreading of a key passage.

14 ibid. p. 34.

15 Not to forget a number of glaring inconsistencies in the text such as why on earth should Jude's old employer in Christminster who had sacked him for drunkenness and absenteeism 'offer[ ] him permanent work of a good class if he would come back.'? p. 234.
16 For this see Marlene Springer's *Hardy's Use of Allusion* (London: Macmillan, 1983): 'Jude is allotted more allusions than any other character in Hardy; over fifty-five groups of them directly concern him, and there are well over a hundred references if counted singly.'
17 C. H. Sisson in the 'Introduction' to the Penguin Classic's edition p. 21.
18 There is a similar sense of material being simply 'dumped' in Hardy's use of standard guide-book material to describe Shaston pp. 259ff. The description of the paintings in Wardour Castle (p. 190) also follows the very order in which they are actually displayed.
19 For the notion of the 'de-signified signfier' see J. Laplanche *New Foundations for Psychoanalysis* trans. David Macey (Oxford: Basil Blackwell, 1989) p. 45.
20 Christine Brooke-Rose op. cit. p. 29 and John Hughes op. cit. p. 96.
21 Sisson op. cit. p. 25.
22 Goode op. cit. p. 140.
23 See Patricia Ingham's 'Introduction' to The World's Classics edition of *Jude the Obscure* (Oxford: Oxford University Press, 1985) p. xvii.
24 Sisson: 'The book is *constructed*, to a degree not to be found in any other of Hardy's novels, and in few English novels of the nineteenth century.' 'Introduction' op. cit. p. 25. For the difference between 'discipline' and 'control', which is germane to much of the discussion that follows see below p. 180.
25 *The Collected Letters of Thomas Hardy* ed. R. L. Purdy and Michael Millgate, (Oxford: Clarendon Press, 1980) p. 93.
26 ibid. p. 99.
27 ibid. p. 105.
28 *Anti-Oedipus* p. 34.
29 ibid. p. 246.
30 ibid.
31 ibid. p. 257.
32 John Bayley, once again, is spot on: '...when he (Hardy) gives up the romantic vision he gives up everything... *Jude the Obscure* has no form... because the appearance of such a form in the realization of the novel is not compatible with the mechanical intentions about 'contrast' in Hardy's original conception.' op. cit. pp. 197, 199.

7 Traversing *The Well-Beloved*

1 It is well known that *The Well-Beloved* (1897) is a revised version of *The Pursuit of the Well-Beloved* which appeared in serial form in *The Illustrated London News* in 1892. There are a number of differences between the two texts, none of which are germane to my argument which will concentrate on the 1897 version. All references will be to the 1985 'Papermac' edition from Macmillan edited with notes by Edward Mendelson and introduced by J. Hillis Miller.
2 Katherine Mansfield *Collected Letters* ed. Vincent O'Sullivan and Margaret Scott, (Oxford: Clarendon Press, 1987) II, p. 218. I am indebted to Tracy Ryan for drawing these remarks to my attention.

3   See J. Hillis Miller's discussion of *The Well-Beloved* in his *Fiction and Repetition* (Oxford: Basil Blackwell, 1982) p. 152. This is a revised and expanded version of his Introduction to the Macmillan edition of *The Well-Beloved* (London: Macmillan, 1985).

4   Introduction p. xii.

5   Patricia Ingham, 'Provisional Narratives: Hardy's Final Trilogy', in *Alternative Hardy* ed. Lance St.John Butler (Basingstoke: Macmillan, 1988) pp. 49–73.

6   Pierston explains his dilemma at length to his friend Somers in Chapter VII. All references to *The Well-Beloved* are to the Papermac Edition.

7   op. cit. pp. 54, 55.

8   Introduction p. xiv.

9   See my Introduction pp. 13–19 above and the chapter on the 'phantasmatic capture' of Tess for this distinction.

10   Hillis Miller *Fiction and Repetition* pp. 161–2.

11   'All love, for Hardy... has this narcissistic component. It is a displacement of the self's love for itself.' (p. 159); 'It [*The Well-Beloved*] is the story of the single consciousness divided against itself, striving to merge again with itself, seeing in others even of the other sex only its own double.' (p. 160)

12   Hillis Miller *Fiction and Repetition* op. cit. p. 168.

13   ibid.

14   ibid. p. 169

15   See Freud 'Beyond the Pleasure Principle' in *The Penguin Freud Library* (London: Penguin Books, 1991) XI, pp. 269–338.

16   Hillis Miller op. cit. p. 169.

17   ibid. p. 167.

18   ibid. p. 167.

19   For this role of the *partial* or *virtual object* see Laplanche and Pontalis and Deleuze's *Différence et Répétition*. See also my summary account of the phantasm in my Introduction pp. 13–19.

20   It might be perhaps worth recalling that these attempts to give the phantasm either a 'transcendent' or an 'endogenous' (i.e. solipsistically centred on the self) status are to be found, too, in Freud's own early attempts to elaborate a theory of fantasy or the phantasm. See my discussion of this in the chapter on *Tess*: the Phantasmic Capture and J. Laplanche and J.-B. Pontalis original paper on the *fantasme*.

21   J. Lacan 'Seminar on *The Purloined Letter*' in *The Purloined Poe* ed. J. P. Muller and W. J. Richardson, (Baltimore: John Hopkins University Press, 1988) p. 40.

22   Gilles Deleuze *Différence et Répétition* (Paris: Presses Universitaires de France, 1968) p. 138 [*Difference and Repetition* trans. Paul Patton (London: The Athlone Press, 1994) p. 105].

23   It is perhaps worth remarking that both Hardy and Lewis Carroll choose this same word – radiant, radiancy – to express this same ineffable moment. See Gilles Deleuze *Logique du sens* (Paris: Éditions de minuit, 1969) p. 280 [*Logic of Sense* trans. Mark Lester with Charles Stivale; ed. by Constantin V. Boundas (London: Athlone Press, 1989) p. 240].

24   For the critical function of *translation* in the phantasm see J. Laplanche *New Foundations in Psychoanalysis* trans. David Macey (Oxford: Basil Blackwell, 1989) pp. 114 & 119.

25   Robert Gittings *Young Thomas Hardy* (London: Penguin Books, 1978) p. 59.

26 From *The Life of Thomas Hardy* (London: Macmillan 1962) pp. 28–9.

27 Robert Gittings *Young Thomas Hardy* (London: Penguin Books, 1978) pp. 58–9.

28 See Hillis Miller *Fiction and Repetition* p. 152 & 164.

29 For a discussion of the schizoid and reparative 'positions' and the Good Object see the chapter on *Tess of the d'Urbervilles*. Here the 'aggressive' aspects of the schizoid position are marked by the soldiers while the chessmen point to the reparative elaboration of the *chequered* surface of the erotogenic body. See Gilles Deleuze *Logique du sens* p. 229 [p. 197].

30 Hillis Miller *Fiction and Repetition* p. 171: Hillis Miller speaks of 'The reduction of the author of *The Well-Beloved* to a subsidiary function of the text, made and unmade by it . . .' and continues: 'The story undermines Hardy's claims to authority as the generating source of the story he writes.'

31 *Fiction and Repetition* p. 168.

32 See the notes furnished by Edward Mendelson p. 152.

8 Retranslating *Jude the Obscure* II

1 *The Life of Thomas Hardy 1840–1928* (London: Macmillan, 1962) pp. 28–9.

2 See p. 349: [Mrs Edlin]:

   'No doubt that's how he that the tale is told of came to do what 'a did – if he *were* one of your folk at all.'
   'What was that?' said Jude.
   'Well – that tale, ye know: he that was gibbeted just on the brow of the hill by the Brown House. . . . But Lord, 'twas in my grandfather's time and it medn't have been one of your folk at all.'

3 See John Paterson 'The Genesis of *Jude the Obscure*' *Studies in Philology* 57 (1960) p. 90. What is more, if, indeed, it was originally a female form that was glimpsed in the fiery furnace then do we not have an echo here of that other phantasmatic figure of a young woman consumed at the stake, Mary Channing? See, above, the chapter on *The Mayor of Casterbridge*.

4 For *radiance* and the phantasm see above p. 162.

5 Revelation XXI.

6 I think this motif of 'reduced' and impoverished representations also accounts for the introductory encounter of Sue with the itinerant image seller with his 'reduced copies of ancient marbles' (p. 140).

7 For a discussion of these levels see the chapter on *Tess*: the Phantasmic Capture, pp. 123–6.

8 For this series see the account of the phantasm in the chapter on *Tess*: the Phantasmic Capture.

9 See the chapter on *Tess*, pp. 136–7.

10 Bayley J. *An Essay on Thomas Hardy* (Cambridge: Cambridge University Press, 1977) p. 212: 'they cannot separate because they are not separable.'

11 See below pp. 178–80 the discussion on '*Autrui*'.

12 Patricia Ingham, 'Introduction' to The World's Classic edition of *Jude the Obscure* (Oxford: Oxford University Press, 1985) pp. xv–xvi.

13 See above pp. 109.
14 See above p. 111 and 123–6 and Laplanche and Pontalis 'Fantasme originaire, fantasmes des origins, origine du fantasme' (*Les temps modernes* vol. 19, jan–juin, 1964) p. 1854–5 fn.45 [p. 11 fn. 23].
15 *The Complete Letters of Sigmund Freud to Wilhelm Fliess 1887–1904* trans. and ed. Jeffrey Masson (Cambridge, Mass.: The Belknap Press of Harvard University, 1985) pp. 207–8.
16 *New Foundations of Psychoanalysis* trans. David Macey (Oxford: Basil Blackwell, 1989) p. 130.
17 For Laplanche's most succinct and programmatic account of these processes of *de-tranlsation* and *re-translation* of the *enigmatic signifier* see his 'Psychoanalysis, Time and Translation' in *Jean Laplanche: Seduction, Translation, Drives* ed. John Fletcher and Martin Stanton (London: Institute of Contemporary Arts, 1992) pp.161–77.
18 *Troilus and Cressida* Act. I sc. 3 l.111.
19 (Paris: Gallimard 1972).
20 G. Deleuze *Logique du sens* (Paris, Éditions de minuit, 1969) Appendix II, pp. 350–72 [*Logic of Sense* trans. Mark Lester with Charles Stivale; ed. by Constantin V. Boundas, (London: Athlone Press, 1989) pp. 301–21].
21 *Logique du sens* p. 352 [p. 303 – where 'Autrui' is translated as 'Others': one of the many problematic translations that make me feel uncomfortable with the English version of Deleuze's text].
22 ibid. 357 [p. 307].
23 ibid. p. 369 [p. 318].
24 There are already here echoes of the function of the *fantasme* which institutes distinction of sex, gender and filiation. See Laplanche and Pontalis 'Fantasme originaire....' p. 1855 fn. 45.
25 See Bertrand Russell *History of Western Philosophy* (London: George Allen and Unwin, 1946) p. 673.
26 Russell op. cit. p. 673.
27 G. Deleuze *Logique du sens* p. 357 [p. 307]; *Différence et Répétition* (Paris: Presses Universitaires de France, 1967) p. 334 [*Difference and Repetition* trans. Paul Patton (London: The Athlone Press, 1994) p. 260].
28 See Leibniz 'Principles of Nature and Grace' §3 in *G. W. Leibniz: Philosophical Texts* ed. R. S. Woolhouse and R. Francks (Oxford: Oxford University Press, 1998) p. 259.
29 For a brief account of a 'Leibnizian phenomenology' see the chapter on *Tess: the Phantasmic Capture*, p. 118 above.
30 In Tournier's novel, Robinson reflects:

I know now that each man carries within him – and as if about him – a fragile and complex scaffolding of habits, responses, reflexes, mechanisms, preoccupations, dreams and implications which is formed and continues to be transformed by the perpetual caressings (*atouchements*) of his peers. Deprived of sap, that delicate efflorescence wilts and decays. *Autrui*, masterpiece of my universe...

p. 53

31 *Différence et Répétition* p. 335 [p. 261] 'It is true that *autrui* disposes of a means for giving reality to the possibles that it expresses independently of the development that we had them submit to. This means is language.'

32 Dylan Evans *An Introductory Dictionary of Lacanian Psychoanalysis* (London: Routledge and Kegan Paul, 1996) p. 133.

33 *Logique du sens* pp. 354–6 [pp. 305–7].

34 *Logique du sens* p. 359 [p. 309].

35 See *New Foundations of Psychoanalysis* trans. David Macey (Oxford: Basil Blackwell, 1989) p.114.

36 ibid. p. 132.

37 My principal reservation both about Tournier's novel and about Deleuze's reading of it is that any moderately attentive reading of Defoe would recognize just how much of Tournier's satiric or ironic revisions are clearly anticipated by the original novel.

38 See Gilles Deleuze's 'Post-scriptum sur les sociétés de contrôle' in his *Pourparlers* (Paris, Édition de minuit, 1990) pp. 240–7. See also Michael Hardt's 'The Withering of Civil Society' in *Deleuze and Guattari: New Mappings in Politics, Philosophy and Culture* ed. Eleanor Kaufman and Kevin Jon Heller (Minneapolis: University of Minnesota Press, 1998) pp. 23–39.

39 Again the *locus classicus* is Laplanche and Pontalis 'Fantasme originaire. . . .' p. 1855.

40 It is only fair to add here that a colleague of mine, here at Essex, Dr. Val Morgan, had quite independently drawn my attention to the 'ritualistic' qualities of the pig-killing.

41 Laplanche has made it very clear that his notion of the *fantasme* has an anthropological as much as a purely psychoanalytical dimension.

42 Jean Baudrillard 'Political Economy and Death' in *Symbolic Exchange and Death* trans. Iain Hamilton Grant (London: Sage, 1993) p. 126.

43 ibid. p.185.

44 *Anti-Oedipus* p. 337.

45 Baudrillard op. cit. p. 127.

46 Which might even account for the fact that he notoriously cannot spell.

47 See J. Lacan *The Four Fundamental Concepts of Psychoanalysis* trans. Alan Sheridan (London: Penguin, 1979) pp. 197–8.

48 Like the pointing finger that points to the dead Mr Tulkinghorn in *Bleak House*.

49 For the connexion between the *lamella* and Ridley-Scott's *Alien* see S. Zizek *Tarrying With the Negative* (Durham: Duke University Press, 1993) p. 181.

50 For this association of the enigmatic signifier and the super-ego and categorical imperative see Laplanche *New Foundations* pp. 137–9.

51 See C. H. Sission 'Introduction' p.22: 'The theoretical chatter of Sue. . . . is rubbish beside what Mrs Edlin has to say.'

52 Gittings *The Young Thomas Hardy* (Harmondsworth: Middlesex, Penguin Books, 1978) p. 58.

53 M. Foucault *Discipline and Punishment* trans. Alan Sheridan (London: Penguin Books, 1979) p. 29.

Bibliography

Anon. *Serious Admonitions to Youth, in a Short Account of the Life, Trial, Condemnation and Execution of Mrs. Mary Channing who, for Poisoning her Husband, was Burnt at Dorchester... With Practical Reflections* (London: Ben. Bragg, 1706 British Library Shelfmark: G.13957

Ansell-Pearson, K. *Germinal Life* (London: Routledge and Kegan Paul, 1999)

Artaud, A. *Antonin Artaud: Four Texts* trans. Clayton Eshleman and Norman Glass, (Los Angeles, Penjandrum Books, 1982)

Bateson, G. *Steps to an Ecology of Mind* (New York: Ballantine Books, 1972)

Baudrillard, J. *Symbolic Exchange and Death* trans. Ian Hamilton Grant, (London: Sage, 1993)

Bayley, J. *An Essay on Thomas Hardy* (Cambridge: Cambridge:University Press, 1977)

Bogue, R. *Deleuze and Guattari* (London: Routledge and Kegan Paul, 1989)

Boumelha, P. *'Tess of the d'Urbervilles*: sexual ideology and narrative form' in the Macmillan New Casebook Series *Tess of the d'Urbervilles* ed. Peter Widdowson (London: Macmillan, 1993)

Brooke-Rose, C. 'Ill Wit and Sick Tragedy: *Jude the Obscure*' in *Alternative Hardy* ed. Lance St. John Butler (London: Macmillan, 1989)

Brown, D. *The Mayor of Casterbridge* (London: Edward Arnold, 1962)

Butler, Lance St. John, *Alternative Hardy* (Basingstoke : Macmillan, 1988)

Carpentier, A. *The Kingdom of This World* trans. Harriet de Onis (London: André Deutsche, 1990)

Colombat, A. *Deleuze et la littérature* (Berne: Peter Lang, 1991)

Deleuze, G. (with Claire Parnet) *Dialogues* (Paris: Flammarion, 1977)

Deleuze, G. (with Claire Parnet) *Dialogues* trans. Hugh Tomlinson and Barbara Habberjam (London: Athlone Press, 1987)

Deleuze, G. *Différence et Répétition* (Paris: Presses Universitaires de France, 1967)

Deleuze, G. *Difference and Repetition* trans. Paul Patton (London: The Athlone Press, 1994)

Deleuze, G. *Logique du sens* (Paris: Éditions de Minuit, 1969)

Deleuze, G. *Logic of Sense* trans. Mark Lester with Charles Stivale; ed. by Constantin V. Boundas (London: Athlone Press, 1989)

Deleuze, G. *Nietzsche and Philosophy* trans. Hugh Tomlinson (London: Athlone Press, 1983)

Deleuze, G. *Le pli* (Paris: Éditions de minuit, 1988). English translation *The Fold: Leibniz and the Baroque* trans. Tom Conley (London: Athlone Press, 1993)

Deleuze, G. *Pourparlers* (Paris: Éditions de minuit, 1990)

Deleuze, G. *Présentation de Sacher Masoch* (Paris: Éditions de minuit, 1967). English translation: *Coldness and Cruelty* trans. Jean McNeil (New York: Zone Books, 1989)

Deleuze, G. *Spinoza, philosophie pratique* (Paris: Éditions de minuit, 1981) English translation: *Spinoza: Practical Philosophy* trans. Robert Hurley (San Francisco, City Lights Books, 1988)

Deleuze, G. and Guattari, F. *Anti-Oedipus* trans. Robert Hurley, Mark Seem, and Helen R. Lane (London: Athlone Press, 1984)

Deleuze, G. and Guattari, F. *L'Anti-Oedipe* (Paris: Éditions de minuit, 1972)

Deleuze, G. and Guattari, F. *A Thousand Plateaux* trans. Brian Massumi (London: Athlone Press, 1987)

Deleuze, G. and Guattari, F. *Mille Plateaux* (Paris: Éditions de minuit, 1980)

Deleuze, G. and Guattari, F. *Qu'est-ce que la philosophie?* (Paris: Éditions de minuit, 1991). English translation: *What is Philosophy* trans. Hugh Tomlinson and Graham Burchell, (New York: Columbia University Press, 1994)

Derrida, J. *L'écriture et la différence* (Paris: du Seuil, 1967) English translation: *Writing and Difference* trans. Alan Bass (London: Routledge and Kegan Paul, 1978)

Eagleton, T. 'Liberality and Order: The Criticism of John Bayley', *New Left Review* 110, 1978

Ellis, H. 'Thomas Hardy's Novels' *Westminster Review* LXIII, 1883

Evans, D. *An Introductory Dictionary of Lacanian Psychoanalysis* (London: Routledge and Kegan Paul, 1996)

Filleul, Rev. S. E. V. 'The History of the Dorset Gallows' in *Proceedings of the Dorset Natural History and Antiquarian Field Club* XXXII

Finley, M. I, *The Ancient Greeks* (London: Chatto & Windus, 1963)

Foucault, M. *Discipline and Punishment* trans. Alan Sheridan (London: Allen Lane, 1977)

Fletcher, J. 'Introduction' to Jean Laplanche's *Essays on Otherness* (London: Routledge and Kegan Paul, 1999)

Foucault, M. *Language, Counter-memory, Practice* trans. Donald F. Bouchard and Sherry Simon; ed. Donald F. Bouchard (New York: Cornell University Press, 1977)

Foucault, M. 'The Life of Infamous Men' in *Michel Foucault: Power, Truth, Strategy* ed. M. Morris and P. Patton (Sydney, Feral, 1979)

Freud, S. 'Beyond the pleasure principle' in *The Pelican Freud Library*, vol. XI *On Metapsychology* (London: Penguin Books, 1984)

Freud, S. *The Complete Letters of Sigmund Freud* trans. and ed. Jeffrey Masson (Cambridge: Mass., The Belknap Press of Harvard University, 1985)

Freud, S. 'The ego and the id' in *The Pelican Freud Library*, vol. XI (London: Penguin Books, 1991)

Freud, S. Schreber Case in *The Pelican Freud Library*, vol. IX: *Case Histories II* (London: Penguin Books, 1979)

Freud, S. 'A note on the "Mystic Writing Pad" ' in *The Pelican Freud Library* vol. XI (London: Penguin Books, 1991)

Garson, M. *Hardy's Fables of Identity: Woman, Body, Text* (Oxford: Clarendon Press, 1991)

Garson, M. '*The Mayor of Casterbridge:* The Bounds of Propriety' in the Macmillan *New Casebook* on *The Mayor of Casterbridge* ed. Julian Wolfreys (London: Macmillan, 2000)

Gittings, R. *Young Thomas Hardy* Harmondsworth (Middlesex, Penguin Books, 1978)

Gittings, R. *The Older Hardy* (Harmondsworth, Middlesex, Penguin Books, 1980)

Goodchild, P. *Deleuze and Guattari* (London: Sage, 1996)

Goode, J. *Thomas Hardy: the Offensive Truth* (Oxford: Basil Blackwell, 1988)

Glynos, J. *A Lacanian Approach to Ethics and Ideology* unpublished Ph.D. thesis (University of Essex, 2000)

Greenslade, W. 'Degenerate Spaces' in the Norton Critical Edition of *The Mayor of Casterbridge* second edition, ed. Phillip Mallett (New York and London: Norton, 2001)

Gregor, I. *The Great Web: the Form of Hardy's Major Fiction* (London: Faber and Faber, 1974)

Grosz, E. *Volatile Bodies* (Bloomington, Indian University Press, 1994)

Guttridge, R. *Dorset Murders* (Wimborne, Dorset, Ensign Books, 1986)

Hardt, M. 'The Withering of Civil Society' in *Deleuze and Guattari: New Mappings in Politics, Philosophy and Culture* ed. Eleanor Kaufman and Kevin Jon Heller (Minneapolis, University of Minnesota Press, 1998)

Hardy, F. E. *The Life of Thomas Hardy 1840–1928* (London: Macmillan, 1962)

Hardy, T. *The Collected Letters* ed. R. L. Purdy and Michael Millgate (Oxford: Clarendon Press, 1980)

Hardy, T. 'The Dorsetshire Labourer' in *Thomas Hardy's Personal Writings* ed. Harold Orel (London: Macmillan, 1967)

Hardy, T. *The Dynasts* (London: Macmillan, 1978)

Hardy, T. *Jude the Obscure* ed. C. H. Sisson (London: Penguin Books, 1985)

Hardy, T. *The Literary Notebooks of Thomas Hardy* ed. Lennart A. Björk (London: Macmillan, 1985)

Hardy, T. 'Maumbury Ring' in *Thomas Hardy's Personal Writings* ed. Harold Orel (London: Macmillan, 1967)

Hardy, T. *The Mayor of Casterbridge* ed. Norman Page (Ontario, Canada, Broadway Press, 1997)

Hardy, T. *The Mayor of Casterbridge* ed. Martin Seymour-Smith (London: Penguin Books, 1978)

Hardy, T. *The Oxford Authors: Thomas Hardy* ed. Samuel Hynes (Oxford: Oxford University Press, 1984)

Hardy, T. *The Personal Notebooks of Thomas Hardy* ed. Richard H. Taylor (London: Macmillan, 1978)

Hardy, T. *The Return of the Native* ed. George Woodcock (London: Penguin Books, 1978)

Hardy, T. *Tess of the d'Urbervilles* ed. David Skilton (London: Penguin Books, 1978)

Hardy, T. *The Wellbeloved* ed. Edward Mendelson with an 'Introduction' by J. Hillis Miller (London: Macmillan, 1985)

Heidegger, M. *Poetry, Language, Thought* trans. and intro. Albert Hofstadter (New York: Harper and Row, 1971)

Heusch, L. de *The Drunken King or the Origin of the State* trans. Roy Ellis (Bloomington: Indiana University Press, 1982)

Hughes, J. *Lines of Flight* (Sheffield: Sheffield Academic Press, 1997)

Ingham, P. 'Introduction' to World Classics Edition of *Jude the Obscure* (Oxford: Oxford University Press, 1985)

Ingham, P. 'Provisional Narratives: Hardy's Final Trilogy' in *Alternative Hardy* ed. Lance St. John Butler (London: Macmillan, 1989)

Irigaray, L. *This Sex Which Is Not One* (New York: Cornell University Press, 1985)

Jacobus, M. 'Tess: the making of a pure woman' in *Tearing the Veil* ed. Susan Lipshitz (London: Routledge and Kegan Paul, 1978)

James, D. *White Mercury, Brown Rice* 1995 (Dorchester County Library)

Jardine, A. 'Women in Limbo: Deleuze and His Br(others)' *Substance* no. 44/5, 1984

Keen, S. 'Narrative Annexes: Mixen Lane' in the Norton Critical Edition of *The Mayor of Casterbridge* second edition, ed. Phillip Mallett (New York and London: Norton, 2001)

Klein, M. *The Selected Melanie Klein* ed. Juliet Mitchell (London: Penguin Books, 1986)

Klossowski, P. *Nietzsche and the Vicious Circle* trans. Daniel W. Smith (London: Athlone Press, 1997)

Lacan, J. *Four Fundamental Concepts of Psychoanalysis* trans. Alan Sheridan (London: Penguin Books, 1979)

Lacan. J. 'Seminar on *The Purloined Letter*' in *The Purloined Poe* ed. J. P. Miller and W. J. Richardson (Baltimore: John Hopkins, 1988)

Laing, R. D. *The Politics of Experience* (London: Penguin Books, 1967)

Langbaum, R. 'The minimization of sexuality in *The Mayor of Casterbridge*' in the Macmillan *New Casebook* on *The Mayor of Casterbridge* ed. Julian Wolfreys (London: Macmillan, 2000)

Laplanche, J. *Essays on Otherness* trans. John Fletcher (London: Routledge and Kegan Paul, 1999)

Laplanche, J. *Life and Death in Psychoanalysis* trans. Jeffrey Mehlman (Baltimore, Johns Hopkins University Press, c.1976)

Laplanche, J. *New Foundations in Psychoanalysis* trans. David Macey (Oxford: Basil Blackwell, 1989)

Laplanche, J. *Jean Laplanche: Seduction, Translation, Drives* ed. John Fletcher and Martin Stanton (London: Institute of Contemporary Arts, 1992)

Laplanche, J. and Pontalis, J.-B. 'Fantasme originaire, fantasmes des origins, origine du fantasme' *Les temps modernes* vol. 19, jan–juin, 1964. Revised edition: Paris: Hachette, 1985; reissued under 'Pluriel' imprint 1999. Translated as 'Fantasy and the origins of sexuality', *The International Journal of Psychoanalysis* vol. 49, 1968, Part 1. This translation was republished in *Formations of Fantasy* ed. Victor Burgin, James Donald and Kora Kaplin (London: Methuen & Co., 1986)

Laplanche, J. and Pontalis, J.-B. *Vocabulaire du Psychanalyse* (Paris: Presses Universitaires de France, 1967)

Lawrence, D. H. *Fantasia of the Unconscious and Psychoanalysis and the Unconscious* (Tennessee: Kingsport, 1977)

Lawrence, D. H. *Study of Thomas Hardy* ed. Bruce Steele (London: Grafton Books, 1986)

Lecercle, J. 'The violence of style in *Tess of the d'Urbervilles*' in *Alternative Hardy* ed. Lance St. John Butler (London: Macmillan, 1989)

Leibniz, G. *Discourse on Metaphysics* in *Philosophical Texts* ed. R. S. Woodhouse and R. Francks (Oxford: Oxford University Press, 1998)

Leibniz, G. *Monadology* ed. Nicholas Rescher (Pittsburg: University of Pittsburg Press, 1991)

Leibniz, G. *Principles of Nature and Grace* in *Philosophical Texts* ed. R. S. Woodhouse and R. Francks (Oxford: Oxford University Press, 1998)

Maxwell, J. C. 'The "Sociological" Approach to *The Mayor of Casterbridge*' in *Imagined Worlds: Essays on Some English Novels and Novelists in Honour of John Butt* ed. Maynard Mack and Ian Gregor (London: Methuen & Co., 1968)

Millgate, M. *Thomas Hardy: a Biography* (Oxford: Oxford University Press, 1982)

Millgate, M. *Thomas Hardy: His Career as a Novelist* (London: Macmillan, 1994)

Miller, J. Hillis *Fiction and Repetition* (Oxford: Basil Blackwell, 1982)

Massumi, B. *A User's Guide to Capitalism and Schizophrenia* (Cambridge, Mass.: M.I.T., 1992)

Morton, P. *The Vital Science: Biology and the Literary Imagination 1860–1900* (London: Allen & Unwin, 1984)

Moses, M. V. 'Agon in the market place' in the Macmillan *New Casebook* on *The Mayor of Casterbridge* ed. Julian Wolfreys (London: Macmillan, 2000)

Musselwhite, D. *Partings Welded Together* (London: Methuen & Co., 1987)

Musselwhite, D. 'Phantasm and Nation: Sarmiento's *Facundo*', *New Comparison* No. 29, Spring 2000

Negri, A. *The Savage Anomaly* trans. Michael Hardt (Minnesota and Oxford: University of Minnesota Press, 1991)

Nietzsche, F. *On the Genealogy of Morals* ed. and trans. Walter Kaufmann and R. J. Hollingdale (New York: Vintage Books, 1969)

Paterson, J. 'The Genesis of *Jude the Obscure*' in *Studies in Philology* 57, 1960

Paterson, J. *The Making of 'The Return of the Native'* (Westport, Connecticut: Greenwood Press, 1963. Reprinted California: University of California Press, 1978)

Paterson, J. '*The Mayor of Casterbridge* as Tragedy' in the Norton Critical Edition of *The Mayor of Casterbridge* second edition, ed. Phillip Mallett (New York and London: Norton, 2001)

Russell, B. *The History of Western Philosophy* (London: George Allen and Unwin, 1946)

Seymour-Smith, M. *Hardy* (London: Bloomsbury, 1994)

Showalter, E. 'The unmanning of the Mayor of Casterbridge' in the Norton Critical Edition of *The Mayor of Casterbridge* second edition, ed. Phillip Mallett (New York and London: Norton, 2001)

Simondon, G. *L'individu et sa genèse physio-biologique* (Paris: Presses Universitaires de France, 1964). A translation of the 'Introduction' to *L'individu et sa genèse physio-biologique* is to be found in *Incorporations* ed. Jonathan Crary and Sanford Kwinter (New York: Zone Books, 1992)

Sophocles *The Theban Plays* (London: Penguin Books, 1947)

Spinoza, B. *The Ethics and Other Works* ed. and trans Edwin Curley (Princeton, N.J.: Princeton University Press, 1994)

Springer, M. *Hardy's Use of Allusion* (London: Macmillan, 1983)

Stavrakakis *Lacan and the Political* (London: Routledge and Kegan Paul, 1999)

Thurley, G. *The Psychology of Hardy's Novels* (Queensland: University of Queensland Press, 1975)

Tournier, M. *Vendredi, ou les limbes du Pacifique* (Paris: Gallimard, 1972)

Wheeler, O. B. 'Four *Returns of the Native*' in *Nineteenth Century Fiction* June, 1959

Widdowson, P. *Hardy in History* (London: Routledge and Kegan Paul, 1989)

Widdowson, P. 'Post-modernizing *Tess of the d'Urbervilles*' in *On Thomas Hardy* ed. Peter Widdowson (London: Macmillan, 1998)

William, M. *Thomas Hardy and Rural England* (London: Macmillan, 1972)

Wittfogel, K. *Oriental Despotism* (New Haven, Connecticut: Yale University Press, 1957)

Wolfreys, J. 'Haunting Casterbridge, or "the persistence of the unforeseen"' in the Macmillan *New Casebook* on *The Mayor of Casterbridge* ed. Julian Wolfreys (London: Macmillan, 2000)

Zizek, S. *The Plague of Fantasies* (London: Verso, 1997)

Zizek, S. *The Ticklish Subject* (London: Verso, 1999)

Index

afterwardsness, 17, 22, 111, 140, 175
  see also Nachträglichkeit
agencement, 16, 18, 20, 21
aggressive-paranoid position, 7
alien voice, 60
Artaud, Antonin, *To Be Done With the Judgment of God*, 5
Autrui, 20, 21, **178–80**, 183
axiomatization, 13
  see also reaxiomatization

Bateson, Gregory, 6
Baudrillard, J., 181–2
  symbolic exchange, 181
Bayley, J., 181
becoming woman, 74, 105, 107
body without organs, **5–9**, 20, 25, 28, 29, 30, 38, 49
  and phantasm, 20–21
Boumelha, P., 114, 116
Brooke-Rose, C., 150, 151
Brontë, Emily/Bell, Ellis, 9
Brown, Douglas, 50, 52
Brown, Elizabeth Martha, 18, 143
Burke, Edmund, 12

capitalism, 12
Carroll, Lewis, 106
categorical imperative, 15, 17, 20, 184
celibate machine, 8, 103
Channing, Mary, **80–88**
coding, over-coding, decoding, neo-coding, scrambling of codes, 2, 11, 12, 33, 145, 182
Comte, A., 58
Conrad, J.
  Heart of Darkness, 24
Corn Laws, 50
corps morcelé, 5, 7–8, 83, 85

Damien, 82
death drive, death instinct, 18, 102, **136–7**, 182

Deleuze, G., 15, 20, 55, 84
  Différence et Répétition, 20, 162 n. 22
  Logique du sens, 20, 108, **123–126**; 'Michel Tourner et le monde sans Autrui', **178–80**
  Présentation de Sacher-Masoch, **99–102**
Deleuze, G. and Guattari, F., 3, 20, 28, 59, 66, 90, 103, 182
  Anti-Oedipus, 1, 2, 3, 7, 19, 20, 38, 44, 52, 58, 90, 145
  A Thousand Plateaux, 1, 20, 58, 90
dephantasmatization, 19, **168**, 169, 170, 190
Derrida, J., 84
Descartes, R., 140
  Malign Genius, 140
designified signifiers, 177, 180, 184
despot, 11, 55
despotic overcoding of alliance and filiation, 58
deterritorialized flows, 32
Dickens, C., 101
  Little Nell, 101
Dracula, 140
drunken king, 53

Ellis, Havelock, 69
enigmatic signifier, 15, 17, 113, 177, 184, 186, 188
Eros, 129
eternal return, 16, 18, 102, 141
ethics versus moralities, 107
être aux écoutes, 24, 113, 141

Finlay, M. I., 60 n. 24, 62
Fleiss, W., 176
flows, 3, 32
Foucault, M., 20, 82, 189
Freud, S., 18, 43, 74, 84, 108–12
  Eros, 129
  Fort! Da!, 16, 17

'seduction theory', 108, 111, 112
Schreber Case, 74

Garson, M., 71, 75–6, 78, 79, 83, 84
Gittings, R., 19, 143, 164
'Go' versus 'Chess', 104
Goldmann, L., 153
Goode, J., 148, 151
Good Object, 125, 126, 128, 130–2,
    135, 139, 166, 175
Gosse, E., 152
Greek/Phoenician alphabets, 60, 62
Gregor, I., 51

haecceities, 106, 107
Hardy, T.
    The Bride-Night Fire, 82, 86
    'The Dorsetshire Labourer', 72
    Far From the Madding Crowd, 146
    He Abjures Love, 86
    The Life, 142, 164, 165, 166, 170
    'Maumbury Ring', 81
    Memoranda Notebook, 81
    The Mock Wife, 82
    Near Lanivet, 1872, 87–8
    *The Romantic Adventures of a Milk-
        Maid*, 39
    The Woodlanders, 111
Heidegger, M., 24
Hercules, 131
Heusch, Luc de, 66
Hitchcock, A., 42
    Psycho, 42
Hughes, J., 148, 151
Humpty Dumpty, 8

incest taboo, **66–9**
Ingham, P., 152 n 23, 155, 156, 175

Jacobus, M., 114
Jardine, A., 74

Keen, S., 78
Klein, M., 22 n. 72, 124–6, 129, 130
    paranoid, schizoid, depressive and
        Oedipal 'positions', 22, 124–6
Klossowski, P., 18

Lacan, J., 15, 135, 160, 179

foreclusion, 135, 179, 182
hommelette, 184
lamella, 184
objet petit a, 18, 160
Poe's *Purloined Letter*, 162
Symbolic Order, 179, (compared
    with Baudrillard's 'symbolic
    exchange') 181, 184
Laing, R. D., 48
    schizophrenic journey, 48
Langbaum, R., 79
Laplanche, J., 17, 176
Laplanche, J. and Pontalis, J.-B., 14–15,
    20, **108–11**, 179
Lawrence, D. H., 1, 25, 43
    Sons and Lovers, 43
Lawrence, Frieda, 43
Lecercle, J., 90
Leibniz, G., 118
    Discourse on Metaphysics, 118
    Monadology, 120
    Principles of Nature and Grace, 118
    'Leibnizian phenomenology', 118
Leroi-Gourhan, A., 58
life drives, death drives, 136
line of flight, 13, 20, 21, 48
linguistics of the signifier, 58
Lorca, F., 6, 106

magic triangle, 59, 60
magic writing block, 117
Mansfield, K., 155
Matheson, R., 47
    The Incredible Shrinking Man, 47
Maxwell, J. C., 51
megamachine, 2, 11
merchant and smith (exclusion of), 11,
    33
metabolization, 179, 180
Miller, J. Hillis, 84, 155
    on *The Well-Beloved*, **158–60**, 166
Millgate, M., 19, 41–2, 86
'miraculation', miraculating-
    machine, 8
moi dissous, 18
molar/molecular distinction, 4, 7, 28,
    37–8, 44, 49
molecular unconscious, 4
Moses, J. V., 51

motivation of the device, 154
Mumford, Louis, 2
Mummers Plays, 32–3

Nachträglichkeit, 17, 22, 111, 112, 162,
    175
'neotenic cache', 122
Nietzsche, F., 16
    Genealogy of Morals, 55
    see also eternal return
nomad (hunter), 10, (migratory), 28
nomadic subject, 103

Oedipus, 46, 184
    Oedipus complex, 4, 16, 40 n. 27, 43,
        44, 49, 122, 126
    Oedipal conversion, 139
    Oedipal phantasm, 19, 109
    Oedipal origins of the Law, 100
    Oedipal threshold, 135
originary phantasm, 16, 20, 24, 48,
    108–11, 122, 144, 162, 167, 170,
    185, 186

paranoid-interpretative ideal regime of
    signifiance, **90–8**
passional, post-signifying subjective
    regime, **90–8**
Paterson, J., 19, 51, 52, 73, 77, 84
    *The Making of 'The Return of the
        Native'*, 19, **38–41**, 44–5
Peter the Great, 131
phallus, 4–5, 11, 126
phantasm, **13–19**, 20, 21, 102, **108–11**,
    126, 135, 175–6, 186, 189
    feudal phantasm, 22, 78
    phantasm/fantasy distinction,
        14–15, 124, 144, 158, 167
    phantasm/instinct/drive, **136–7**
    phantasm/nation, 16, 22
    phantasm/'symbolic exchange', 181
    phantasm/Symbolic Order, 179, 185
    phantasmatic translation, 180
    traversing the phantasm, 15, 141,
        186
    see also 'originary phantasm'
phenomenological palimpsest, 117
phenomenological heritage, 126
'phenomenological residue', 122

phylogenetic memories/heritage, 110,
    115
physio-biological genesis, 126
placenta, 7, 46
plane of consistency, 5, 6, 20, 38
    versus plane of organization, 21
plateau, 5, 7
potlach, 57
pre-signifying/signifying/post-
    signifying systems of
    representation, 58, 65, 90
Proust, M., 6, 155, 168

quasi-cause, 18

radiance, radiancy, 18, 162
reaxiomatization, 34, 153
regimes of signs, 90
    authoritarian/despotic distinction,
        91, 103
    paranoid-interpretative ideal regime
        of signifiance, **90–8**
    passional, post-signifying subjective
        regime, **90–8**
    pre-signifying/signifying/post-
        signifying regimes, 90
Revelations, 173
Robinson Crusoe, 8
Russian Formalists, 154

sadism/masochism, **99–102**
Saussurian linguistics, 60, 91
Seymour-Smith, M., 19, 86
Shakespeare, W.
    Troilus and Cressida, 22, 178
Showalter, E., 73–2
signifying/post-signifying regimes,
    90–8
Simondon, G., 118, 129
    *L'individu et sa genèse physico-
        biologique*, **118–20**
singularities, 38
Sissons, C., 151
socius, 2, 3, 10, 11, 26, 134
speech/marking/writing, 58, 60
    see also voice/graphism
Spinoza, B., 24, 106, 107
    Ethics, 6
Stephens, L., 39

Cornhill Magazine, 39
strata, 20, 21, 133–4
sujet d'énoncé/sujet d'énonciation, 94–7

territorial/barbarian systems of
    representation, 58, 59
territorial, despotic, capitalist
    machines/regimes/social
    formations, 1–2, **9–13**, 21, 34, 44,
    89, 90, 145
territorial, despotic and oedipal
    regimes, 44
territorial coding, despotic over-
    coding, capitalist decoding, 3, 52,
    191 n. 5
    see also coding, over-coding,
        decoding, neo-coding,
        scrambling of codes
territorial (mega)machine/regime,
    10–11, 25–6
territorialization, deterritorialization,
    neo-territorialization,
    reterritorialization, 2, 13, 34, 89,
    145, 153
Tournier, M., 178

Vendredi: ou les limbes du Pacifique
    178–80
Thurley, G., 146 n 4
translation, de-translation, re-
    translation, 15, 17, 109, 135, 140,
    162, **176**, 177, 187
failure of translation, 176, 179, 180
self-translation, 176, 181
traversal of (traversing) the phantasm,
    15, 17, 141, 209 n. 73, 181, 186

virtual object/real object, 18, 162, 167
voice/graphism, 58, 60
    see also speech/marking/writing

War Machine, The, **103–5**
Widdowson, P., 105, 116
Wilde, O., 101, 157
    Dorian Grey, 157
Wolfreys, J., 83–4
Wren, Sir Christopher, 80
writing and incest, 58–69
    see also incest taboo

Zizek, S., 15 n. 52, 16 n. 53, 141